WAR AND REDEMPTION

A Civil War Tale

By

David Cleutz

June 2016

About the Second Edition:

The original printing of War and Redemption was successful beyond expectation, selling out in less than a year after its first publication in mid-2004. Reviews of the book in newspapers of the area in which the story of War and Redemption takes place have been generous in praise of both the fictional tale and the real history in the book. An outpouring of positive comments from both casual readers and avid Civil War buffs, coupled with continuing demand for the book from bookstores, has motivated the production of the Second Edition from a new publisher, Coastal Publishing, Inc.

The Second Edition includes a chapter index, omitted from the first edition, to help the reader follow the story locales. Several small errors of fact, spotted by knowledgeable readers, have been corrected. The author thanks these readers for their assistance.

As the author proceeds with the research and writing of a History of Col. David Ireland and the 137th New York, it becomes ever more apparent that Col. Ireland and the 137th were an unusually important factor in the winning of the Civil War. First at Gettysburg (as described in War & Redemption), and subsequently at Chattanooga, Atlanta, and Savannah. The author hopes the reader's interest in this exceptional but largely unsung regiment will be sparked by the accounts of its bravery in this novel, and go on to learn more about its many subsequent contributions in the preservation of the Union. The letters from the men of the regiment to their hometown newspapers provide unsurpassed insight into the extraordinary contributions of these ordinary citizen-soldiers. The author has compiled a collection of these in a book entitled *"In Their Own Words – Col. David Ireland and the 137th New York"*, just released in May 2005.

Coastal Publishing, Inc.
504 Amberjack Way
Summerville, SC 29485
1-843-870-9352

War and Redemption

Designed by Rae Siebels, design@american-book.com

Publisher's Note: This is a work of fiction. Names, characters, places, and incidents either are the product of the author's imagination, or are used fictitiously, and any resemblance to actual persons, living or dead, events, or locales is entirely coincidental.

Library of Congress Cataloging-in-Publication Data is available upon request.

ISBN 1-931650-41-1

Cleutz, David, War and Redemption

Special Sales
These books are available at special discounts for bulk purchases. Special editions, including personalized covers, excerpts of existing books, and corporate imprints, can be created in large quantities for special needs. For more information e-mail orders to:
coastalpublishing@earthlink.com

TABLE OF CONTENTS

Prologue

Epilogue

Chapter One
Jack

March 22, 1852

High up on the eastern slope of Lost Mountain, in the Blue Ridge Mountains of northern Virginia, the morning sun was melting the snow-covered banks of the little stream, the headwaters of Goose Creek. In a few spots, bare earth showed through the snow. Violets in bloom added color to the scene.

Ten-year-old Andrew Jackson Lewis checked the crude snare he'd set the day before, in the hope of catching a fat rabbit for the family supper. Jack was hungry. Very hungry. He often was.

His father had died. Kane, never a good provider for his family, had come home empty-handed and drunk, as usual, after helping out at Eben McCraw's whiskey still. Ashamed of his inadequacy, his brain inflamed by the corn liquor, Kane vented his frustration on his long-suffering wife, Rachel, by taking a vicious swing at her.

Jack, scared, but determined to protect his mother, tried to stop him. The boy caught a hard blow to the head and stumbled into Kane, who pushed him aside and slapped Rachel mindlessly, once, twice, three times, until the blood trickled from her mouth.

Jack picked up one of the few implements the poor family had, the fireplace poker, swung it high, and brought it down with all the force he could muster. "Gawddam brat!" his father howled, holding his broken arm.

"Git out! Git out o' here now, ye drunken brute!" With that, Rachel had pushed her husband out into the night, and slammed and barred the heavy door behind him. After a few more drunken curses and banging on the door, Kane staggered away toward the shed across the barren yard.

It had begun to snow again, and a cold wind blew hard up the hollow. Kane tried to open the door to the shed, but couldn't maneuver the wooden peg from its hasp. In a stupor, he sank down to the ground by the shed door and passed out.

The next morning, Jack and his mother found Kane, dead and frozen. They dragged the body up into the woods, laid it on a little hillock, and covered it with stones. They fashioned a crude cross, laid it on the stone cairn, and Rachel said a prayer. He wasn't mourned.

Since then, their sustenance had consisted of game Jack had trapped, nuts he'd robbed from squirrel holes, and the few remaining potatoes and turnips left in their crude root cellar from last year's lean harvest.

Now Jack saw the small rabbit, caught in the snare. He took out his father's long knife, slit the animal's throat, and slipped it into his game bag. Back at the cabin, he skinned and gutted the animal and gave it to his mother to add to the pot, along with one turnip and one potato from their dwindling stock. He wrapped the rabbit's skin, fur side in, around his right foot, closing a gap in the hides that provided meager protection to his nearly frozen feet.

Rachel looked at the thin, shivering boy and shook her head sadly. "Jack, we cain't make it like this no more. I'm gonna move down to the valley with my sister and your Uncle Cletus. Her boy Will is gonna work fer Mr. Harry Pettis at his horse farm by Upperville, an' you kin jine him."

"No, Ma, we'uns'll be all right here. I kin take care of us."

"Jack, you're a good boy, and I love ye. But I cain't stand t'see ye wastin' away hereabouts. Mr. Pettis is a good man, I hear, and he'll do right by ye. Missus Pettis'll fatten ye up some. Learn ye 'bout horses.

Learn ye t'read and write, an' likely learn ye t'talk good. Even git ye a trade. No, we-uns got t'cut loose o' this here gawd-fersaken place!"

The next morning Jack and his mother had packed up their few meager possessions and walked the two miles down Lost Mountain and out into the valley to his uncle Cletus Gresham's small farm on Gap Creek. Satisfied that his mother was in good hands, Jack agreed to leave her. Two days later, he and his cousin Will walked down the road to the Pettis farm outside Upperville in the Loudoun Valley.

Over the next six years, the two boys had thrived under the regimen of good and plentiful country cooking, hard work, and reading, writing, horsemanship, and husbandry. Will Gresham was stocky and moon-faced with an unruly mop of light brown hair and an infectious grin. Jack Lewis had grown taller—he was almost six feet—and broad shouldered. His angular face, made serious by his strong jaw and prominent cheekbones, was relieved by the twinkle in his blue eyes that you could see if you looked closely. He was lean and wiry from hard work and riding. Will admired Jack and loved him like a big brother. Minerva Pettis was pleased that the handsome young man had taken so well to her teaching, his speech becoming more correct with each passing year. Harry Pettis was particularly pleased with Jack. His young apprentice was hard working, responsible, and showed unusual aptitude with horses, learning, and people. At age sixteen, he looked much older. Jack had earned Pettis's complete trust and confidence.

Early one bright spring morning in 1858, Pettis found Jack in the stables, grooming one of the farm's finest horses, talking to the horse soothingly, the horse responding to the boy with what Pettis could only describe as affection. "Jack, how'd you like to see Pennsylvania?"

"Pardon, sir? Pennsylvania? Up north? T'other side o' the Line? Oh my, I do allow as how I'd like that, sir!"

"Then tomorrow daybreak, I want you to come with me to take a string of horses up to some farmers up there."

Five days later, back at the farm, Jack and his cousin Will were working on harnesses.

"Jack, what was it like up there?"

"Will, those folks're pretty much like folks here. Some o' the nicest farm land I ever seen. Good pasturin' for horses, too. An' lots o' good eatin'. Those Dutchmen's wives can cook! Mr. Pettis says now I know the way, he's gonna let me go by myself next trip. I'm lookin' forward to it, for sure."

In May and June, Jack made two more trips north. The first was to a Maryland farm in the Middletown Valley, west of Frederick between the Catoctin and South Mountains. On the second trip, he delivered three fine horses—a gray, a sorrel mare, and a black stallion named Midnight—to a Pennsylvania farmer named Dubs, just over the Mason-Dixon Line near Hanover.

The sun rose bright and shining one warm morning in July. Jack had just finished currying Katrina, the finest mare on the farm, when Harry Pettis strode into the barn. "Jack, how'd you like to go back up to Pennsylvania?"

"I'd like that just fine, Mr. Pettis! When can I go?"

"Tomorrow, first light. You're to take Katrina to a place President Buchanan owns outside Mercersburg, called Patchwork Farm. While you're at it, you'll deliver two horses to the farm at a place called Irwinton Mills. The fourth horse you take to a farmer named Brunebaugh. His place's just a few miles further on."

"Yessir. I remember when we was there back in April. Didn't much like the man, but he paid cash money. I'll be sorry to see Katrina go. She's sure a fine mare. Did the president buy her from you?"

"Not directly. A man came out from Washington, German fella, said he was buyin' my best horse for his master, the Duke of Westphalia, for to be a present to the American president. Then I got word that Buchanan wanted the horse kept at Patchwork Farm 'stead of at his home in Lancaster. That's why you're to take Katrina there. Now, a lot of folks are unhappy with the president, and might try to do somethin' to show it. I'm trustin' you, Jack, to make sure Katrina gets there safe and sound. As for Brunebaugh, didn't you tell me 'bout a pretty little girl he's got workin' there? Now don't tell me you wouldn't like to see her again, Jack."

"Wouldn't mind, that's for sure. Anyway, that's pretty country up there. I'll be happy to go back again. And thanks for trustin' me with Katrina. I'll make sure the president gets his mare!"

The next morning before dawn, Jack saddled up and led his string of horses over the Blue Ridge at Ashby Gap down into the Shenandoah

Jack

Valley. The air was clear, the mountains green, the river blue and glittering under the bright sun. The sixteen-year-old was happy to be alive on such a day, and proud to have his master's complete trust. He felt the weight of responsibility for Katrina, but he had the abundant confidence of youth. He was feeling hungry when he reached Berryville, and figured the horses would be too. He stopped for an hour at a shady spot near a small brook carrying cool, clear water off the Blue Ridge slopes just east of him. The horses grazed in a field of timothy and drank from the brook, while Jack sat beneath a tall chestnut tree and ate the lunch Mrs. Pettis had packed. He'd only dozed for ten minutes when his horse nuzzled him as if to say, "C'mon boss, let's keep movin'!"

The sun was hot and the road dusty, but Jack was whistling as he rode through Charles Town. He leaned down and spoke to his mount as he would to a close friend or his cousin Will. "What d'ye think, fella, should we take our time and spend the night in Martinsburg, or should we push it on t'the Potomac and Williamsport yet today?" His horse shook its head and whinnied emphatically. "Well, I guess I know what you think! All right, we'll spend the night at Martinsburg and go on to Pennsylvania tomorrow. I've stayed before at the Apple Valley Inn an' they've got good eatin' for both of us. Come mornin', we'll go up an' cross the river at Williamsport an' take the short way through Cearfoss up t'Mercersburg. We can spend the night there an' deliver the horses the next mornin'. Soon 'nough."

Late the next afternoon, a weary Jack Lewis and five tired horses moved down the pike past Fairview Cemetery into the little town of Mercersburg. Jack led his string of horses to the watering trough on the town square. He let them slake their thirst before leading them down the alley to Ott's livery stable. "Give two measures o' good oats, and I'll be along for them in the mornin'." His valuable charges safe and cared for, the Virginian carried his gear back up to Murphy's Hotel on the square.

Jack was hungry. It had been a long two-day ride, and he was ready for a good meal. He washed up in his room and came down to the tavern, looking forward to a good supper. The bar room was full of men, arguing in animated discussion.

"What's all the excitement about?" He stood at the bar, meaning to ask the barkeep where he should sit to be served dinner.

The barkeep heard his drawl, different from the local twang. "You ain't from 'round here, are ya, son? Everyone's bettin' on the cradlin' record bein' broke t'morra out t'Hoke's wheat field."

" 'Cradlin' record'?"

"Y'know, wheat. Big scythe with a big rack on it t'catch the wheat when it's cut. That's a cradle. Good man workin' hard might be able to cut five, six acres a day usin' it. We got a man here in town, carpenter by trade, big man, stands well over six feet, somethin' of a legend with a cradle in his hands. Michael Cromer. Once cut ten acres in one day. Company in New York got wind of it, Millard Scythe, an' made him an outsize cradle only he's big enough to swing. Blade's supposed t'be five inches wide an' five feet long. Now he's supposed t'use it t'break his old record. Some fellas think he will, most don't. That's what they're bettin' on. If ya wanna try yer luck, there's lots a fellas here t'take yer money."

Jack laughed. "I'm a horseman, not a farmer. But sounds t'me like a tall order. Don't know enough t'bet on 'im, but I wouldn't care t'bet agin' 'im, neither." Jack figured either way he'd risk getting some people mad, maybe potential customers for Pettis horses. And he wisely figured that wasn't good for business. Still, he was curious about the whole thing. Might be interesting to see if the man Cromer could actually do it.

In the morning, Jack went to the livery stable, retrieved his horses, and rode out to the Hoke field to watch the start of this prodigious feat. He only watched for a quarter of an hour, leaning on the rail fence at the side of the road with a number of other spectators. The tall man in the field was swinging the scythe and its cradle in a smooth, steady, unbroken ribbon. Stripped to the waist, the big man was glistening with sweat, even though the heat of the day was still hours away. Jack turned to the man on his right. "How many acres you think he's cradled so far?

The man spit a stream of tobacco juice into the dust. "Figger an acre since sunup."

Jack thought a bit. "With sixteen hours o' daylight, that means he could cut near twelve acres!"

Jack

"It ain't hot yet, son. An' like as not, we'll git us some good storms come afternoon. That'll sure slow him down. Naw, breakin' records ain't no sure thing. But I'm bettin' he'll do it."

"An' yer gonna lose, Duane. He's gonna slow down come noon, I tell ya!" The observer on Jack's left made his opinion known. Duane countered, and the two began to argue. Jack figured this was the time to make his exit.

"Well, I wish 'im luck." He untied his horse's reins from the fence rail, mounted up, and led his string of horses on to Patchwork Farm.

The farm sat on a bluff overlooking the Conococheague Creek's West Branch. The house and barn built by President Buchanan's father were solid, handsome buildings and the grounds were well cared for, with lawn and large oaks in the front yard. Several fine horses stood under a shady maple in the pasture to the side of the barn on the other side of the lane.

"Mornin'!" Jack hailed the farm manager as he came out of the barn to meet him. "I'm Jack Lewis. Here with the president's mare from Pettis in Virginia. You'll want t'look her over, I expect. Her name's Katrina, an' she's a good horse."

The farmer came over and inspected the horse carefully. "Well, son, she looks to be one fine mare, as we might expect, bein' she's a gift to the president." Katrina stood patiently. "Not skittish, is she, son. Well, you can tell Pettis the mare arrived in fine shape. Just hope the president gets a chance to come see her soon. We don't see much o' him here lately, what with all this fussin' 'bout Kansas and Missouri bein' slave or free. He must feel 'bout like a one-arm man in a three-man wrestlin' match, tryin' to keep ever'body happy down there in Warshington. Seein' this fine mare'd give him reason t'smile, that's fer sure!"

Jack gave Katrina one last pat on her neck, and the mare nuzzled him in return. "Now Katrina, you be a good girl an' be nice t'the president." It saddened him to say farewell to this mare that he'd spent so much time with, but he understood the nature of the business and was proud her quality was appreciated here. He knew the horse would receive only the best of care at a presidential farm. He mounted up once more, then spoke to the farmer.

"I'm to deliver two o' these horses t' Irwinton Mills. What's the best way t' get there?"

"It's easy, son. The mill's downstream on this here crick. Just go back the lane t'the Pike, go east 'bout a half-mile, take the road t'the right an' follow it 'til ya see the mill. I must say, Pettis must think a lot o' you. You're a mite young t'be deliverin' such valuable horses by yerself. But you sure are doin' a fine job fer 'im. Well, safe journey!"

Jack led his string of horses down the lane away from Patchwork Farm. He could tell from the meandering line of trees off to the right that he was following the creek south. He reached the Greencastle Pike at the east end of a stone arch bridge over the Conococheague. A hay wagon was headed east. Jack rode up alongside it.

"Nice lookin' horses, son. Where ya headed with 'em?"

"Irwinton Mills. I'm told I'm t'turn right up here aways t'get there. Heard anything 'bout that fella tryin' t'break his cradlin' record?"

"Cromer's to five acres, and it's not yet noon. The record'll be broke fer sure! An' there's yer turnoff t'the mill. Ya gotta cross the crick, then take the next left, go 'til ye cross the stone bridge, then the mill's just up the road. Good luck to ya."

Jack waved to the teamster and turned off the pike. Following the man's directions, he crossed the creek and rode down the road until it came to an end, then he turned and rode east. He stopped to let the horses drink where a side lane forded the Licking Creek, its juncture with the Conococheague not a hundred yards downstream. "If this was in Virginia," he said to his mount, "I'd love t'own the farm just up there on the hill. It's got a neat little springhouse just up the hillside past the ford. I'll bet its spring water's cold an' clean—keep milk an' butter fresh for weeks in there. An' I'll bet the fishin's good in these cricks!" Turning back to the camelback stone bridge and drinking in the view, he followed the road along the Conococheague.

A beautiful place, he thought. The placid water reflected a cedar tree precariously perched on the low limestone bluff beyond the bridge. There were several holes in the rock cliff, shallow caves big enough for a short man to stand in, carved out by the creek at some point in the distant past. A narrow, grassy pasture lay between the road and the creek the whole way to Irwinton Mills. He delivered all but one of the remaining horses—fine animals, if not quite the same caliber as the presidential mare now safely in the meadow at Patchwork Farm. Jack was impressed by the stately limestone house of the Irwin farm, but he'd seen some nearly as imposing back in Upperville. Walking the few yards across to the mill now run by J. W. Henkel, he was even more impressed by the size of the operation. "This place looks bran' new!" Then he saw the cornerstone that told him he was right—it wasn't but a year old.

At the mill, farmers unloading grain from wagons backed up to the front of the mill continued to discuss Cromer's chances of success. A sudden thunderstorm swept in over Cove Mountain to the west, driving the men into the mill for cover. Crowded into the small mill office, they tried to dry off by the potbellied stove. "That rain'll slow Cromer down, fer sure!" they said, shaking their heads. "Doubt he'll beat his record, now. Sad. Hoped he'd do it. Like no man I ever seen with a cradle in his hands, though!" They turned to the stranger in their midst.

"Where you from, boy?" one of them asked.

"Virginia. Upperville. Brought some horses t'farms hereabouts. I watched that fella Cromer a bit this mornin'. Never seen a man that big work so hard. I'd say he's still got a chance o' breakin' that record. Teamster up on the pike told me he was up t'five acres 'fore noon!"

When the storm passed, a bright sun emerged, arching a brilliant rainbow above the road to the east. Jack rode off with one remaining horse in tow. He saw that the end of the rainbow lay somewhere north of Greencastle. In his mind, it lay at the Brunebaugh farm, where he'd get payment for this one last horse. He'd met Bartholomew Brunebaugh a few months before, and didn't much like the man. But his wife had a pretty and perky young girl named Sally working for her in the kitchen. Sally was slender, with chestnut curls peeking out from under her little white cap, sparkling blue eyes, and a ready smile for the young Virginian. Jack thought that Sally would make a fine wife for a lucky man in a few years, and he looked forward to seeing her smile again. If she were a few years older…but he pushed such thoughts from his mind. No sense getting himself excited over something not possible.

Later, at the Brunebaugh farm, he took payment and accepted their dinner invitation. Casually observing the young serving girl as she bustled about, he could see her quick smiles aimed at him when the others weren't looking. Brunebaugh expressed his satisfaction with the horse's condition and indicated that he'd do more business with Mr. Pettis if this was the quality of the horseflesh he sold—"damn sight better than most hereabouts!" Jack knew his employer would be pleased when told of Brunebaugh's comments; still, he longed for an opportunity to have time alone with young Sally.

After dinner, Jack was out in the barnyard readying his horse when Sally came out to get water at the pump. He walked his horse over to the watering trough next to the pump, and spoke softly to her.

"So you're Sally?"

"Yessir. Sally Keefer, sir."

"You needn't say 'sir' to me, Sally. My name's Jack, an' I'm sixteen, only a few years older than you, I'd reckon."

"Yessir—I mean, *Jack*. I'm fourteen last March." She looked up at him, bashful but admiring. "I hope we'll see you up this way again before too long!"

"Well, Mr. Brunebaugh appears t'be pleased with Mr. Pettis's horses, and if he buys some more, I'll make sure it's me that brings 'em! I'd be right pleased to see you again, Sally, for sure."

"Take this, Jack, so's you won't forget me. Maybe it'll bring you back again." Sally took the simple necklace from her neck, one she had woven from dried cornhusks and embedded with small red quartz pebbles found while gathering wildflowers for the Brunebaugh table. She slipped the necklace around Jack's head as he bent down to receive it.

"I'll treasure this, Sally, an' it will bring me back—count on it!" He bent down and gently kissed her forehead, then mounted his horse and rode out the lane toward Marion and then Greencastle, as she watched wistfully, her heart beginning to pound with feelings she didn't yet comprehend.

The sun was low in the sky, and as Jack approached Greencastle it disappeared behind Cove Mountain, leaving a vermilion-magenta glow in the western sky. He spent the night at the Antrim House, and in its tavern room heard the news. The excited patrons were talking about the prodigious feat by Michael Cromer.

"Kin ye believe it? That fella Cromer cut twelve an' half acres! Hot as it was t'day, an' even with that thunderstorm. Won't see the like again in our lifetime, I reckon."

Jack got a measure of satisfaction that twelve and a half acres was what he'd reckoned, based on what he'd seen earlier in the day. "I'm sure glad I didn't bet agin' it!"

Over the next two years, Jack Lewis was to make more trips north with breeding stock and fine riding horses to farms in Maryland and nearby areas of Pennsylvania. In the process, he got to know the lay of the land, the main roads and backcountry roads and farm lanes, the creeks and rivers, the fords and bridges.

He got to know the people, and how they felt about the growing split between North and South. He found strong opinions among Maryland slaveholders to keep the Union intact, and equally strong opinions among some Pennsylvania Democrats in support of states' rights. President Buchanan, who he learned had grown up in Mercersburg, had both supporters and detractors there and in the surrounding country. Old Buck was trying desperately to keep the United States from tearing apart, but from what Jack could determine, his chances of success were diminishing with every passing day.

As the election of 1860 approached, the Republican Lincoln's platform of "Union at All Costs" looked like it would lead to secession by Southern states if the man from Illinois actually won the presidency. Jack knew that his trips north, which he enjoyed so much, would be at an end. He little realized that in a few years he'd be riding north again, but with thousands more like him, looking to repossess the same horses he'd conveyed to these prosperous Pennsylvania farmers.

On 16 October 1859, a wild-eyed Northerner named John Brown tried to raid the U. S. Army armory at Harper's Ferry. His small band of radical abolitionists intended to arm a slave insurrection with guns from the armory. Beaten back, Brown and his men took hostages and barricaded themselves in the firehouse. The army took swift action, sending Colonel Robert E. Lee and a young cavalry officer named J.E.B. "Jeb" Stuart to lead a small contingent of soldiers to storm the firehouse and capture Brown. Lee's men quickly breached the firehouse, rescued the hostages, and took Brown and his gang prisoner. Virginians, Marylanders, and southern Pennsylvanians alike applauded this swift and sure action in ending the crisis. "Them damn abolitionists! Bad as them Southerners talkin' secession! Between 'em they gonna pull this Union apart for sure, they keep this up," Jack heard more than one of his customers up north say. Jack, an attuned listener, knew what that meant. These Northerners may not all be abolitionists— far from it—but they were strong for Union!

Virginia was in an uproar after John Brown's raid. Slave insurrections were a real threat in the mind of every Virginia slave owner. Whether they had a huge tidewater plantation with hundreds of Negroes or just a small farm in the Piedmont with one or two, the fear was the same. For most, if not all, the fear was completely irrational. In many cases, these servants were almost like members of the family, and treated as such, unlike in the Deep South, where field hands were treated like oxen, or worse.

Irrational or not, the fear was a motivator for the powers that be, from tidewater to Blue Ridge. Militias were formed, reporting to Governor Letcher, in almost every Virginia county. In Fauquier County, which included Upperville just inside its northwest border, the leading men of Warrenton established the Black Horse Troop, a mounted militia. The service of the Black Horse in guarding John Brown after his capture was well appreciated by the citizens of Fauquier County, and indeed, by all Virginia.

Jack was caught up in the patriotic fervor. One September morning he thought Harry Pettis was in a particularly good mood. "Sir, I'd like your permission t'go t'Warrenton and sign up with the mounted militia. I can ride and I can shoot, and as you know, I know how t'take orders."

"Jack, I'm proud of you. 'Course you can. You're the kind of man this state is gonna need. All too soon, I'm afraid. Go join up, with my blessing."

Jack stood a little taller when Pettis called him a man. Pettis wasn't merely flattering him. He'd come to trust Jack completely, a confidence borne out by the always-successful trips north Jack had made. Horses went north; the money came back, with never a hitch.

Andrew Jackson Lewis, though only seventeen, was well known in the Loudoun Valley as a skilled horseman, intelligent and responsible. When he came to enlist, he was welcomed enthusiastically by the Black Horse Troop's founders, John Scott and William Henry Fitzhugh Payne. Jack spent the weekend drilling with the company, then returned to the Pettis farm and his duties there.

Jack had not lost his hunting instincts since moving down off Lost Mountain. He and his cousin Will regularly hunted small game, grouse and quail, and deer in the local fields and woodlots and nearby forests of the Blue Ridge. Their eye was keen, their aim steady, their shots quick and on the mark. They shared their catch with Jack's mother Rachel and Will's parents, taking their share to Mrs. Pettis for the farm's table. Rachel was particularly partial to roasted partridge and quail, while Mrs. Pettis's household found her marinated venison steaks to be a fine treat after a hard day in the fields and stables.

Minerva Pettis, who had been a schoolteacher, took pains to teach the boys whenever their work schedule allowed some time. She found the boys' speech to have improved, replacing the mountain-corrupted English in favor of the right words, properly pronounced (albeit with a proud Virginia soft drawl). But when they were in the woods, and their blood was up, hot on the trail of game, the polished veneer slipped away, and the mountain tongue of their early boyhood just naturally came out. "Hot damn! Ye got that there buck, Will, but he's done skedaddled 'crost them rocks into them burry bushes!" But back at the farm, he told Mrs. Pettis, "Yes ma'am, we shot a good-sized buck, but he got into some berry bushes and we had ourselves a time gettin' him dragged out. But I expect he'll taste pretty good, the way you prepare venison."

The Black Horse had regular drills, and included practice with saber and carbine. With all his riding and hunting skills, Jack soon proved to be a natural warrior and was given the rank of Third Sergeant. Jack had instinctively known how to blend his rough mountain talk with the refined language he'd been taught. That way, his militia comrades neither looked down on him as an ignorant hillbilly nor despised him for "putting on airs." He soon earned their respect and friendship. Captain Payne saw that Sergeant Lewis was a man he could depend upon, no matter what the future held for the Black Horse Troop.

Will, a year younger, envied Jack his status as a Black Horse trooper. He constantly begged Jack to intercede for him so he'd also be allowed to enlist. But Jack put him off, telling him he'd have to wait a year or two—he was just too young. Will continued to grumble, and occasionally tested Jack, to see if he'd relent. But Jack would just smile, telling the younger boy to be patient and pay attention to his chores.

Chapter Two
Sally

August 1860

Harry Pettis needed to send his most trusted hand, Jack Lewis, north to Pennsylvania with another string of fine horses. Captain Payne had taken Jack aside. "Sergeant, I'll ask you to keep your eyes and ears open when you're in Maryland, and especially in Pennsylvania. Learn as much as you can. Who are our friends, and who aren't. What roads are good, which aren't. Where the fords are. With this election coming up, if the abolitionists win, and Virginia is forced to secede, we may find the Black Horse ordered north at some point. We'll depend on you to guide us."

Jack was looking forward to this trip. In the string was a fine black stallion destined for the farm of Bartholomew Brunebaugh, whose prosperous Pennsylvania farm lay in the Cumberland Valley near Marion, midway between Greencastle and Chambersburg. Jack thought once more of the pretty Sally Keefer, working for Brunebaugh. He had thought of her often in the past two years, frustrated that his trips north had all been well to the east of the Cumberland Valley, too far east to have an excuse to call at the Brunebaugh farm. Until now. Finally, he'd be able to see her again.

His cousin Will teased him about it. "So you're gonna go see a pretty one, Jack. Better be careful. This time she'll tie ye up with a stronger cord than that little flower neck piece she give ye back in '58!"

"C'mon, Will. I only met her that once. She may not even be there. Doubt she's old enough to have gotten married yet, but who knows? A lot can happen in two years time. Still, I'm some curious t'see how she's grown. Let's see, she'd be sixteen by now. Near a full-grown woman! But I'm Black Horse now. No time for worryin' with a woman in tow."

Will laughed. "Oh sure, Jack. Now you're gonna tell me that if ye 'jine the cavalry,' they don't let ye have women? Not what I heard!" He laughed again, harder this time. Jack punched his younger cousin playfully in the arm and walked off to finish his trip preparations.

Jack set out early the next morning with the horses. He dropped off all but one at a farm outside Sharpsburg on the Antietam Creek in Maryland the next morning, then continued north to Hagerstown, crossed the Mason-Dixon Line into Pennsylvania, and rode on through Greencastle. The sun was getting low in the western sky when he reached Marion and rode down the lane to the Brunebaugh farm.

"Well, Jack Lewis, you've grown some. You look to be over six feet, an' you've put some meat on your bones. You're no boy no more, for sure." Brunebaugh saw more than size. The man before him had a presence about him that, despite his relaxed and easy manner, clearly indicated he would brook no nonsense. Brunebaugh decided quickly that he wouldn't try to beat down the price he'd agreed to with Pettis some months before. "This horse is in fine condition, Lewis. Pettis is as good as his word. I'll not haggle price with you."

Brunebaugh was a man normally full of bluster, who would try to intimidate whenever he could get away with it. He wasn't a coward, but he had no desire to get on the wrong side of the now-grown Jack Lewis. In fact, he figured he'd better try to get on the young man's good side.

"You've had a long ride here and another one back coming up. Have supper with us. And you're more than welcome t'spend the night. My boy Henry's bed's big enough even for you."

"Thank you, Mr. Brunebaugh. I'm glad the horse suits you. He's one of Mr. Pettis's best. I hated to see him leave the farm. And thank you for your hospitality. I'd be pleased to stay for supper, if Mrs.

Sally

Brunebaugh wouldn't mind settin' an extra plate. But I'd be pleased to just pitch my bedroll on some straw in your barn tonight."

Jack knew that the meal would be delicious and more than ample to satisfy the hollow spot in his belly—roast pork, potatoes and yams, sauerkraut, beans, stewed apples, fresh hot bread with *schmierkase* and apple butter, and apple and mince pies with hot coffee. He also knew that the presence of the pretty young serving girl he'd met here in the Brunebaugh kitchen back in '58, Sally, would ease the hollow spot he'd felt in his heart ever since. But he had no desire to sleep in a bed with pimply, fifteen-year-old Henry. Something about the boy just didn't seem natural. No, he'd sleep a lot more comfortably in the barn's haymow.

Sally Keefer was overcome with joy at the return of this boy she'd dreamt about constantly for the last two years. She'd let him know of her affection, without arousing the suspicion of the Brunebaughs.

At dinner, while serving the family and their guest, she found ways to press an arm, a thigh, and, for one brief instant, her breast, against the handsome young visitor. Jack felt each touch as if he'd been hit with a hot iron, but didn't so much as move a muscle that might give away the girl. To the Brunebaughs, he gave every appearance of ignoring the servant completely as he ate ravenously (much to Sadie Brunebaugh's delight) and conversed knowledgeably with Bart Brunebaugh and Henry about horses, breeding, and the impact of the dry weather on the corn crop that fall. But his mind was on the beautiful young woman serving him. *She's no longer a young girl,* Jack thought. *Some fella'll be tryin' t'court her, if they haven't already. Wish I was closer so it could be me courtin' her!* Whenever he could, he flashed a quick smile and wink to the pretty girl bustling about. Equally careful not to be observed by anyone else, she returned his smile with one of her own.

After Sally cleared away the final dishes and cups, Jack pleaded tiredness and the need to be fresh for the long ride back to Upperville the next day. He excused himself and headed to the barn.

Sadie Brunebaugh gave her orders to the serving girl as first her son and then her husband headed upstairs to bed. "Red up the table an' warsh the dishes 'fore you get up to bed. An' don't forget to outen the lights! We got us a hard day comin' tomorra, cannin' all them peaches

23

Henry picked t'day." Sadie burped, scratched her ample belly, and walked heavily up the creaking stairs to her bed.

Sally cleaned off the table, washed and dried the dishes, and set the table for breakfast. Hearing the activity upstairs cease, followed shortly by the snores of the family, Sally decided it was safe to sit out on the side porch for awhile before bed. It was a warm night, and she'd been cooped up inside working all day and all evening.

Sally took off her apron and hung it on the door peg. On the porch, she sat on the rocker and gazed at the half moon shining brightly across the fields. Still feeling warm from the hot kitchen, she took off her little white cap, allowing the chestnut curls of her hair to spill down across her shoulders. She raised the hem of her skirt to the knees, unbuttoned the top four buttons of her high-collared blouse, and leaned back to enjoy the cool air on her skin. "Good thing Henry can't see me like this, skin exposed in plain sight!"

She knew Henry lusted for her, just like Reverend Coldsmith said young men do. She saw how he'd watch her on a hot day when she carried out the wash and hung it on the line, her thin dress clinging to the ripe curves of her sweaty young body. She saw him slink off to the out-house and not come out for ten minutes. Once, curious, she walked quietly up to the side of the privy and listened when Henry was in there after watching her. She grimaced when she heard his sharp heavy breathing and the strange rhythmic sounds, and heard him softly saying her name—"Sally, yes!"—over and over. "Well, that's the most you'll get from me, young Mr. Henry!" she thought to herself as she went back to her chores. "No danger of my goin' to hell for lustin' after you!"

It bothered her more when she caught Mr. Brunebaugh staring at her the same way. The farmer had just come from the fields and was on his way to the pump by the washtub to clean the grime from his face and hands when he noticed Sally, bent over the washboard, scrubbing his underwear. Her dress, wet with splashing from the washtub, clung to her hips and breasts. After he'd washed, he asked Sally for a towel, but she had none. "Well, this'll do fine!" said Brunebaugh, and he wiped his wet hands dry on her dress, making sure to feel her bottom and thighs in the process. That bothered her a lot. After that incident, she began to notice him staring at her more and more, clearly lusting for her. "Well, Reverend Coldsmith, it ain't just young men that court hell with lustful thoughts. An' I surely don't have no lust for him!" She began to worry that he might visit her little room over the kitchen some night when his wife was exhausted and asleep. Lacking any bolt on the door, she had fashioned a rope loop fastener to secure the door latch. She hoped it would hold if he ever attempted to enter while she slept.

But tonight the Brunebaugh men were in their rooms. Asleep, she hoped. The tingling she felt in her ripening body was not for them. No, it was brought on by the contact and flirting with the handsome young Virginian, now asleep in the barn. Romantic images of him lying with her under an apple tree in spring by a meadow, white petals slowly drifting down on them as they hugged and kissed, had long filled her head as she lay alone at night. Lost in the fantasy, aroused, Sally allowed herself to rise, walk off the porch, and go off in the moonlight to the barn.

Jack lay on his blanket above her in the loft. Tired as he was, he couldn't sleep for thinking of Sally. She had indeed blossomed from a pretty girl just out of childhood, into a lovely girl nearly into full womanhood. Even with the high collar and the many pleats of her skirt, he knew she had a fine figure to go with the oval face, high cheekbones, cornflower blue eyes, full mouth, and the chestnut hair which, mostly hidden under the prim white cap at dinner, now hung in curls to her shoulders. "Lordy, I'm in love with this girl. I can't hardly believe how beautiful she's grown." He felt himself getting aroused at the image of her moving under him, moaning in delight. Then he stopped himself. In his fantasy, he thought of her as a chaste young virgin, flirtatious but pure. Not like the whore he'd been with once in Baltimore.*'Course,* he thought, *that Maryland girl sure knew some tricks that could drain a man dry and leave him comin' back for more! But I can't be thinkin' of sweet Sally like that.* His reverie was broken by the hushed call from below.

"Jack. Are you awake?"

"I'm awake," he answered.

"May I come up?"

"Surely! Just take care on that ladder." Jack went to meet Sally at the top of the ladder at the edge of the hayloft, gave her his hand, and swung her up onto the loft floor. He gathered her into his arms, lifted her up, and held her tight against his chest as he kissed her. Arms around his neck, she kissed him back and hung on while she wrapped her lithe legs around his waist. Their youthful desires got rid of any inhibitions they might have been feeling, as each strove to make the fantasies nurtured during their two-year separation come true.

Jack pulled Sally down onto his blanket on the hay, their mouths eagerly exploring one another's. He felt the points of her firm breasts pressing into his chest. She felt his arousal pressing against her. She took his hand and slipped it into her blouse. She wore no corset or binder cloth to hide her ripening figure. Sadie said she was too young, her breasts too slight to need one. "Just something else to make and wash," she'd said. *If Mrs. Brunebaugh knew how her husband looked at me in a wet dress, she'd change her mind in a hurry,* Sally had thought. But now she was glad nothing hindered her lover's touch sending thrills through her.

As Jack caressed the smooth flesh and the hard nipples at their tips, Sally's body suddenly shuddered. She rubbed herself urgently against him. Still kissing feverishly, they both reached climax together. Sally cried out in a passionate release of emotion and pleasure, disentangled herself, then lay back in the hay, her head on his chest. She had never enjoyed such sheer physical release. She felt flooded with love and happiness.

Jack lay there, quietly stroking and kissing her hair. He too had felt the surge of release, and then a swelling of love for the vibrant girl who had come back into his life today. The deep pleasure and satisfaction he felt at this moment were incomparably greater than any feelings he'd ever experienced. And this wasn't even real intercourse! Sally was still as pure as she had been before they met. He felt the sharp edge of conflict within his mind. Animal lust had urged him to take her completely, but moral rectitude silently praised him for not yielding to that ultimate lustful act.

Sally was in rapture, and she didn't care if Reverend Goldsmith would condemn her lustful thoughts. She loved this man, had given him pleasure, and had received it in return. And her chastity was intact!

"I love you, Sally Keefer!"

"And I love you, Jack Lewis!"

"I'll come for you on my next trip north an' take you back with me."

"An' I'll be waiting for you, dearest Jack!"

As the moon rose higher, shining through the open haymow window, Sally reluctantly got up, bending over and kissing him one last time before she clambered down the hayloft ladder. She slipped back into the house and up the back stairs to her bed, her tryst undetected.

The next morning, Jack saddled up and rode back to Virginia.

Before a return trip could occur, South Carolina militia fired on Fort Sumter, and the War of Secession had begun. Sally often cried herself to sleep, knowing that Jack would have been among the first to join in defending his Virginia from Lincoln's armies. She feared she'd never see him again, but wouldn't give up hope.

The Brunebaughs had no idea that she harbored this love, but around the dinner table she'd hear them discussing the war, the danger they faced, and the results of the battles, decrying the series of defeats suffered by the Union at the hands of the Army of Virginia.

Sally silently cheered, hoping that meant that Jack would be safer on the winning side. She prayed that somehow the Peace Democrats in the Union would force Lincoln to abandon this war, and that Jack would return to her and take her away. She didn't care about preserving the Union or freeing slaves. She just wanted her man—and to relive the fantasy that had become reality in the barn that night.

In the fall of 1860 and early in 1861, Sally had been able to write a few letters to Jack and had received a few. In the last, written shortly after the firing on Fort Sumter in Charleston, Jack had told her of how he had joined a Virginia cavalry regiment. Only later would Sally learn which regiment he had joined. More importantly, she knew he loved her, and treasured his promise to come for her after the South won the war.

One hot summer afternoon in 1861, Mrs. Brunebaugh asked Sally, now seventeen, to go down by the creek and pick blackberries for the pies she wanted her to bake. Sally was eager to go. For several summers she'd used every such occasion to take a refreshing dip in the Conococheague Creek, washing away the accumulated sweat of the summer chores, relishing the feel of the cool water rushing over her body and the tingle on her skin as she dried off on the creek bank.

On this day, she soon gathered two large wicker baskets full of berries. There was time for a bath. Her special spot was in a secluded glade at a sharp turn of the creek. A steep limestone cliff formed the opposite bank. Forced by the cliff into a narrow channel, the current had scoured out a deep hole in the otherwise shallow creek. Tall hickory trees shaded the small glade. But in the early afternoon, the sun's rays shed a warm light on the water.

Believing her privacy to be assured in the wooded glen, Sally sat down on a large rock, took off her high-top shoes, then stood and slipped her dress up and over her head. She removed her little white cap, let her hair hang down, and slipped out of her undergarment and stockings. Naked as Eve, she jumped from the rock into the water.

The cool water took her breath away as her body reacted to the sudden change from hot to cool. But a young body adapts quickly, and she soon was splashing happily, running her hands over her smooth skin, washing away the sweat. For the time being, she found a measure of happiness. As she touched herself, her mind turned again to the memory of the pleasure she'd felt in the barn last year with Jack. Oh, how she wished he were here now, with her, in the water. How she longed to give herself to this man she loved!

Sally knew she must get back to her kitchen, or Mrs. Brunebaugh would show her displeasure in a hundred small but unpleasant ways. She waded over to the bank and clambered up on the rock, careful not to let any mud touch her now-clean and glowing skin. She dried herself on the warm rock, enjoying the sensual warmth of the bright sun shining through the opening in the tree canopy around her.

Bart Brunebaugh had been walking in a field that ended in a line of trees at the top of the cliff opposite the little glade. He heard splashing in the creek as he approached the trees. Peering down at the water from behind a large hickory, he saw the naked form of a shapely maiden emerge from the water and stand on a sunny rock. "My gawd, that's Sally—buck naked!" He stood transfixed by the sight of her ripe young body, fully exposed to his view. He'd never seen such beauty in all his life—certainly not in his wife! He watched intently as Sally slowly dressed. A devilish desire to possess her began to grow.

Sally

Only his fear of being caught in the open raping a young girl kept him from rushing down to the creek, taking her, and satisfying the long-suppressed lust that now threatened to overcome him. He'd wait for the right time and place to fulfill his urge. The little tease! The harlot! She'll find out soon enough what happens to women who flaunt their naked bodies!

Bart Brunebaugh knew what a harlot was, from personal experience. Last summer he'd made an unexpected extra profit at the livestock auction in Greencastle, money his wife would never know about. Flush with cash, he had ridden across the state line to Hagerstown and headed for a house of ill repute on East Franklin Street run by a buxom woman named Isabel, a place he'd heard about at the auction many times but never visited. Inside, he looked over the scantily clad girls and chose a thin young thing, about as opposite from his stout wife as he could find. She lay beneath him, going through the motions until he finished and got off. Bart had loved it! Now, he thought, if he could just finagle a way to come back and use this harlot again! But Sadie kept a close eye on the cash and this had been his one and only time.

Now he drank in the view of a naked and far prettier young girl at the creek below. He thought the Hagerstown whore he'd been with probably started the same way, showing off and just waiting to get it! His wife's servant girl was heading down the same path. She'd wind up working at Isabel's for sure in another year. Why should he wait? He might as well get his before Isabel charged him cash money for it! Not this afternoon. Too risky here. But soon.

After Sally was fully dressed, he forced himself to turn away and walk back to the team of horses and the hay rake he'd left standing in the field. He finished the raking, but thoughts of the girl and her ripe young body consumed him. He could scarcely wait to feel her writhing under him as he vented his passion on her. That evening at the dinner table his eyes followed her as she moved about the room serving the meal. He mentally undressed her, recalling his afternoon vision, feeling the arousal of her presence so close to him.

Brunebaugh now realized that his son Henry was looking at Sally in the same lustful way. *Why, the little devil! I'll wager he's snuck down and watched her naked at the creek before!*

Sadie Brunebaugh, a big woman who liked to eat, was noisily chewing a big mouthful of ham, oblivious to the lustful glances her son and husband were casting on her serving girl. The idea that men would be interested in Sally never occurred to Mrs. Brunebaugh, who thought her entirely too thin and insubstantial for childbearing, despite her best efforts to fatten the girl up.

Brunebaugh had been given a jug of fine whiskey from a renowned distillery in the nearby Catoctin Mountains of Maryland. After dinner, he sat down on the porch and began to sample the jug. Like molten lava, the potent Maryland rye slid down his throat, setting his belly afire, the heat quickly rushing to his brain. One swig led to another, and another, and another.

Sadie Brunebaugh had complained of indigestion after dinner, left Sally to do the cleaning up, and had taken to her bed. This happened often. Sally was exhausted trying to keep the demanding Mrs. Brunebaugh satisfied while doing all the cooking for the household and feeding the farm hands, cleaning, washing, and tending the garden.

While Bart Brunebaugh sat on the porch sampling his jug, Sally checked on Mrs. Brunebaugh, who was sound asleep and snoring loudly. Henry, too, had gone to bed. Sally went off to her room, changed into her thin cotton nightgown, slipped under the thin sheet, and fell into an exhausted sleep.

Brunebaugh sat rocking on the porch, his mind now deeply under the influence of the powerful spirits. The afternoon's images of Sally's bared body returned. In the heat of the night, he began to feel a strong lustful need growing in his loins. He felt like a rutting buck, needing to find a doe in heat, and ready to fight anything standing in the way of his conquest. He envisioned his stout, doughy wife Sadie, snoring in their bed. The prospect of coupling with her made him shudder with disgust.

On the other hand, their young serving girl would be lying alone in her bed, in her room up over the kitchen. He vividly recalled the image of her nudity in the glade. So beautiful. So young. So desirable. So available! He thought of how she looked serving dinner that evening, her dress so prim and proper, hiding beneath it the ripe body of a young woman. Sleeping in his own house, she was his for the taking. Fueled by courage from the jug, he no longer felt any fear of discovery.

His alcohol-soaked brain quickly constructed the rationale he needed: she was just a harlot, having a body like that, teasing him by hiding it under prim clothing. Well, he'd seen it. Seen its ripeness. Seen how she'd exposed herself fully, in broad daylight, for the amusement of strangers. The tease! She needed to be taught a lesson. She needed to be taught a lesson in what a man does to a harlot when she teases him like that! He helped himself to a few more swigs of good Maryland rye. Yes indeed, no time like the present for her to get that lesson. And he was just the man to do it. By morning she'd no longer be a teasing virgin, she'd be the well-used harlot he knew she really wanted to be.

Brunebaugh went into the kitchen and crept up the back stairs to Sally's room, taking care not to wake his wife. He didn't want her to interrupt the lesson he was going to administer to their servant girl. He stealthily raised the door latch. Tired, Sally had forgotten to put her rope loop fastener on the latch, so he was able to push open the door unhindered, noiselessly.

Stepping to Sally's bed, the big man put his hand over her mouth, pushed up her nightgown, held her down on the bed, and brutally entered the innocent girl. Terrified, Sally struggled. But she was no match for the burly farmer. She nearly passed out from the pain as he violently took her virginity. When he had emptied his seed, Brunebaugh slid away. Warning her not to make any fuss, lest he beat her without mercy, he took his hand off her mouth, calling her a harlot and the devil's handmaid. He ordered her to get out of his house before his wife got up and treated her like the harlot she was. Then he left the room, leaving her shaking in anger, disgust, and fear of what might follow if she stayed one minute longer under this brutal man's roof.

She sobbed into her pillow, praying that God wouldn't condemn her to hell for what had been done. This was worse than anything she'd imagined. Worse than any sin Reverend Goldsmith had warned against. If only the war was over, and Jack Lewis were here! But the war wasn't over, and he wasn't here. Mercifully, she fell into a deep sleep for a few hours.

Rising before dawn, Sally packed up the treasured letters from Jack, put her clothes and a hair brush in a sack, and slipped out of the house before the hung-over Brunebaugh, his wife, or their son Henry were awake. When Henry came downstairs, there was no Sally, no fire in the stove, no breakfast. He stormed up the stairs to her room, found her things gone, and roused his father and mother. "Ma, Pa, Sally's done run off!"

"Good riddance," said Bart Brunebaugh. "Henry, get yerself back down t'the kitchen an' get the stove goin.' Fix some bacon and eggs fer us." When the boy left the room, Brunebaugh turned to his wife. "We're well rid of her. You seen the way Henry looks at her? It ain't healthy, Mother. She's ripe, and he'd soon be gettin' her in the barn an' gettin' her pregnant, fer sure. She's been teasin' him, askin' for it. We oughta be gettin' us a younger girl anyway. Cost us less."

Sadie Brunebaugh, though she didn't much like not having kitchen help at the moment, nodded in agreement. "The hussy! Yes, I seen how she flaunts herself at Henry. Poor boy. She'd like to take advantage of him, fer sure. She's too skinny, anyway. Good riddance is what I say. Wonder where she'll go to, though? She got no family around now. Bet she'll be back here beggin' t'stay 'fore long."

Bart thought he knew exactly where she would go. *The harlot's headed to Hagerstown and Isabel's, for sure. Men'll pay good money to have her!*

Sally, sore and aching from Brunebaugh's brutal attack, had walked down the lane to the Chambersburg Pike. Normally a six-mile walk into town wouldn't bother her at all, but the violation she'd suffered made every step a trial. She knew nothing of houses like Isabel's in Hagerstown, and would have died before she'd let herself wind up in such a place.

She said a silent prayer of thanks when she was given a ride by a farmer taking milk into town. He told her about his cousin who had married a well-to-do Chambersburg lawyer. Right now she was looking for a comely, hard-working girl to help with the house and children. Seemed she had trouble keeping good help. The farmer thought Sally was just the girl she'd want. This kind man dropped off his load at the creamery, then drove Sally to his cousin's house. Sally was hired on the spot.

She began to feel content at the Chambersburg home of Joseph Baird. His wife Martha was a kind mistress; the children were likeable and responded well to Sally. Their house on Queen Street was large and comfortable, and her room was cozy. She immediately took over the chores and fit into the household routine. A delighted Martha Baird was quick to praise her.

In time, Sally lost the feeling of helplessness and guilt she'd felt that horrible last night on the farm. She came to realize she'd done nothing to deserve Brunebaugh's violent rape, that the guilt and blame were his. He'd be the one to see hell, not her. Remembering the happiness of the night with Jack Lewis in the barn, she let the anticipation of someday seeing him again blot out the horror of rape. Sadly, the pretty young girl would face more such abuse from a master.

Joseph Baird and his wife had been happy in their marriage. But after the difficult birth of their second child, when Martha nearly died, she moved her things to a separate bedroom in their spacious house. She began to lock the bedroom door. Baird complained at the loss of his marital privilege, to no avail. He was a healthy man with strong sexual urges. His wife still dearly loved him. Martha just felt no need for physical intimacy with him, and feared another pregnancy. She sought out a discreet way to let him satisfy his normal hunger without risking a scandal outside their house.

Mrs. Baird hired a succession of young women to "help around the house." They soon learned that their most important duty, though one never to be mentioned, was to service the master of the house in their bed. Some, disgusted or horrified, left immediately. Others, those who desperately needed the job, suppressed their feelings of shame and guilt long enough to stay on for a few months, until they could bear it no longer. Baird was a demanding and inconsiderate lover. These were, after all, in his mind, just hirelings meant to satisfy his needs. He felt no obligation to let them share any pleasure, let alone be concerned about their feelings of shame.

And now Sally Keefer had been thrust into this odious situation. Baird allowed her a few weeks to become comfortable with the new house, job, mistress, and children before he bothered her. Then, just when she thought she'd found a real home, with warmth and some measure of happiness, Baird came to her bedroom. She was in her room, undressing before putting on her nightgown, when he entered without a knock. The view of the young beauty, nearly naked, stirred his lust to its fullness.

Shocked and frightened, she tried to cover herself, shrinking away from the man. Was this to be a repeat of the horror she'd had at the farm? Undeterred by her obvious fear, Baird strode across the room and drew her into an unwilling embrace.

"Stop your struggling, girl, if you know what's good for you! I will not rape you, but you will allow me the use of your body, Sally. This is the condition of your continued employment in this house. You will be the surrogate for my dear wife, any night that I desire you."

He swiftly undid his trousers, freed his erection, and placed her hand on it. "You must give me pleasure, in any way I demand." He described all the acts to which he intended to have the girl submit. She protested, claiming in all honesty her innocence and ignorance of what he was demanding. Sadly, over the next few weeks, he compelled her to learn all the perverse methods he demanded for his gratification, acts that his wife had always refused. At least he hadn't violently raped her. Seeing no way out, she passively accepted Baird's use of her body while detesting his touch and loathing his presence in her bed.

Sally tried to complain to her mistress. Initially, Sally had come to feel fondness and trust for Martha Baird. In every other respect, Mrs. Baird had made her a happy and contented member of the household. But Sally soon realized that Martha put her husband's needs and desires above all else, and would do whatever was necessary to satisfy those needs and desires, except personally submit to them.

In compensation for the sexual usage she abhorred, and knew that Sally had to endure from her husband, Martha lavished exceptional consideration on the young girl, buying her lovely clothes, expensive shoes, and perfumes. After a few months, she gave Sally a large oval gold locket. It was finely made, its front and back sections hinged, with a tiny clasp to seal the sections tightly together. Its slim gold chain was long enough to easily slip over the wearer's head, displaying the locket just below the top of the valley between the breasts. She had a woman on King Street do Sally's hair—"Such lovely chestnut curls deserve fine style." Then she had Sally's likeness captured in tintype and mounted inside the locket. "Someday, Sally, you will marry. Your husband will be proud to have a locket with your likeness to wear beneath his shirt, close to his heart."

Sally

Sally was awed by her mistress's generosity. That her image could be captured and preserved through this magical process was something she'd never have imagined. She hugged her mistress and thanked her profusely. Martha assigned Sally to be responsible for the children, and hired a hard-working woman from the Chambersburg colored community to do the cooking and housework. Martha spent long hours grooming Sally to become a gracious young lady, in order to be a fit model for her children.

Not wanting to lose the many positive things Martha Baird had introduced into her life, Sally resigned herself to the situation. When Baird came to her room at night and used her for his perverse gratification, she'd shut her mind to what was being done to her. Afterward, she'd cry herself to sleep, praying that her God would not punish her. In her mind, she was not the sinner, but the sinned-against, a vessel for the execrable exertions of the lustful Baird, certainly. But having no love, and taking no pleasure, she felt herself to be as chaste a virgin as she was when her true love Jack Lewis last left her. But, oh, how she prayed that God would somehow find a way to send Jack back to her. Jack would take her away from all this, then her bed would be shared with the man she loved, not a man she detested.

Chapter Three
Luke

November 1861

Luke Kellogg urged his team to go faster as his wagon left the little crossroads community of Owasco. The seventeen-year-old from the tiny New York hamlet of New Hope was anxious to get to Auburn before mid-morning. He still had to unload the fifty sacks of buckwheat flour before he could get over to the Cayuga County Courthouse and enlist. The Seventy-fifth New York Volunteer Regiment was being formed, and its quota was filling up rapidly. Young men from this northern Finger Lakes region were caught up in the patriotic fervor, leaving farms and villages to join the army, eagerly responding to President Lincoln's call to arms. They were all determined to put down the secessionist rebellion and save the Union.

His younger brother Andrew hung onto the seat as the wagon jolted over the ruts in the dusty road. "Luke, ease off! You'll bust the wagon at this rate. We got time to get this load delivered and get home before dark. C'mon, slow down!"

Luke hadn't told Andrew that he intended to join up today, hadn't let him see the traveling bag he'd packed and concealed among the flour sacks. He'd brought him along just to drive the wagon back home after he'd joined the Seventy-fifth. "Andy, hang on. I mean to get to town soon as this team'll get us there."

Soon the road turned north, following the east shore of Owasco Lake. The team slowed down under the weight of the loaded wagon as they ascended a long hill. At the top, Andrew looked west across the sunlit waters of the lake to the hills on the far shore. The sky was clear and bright, with no sign of the low gray clouds that foretold autumn snow in this upstate New York region. *Maybe Luke'll let us take some time to fish some on the way home,* he thought. But then Luke shook the reins, gave out a "gee-haw!" and set the horses back into a canter toward Auburn.

Then they were into the village, following the east shore of the Owasco Creek until they reached Calvin Avery's warehouse. There they unloaded the sacks of flour, collected the cash and drove on to the courthouse. Andrew tied the team to a hitching post, and Luke went into the building to search out the recruiting agent. He ordered Andrew to stay with the wagon.

Inside, he found a small office with the sign "Enlist Here" above the open door. Sergeant Keeler was behind the desk, filling out the forms for a gangly youth. Keeler looked up at Luke and said, "You here to enlist, boy?"

"Yessir!" Luke responded.

"You over eighteen?"

Luke couldn't bring himself to lie. "No sir, not 'til next year. But can't I sign up now? I'll surely be eighteen before we see any fighting."

"Sorry, them's the rules. Besides, this boy here's the last recruit. We've met our quota. Can't take no more. I expect we'll be geared up and leavin' for Albany before the week's out." And Sergeant Keeler went back to his forms.

Crestfallen, Luke slowly walked down the corridor, out the entrance, and down the granite stairs to the street. Why should he be left out, when his friend Henry, only sixteen, had gotten in? How had Henry gotten around the age requirement? He knew Henry would never lie.

Andrew was impatiently waiting. "C'mon, Luke. It's early enough, we can do some fishing on the way home. Can we?"

Luke

Luke hid his disappointment. No sense letting Andrew know what he'd intended, for he would probably tell their father, who would then forbid Luke to sign up. Even though the fall harvest was over, all hands were needed to take care of the never-ending chores at the family farm, as well as to help out at the mill at New Hope. The mill, built into the side of a steep ravine with its tall overshot waterwheel fed from the mill pond above, had been built almost thirty years before by Luke's great-uncle, Charles Kellogg. Luke's father had long helped his uncle Charles. But the mill had been sold. It was now Horace Round's buckwheat flour the boys had delivered—a regular job for them, since Horace's mill hand had gone off to the army some months ago. Well, he'd heard that another regiment, the Seventy-sixth, was going to be formed in Cortland in December. Maybe they'd not ask about age. Or maybe he'd do what his friend Henry did.

Henry Wilcox lived on a farm at the edge of Bear Swamp, a few miles south of the mill at New Hope, on the top of the ridge overlooking Skaneateles Lake. Luke and Henry had gone to a one-room school at New Hope together for a few years. It was a six-mile walk, every day, each way. But Henry was passionate about learning, and hoped even as a lad to find a way to learn more about the world beyond Bear Swamp. An inventive boy, he had made a small boat that he sailed on the emerald green waters of Skaneateles. He'd made a trail through the woods down the side of the ridge, and kept the boat in a small cove in the southwest corner of the lake at Glen Haven. Out on the lake, he fished and caught trout and bass, supplementing the meager fare so hard-won by his family from the thin soil on the ridge-top farm. Living there was hard, and Henry longed to look for better prospects. His father had died some years before, and he and his widowed mother lived on the farm with his uncle Josiah. They needed him on the farm, but his mother finally persuaded Josiah to let Henry join the army, praying to God that this was the right decision.

Henry was only sixteen when he went to Auburn to enlist. Knowing he might not meet the army's age requirement, he inquired of several young men, who didn't look to be much older than he, how they had managed to be accepted. "Why that's easy. We didn't exactly lie, neither. Y'see, you take a piece of paper and write '18' on it. Put it in your shoe. Then, when they ask, you say, 'Yessir I'm over eighteen.' "

Needless to say, it didn't take the clever Henry long to equip his boots with the needed paper lining. And while Sergeant Keeler gave the boy a long look, he took him at his word and signed him up.

Henry's mother cried and Uncle Josiah and Aunt Mary waved goodbye as they watched the new regiment board the train for Albany. They knew Henry would fight honorably for his country, for the Union they all believed in. They had heard of the colored woman, Harriet Tubman, who had been working to help escaped slaves make their way north, leading them through nearby Auburn and on to freedom in Canada. But while the Wilcox family thought slavery was wrong and un-Christian, they had no desire to see Henry die for that cause. They had no desire to see him die for any reason! But they knew life could be fragile. They knew death was always about—from disease, accident, or overwork. At least Henry was risking his life for his country, for freedom, for those who would come after.

And so Luke envied Henry, and had wanted to join his friend in the Seventy-fifth New York. But it was not to be. He could not know that his friend would die, not of wounds in battle, but of typhoid, in the trenches, as the Union Army besieged Richmond, on August 8, 1864.

In later years, after the war, when he visited his family at New Hope, Luke would make the pilgrimage to the Wilcox Cemetery on Ridge Road, high above Skaneateles Lake. He would say a prayer for the childhood friend who had given his life for his country. Luke would make it a point to always bring something for Henry's family. Henry's mother Jane, widowed since 1855, with her son now dead, and his aunt Mary, widowed when Josiah Wilcox died in February of 1863, were struggling to keep the farm going. Others in the family gave support, and the women managed. But while they were thankful to Luke for his kindness, a small part of their minds harbored some resentment that Luke had survived the terrible war in which their beloved Henry had perished.

Mary Wilcox treasured a letter from Henry, written in January of 1863, from Bayou Teche, Louisiana. She read it to her husband before he died. They talked about how Henry had wanted to see beyond Bear Swamp. Now he was in Cajun country, near New Orleans. Henry had gotten his wish. He was about as far from their New York farm as his family could envision. Then Josiah had died.

Luke

A year later, while still mourning Josiah, the family had gotten the letter from Harrison Root, Lieutenant, Seventy-fifth Regiment, New York Volunteers, telling them of Henry's death in Virginia. Lieutenant Root wrote of Henry's bravery in numerous engagements in Florida and Louisiana in '61 and '62, the dark early days of the war, and especially of his courage during the battle of Sabine Pass, Texas, in September of '63. In the late summer of 1864, the family met the train at Cortland, set the coffin on their wagon, and drove Henry home to his final resting place, among the oaks on the crest of the ridge above Skaneateles Lake.

After the war, when Luke stood before the simple stone marker in the Wilcox family cemetery, he remembered that Henry had lived the life he had wanted—he'd traveled far beyond his Cayuga County home and had died in defense of the country he loved. "And Henry, you couldn't know it then, but you won. The Union is preserved!"

But in the fall of 1861, all Luke could think was, *Lucky Henry. He's gone off to serve our country, and I'm stuck here on the farm, unless I go to Cortland and use Henry's trick. And why shouldn't I? Henry's younger than me. I'm only fooling them by some months. He did it by two years!* As he and Andrew slowly drove the wagon home, Luke resolved to see that the next load of New Hope flour went to Cortland.

But first, he decided to meet his younger brother's request. They'd detour down a narrow lane to Owasco Lake and drown a few worms. While the ground might be frozen elsewhere in upstate New York in November, the Finger Lakes still held some warmth, and the ground on their shores was easy to dig. The boys found a few worms, cut two willow switches for poles, tied hooks on some line that Andrew had tucked in his pocket, anticipating this opportunity, and proceeded to do some serious fishing. Luke was still too distracted to develop appropriate fishing tactics, but Andrew filled the breach. He scampered along the lakeshore until he found a tree that had fallen into the water, creating the ideal hiding spot for the bass he coveted. "C'mon Luke. Over here."

Andrew knew his beans. He saw the late afternoon sun reflected on the surface of the lake. The long shadows made a dark patch under the fallen tree. He knew that fish would love to loll there. He swung his arm in a swift arc. The small pebble he'd wound in the line as a sinker flew through the air and, with a splash, sinker and worm sunk beneath the shimmering surface. With no insects hovering over the water on this cold afternoon, the bass hiding under the tree was hungry, and struck instantly at the morsel that suddenly appeared before his eyes. Too late, he felt the sting of the hook as it lodged in his mouth. His instincts took over, and he dashed out from under his log at top speed, only to be jerked to a halt. The big fish leaped high out of the water, trying to free himself. Instead, he fell back and felt himself being drawn backward, out of the water, onto the bank. He flopped and gasped, but his gills, while superbly designed by the Creator for efficiency in extracting oxygen from water, were completely inadequate in the cool November air.

"My gawd, Andy!" exclaimed Luke, rushing over to help his younger brother. "This bass is huge!"

Andrew beamed at the praise from his older brother—he didn't get that very often.

Together, the boys took the fish off the hook, cleaned it, and slipped it into a flour sack that Andrew had tucked into a corner of the wagon, just in case the opportunity to fish came along, knowing that he'd sure catch something if it did!

They reached home just before the sunlight died away over the western hills, enjoying that orange glow of the autumn sun so treasured in upstate New York. Knowing that darkness descends in a matter of minutes after the sun sets, they were grateful to be pulling into the barnyard as the last rays spread across the still clear sky, mingling with deep-hued blues, magentas, violets, and dark purple.

Luke unhitched the horses from the wagon, led them into the barn, wiped them down, and forked out some hay into their stalls before heading to the house. He hoped Andrew hadn't figured out why he was in such a lather to get to the Cayuga Courthouse. As he entered the warm kitchen, he heard Andrew happily bragging about his fishing success that afternoon at Owasco.

His mother was hugging Andrew while the boys' father was admiring the size of the catch. Luke was grateful that the dinner was good, the fresh fish delicious, and Andrew content to talk of nothing but fishing. Perhaps his secret would be safe.

Luke

The next day, Luke and his father went into the woods on the ridge to cut firewood. They took their horse Kate to pull the log out of the woods after they cut the tree down and trimmed off the branches. His father swung the axe skillfully, cutting a notch on the side where the tree was to fall, then another above it on the opposite side. But the tree didn't fall. They wrapped one end of a rope around the trunk and the other end to Kate. Luke set her off. Kate pulled. The tree creaked, bent, then snapped. But it didn't fall exactly as planned. It careened off to one side, and its largest branch, nearly a foot across, clipped Luke's father in the head, knocking him down. Luke rushed to his father, who lay unconscious on the ground, blood streaming from the gash on his head.

"Father!" cried Luke. But there was no reply.

Luke placed his fingers on his father's neck, felt the pulsing of the artery. "Thank God. You're alive!"

Luke took off his jacket and shirt. Tearing a strip of cloth off the shirt, he bound the wound on his father's head. He put his jacket back on, hoisted his limp father onto the horse with some difficulty, then climbed on the horse's back, holding his father up during the short ride back to the house.

"Andy—get out here quick!"

Andrew rushed from the barn where he'd been cleaning out Kate's stall.

"Father's hurt. Help me get him in the house!"

The two boys carried the unconscious man into the kitchen.

"Oh my Lord, boys, what's happened to your father?" Mrs. Kellogg quickly took charge. She had the boys carry her husband into the parlor, laying him on the settee. She removed the shirt bandage, cleaned the wound with soap and water, and rebandaged his head. He began to stir.

"What? Where am I? Who are you? My head hurts." He managed to get out the few words before drifting off again.

She knew the doctor was too far away to get to them. And she had no confidence in most of the doctors anyway. It seemed they had three remedies for every sickness or injury—purgatives, bleeding, or amputation. Instinctively, she knew none had any application here. Over the next few days, she made him teas from roots and herbs, especially willow bark. The bleeding from the scalp wound had soon stopped, though the wound would leave a scar. Her home medicine had brought him back to full consciousness. But his memory was affected, and his right leg and arm were paralyzed.

The boys did all the farmwork while their mother handled all her normal chores, which now included being a nurse to their father. They were tired and short of sleep, but grateful that Kellogg was alive and improving, if but slowly.

A week later Mrs. Kellogg sat with the boys after supper to discuss their situation. "Father's doing better, but he can't do anything on the farm for who knows how long. Thank God you boys are here and healthy. Not like our neighbors, whose boys are off somewhere in the South fighting rebels."

Luke pushed the desire to enlist to the back of his mind, concentrating on the running of the farm while his father slowly recovered from the effects of the blow to his head. In the long winter he and Andrew chopped wood, fed animals, cut holes in the ice of the creek for the animals to drink, threshed oats, mucked out stables, and did some hunting and trapping. By the beginning of spring, their father's memory had largely been restored, if not his strength. So the boys carried out his directions for plowing and planting, readying the fields for the season. Over the summer, they cut hay, cradled oats, built and repaired fences, and prepared for the harvest. Filling in for their father, they joined their neighbors in repairing the township roads. When the roads were passable, they drove the wagon to carry loads of flour from the mill at New Hope to Auburn, Cortland, and a few times to Ithaca.

In late July, Luke and Andrew drove a wagonload of flour across the county to Aurora, due west of New Hope, beyond Owasco Lake, on the east shore of Cayuga Lake. While unloading, they were asked by several boys their age if they were going to enlist. The local men were angry at the Secessionists for dragging out what was supposed to be a quick victory for the Union. Many young men were eager to join the army. They talked excitedly about the organizing of the 111th Regiment of New York Volunteers at Auburn. There were a number of volunteers from Aurora and the surrounding farms in the town of Ledyard who had already signed up.

Luke

Hiram Ellis, Rufus Myers, and Ansel Smith were gathered at the store that morning, talking and eagerly anticipating their chance to "give it good to Johnny Reb." They were convinced that they and the rest of the men of the 111th would do Cayuga County proud. They'd go and teach the Secessionists a lesson, and restore the rebellious states to the Union for once and for all! Luke questioned them intently. Did they think he'd be able to join? Was the roster yet full? Should he go back to Auburn once more? Hiram and Rufus were nineteen, and Ansel was twenty. They looked at Luke, taller than any of them by several inches, and proportionately heavier—smooth-shaven, but with a clear dark shadow of beard. His thick black hair set off a high forehead above a well-proportioned face with dark brown eyes, a strong mouth, and a firm jaw. "Well, you sure look old enough. An' tough enough. An' you're sure big enough! Join us, and we'll lick those Rebs!"

Andrew overheard, worried. Their father was getting better, but could they manage the farm without Luke? *Not yet,* he thought. He'd better tell his parents, or Luke'd be off to Auburn and into the army, for sure.

It was twenty-five miles back to their home outside New Hope on Old Salt Road. It would be early evening before they completed the day's journey. Luke was excited, laying out in his mind the reasons he'd give to persuade his parents to accede to his enlisting. *I'm eighteen now. Age can't deprive me of my chance this time. Father isn't quite his old self, but near enough. Andrew is older, taller, stronger. The family can spare me now. And my country needs me!.* He knew his parents were firmly against slavery, and were proud of their neighbors in Auburn, rumored to be involved with the Underground Railroad, shepherding escaped slaves to freedom in Canada. They were firm believers in the need to hold the country together and fully agreed with President Lincoln's drastic measures to put down the secessionist insurrection. *Now they must allow me to do my part in this struggle.*

The boys rode in silence, each preoccupied with his own thoughts. Andrew tried to compose in his mind a list of all the farm tasks that needed doing, tasks that needed Luke in order to get done. The haying, the cradling of the oats, the repair of the fences, the clearing of the woods on the ridge to provide needed pasture...on and on, Andrew enumerated all the many tasks that a thriving farm required.

Luke considered making a detour towards the north to let Andrew fish for a bit in Owasco Lake. But he was in a hurry to get home. He was eager to say his piece. So instead of turning north, he stopped briefly in Moravia, just south of the lake, to water the horses and quench their own thirst. At Hanford's Store he told Andrew to go in with him. "I'll buy you a present, Andy, for helping me today. See them traps up there? Be just right for muskrat trapping over in Bear Swamp, don't you reckon?" He figured this might help make Andrew more agreeable to the family decision Luke wanted so badly.

As they continued on up the steep hill out of Moravia, Andrew talked happily about his plans to expand his trapping, happy to contemplate the things he could do with the money he'd get selling skins. Luke's generosity had driven away his sad and gloomy thoughts. Luke smiled and began to enjoy the ride up and down the rolling hills. Now he felt certain the way was clear for him to join up.

When they reached the Kellogg farmstead, Andrew unhitched the team and tended to the horses before turning them loose in the adjacent pasture to graze. Luke went inside. His father, paralysis long overcome, was still out in the fields, riding the hay rake.

Luke decided he'd better get his mother on his side before he confronted his father. He handed her a few items he'd bought in Moravia. "Why, thank you, son! These needles are just what I needed, and I'd been wanting the spools of thread to finish mending that tear in your father's good trousers. But this perfumed soap is an extravagance! You shouldn't have spent your money on me like that." But she was deeply touched, and pleased at her son's thoughtfulness, not yet realizing his ulterior motive.

Luke grinned as she gave him a big hug of appreciation. *Now if she'll only back me up when father's here,* he thought, and took the plunge. "Mother, in Aurora the men are forming a new regiment. They asked me to join. They're recruiting in Auburn now. Mother, I'd like to go. Father's much better, Andy's nearly grown, and most of the chores are done. Andy can get our friend Billy Weed to help him with the mill deliveries. There's no reason for me to delay serving my country, Mother. Will you help me persuade Father to let me join up?"

His mother hugged him again, even tighter this time. Tears began to form in her eyes. He felt a teardrop as he bent down to kiss her cheek.

Luke

Now he began to feel remorse. Maybe it was too soon, after all. Maybe the family wasn't ready to let him go. Maybe he should wait just a bit longer, at least until the early September corn was harvested. These boys over on Cayuga Lake weren't his close friends, after all; his friends had all gone off with the Seventy-fifth Regiment last fall. He steeled himself against the immediate disappointment, but figured now he had an even stronger argument for his father to consider.

Andrew and his father came through the door together. Kellogg was visibly exhausted. Mrs. Kellogg clucked disapprovingly. "Oh, Father! You've overdone it again today. Come sit down here and have a tot of hard cider. Supper's near ready." She brought him a basin of hot water and a washcloth and bathed his face and neck while he took a deep draw on the hard cider. "Mother, that's just what I needed. I'll be fine. I'm really starting to gain my strength back."

Andrew figured it was all right now to relate the news from Aurora. "The fellows in Aurora are all excited about the new Cayuga regiment forming up in Auburn. They want Luke to join up too. I'm against it, Father, we can't do without him just yet, can we." He said it as a statement, not a question.

"Just hold up, Andy. Who said I was goin'? Maybe it is a bit too soon. Maybe you're still too little to take it all on. Can't dump it all on Father, for sure. Not now." Luke worked hard to hide his disappointment, but his father was very observant, tired though he was, and he could see the signs.

"I am not too little! I can do anything around here you can!" Andrew protested, then realized he'd trapped himself.

As Kellogg spoke to his sons, his wife sat quietly listening. She knew her menfolk.

"All right, boys. Here's what we'll do. If you can hold off a month or so, Luke, we'll have most of the corn in; the hay's almost done now, and the oats are coming along. Then Andrew and I can manage the farm, and you can go thrash Johnny Reb!"

The mill at New Hope was busy Monday morning with farmers bringing grain and loading up with flour. Luke Kellogg was waiting for his load when Billy Weed came up to him, all excited and blurting out his news.

"Luke, I'm goin' off to enlist in the 137th New York!"

"Whoa, Billy. Slow down. I never heard of the 137th. Cortland? Auburn? Syracuse?"

"You probably never heard of it 'cause it's forming up all the way down in Binghamton. But it's men from all over. Up this way as far as Ithaca an' Groton. My father's cousin, Sam Weed, told us about it. He owned a hotel down in Binghamton, the American. He was up here visiting yesterday, an' said a Cap'n Ireland was recruiting for a new regiment, the 137th. Father said I could go down on the cars from Cortland on Wednesday an' join up. Come with me, Luke! I know you've been wantin' to enlist for the last year. Here's a chance for us to go in together!"

"Well, this sounds like what I been waiting for, Bill. I think my father's good enough to let me go, and Andy's big enough to do a lot. I'm not too keen on going all the way to Binghamton…but if you're going, I'll go."

"Well, now, that's good news! You're gonna need me to keep you safe from all those pretty girls in Binghamton, Luke, so we better go together!"

"I just have to convince my folks it's all right for me to leave them now, Bill. My mother's been after me to read law like Father's uncle Charles. She thinks I might even get to be a judge someday, like he was. I think that's why she worked me so hard home schooling me."

"You mean Judge Kellogg was your uncle, Luke? I knew he built the mill, an' Kelloggsville was named for him, an' was told he'd been in Congress years ago. Guess I shoulda known you and him were family."

"Well, he moved out to Michigan before I was born. I never knew him. Say, Bill, looks like my flour's ready. I'm going to load up, get home, and tell my folks the news. I'll ride over to your place later and we can talk more."

"Just tell 'em you'll be fine, Luke, you're with me!"

True to the elder Kellogg's word of the previous month, Luke was allowed go off to war with his father's blessing and his mother's apprehensive prayers. He and Billy Weed packed their gear and set off with Andrew for Cortland, where they'd get the train to Binghamton.

At the depot in Cortland Andrew shook his brother's hand solemnly and then was embarrassed, but not a little pleased, when his big brother pulled him into a last embrace between these two brothers and best friends. "Now you take care, an' send us letters when you can. And thrash those Rebs!" Andrew watched him board, waved good-bye, and drove the wagon back to the Kellogg farm.

As the train's engine spewed black smoke from its stack, Luke looked out the car's window at the Tioughnioga River. The tracks would follow it from Cortland to its junction with the Chenango River, then turn south for the final eight miles, once again following the Chenango toward its confluence with the Susquehanna River at Binghamton. In less than a month, Luke and Billy would be on another train, this time following the Susquehanna south to Baltimore, then Washington, and the war.

War

Chapter Four
Black Horse Troop

April 1861

Southern states reacted in a predictable way to the election of the Republican candidate, the man from Illinois, Abraham Lincoln. Certain he'd oppose the introduction of slavery into western states, and fearful he'd condone its abolition in their home states, they took action. The Confederate States of America was formed, with Jefferson Davis as its president and its capital in Montgomery, Alabama (soon to be moved to Richmond, Virginia). The battle lines were drawn. South against North. Slave against free. States against Federal. High tariff against low. Irresolvable policy differences. Both sides convinced that God and the Scriptures justified their action and would be on their side in this fratricidal confrontation. Not since Cain and Abel had two family members resorted to such never-to-be-forgotten mayhem. Fort Sumter in Charleston Harbor was fired upon, and the insurrection began. The President of the United States had no intention of backing away from this challenge. The Constitution established "a more perfect union." One nation, not two. And Abraham Lincoln meant to keep it so.

Equally adamant were the people of Virginia. Less than a hundred years ago, one of their own, Patrick Henry, had said, "Give me liberty or give me death!" They were not about to yield their liberty to some tall, ugly man from Illinois who sat in Washington as if he were the reincarnation of King George of England and could dictate to free men! The inconsistency of their position—defending free expression while holding colored people in slavery—did not trouble them at all. When the Declaration of Independence was signed by Southern states' representatives, they fully understood that blacks were not "men"; they were just "chattel," not unlike their mules or horses, beasts to be used productively and to be taken care of as you would a useful mule. And not housed any better, certainly.

Now some of these ungrateful wretches had run away, crossing the Potomac with the help of ignorant Northerners, into Canada beyond the reach of law and bounty hunters. This was no less than theft of property, and had to be stopped. The tyrant Lincoln would not be allowed to interfere with people's property rights without a challenge! And so Fort Sumter was fired upon, and the War of Rebellion, the War of Secession, the Civil War, was begun.

The business world, as always, dealt with this turn of events in its own way. Northern cotton mills needed raw cotton to stay in business. Southern enterprises needed manufactured goods only available from Northern businesses. As enterprising businessmen do, both North and South found ways and channels to maintain a flow of merchandise, enough to ensure survival of the businesses. Meanwhile, the politicians riled the populace into a fury of political and patriotic furor. Young men were exhorted to enlist in their regional units to defend the beliefs the politicians proclaimed, with God's certain justice to back their efforts.

America, a young country, had trained a cadre of fine officers in its two official military institutes, West Point and Annapolis, Army and Navy. Now these fine officers, classmates, would find themselves fighting for an honor they'd been taught to defend, against each other.

Ordinary people, moving across the developing countryside of America, would find themselves on opposite sides of a strange divide. A young engineer from a small village along the Susquehanna in upstate New York would find himself, as a recent citizen of the Shenandoah Valley of Virginia, serving willingly as the mapmaker for Stonewall Jackson, helping him to kill young men from his family's home county in New York.

So now here was young Jack Lewis, born on Lost Mountain, working happily on a horse farm in an idyllic location in Virginia, eagerly going off to fight against the very people who had bought his horses. To another age, this made absolutely no sense. As Jack might have said, "you had to be there."

Jack had no slaves. Pettis did, but they were as well treated as Jack himself. Jack, at age nineteen, certainly never gave a thought to the fact that he had an inherent freedom that a black man on Pettis's farm was denied. To Jack, the black folk were no better, no worse, than he or any of the other help. The slaves understood the vast difference between their situation and Jack's, but also were wise enough to never call attention to it, in front of white people.

Jack just knew that Virginia was being threatened by a tyrant in Washington, that the Union was threatening everything a free Virginian stood for, and that the Black Horse Troop was being called by Governor Letcher to defend the state. This Jack would do. To his last breath!

At the Pettis house the situation was discussed endlessly. Jack knew that Harry and Minerva Pettis, while fearing any harm that might come, were immensely proud of Jack and his membership in the Black Horse. Cousin Will was almost embarrassingly proud of Jack, and eager to join as soon as he was of age. Jack knew he could count on the Pettis's support for him in any endeavor.

Young Will he was concerned about. So eager to join up, to "jine the cavalry." Jack talked to him at length, urging him to wait, that his time would come soon enough.

"But the war'll be over quick, Jack. Them Northern boys ain't gonna want t'fight. Why should they? D'ye think they care what we do?"

"I don't know, Will. Maybe not. But I have a feelin' this ain't gonna be as easy as some folks'd like t'think it'll be."

In April of 1861 the Black Horse Troop became active, and was sent to Harper's Ferry to occupy the arsenal. Jack Lewis left the comfortably familiar life of the Upperville horse farm for the demanding and perpetually changing life of a warrior. For the next six months, the men of the Black Horse fought battles in Virginia, helping to frustrate the Union Army in its desire to capture Richmond and end the War of Rebellion.

In late September of 1861, Sergeant Jack Lewis was given permission to return to the farm at Upperville. Jack rode up the lane to the farm, tired, but happy to be home. He was greeted as a hero.

"Jack, welcome back!"

Minerva Pettis gave him a big hug and insisted that he sit right down to a hearty dinner.

"My, Mrs. Pettis, you have no idea how good this tastes to me! I've been livin' on dried beef with a little salt and flour cakes, and a little rye coffee with sugar." Jack cleaned his plate, which the pleased Minerva Pettis then heaped again with country ham, sweet potatoes, cabbage, and fresh hot biscuits, refilling his cup with hot coffee. When he'd finished his pie, he sat back and let out a contented sigh of satisfaction.

"Oh, that was delicious. I surely have missed your cookin'! "

"Now, Jack, you must tell us all about your adventures while you've been gone."

His cousin Will pulled his chair closer, not wanting to miss a word.

"Well, we've been in a lot of fightin', for sure. But it hasn't been all glory. Startin' out, it looked like we might lose more men t'measles than Federals. Forty men over in the Powhatan Troop nearly died in camp at Culpeper Court House. We were itchin' t'take on the Union Army, and on May 31 we got our chance. We were saddled up before dawn and rode to Fairfax Court House to reinforce Captain Thornton's troop that was supposed t'be battlin' the Second U. S. Cavalry on Little Falls Church Road. But when we got there at sunup, the Federals had skedaddled. We were all pretty disappointed. But Captain Payne told us our time would come.

"In June and July, we were operatin' out of Centreville, supportin' Gen'ral Beauregard, picketin' an' scoutin' on the Potomac frontier. In July, I got t'be part of Gen'ral Johnston's escort. I soon came t'see Gen'ral Johnston was right smart and a damn fine—'scuse me, ma'am—a good leader.

"Then came the twenty-first of July. At Manassas, our troop almost got into some real action. We came onto the battlefield just as the battle was windin' down. The Blue Coats, infantry an' artillery, were movin' back t'Washington 'cross the Cub Run bridge when it collapsed under their weight. Us Black Horses, we charged! The Federals ran. Congressmen, come out from the Capitol in their buggies, fled in confusion. Some of the boys stopped to gather up cannon, but the rest of us galloped on, chasin' the Union forces back to Centreville. We were some disappointed at not yet gettin' t'take on, head to head, a worthy cavalry opponent. Instead, we worked through the night to gather up abandoned artillery pieces an' other equipment the Federals left behind when they ran off t'Washington."

"Minerva, we got t' let this boy get t' bed," said Harry Pettis. "Jack, thank you for tellin' us about all your adventures soldierin'. We're just glad you're alive, boy. But that's enough talkin' for one night. You get off t'bed an' a night's sleep on a real mattress!" Harry Pettis smiled proudly as the young cavalryman pushed back his chair, rose, said his good nights, and went off to a good night's sleep.

In the morning, with a fresh horse and clean gear, Jack rode back to the Black Horse Troop, feeling completely rejuvenated, ready to go again.

It would be nearly a year before he got back to the farm on another furlough, but in late September of 1862, just after the Battle of Antietam in nearby Maryland, Jack was once again at the Pettis table, enjoying a cup of real coffee after another delicious meal. Once more, he was recounting his experiences since his last visit.

"Our Black Horse Troop was made part of the Fourth Virginia Cavalry Regiment last September, under Colonel Beverly Robertson. We soon figured out that Robertson was good at trainin' men, but seemed to have no belly for a fight. I wasn't much disappointed when the Black Horse got detached to another command.

"Not much went on last winter. Like I said, the food was a far cry from what your kitchen turns out, Mrs. Pettis. We didn't have what you could call any real entertainment, but at least we got a prayer meetin' almost every night. Bad weather kept us confined to the log cabins we'd built while we were at Camp Ewell, two miles below Manassas.

"When the spring thaw came in March, most of the cavalry rode down the Peninsula to take on the Federals gatherin' at Fortress Monroe. But our Fourth Virginia stayed behind to keep watch on the

Federals along the Potomac frontier. 'Bout this time, Gen'ral Jeb Stuart got t'be in charge of all the Virginia cavalry. On March 28, a Federal Corps started movin' south 'long the Orange and Alexandria Railroad. Gen'ral Stuart ordered us t'harass and delay 'em. We captured some fifty stragglers, but still didn't feel we'd been part of any real fightin'.

"We rested awhile near Richmond, then our regiment moved on down the Peninsula to Yorktown. Late in April, the Regiment held an election of officers an' we threw Robertson out an' voted in Colonel Wickham, the company commander of the Hanover Troop. I was surely pleased. Wickham's a man we can fight for!

"Then a few days later, on May 4, outside Williamsburg, Wickham proved we were right about him. Stuart ordered our regiment t'go after the Federals attackin' our Fort Magruder, an' Colonel Wickham led the charge. We was on the Federals so quick, we drove 'em down the road an' captured a six-gun Union battery t'boot. The Federals came back at us, an' Colonel Wickham took a saber thrust to his side. But he's one tough officer. He stayed in the saddle 'til the Yankees were beaten back and the area secured. An' then we got into another skirmish an' our Black Horse commander, Major Payne, got wounded an' none of us could get him out, so he got captured. But, thank the Lord, he recovered from his wounds, got exchanged, an' got back t'the Fourth Virginia in August. I felt bad I hadn't been any help t'Payne, but I had my hands full. I was gettin' all the fightin' I wanted this time. Turns out I'd got a cut of my own. One of the boys, Rob McCormick, come up t'me an' says, 'Well, ye got yerself a nice remembrance o' this little set-to, Lewis. That's quite a little slice you got on that there cheek!'

"I looked at McCormick like he was joshin' me, 'cause I hadn't felt nothin'. But then I put my hand up an' felt my face, all warm and sticky. I pulled my hand down and saw blood on my fingers.

" 'I'll be damned,' I said to McCormick. 'I thought that bluebelly saber'd missed me clean 'fore I speared him. Well, I'll wear it with pride. I finally feel like we've earned our pay and got us a few Yankees!' Praise God, that Yankee saber was sharp. It left a clean slice, not deep, an' healed up fast. I've got a lot more respect for Federal sabers, for sure. I know gettin' careless, or foolish, can get you killed quick. I'll have this scar on my cheek t'remind me that war ain't glory, it's deadly!" He looked straight at his cousin when he said this, hoping the boy would get his message and stop pestering him about "jining the cavalry" for a while at least.

Minerva Pettis reached out and traced the scar with a gentle hand. "Oh my, Jack. You were just so lucky not to be killed. You had an angel on your shoulder this time, for sure." She tried to hide her worry, her fear for him, this boy she treated like a son. But of course he was no longer a boy, but a man, and a warrior, fighting for Virginia. She couldn't do anything for him now but pray for his safe return when the war was over, but she resolved to try hard to dissuade young Will Gresham from enlisting, at least for now.

"I'll not bore you with all the fights we had, except t'say that Gen'ral Stuart is some leader. Seemed like nothin' the Federals could do could stop us. I got to worryin' we'd think we couldn't ever get licked, when I knew durn well what the penalty was for gettin' careless. But on the eleventh of June, Gen'ral Stuart took us on a raid down by Dumfries, ridin' around McClellan an' that big Army of the Potomac. After an easy one like that, it's hard not t'feel like nothin' can stop you!

"Back in July, Gen'ral Stuart reorganized the cavalry, an' our Fourth Virginia got put in Gen'ral Fitz Lee's brigade. 'Bout the same time, Colonel Wickham came back t'command the regiment an' Major Payne got back t'command our Black Horse. Sure is good havin' leaders that you can respect and count on.

"We had us a good one in August. Gen'ral Stuart led us in a raid on Federal General Pope. We whipped him good and came away with five hundred horses, $500,000 in greenbacks, and $20,000 in gold!

"I guess you heard 'bout the big battle up in Maryland earlier this month in Sharpsburg, on the Antietam Creek. Well, we got there too late. We'd ridden up t'Frederick, went up over South Mountain to a town called Boonesboro. 'Member, Mr. Pettis, you had me deliver a horse there back in '59? I don't know why, but Gen'ral Lee had Gen'ral Stuart hold the Fourth Virginia back, in reserve, I guess. So we missed the fightin,' pretty much. We just covered our infantry when they pulled back over the Potomac. Then we crossed over ourselves into the Shenandoah, and that's when I got permission to come home.

"Major Payne's hopin' you'll be able to let me switch to a fresh horse an' get my gear mended, Mr. Pettis. I get the feelin' Gen'ral Stuart's itchin' t'make another raid t'embarras McClellan and the

Union Army layin' up there below Hagerstown. Thanks to you, Mr. Pettis, an' all the trips you sent me on, I know the country up there pretty well. If Gen'ral Stuart does it like we did McClellan before, back in June, we'd likely be ridin' through Pennsylvania. Who knows—I might be able t'see Sally. You haven't got any letters from her for me, have you?"

Minerva Pettis shook her head sadly. "No, Jack. But it's real hard to get a letter through the lines with all the fightin' up there. Seems nobody wants to risk carryin' one."

"I can understand that. But I sure hope she's all right. The more I saw of that farmer Brunebaugh, Mr. Pettis, the less I trusted him. An' she's a right pretty girl...." He left his concern for Sally unstated, but the adults knew what he worried about. They knew of too many young serving girls who had been victimized by their masters.

Harry Pettis wanted to be helpful to this young man he treated like a son. "Jack, would you feel better about Sally's safety if I sent Will up to get her and bring her back here to work for Minerva, once things settle down in Maryland?"

Will quickly chimed in. "I kin do that, Jack. You kin tell me the back roads t'follow an' I kin get in, get Sally, an' get her back here safe in no time."

"Thanks, both of you. It's truly tempting to say 'yes,' but it's too dangerous right now, Will, for you an' for Sally. I got no real reason t'worry for her safety, an' certainly no real reason t'think the war'd get into Pennsylvania. Other than maybe a quick raid by Gen'ral Stuart. An' Sally's got no cause for worry from us, for sure!"

That issue appearing to be settled for now, Will was sent off to tend to chores in the barn. Harry Pettis proceeded to tell Jack about a new man he had hired a month ago, one Lathrop Emmons.

"Jack, he has some good traits. He's a true Virginian. Eager to fight, in fact. Would like to 'jine the cavalry.' But he's hard on the horses. I have a suspicion he may be harborin' a real mean streak deep down, waiting to come out. He worries me some. Frankly, you'd be doing me a favor if you could get him into the cavalry and off my hands. He seems like just the type that would make a good Yankee killer!"

"What about Will?" Jack was concerned about his younger cousin, who was always entirely too eager for the taste of combat.

"He's still a year away from being old enough to go. And I really need him here. He's like you. Good with horses. Gentle with 'em. Seems to think like they do. The horses really respond to him, like they always have with you. By the way, I have a big strong stallion with a lot of endurance. I'd like you to take him when you leave here." Pettis was proud of Jack Lewis. He wanted to make sure that if the speed of a swift mount would save a life, Jack would have that mount.

"Thank you, sir. I'm afraid I'm owin' you a lot for the horses you've provided, but somehow I intend to repay you."

"Nonsense. I want to do this. You owe me nothin'."

After a good night's sleep and a hearty breakfast, Jack rode his new stallion back over Snicker's Gap to rejoin the Black Horse. It was October 8, 1862.

Rob McCormick welcomed him back. "Just in time, Jack. We're off on another raid. Gen'ral Stuart won't say where, just t'gather at Darkesville by noon tomorrow an' be ready to ride! I have a feeling we're goin' north, into Yankee country, for another ride around the Yankee army that's still sittin' at Antietam Creek. Betcha we kin git some good stuff up there. Yahoo!"

Jack took this in quietly. He immediately thought again of Sally Keefer, up there over the border, still waiting for him, he hoped. *Damn, I wish these Yankees would give it up and go back to their business, and let us go back to ours! Then I'd go get Sally and make her my wife. Well, if we're headed north, maybe I'll get a chance t'see her, anyway.* The warm feeling that thought engendered would linger through the night and stay with him as they saddled up and rode on to Darkesville.

Rising well before dawn on October 10, General Jeb Stuart led fifteen hundred cavalrymen through the Potomac waters at McCoy's Ford. He proceeded north past Clear Spring, up into the mouth of the narrow Blair's Valley, the nearly hidden southwestern gateway into Pennsylvania's Cumberland Valley, headed for an unsuspecting Mercersburg. He dressed General Wade Hampton's lead regiments in captured Union blue coats to further deceive the citizens, thus preventing them from being forewarned in time to hide their valuables, livestock, and store goods. Stuart aimed to gather up as much treasure as he could without harming any civilians unnecessarily. Fitz Lee's brigade was allowed to follow Hampton's, wearing their usual gray and butternut. Jack was relieved. He had no desire to wear the despised Yankee blue, though he thought Stuart's ploy was a damn fine trick.

The column rode in formation, in fours, almost a mile long. The day was cloudy and it was apparent rain would fall before the day was over. But at this point, none had fallen, and the roads were dusty. The rebel column raised a very visible cloud. Jack knew there were Federal cavalry pickets around the Potomac, that Stuart was skirting the very edge of the Union army—the mouse daring the cat to pounce. He knew they were in for a hard ride, that speed and stealth were life for this daring raid. He just hoped somehow he'd find a way to pass by the Brunebaugh farm and see his beloved Sally. But first came the business of war.

As the column emerged from the northern end of Blair's Valley, General Wade Hampton led his North Carolinians dressed in blue up the Corner Road into Mercersburg. General Fitz Lee had instructed his regimental commanders to organize squads to forage through the rich farmland to the east, commandeering horses, wagons, and anything else of military value. To the troops, this meant anything they could eat, drink, ride, or wear. Major Payne rode up alongside Jack.

"Sergeant Lewis, remember two years ago I told you to learn the roads up this way? Well here's your chance to use that information for Virginia! I want you to take three men and head east from here. Gather up the best horses you can find, anything else that's useful to us. But beware of Federal pickets. We're skirting the whole Union Army hereabouts. General Fitz Lee says we're headed through Mercersburg, then on to Chambersburg this afternoon. There's supposed to be a village called Bridgeport between the two—d'you know where it is? You can rejoin the regiment there in early afternoon, I'd think."

"Yessir, Major. I know where Bridgeport is. 'Bout three miles northeast of Mercersburg. An' I know these back roads well. I delivered some fine horses hereabouts, an' with luck they'll be in Virginia's service before evening!"

Jack picked out three men he knew well.

"C'mon, McCormick. You, Martin, Towson. Come with me. We're goin' t'Irwinton Mills an' get us some fine horses!"

The four troopers rode off, following Licking Creek around the tip of Kasies Knob out into the broad stretch of rolling hills and cavern-riddled limestone fields of the Cumberland Valley. Jack warned his men. "Stay together on the roads. Keep an eye out for signs of Federal cavalry pickets. Look for likely farms with good horses. When you go to a pasture for horses, watch out for sinkholes. That tells you there's caverns under, in the limestone, and the holes leadin' in can catch you unawares. I don't want none of you disappearin' into some hole in the ground."

"Have t'be pretty big hole t'swallow up my horse an' me both, Sergeant!" McCormick was laughing at the thought. "I'd have t'be blind not t'see it!"

Jack grinned back at his friend. "Have your fun, Rob, but just you boys be careful on strange ground."

They had ridden a little over two miles, and were on a narrow country lane in the midst of fields covering the broad belt of limestone that lay just beneath the surface. Sharp rocky outcrops jutted up here and there; cedar trees dotted the fields. Jack saw something and pulled up, as did his three men.

"Now Rob, look over there t'the right, in that field. See that sinkhole? And see them cedars there by it? Look close. What d'you see?"

"All right, Sergeant, I see it. Looks like a hole. Well, I might fit in there all right, but my horse'd have t'be in pieces for it to fall in! But I take your point."

"Just you keep your eyes open. Now come on, I think this lane goes up this rise, then drops down to a fording 'cross the crick we been following. And up the road's a gristmill where I delivered some of Harry Pettis's best horses a few years back. Let's go get 'em, boys!"

As they crested the rise, they saw no one around the barn and house on their right. But below them, splashing through the ford of Licking Creek, was a rider on a fine-looking roan stallion, who came to a skidding stop at a willow tree by the creek at the base of the hill. He'd seen them. Was he a Federal picket, or one of their civilian guides?

"Let's go see what this fellow is, boys." Carbines raised and ready, aimed at the rider in front of them, Jack and his men rode slowly down the hill.

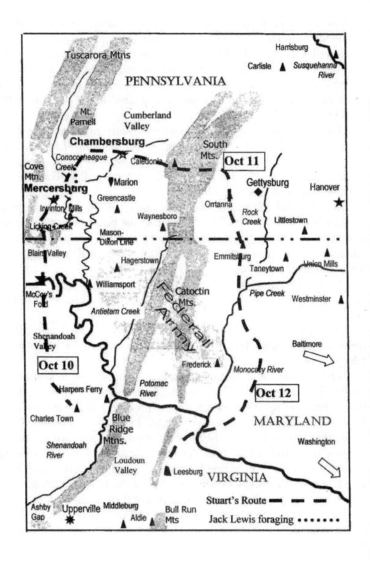

Stuart's Raid of October 1862

Chapter Five
Blair's Valley

October 10, 1862

Eight miles to the south of the mountainous southwestern corner of Pennsylvania's Cumberland Valley lies the Virginia bank of the Potomac River; three miles north sits the borough of Mercersburg. Here the ridges of the Tuscarora Mountains, long ago folded into an acute angle, are locally referred to as The Corner. Cove Mountain forms the southwest wall of the Cumberland Valley, terminating at the Maryland border to form one leg of the angle. Cross Mountain, the other leg of the angle, runs east along the border for a mile to merge into Two-top Mountain, forming what locals call The Punchbowl. Two-top straddles the Mason-Dixon Line, extending about a mile both north and south of it. Just east lies a similar short ridge, Kasies Knob. Their wooded slopes meet to create the narrow defile of Blair's Valley, where a dirt road follows a little stream south to the Potomac River near Clear Spring and McCoy's Ford. While there are many avenues leading north from the Potomac into the Cumberland Valley, all lie to the east except this nearly-hidden mountain passage.

On a cool, cloudy fall morning, high up on the east slope of Two-top Mountain, young Samuel Pine watched a fat gray squirrel run up the trunk of the large oak tree a few yards away across the small clearing. The boy aimed carefully and let the stone fly off his slingshot. The missile found its mark. The squirrel fell to the ground. Sam ran across the clearing and picked up the lifeless animal. As he was putting it in the game bag slung over his shoulder, movement in the valley below caught his eye. He turned and looked intently at the dust cloud rising at the far end of the valley to the southeast, down in the Maryland end of Blair's Valley.

What could it be? Sam knew that in the year since the War of Secession began, people had been traveling north in numbers to escape the dangers of combat surrounding their homes in Virginia and Maryland. Just before the great battle in nearby Maryland on the Antietam Creek a few weeks ago, the stream of refugees had increased. Most traveled the roads east of the mountains, with only a handful coming up Blair's Valley. There had never been enough of them at one time to make such a dust cloud. No, this had to be something else.

Was this the rebel attack they had feared? The rumors had been conflicting—rebels were headed for Pennsylvania to raid and pillage; Union troops had driven all rebels far south into the Shenandoah Valley. Still, fear had been rampant. Some farmers had already sold out and moved west to Ohio. More were said to be getting ready to sell and join them. Today the people in Mercersburg felt secure, knowing their own men, soldiers in Company C of the 126th Pennsylvania Volunteers, were in camp in nearby Maryland. Surely no rebels would dare disturb the town's peace with Union forces so close at hand. Yet something sizeable was coming up the valley from the direction of Virginia.

The young boy's curiosity overcame his uneasiness. Sam wanted to move closer, down the mountainside, to see whether this was indeed the dreaded Southern invasion about to occur. Maybe his "dust cloud" was just mist hanging from the low clouds that had moved in over Cove Mountain to the west. But he had to see, know for sure, then warn folks if he could.

The boy ran back through the woods to the clearing at the upper end of the mountain path where he'd tethered his horse at sunrise before walking stealthily through the woods in search of a fat squirrel, and maybe even some chestnuts he could sell in town for cash money.

Once in the clearing, Sam made reassuring noises to the whinnying horse—as much to reassure himself as the animal. He untied the reins, put his left foot in the stirrup, and swung up on the bay mare. Pulling on the reins, he turned the horse back down the mountain path at a trot. He turned south where a rock outcrop made a break in the trees that gave him a clear view south to the Blair's Valley Road. What he saw shocked him.

A seemingly endless column of blue-coated cavalry, four abreast, was raising the dust cloud. But the battle flags looked different, and no familiar Stars and Stripes flew at the head of the column. It appeared that the horsemen toward the rear of the column were clothed in gray or butternut, with black slouch hats instead of blue caps. Sam was confused. Were these indeed Union troopers, coming to intercept some rebel force? Or were these the rebels themselves?

He instinctively knew he shouldn't delay, but ride swiftly back into town and warn people of this fast-approaching threat. He dug his heels into the horse's ribs, urging the animal on, moving down the narrow mountain trail as fast as they could go, Sam ducking low branches, his horse picking its way over rocks and fallen trees. Soon they emerged from the woods by the little church where the Blair's Valley Road met Corner Road.

Sam reckoned the cavalry would turn east and take the wider road through Claylick to enter the town. Figuring to avoid them, he swung to the west before turning northeast along the base of Cove Mountain, heading up the Corner Road toward town at a gallop.

He figured wrong. The main body of the invading army was following behind him, marching up the Corner Road!

Reaching the town, the boy turned his horse to the right at the old stone Presbyterian Church of the Upper Conococheague, then rode up the hill of Seminary Street to the Mercersburg town square. He pulled his sweating mount to a halt in front of Brewer's store, dismounted, threw the reins over the hitching post and ran into the store. "There's cavalry coming up Blair's Valley!"

Brewer and his several customers looked up, startled, at the excited boy. "What do you mean, Sam?"

The nearly out-of-breath youngster quickly related what he'd seen, what he'd concluded, and why he'd rushed back to warn the town. Brewer's customers laughed. "C'mon, Sam. You're jumpin' at your own shadow. McClellan whipped Lee good at Sharpsburg last month, an' he's still down below Hagerstown. Our own boys in the 126th are right there with 'em. Ain't no rebels foolish enough to come up here now! Besides, didn't you say they was in blue uniforms? That's our boys, just patrollin', most likely." They paid their bills, laughed some more about a young boy's fears, and left the store.

Brewer was more thoughtful, and more deliberate. No harm in being prudent. He called down to the basement storeroom where his clerk was sorting out a recent shipment of hardware. "Jake, I need you up here now!" Brewer set Jake Suffecool to gathering up the cash box, watches, and other valuables to hide in a cellar cubbyhole hidden behind a storage cupboard, just in case. Brewer was a cautious man. Then he walked quickly down Main Street to the Fallon house.

The basement of this large stone house served as the home of the Mercersburg Savings Fund. It wasn't yet open for business, but Brewer, as a senior director of the fund, had a key to the heavy oak door. He knew Seth Karper had brought two moneybags for safekeeping overnight. Brewer had no idea how much was in the bags, but he didn't want the Savings Fund to be responsible for their safety— not if it really was a rebel force about to enter the town. Karper hadn't actually deposited the money in the fund, and he could jolly well deal with the problem of the money's safety himself. He walked two doors further down the street to Karper's door.

Brewer had known Karper for many years. The old widower was childless, cantankerous, and something of a skinflint. But he made good brooms, and he'd been good to the orphan boy that worked in his broom shop. Some folks thought he'd not been entirely fair in his land deals over the years, but Brewer felt he was just a canny trader. Brewer wasn't sure how the old curmudgeon would react to this news. He raised the brass knocker and banged it down hard.

The day before, Karper had gone to the bank in the Franklin county seat, Chambersburg, and drawn out $20,000 in twenty-dollar gold pieces, two hundred and fifty coins in each of four sacks. Tired of living under the constant threat of a rebel invasion, after months of hoping for a better price, four farmers east of town had finally decided to accept even Seth Karper's stingy offers for their land. Last month's battle nearby at Antietam Creek clinched it. They'd take what they could get and move west. Half price was better than death and destruction! Karper was to close the deals tomorrow, hard cash for each deed.

Hearing Brewer's knock, Karper opened the door. "What do you want already this morning, Brewer?" he grumbled.

"Come up street and get those money sacks. Now."

"Leave 'em there, dammit, Brewer. I don't need 'em until tomorrow, when them farmers come in with their deeds."

Brewer ignored the man's attitude—he'd long since gotten used to it. He explained the urgency.

"Well, damn, why didn't you say so right off! Cavalry? Maybe rebels? Oh my gawd! I'll come get those sacks. The first place they'll look for hard cash is at the fund! I'll get it and get it hid—quick!"

The two men returned to the Fallon house and went through the basement door to the Savings Fund. Brewer got the sacks and handed them over to Karper, who rushed out with them, out the back door, strode quickly across the yard, and into the long wooden building by the alley, looking for the young man who made the brooms for him.

Chapter Six
Irwinton Mills

October 10, 1862

Nicholas Mellott sat on a stool in Seth Karper's broom shop, feeding corn straw into the binding machine. Only fifteen, he had been apprenticed to Karper for the last year. He had come to Mercersburg from a small farm on the side of Scrub Ridge, in the Allegheny Mountains some twenty miles to the west. His mother had died when he was born, and his father had caught pneumonia and died last winter. His married older sister Jane had moved west to Iowa when Nick was only five. For all practical purposes, he was alone in the world.

Mellott's employer was a hard man, a demanding boss. Still, young Nick was grateful for the chance to learn a trade and have a roof over his head and the food from Karper's kitchen. Alice Frisby, Karper's cook and housekeeper, had taken a shine to the boy and made sure he got enough to eat. While the making of brooms was rather monotonous, he looked forward to the times Seth had him take his fine roan stallion out for an exercise ride, as he had done earlier this gray October morning. Nick, invigorated by the fast gallop in the brisk air, had returned to his workbench with renewed energy.

He looked up when his employer rushed into the room.

"Nick, drop what you're doing, right now. Get down the alley and across the street into the meadow and get that roan stallion of mine. Bring him back to the stable, saddle him up, and come up to the back door of the house. Now! Fast!"

Nick did as he'd been told, and ten minutes later knocked on the back door. It opened immediately. Karper handed him a set of saddlebags, heavily loaded. He gave Nick his instructions. He was to ride out to the John Meyers farm three miles east of town, just up the Licking Creek from Irwin's mill, taking only the back roads. Once there, he was told to put the saddlebags—"don't open them bags! What's in there's no concern of yours!"—in the darkest corner of the springhouse. Then he was to come back to the shop.

Karper warned him to get his horse out of sight and into the woods if he saw any men on horseback riding his way. He warned Nick— "You keep your eyes open and your wits about you. They're sayin' cavalry's headed this way. Brewer says they're our boys from Hagerstown, but I'm thinkin' it may be that damn Jeb Stuart! Reb cavalry'd as soon steal the horse as breathe, boy. So if you see them, don't let them see you! Now get goin'!"

The day had turned gloomier, low clouds scudding swiftly overhead. Rain was surely coming. Scarlet and orange leaves skittered through the air. The trees that overhung the lane spread their partially denuded branches like black tracery against the gray sky. The day no longer held pleasure, only foreboding.

Nick rode off at a trot, heading east out of the lane past the large main building of Mercersburg Seminary, past the McFarland farm. Crossing the Conococheague Creek, he swung right at Patchwork Farm, trotting down a lane that led to the Greencastle Pike. Once more he pulled the reins, turning the roan stallion to the right and trotting down the lane to the Irwinton Mills, where he slowed his mount to a walk. So far, so good. He had encountered no rebel cavalry on these backcountry lanes.

The gristmill stood on his left, next to its dam on the Conococheague. Across the way, on his right, was the large two-story house, the seat of the Irwin family. The Irwin house was classic early Pennsylvania—silver-gray limestone, two-story, with a steep pitched slate roof, massive stone chimneys at either end, four four-over-four windows above, three tall six-over-six windows below, with an imposing recessed front entry. He'd been told the story about the Irwin sisters, how Jane and Elizabeth had married into the Ohio Harrison family, Jane serving as mistress of the White House in 1841 for her father-in-law, William Henry Harrison, and Elizabeth marrying another presidential son, John. But Nick's attention was brief, and focused more on the activity at the mill.

There were two farm wagons tied up, loads already extracted, teams munching on oats from feedbags. The farmers were inside, taking the chill off by the woodstove while they passed the time discussing the presence of the Union Army in nearby Maryland, seemingly undecided about where to move after the Battle of Antietam.

Nick took it all in, considering whether to stop and warn the men about the mounted columns that had been seen to the southwest. But he'd had his instructions; he knew he had valuable cargo and dared not take time to stop. Instead, the boy spurred his horse into a gallop. He rode west along the Conococheague Creek to where it turned abruptly to the north, crossed the stone camelback bridge, turned south onto the left fork of the diverging lane where he forded the Licking Creek beside a low-hanging willow tree. The Meyers springhouse was on his left, just a few yards up the side of the steep hill that ran down to the creek.

He had pulled his horse up to a skidding stop. There, near the Meyers barn, at the top of the hill, silhouetted against the gray sky, were four horsemen in the lane. No blue coats here. Just gray, and butternut tan, and well-worn black slouch hats. And sabers, and carbines, and pistols. The boy froze, his worst fears realized. Rebel raiders! The four riders were down the hill and at his side before he could react. Private Josh Martin seized the roan stallion's bridle. Private Isaac Towson had his carbine aimed right at Nick. "Hold up there, fella. That's a fine lookin' animal yer ridin'! What say we trade mounts?"

"Damn sight better'n that worn-out nag yer settin' on, Towson, that's fer sure!"

"Watch yer mouth, Josh. That ol' gray o' yers don't look none too swift, neither!"

Sergeant Jack Lewis laughed. "Go on boys, get t'the mill and seize all the horses you can find, 'fore they find out we're among 'em. I'll handle this here fella."

The three troopers spurred their horses, splashing through the stream, then quickly disappeared over the stone arch bridge, trotting down the road to the mill. Jack had told them about the fine horses he'd sold there before the war, horses that would just be waiting for them to "reclaim."

Nick looked nervously at the trooper in front of him. The big man was unshaven, his coat and pants dusty, his slouch hat sitting ominously low above the piercing gray eyes.

"You gonna take my mount? This ain't my horse. It's my boss's. An' I'll catch Hail Columbia if I don't get it back to town in the next hour!"

Jack stared at the rider in front of him, sizing him up. In the floppy hat and long coat Nick Mellott had worn against the threat of a cold rain, his youthfulness was well disguised. Jack was having trouble deciding if this fellow was a civilian guide for Federal pickets following just around the bend to the west, or only some local citizen out on an unknown errand. Jack had taught himself to be alert and ready for the worst: he wanted to live out the war. *I'll get this fellow's horse—it's too fine to pass up—and send him on his way. If some Federals do come around the bend, I can cross the ford and get to the mill before they cancatch me. That mill's stout-me an' the boys can hold off a squad of Federal pickets. In fact, the Bluecoats will likely skedaddle as soon as they come under fire from us four tough Virginians!* He gave his immediate attention to the man in front of him, his carbine lowered non-threateningly, but ready for instant use.

"Well, fella, I'm bound by Gen'ral Stuart to not steal your horse—just commandeer it in the name of the Confederate States of America. You'll have this receipt to give to your boss, signed by Gen'ral J. E. B. Stuart himself. Now, what you got in them saddle bags?"

By now, Nick had recovered his wits. His fear of Seth Karper's wrath overrode his fear of the horseman in front of him. The rebel trooper hadn't drawn his saber, and his pistol remained in its holster. Maybe he thought this Pennsylvania boy was too timid to challenge one of Jeb Stuart's legendary Virginia Cavalry. *Well,* thought Nick, *I ain't afraid of him. He don't know just how fast this roan of Karper's can run! No Reb's gonna take this horse, or the saddle bags, if I can help it!*

Nick kicked his heels into the roan's ribs, and the startled animal bolted up the hill. But not far or fast enough. Jack's combat-hardened reflexes took over as he raised his carbine and fired at the fleeing rider. Nick pitched forward, then jerked back in the saddle and fell to the road, dragged along with one foot still in the stirrup as his terrified horse ran halfway up the hill. Jack had spurred his own mount into chasing the roan. He came alongside and grabbed the runaway horse by the bridle, pulling it to a halt. Dismounting, Jack bent down and inspected the rider lying lifeless in the narrow lane, instantly regretting his decision to shoot.

"Why, he's only a boy! He's dead. Only a boy, an' I've killed him! Why in blazes didn't I just let him go!"

Jack was in trouble. General Stuart had been clear in his orders for this raid—once into Pennsylvania, his men were permitted to take every available suitable horse, for riding or wagon teams, any food, clothing, boots, shoes, or other supplies. Every Pennsylvania farmer or merchant would now be a Confederate quartermaster! But other than taking a few political hostages for swapping later, no civilians were to be molested. No thieving or pilfering would be tolerated, under penalty of death.

Now Sergeant Jack Lewis had just shot a civilian—and a mere boy at that. Still, no one was in sight on that lonely back road, on such a threateningly gray October day.

He'd just have to make the best of it. Make it as if it never happened, and then block it out of his mind. For Jack was a God-fearing man. Killing the enemy in a just cause was inevitable, and couldn't be helped. But this was an unarmed civilian. This was more like murder. Jack could only hope that a merciful God would understand, would recognize his repentance for what he had done, forgive a valiant soldier's mistake, and grant him redemption in spite of it. He feared the loss of God's grace—a grace he counted on to carry him safely through the dangers of war.

Surely God recognized that in wartime such civilian casualties happened. Goodness knows, enough of his fellow Virginians had suffered as much at the hands of Yankee troops. And when he fired his carbine, he hadn't realized the youth of his target, and that he wasn't a Federal civilian guide. Still, he didn't want to go through a big explanation of his action, even if he thought the action understandable in the circumstances. Instead, Jack resolved to appropriate the fine roan stallion for the regiment, and then somehow make the boy's body disappear.

First, he'd see what was so valuable in those saddlebags that the boy would risk his life by challenging an armed cavalryman. Jack undid the straps, pulled back the flap, reached in, and removed a sack. A very heavy sack. Untying the cord that held the neck of the leather bag shut, he reached in and removed a coin—a twenty-dollar gold piece! "My gawd, there must be hundreds of double eagles in them sacks! I never seen so much money in my life! This'd let me pay off Mr. Pettis for the horses I've used up this year and last, an' then some!"

Jack slipped a few of the double eagle coins into his pocket, but knew if he took the sacks back to Major Payne he'd not have a believable explanation for how he'd come by them. Not without the boy's death coming to light. Not without being seen as violating Stuart's orders. So he looked for a secure place to keep the gold hidden until he could safely retrieve it.

Sometime in the future, on another raid, or once the States had won their independence, he'd slip back over the Mason-Dixon and take that money back to Virginia. Jack's mind was quick to justify his plan. *Yep, it's only fair. Yankee money to pay for our horses we've used to defend Virginia from Yankee armies, an' to pay for destruction Yankees've done to our folks' places.*

Looking around, Jack spied the low silhouette of the springhouse on the hill, a few paces away. He covered the dead boy with a blanket in case someone happened by. Hefting the heavy sacks, Jack strode across the grass, opened the low springhouse door, bent down, and entered. It was dark inside, but enough light came through the door for him to see, in the back, lidded pails sitting on the straw-covered earthen floor. He set the pails aside, pushed away the straw, drew his knife, and used it to quickly dig out a deep, narrow hole. He took two pails of milk and dumped their contents in the corner, scoured them dry with straw, and set them in the hole. The sacks went in the pails, the lids back on top, and the dirt back into the hole over the pails. Jack spread the remaining dirt evenly, then restored the straw and set the remaining pails back in place, rearranged so that the buried pails were unlikely to be missed.

Backing out, he swept away his footprints from the dirt floor, shut the door, and ran back to the horses. Jack removed the blanket, rolled it up, and strapped it to his saddle. Trying to avoid looking at the dead boy's innocent face, Jack hoisted the body across the roan's saddle. He mounted up and led the stallion back up the hill and down the lane. Always observant, Jack had seen the collapsed depression in the field not far from the road—the tell-tale sign of a sinkhole, which he had learned were common in this limestone-rich part of the valley. He had pointed it out to his men as a hazard to avoid, never dreaming he would soon be using it to eliminate a problem. Reining the horses to a stop at the edge of the depression, Jack saw what he anticipated—the small hole led deep into the limestone. As Rob McCormick had observed, the cavern's entrance was big enough for a man's body to fit through. A minute later, Nick Mellott's body and the now-empty saddlebags had disappeared into an anonymous subterranean grave. Confident that every trace of the deadly event had been erased, Jack headed off to the mill to rejoin his men, leading the roan stallion.

In the brief ride to the mill, Jack was still thinking about what had just happened. He was never one to avoid a fight and had proved to himself he wasn't afraid to risk death when he had to. He had no qualms about taking another man's life in battle. But this time his reflexes had misfired. This wasn't an enemy soldier, just a civilian. Not many years younger than Jack himself, but a boy nonetheless, not yet a man. Jack again felt deep remorse for his impulsive action that had snuffed out an innocent life. He silently vowed that from now on bravery would be tempered by prudence, and not driven by impulse. *How I wish I'd seen how young that rider was. How I wish I could have the last fifteen minutes t'live over. I'd let that boy ride off unharmed, gold an' all. Ten times that gold wouldn't make my killin' him worth it.*

Too late now. He was in front of the mill. His men were waiting with a string of fine horses, both saddle horses and draft animals. They looked up expectantly as he pulled up with the roan in tow. Private Rob McCormick laughed. "Well that took ye long enough, Sarge. We thought mebbe ye found some farmer's likker an' fell in the crick. I was watchin' t'see if you was gonna float by an' git caught at the dam!"

Lewis quickly concocted his story.

"The boy tried his damnest to talk me out of takin' his roan. Can't blame him. One fine horse! I let him talk hisself out, then made him get down and take 'Shank's mare' home. He seemed like a strong enough fella. The walk back t'town won't hurt him none. There was only some apples in them saddle bags, green ones at that. I give him Jeff Davis dollars for the horse, and sent him running back t'town afoot. I expect y'all got some good animals here?"

Jack liked Rob McCormick. He was a fine horseman, a good friend, and a credit to Company H, the Black Horse Troop. Maybe if he'd kept McCormick and the others with him, instead of sending them on to the mill, the boy would still be alive. Well, he hadn't, and he couldn't undo what was done, terrible as it was. No point in making any further issue of it.

Jack had no crystal ball. He couldn't see the future. He couldn't know that late the very next day his friend Rob McCormick would be wounded and lose his leg. The war was going on. Even this nasty incident here would be quickly overcome by future events.

As Jack had expected, his men had rounded up three fine stallions and two mares from the pasture by the mill—horses Jack had delivered there before the war. They also commandeered wagons and teams, over the loud protests of their drivers.

The Virginians had eaten nothing since a rough breakfast of hard biscuits and wheat "coffee" before dawn, while still on the south bank of the Potomac at McCoy's Ford. McCormick and the others eagerly dug into the large midday dinner of cured ham, cabbage, new potatoes, apple pie, and real coffee that the miller's wife had prepared for her family and a visiting farmer. Jack contented himself with coffee. He had left his appetite back at the sinkhole.

Jack knew these Franklin County back roads from his pre-war horse delivery trips. Feeling pleasantly full for the first time in many days, the troopers followed him north on the road to Church Hill and then toward McDowell's Fort, bypassing Mercersburg. The men rejoined Fitz Lee's brigade at Arch McDowell's farm near the foot of Mt. Parnell as the long gray column was moving on toward Chambersburg.

Sergeant Jack Lewis was commended by Major Payne for his squad's success in obtaining both quality and quantity of horseflesh. Other foragers from the Fourth Virginia had also had success in resupplying the brigade, cleaning out all the merchants in Mercersburg and Bridgeport, gathering up every fit horse from that part of the valley that the locals hadn't quickly taken north or west into the mountains. No suggestion was made by anyone in the brigade that even a small violation of General Stuart's order had been committed. Jack recalled Stuart's raid two months ago on the Federal General Pope, when the cavalrymen had taken twenty thousand dollars in gold. *Probably more'n that in those sacks I hid,* he thought.

He debated again whether to go back and get the gold and turn it over to his superiors, but quickly decided that that would likely get him shot, not commended. So Jack pushed aside the vivid image of Nick Mellott's body slipping into its anonymous tomb and tried to be content with his superior's praise for the visible success he had had. The killing of the young Pennsylvanian was regrettable, but sometimes such things happened in war. Now he had to put the incident behind him and get on with it.

Chapter Seven
Chambersburg

October 10, 1862

Company D of the Fourth Virginia Cavalry, the Little Fork Rangers, rode east through the rain on the Bedford Turnpike into Chambersburg. The citizens had been alerted earlier that General Jeb Stuart's Confederate Cavalry was in Franklin County, presumably looking to plunder the Union storehouses in Chambersburg. Unfortunately, the local Union Army commander chose to ignore the warning he'd received. Town folk waited in trepidation. Some had loaded prized possessions in buggies and wagons and ridden off to hoped-for safety in the mountain ridges northeast and northwest of the town. Others secured valuables in presumed safe hiding places in their basements or outbuildings. Some hid in their cellars. But many were driven by curiosity and excitement to watch the columns of rebel cavalry, pennants flying, ride past their porches and below second-story bay windows and balconies that overlooked the street.

On the side porch of a stately house on Queen Street stood eighteen-year-old Sally Keefer, disturbed by the mixed feeling of fear and anticipation. Servant of the Baird family, she had been left behind, charged with watching over lawyer Baird's property while they fled with the children and valuables to their summer cabin at South Mountain near Walnut Bottom. She had been told that Joseph Baird had to go into hiding since the rebels typically took prominent citizens as prisoners to exchange for Confederate officers held in Union prisons. Still, she felt the weight of a great responsibility, knowing she had no means of stopping any invaders who might choose to enter the Baird homestead and take whatever they wanted.

Sally's fear was tempered by anticipation—was it possible her Jack Lewis was one of the cavalrymen entering the town? She felt a tingle of excitement course through her body at the thought of seeing the handsome young Virginian again.

She silently chided herself for wishing he might ride up and carry her off and satisfy her desire. Reverend Goldsmith had always railed against young people and their lustful thoughts. Hell awaited a young man or woman who looked at the other with carnal desire. Chastity and purity were the only way for a young woman to be worthy of heaven.

In her mind, Sally blotted out the horror of the unwanted intercourse she'd been forced into. First farmer Brunebaugh's rape of her innocence, now her current employer's continuing abuse of her body. She knew a merciful God would not count the sins of others against her. Only by the grace of God had she been spared an illicit pregnancy. In her soul, she was still chaste and pure, waiting for her lover to fulfill her in the way God intended for man and wife. For two years, she had prayed each night that God would send Andrew Jackson Lewis back to her.

Now perhaps God was answering her prayer. Seemingly out of nowhere, long columns of Confederate cavalry were passing by her doorstep, their regimental pennants flying in the wind and rain. She waved her handkerchief to draw their attention to where she stood on the side porch, where no nosy neighbors could see her and brand her as a sympathizer. She didn't want the Bairds to be accused of harboring a Copperhead, as Southern sympathizers were called in the North.

A dismounted trooper from the Third Virginia saw the pretty girl wave, and walked over to the porch railing. It was raining harder, and he was well soaked.

"Please come up out of the rain, sir, I would like to inquire about a Virginian of my acquaintance." Sally almost shook with anticipation.

The trooper stepped up under the porch roof, happy to have even a minute out of the rain and mud. Who knows, maybe this young woman would spare a hungry soldier a real, soft, biscuit, maybe even with a dab of apple butter!

"'Scuse my boots, Miss. Them streets're powerful muddy. An' I ain't no 'sir,' miss—just a private in the Third Virginia, under Gen'ral Fitzhugh Lee, miss."

"Oh my, excuse my manners, Private—wait right here." Sally ran inside, scooped the morning's leftover biscuits into a sack, took a small crock of apple butter from the well-stocked Baird pantry, and brought it back out on the porch, where she thrust them into the hands of the delighted trooper.

"Smells powerful good, miss—thank ye. Thank ye! Now, how kin I be of assistance?"

Sally proceeded to describe Jack Lewis and the little she knew of his Virginia origins. "He worked at a horse farm in Upperville for a man named Pettis. He told me in a letter last year he'd joined a company of Virginia cavalry, but I don't know which. I've not had another letter since the war started. Do you think he might be among your men here tonight?"

"There's a powerful lot o' us here, miss. I don't dare say how many or what regiments, but it's the men of Gen'ral Stuart's cavalry. If'n yer man's in our cavalry, and ain't been kilt, he's likely somewheres hereabout. An' if he's from Upperville, it's most likely he's part o' th' Black Horse Troop. You're a right special pretty lady, an' I'll pass the word tonight in the camps that yer looking fer Lewis. Hope he's here fer ye, miss. An' thank ye agin fer yer kindness!"

He turned and ran to catch up with the rest of his company. Sally was elated at the private's words. Jack was nearby, she just felt it in her bones. The private would surely get word to him that Sally was here, in the house on East Queen Street. Somehow, Jack would find a way to come to her. And she would this time show the complete depth of her love for him. If she never knew another moment's happiness in her life, she would know it tonight. Filled with certainty and anticipation, the excited girl ran into the house and began to prepare him a welcome fit for her hero, her love.

In a muddy field on the south edge of town, by the road to Greencastle, the Fourth Virginia Cavalry was bivouacked for the night. Despite the rain, the Black Horse Troop had its fires going, and the men were preparing hot meals with the food they'd "requisitioned" from the townspeople and nearby farmers—smoked hams, sausage, chickens, turkeys. To the veterans of Stuart's fast-moving raids, a night with this kind of food was a rare feast, to be savored and remembered in the lean times they knew lay ahead. A meal such as this almost made them forget the wet feet in their muddy boots squishing through the mud and puddles.

Among the talk of the day's events—the swift ride from Maryland, the fine horses confiscated, the protesting hostages taken in Mercersburg, the many stores and provisions available for the taking there and in Chambersburg, the burning of the train depot and of the stubborn railroad bridge at nearby Scotland, the speculation as to the whereabouts of pursuing Union forces—the word was passed that a beautiful young woman of the town was asking for Jack Lewis of Upperville, Virginia. Every trooper, even the married ones and those with sweethearts back home, wished he were Lewis that dreary October evening. The man of the moment was at that time talking to Major Payne about the return route south to be taken the next day. Before the war, Jack had delivered Virginia horses to the peach orchard owners near Orrtanna, on the far side of nearby South Mountain. He had heeded Payne's pre-war orders, learned the Pennsylvania terrain, and knew the routes which avoided main roads south that might have pickets from McClellan's Union Army, still camped in Maryland's Antietam Creek valley.

The men of Company D of the Fourth Virginia, the Little Fork Rangers, were discussing the pretty girl and the whereabouts of Trooper Lewis. Private Gideon McDonald overheard the name and moved over to the group. "What about Lewis?" The men relayed the story. "From Upperville? Why, o' course, he'd be with the Black Horse. Fact, I think I just seen Sergeant Lewis with Major Payne over by Colonel Wickham. This is a good'un! I'll git right over there and tell 'im."

And so the amazed and delighted Sergeant Lewis was given permission to go into the town to visit the pretty young lady whose story had entertained the troopers around their campfires that evening. The events of that afternoon near Mercersburg and his commander's need for Jack's help in planning their return route had until now pushed thoughts of Sally to the back of his mind. Then the corporal from Company D rushed up with news of a girl on Queen Street who was asking around for Jack Lewis. She was here somewhere, away from Brunebaugh, safe. A wave of relief washed over him. Visions of her and memories of that night in Brunebaugh's barn flooded back, and the desire mounted—to see her, hold her, to consummate the love they'd begun in the hayloft. War or not, somehow he intended to make her his wife, then figure out a way to get her safely to Virginia.

Jack rode swiftly up the pike and turned onto Queen Street. Thinking of the need to keep this meeting from the town gossips, he rode on past the house and turned into the next puddle-filled alley. Despite the dim light and the drizzle, he found the gate in the side fence, reached down, undid the latch, and pushed it open. Entering the yard, he saw the stable where he dismounted, opened the door and led his horse into a warm, dry stall. He wiped the horse down and threw several scoops of oats from the bin into the feed trough. With his mount taken care of, he ran across the muddy yard onto the porch, wiped his feet as best he could, and banged the fancy brass doorknocker. "Sally? It's Jack—Jack Lewis. I'm here! Open up!"

Sally was just finishing up in the kitchen, still full of apprehension and hope, when she heard the knock followed by Jack's call to her. She ran to the door, unbolted it, and opened it. There stood Jack, wet, dirty, and bearded. That didn't matter. She flew into his arms, pulled him inside, and pushed the door shut and bolted it with her free hand. She kissed him deeply while he lifted her up and held her tightly carrying her into the parlor.

"Oh Jack, I had hoped against hope that you'd be here, that somehow you'd find me."

He set her down and took a step back. "Let me look at you, girl— my gawd, you're beautiful!" He looked her up and down as she beamed and pirouetted around. Now a near-grown woman at eighteen, her figure was even shapelier than he'd remembered. But the blue eyes, full mouth, and chestnut hair were the face he'd remembered and conjured up when lying awake under the stars on so many nights, after so many battles. She looked at him, caressing his beard, touching the raised ridge of the saber scar on his cheek.

Sally chattered away: what he'd been through, whether he'd married, how long he'd be here, was he hungry or thirsty, did he want to wash up. She told him about herself, and the good aspects of life with the Bairds—"Oh, they've gone up to the mountain. I'm alone here"—but nothing about her last night at the Brunebaughs. And nothing about the shameful duties imposed on her by Baird. She figured rightly that if he knew of her rape, Jack would ride off tonight to Marion, and Mrs. Brunebaugh would be a widow in the morning. And Baird would be made to suffer as well. She wanted nothing taken away from the happiness she hoped to find this night with Jack.

"No, I don't need food. I ate earlier, an' I'm not thirsty. But I'd dearly love to get these muddy boots off an' wash up a bit. My face an' hands feel like I been swimmin' in mud—which is about right, I guess!" Jack chuckled, just happy to be here with this girl he'd dreamed about for so long.

Jack pulled off his boots and set them aside. Sally brought him a basin of warm water and large towels, and helped him take off his tunic and shirt. He set his pistol on the sideboard, having left his saber and carbine in the stable. She stood and admired his well-muscled physique. Jack was thinner than she remembered. There had been too many days riding with Stuart with slim rations, and too few days of hearty meals while on leave at the Pettis farm. Sally happily helped him wash up, dipping his head in the basin while she soaped his hair and rinsed it with clean water She scrubbed his broad back and then relished the feeling of running her hands over his chest, just to assure herself this wasn't only a dream. He toweled off, feeling cleaner than he'd been in weeks. He felt like he'd washed away any regrets over the afternoon's encounter at Irwinton Mills. The perfumed vision of loveliness beside him, touching him, erased for the moment the images of sacks of gold and the dead boy thrown down the sinkhole.

"Why don't we get all of you clean," she said with a soft smile, pushing him back into a chair. She unbuckled his brass belt buckle, unbuttoned his pants, and pulled them off, exposing his dirty and torn drawers. She laughed at them. "Jack, dear, these are disgraceful! You're 'bout Mr. Baird's size. I'll get you a pair of his and we'll burn these!" Then she yanked them off the surprised Jack. He grabbed for the towel to cover himself and preserve some appearance of modesty. Too late.

"Oh my goodness, Jack!" she gasped. There sat Jack with his manhood fully erect. The stimulation of her beauty, her perfume, her washing and toweling and touching, had been more than he could control.

"Forgive me Sally, I don't mean t'embarrass you." He laid the towel across his lap."

"Oh, Jack, this is no time to be so modest. We're going to get you clean—all over!"

She took away the towel then used the freshly wrung-out washcloth to gently wash his loins. Jack thought he should protest at her intimacy, but only groaned in satisfaction. Sally was determined to fill her heart and mind with images of romantic loving to push away the bitter memories of brutal, unfeeling sex—the only experiences she'd known until now. She set the washcloth aside. This time she'd take the skills the insensitive Baird had forced her to learn and willingly use them to give pleasure to the one man she truly loved.

"Oh my gawd, Sally, stop now or I'll explode! Let me make love to you!"

Delirious with joy, she led her beloved Jack up to her room, where she disrobed. Her slender body glowed in the candlelight—more lovely than he'd imagined! They lay down on the bed facing each other. He drew her to him and caressed her body, slowly, then more urgently, loving the feel of her smooth, warm skin, her pliant curves, her most sensitive places. She was more than ready to give herself completely. Her body, chaste in spite of its past violations, would be given to him, as he gave his to her, in an act of purest love. Jack let Sally guide him, every movement slow and gentle until her body took over her brain. Then slow became fast, and gentle gave way to more forceful, more urgent movements. Her little whimpers of joy became cries of release as they moved together, and she felt his climax deep within her as she reached her own pinnacle with a joyous cry of complete fulfillment. Now she was finally rid of the horrid images of brutal sex. She would only remember this magical joining, the joy of true love. Afterward they lay in each other's arms, not wanting to forget a moment of this consummated love.

"Sally, I swore that somehow I would marry you this day. Oh my, I haven't even asked you! Sally Keefer, will you marry me?"

"Oh yes, Jack Lewis. Yes! Yes!" She hugged him tightly and kissed him, and then kissed him again, nearly overcome with her happiness.

Together, they said the sacramental vows that sanctified their marriage, though no minister or witnesses or legal papers would ever be able to attest to it. Jack explained the marriage sacrament to Sally. "We need no minister. We marry ourselves. The minister is just a witness. Ours is a true marriage in the sight of God!"

Then Jack fell into an exhausted sleep. Sally lay next to him, reveling in the presence of this strong, loving man. She feared wakening him, knowing how badly he needed sleep, but she couldn't resist pressing herself tightly to his lean, muscular body. This feeling of safety, of protection, of enveloping unconditional love was so rare, so precious to the girl who had been denied it for so many years. She understood it was fleeting, this feeling, that her lover would be leaving her so soon. She lay awake, almost bursting with happiness, not allowing the certainty of his leaving to interfere with the joy she had had for these all too brief moments.

Jack woke up at three in the morning. Sally pulled on a robe while her new husband dressed. She fixed him a quick meal of eggs, cured ham, fried potatoes, and coffee while he went out to the stable and readied his horse. Back in the kitchen, he ate deliberately, savoring each bite: their marriage breakfast, the only meal they could share until this war was ended. He asked for a sheet of paper, pen, and ink, which she brought from her employer's desk in the library. He wrote out a simple statement: "I, Jack Lewis, on October 11, 1862, did take in marriage Sally Keefer. To her I leave all my earthly belongings in the event of my death. Signed, Sgt. Jack Lewis, Co. H, 4th Va. Cav., CSA—Chambersburg, Penna., Oct 11, 1862." She folded it, put it in an envelope, and set it aside, to place it later in the small walnut keepsake chest on the dresser in her room.

"I got no ring t'give you, Sally."

"Yes you do." She took a scissor, cut off a long length of his hair, wove it quickly together into a circle, and slipped it on her finger.

"And I give you this, Jack." From her neck, Sally took off the large gold locket, a guilt offering from Mrs. Baird. She opened it, showing him her likeness on the tintype, then wrote on a little slip of paper, "To Jack with all my love, Sally." She folded the paper, put it in the locket, snapped it shut, and placed it tenderly around his neck, and kissed him. He slipped the locket down inside his shirt, to lie next to his heart. There it would remain throughout the battles he knew were to come.

He stood up from his chair. "I'll treasure this, dear wife, until Virginia's won its freedom and I can come for you."

Jack reached in his pocket for the double eagle coins he had earlier removed from the sacks safely hidden in the springhouse. "Now I want you to have these, Sally. I wish it were more. Sew them in the hem of your coat. Let them be your nest egg when times get difficult. And Sally, if anything should happen to me, I've told my cousin Will to come look after you. He's a good boy; you can count on him."

"Oh Jack, please let's not even talk about such things. I can't bear to think of losing you. I'll wait for you, dear Jack, just please promise you'll come back to me!" Sally pressed tightly against him, kissed him, and bade him good-bye and safe journey, until they met again.

When he left, she sat down and cried. Tears of happiness, full of love. Tears of sadness, full of fear. Would this war destroy their lives? Dare she dream of seeing him again? Yet she silently praised God for bringing her lover to her this night, for erasing the horrors of the past, for making them husband and wife, if only in the sight of God. She looked at the handful of gold coins in amazement. She wondered how he had come by such a sum, grateful for the freedom of action these coins might provide to her.

A month later, she knew she was pregnant. With all the events surrounding Stuart's raid, Baird had been too preoccupied to bother her at night. She knew she'd have to tell Mrs. Baird of her condition. The baby was Jack's, but Sally couldn't tell her she was married, and to a rebel soldier at that. Sally wouldn't lie, she'd just tell Mrs. Baird of the pregnancy, and Martha would automatically assume it was her husband's. The woman did just that. She was shocked, and saddened, but knew it was inevitable.

That evening Martha Baird informed her husband. He was angry at first; and wanted to cast poor Sally into the street. He quickly realized the scandal that could cause, even if he denied it and called Sally a loose woman. So the Bairds decided to send her away to Martha's sister's home in Harrisburg, where she was to remain in seclusion until she gave birth to the baby, born prematurely in May. In June of 1863, Sally was told to return to Chambersburg with the baby. The Bairds would tell people the baby was an orphan whose father had been killed in the war, and whose remaining family had died of the fever.

The Bairds adopted the baby and named him Elias, or Eli for short. Sally was to be nurse to the child in the Baird household. From this time on, Baird avoided any physical contact with her. At night, Sally would lie awake thinking of her beloved Jack, wondering if he was dead or alive, wondering how she might get word to him of his son, how she could tell him once more of her undying love.

Chapter Eight
Mercersburg

October 10, 1862

By mid-afternoon of October 10, the columns of Stuart's Cavalry had ridden out of town, taking with them all the good horses they could find, along with everything useful from the shops in the town. The stunned townfolk in Mercersburg began to tally up the losses they'd suffered due to the rebel raiders.

Angered at being initially put off guard by the rebels' use of Union uniforms, they were most concerned about the fate of the hostages that Stuart had taken off with him to Chambersburg. These were mostly prominent men of the town, such as Burgess G. G. Rupley. But the rebels also took one ordinary householder who'd had the misfortune to fire his gun at a backyard chicken slated for the evening's dinner plate (or so he claimed.). Nervous troopers had seized Daniel Shaffer despite his protest that that his bullet was meant for a hen, not a Johnny Reb. If truth be known, the troopers were right – a quick wring of the neck would fix the chicken, but rebel invaders deserved a patriotic citizen's deadliest dispatch!

Later that rainy evening the townspeople felt some relief when word spread that George Steiger, local butcher and dealer in livestock, had escaped from his capture by rebels on the road near Bridgeport, and had made it back to his home, Bridgeside. Ironically, General Stuart and his staff had made their noontime headquarters at Bridgeside and had been well fed by Mrs. Steiger. Had the good woman known that her husband would later be seized by her ungrateful guests, she would have slipped some country purgatives into the mashed potatoes. The rebel commanders would have been out of their saddles and into the woods every half hour before their bowels settled down!

At the broom shop, Seth Karper grew ever more angry, then concerned, as the afternoon wore on, the gloomy gray day grew darker, and still young Nick Mellott hadn't returned. He stood on his front porch on Main Street, questioning every neighbor and passerby, to no avail. No one had seen Nick since the morning.

Karper was stewing over the loss of the huge sum he'd borrowed from the bank. Without that money, he couldn't buy the farms he'd expected to gain title to on Saturday. Damn the rebels! Damn Stuart! Damn the army! A hundred thousand men? Why hadn't they blocked this huge rebel force at the Potomac—were they asleep? Scared? They'd left the border open to these damn raiders. And now Mercersburg was paying the price. Damn them all!

Then it dawned on him that more than his financial well-being was at stake. What about Nick? What had befallen the boy on this terrible day? Where could he be? Karper wasn't known as a man who showed much concern for others, but his duty was inescapable. At least Karper hadn't lost his old shop wagon horse to the raiders—poor Kate was too old and slow to interest the cavalry. He hitched Kate up to his buggy and set out in the rain to look for his apprentice.

Going through the town square, known as The Diamond, he saw Constable Wolfe on the steps of the Mansion House hotel. Karper hailed him. "George! Constable Wolfe! My apprentice is missing. Didn't come back from out by Irwinton Mills this afternoon. Have you heard anything?"

"Can't say as I have, Seth. Are you headed out to look for him? I can't help you now, but if he ain't home by mornin', I'll get some of the boys at the college to help us search. Let me know, and I'll keep my ears open for any news. You be careful out there tonight, in case those damn rebels weren't lyin,' an' Stonewall Jackson is indeed comin' this way with twenty thousand men!"

Karper drove the buggy over the muddying roads to Irwinton Mills, where he stopped and asked whether young Nick had been seen that day. He got an earful about the four Virginia troopers who had taken their best saddle horses and teams, but no one had seen Nick Mellott. Karper continued his melancholy journey over the camelback bridge, through the ford, and up the hill to the Meyers farm. He listened dejectedly as Meyers told him that he'd been in the barn husking corn and repairing a plow all afternoon. He confessed that he was just relieved that the raiders had left him and his family alone. And no, he hadn't seen Nick. Meyers paused, stroked his beard, and looked at Karper.

"No, now, wait a minute. I did hear somethin.' Late this mornin,' before the rain started. Thought it mighta been a gunshot. But I just figgered it was old man Witter shooting after pheasant or squirrel down by the crick. I did go take a look after a bit, an' I seen one of them rebels riding back out of my field over there. Mighta been him shootin' at a pheasant. Least he wasn't shootin' at me! I ducked behind the barn so's he didn't spot me and come lookin' for my horses. When I looked back out, he was gone. I guess toward the mill. Just wisht he'd fell into the sinkholes out in that field! "

Now Karper was really concerned. Could these rebels have found Nick and taken off with him and the gold? Karper couldn't pass up the chance to see if Nick had been able to hide the sacks of coins in Meyers' springhouse. "D'you mind if I check out the springhouse, Meyers?" Meyers couldn't imagine that the man expected to find the boy in there, but he had no wish to antagonize the crotchety Karper.

"'Course not, Karper, go ahead."

Karper pulled his broad-brimmed hat down lower over his eyes against the drizzle. He walked down the hill to the springhouse, undid the catch, opened the door, and ducked inside. He waited for his old eyes to adjust to the dim light, impatiently moving milk pails around, even feeling through the straw on the floor. He neither saw nor felt any sign of the saddlebags with his precious hoard of gold coins.

Shaking in fear and anger, Karper began talking to himself, his voice echoing in the small dark room. "Oh my God, my money's gone.

I know it! Damn Rebs must've got to Nick 'fore he could get here! Sons a bitches! Now I'm done for. I can't close on them farms, and I owe the bank that money, with nothin' to back the loan, now, except my house and business. I'm ruint! I never shoulda sent that poor boy off with them sacks! Shoulda just left 'em at the Savings. Rebs never even touched that. Now, the boy's gone to who knows where, my money's gone, an' I'm soon ruint!"

He trudged dejectedly back up the hill to the farmhouse, where he stood dripping just inside the Meyers' kitchen doorway. "Well, Meyers, you'll have to find another buyer for this here farm. I'm goin' back the orchard road to town, see if maybe Nick's holed up in a farmhouse out of the weather."

"Hold on, Karper. You ain't gonna buy my farm? But we shook on it! I was plannin' to come in to town tomorrow with my deed and get my cash! My wife's already plannin' us joinin' her brother out in Ohio. Where it's safe. Where the Rebs don't come. What's happened? Why you backin' out?"

"It's them damn rebels. I don't want to talk about it now, Meyers. Just save yourself a trip an' don't come in tomorrow. Hear? Right now, I need to keep lookin' for my boy!"

Karper stopped at every farmhouse on the way, with no luck. It was as if Nick had been swallowed up by the earth—as, of course, he had. Karper finally drove home, discouraged and dreading having to tell his cook and housekeeper that Nick had not been found. Alice Frisby began to cry softly at the news, but held out a slim hope that the boy had been taken along to Chambersburg as a hostage.

The next day, Saturday, two of the Mercersburg hostages were turned loose and allowed to return home. Old John McDowell, released because of his age and delicate health, was barely able to talk, worn out by the physical and mental stress of his brief captivity and journey. Still, he was able to confirm that young Nick Mellott wasn't one of the rebels' captives. Karper cornered Constable Wolfe and insisted that a search be mounted immediately. Most citizens were much too busy with their own misfortunes to help. So Constable Wolfe prevailed upon Dr. Philip Schaff, head of Mercersburg's Reformed Theological Seminary. And so a number of students agreed to walk the roads east of town that afternoon, searching the tree lines and hedgerows, inquiring of anyone they met.

But all was to no avail, of course. Nick Mellott had become the one Friday casualty of Stuart's Raid—killed at the confluence of the Licking Creek and the Conococheague, his body resting in the subterranean limestone cavern beneath an anonymous sinkhole, never to be discovered. The only witness was his slayer, and Sergeant Jack Lewis, Fourth Virginia Cavalry, would carry that knowledge to his grave.

Lying in his bed one cold night in December, facing the loss of his business to bank foreclosure, Seth Karper suffered a massive stroke. He was dead in minutes. The knowledge that both the gold and Nick Mellott had vanished without a trace died with him. Only Brewer knew about the gold, so only he would wonder what Karper had done with it. Brewer had a thought that perhaps the boy had just decided to take off with the gold and the roan, riding west on the National Pike to Ohio or beyond. He quickly dismissed the thought. Nick Mellott was too young, too honest for that. Others speculated about what might have become of Karper's apprentice, but in time, the gossip died down. Only Alice Frisby, kind woman that she was, continued to mourn the young boy. Each Sunday the good woman asked God's grace for Nick Mellott in her prayers at the Bethel African Methodist Episcopal Church. Except for the good-hearted Alice, the town had already forgotten the incident.

Jack Lewis's complete success in wiping away any trace of his deadly encounter with Nick Mellott was apparent in the Reverend Dr. Schaff's diary account a year later: *"The present state of things in this community is certainly much worse than the rebel raid of General Stuart's cavalry of October last when they suddenly appeared in Mercersburg at noonday, seized a large number of horses, shoes, and store goods and twelve innocent citizens as candidates for Libby prison, but did not allow further harm and left after a few hours for Chambersburg."* The culpability of Jack Lewis in the looting and hiding of Karper's gold and for the death of Mellott would forever be lost to the pages of history.

During the next two years of the war, there were new rebel raids and depredations in Mercersburg, providing new fears and hardships for its citizens—more than enough to push all speculation over Karper's death and Mellott's disappearance into the background.

In June of 1863, General Imboden's Confederate cavalry and General George Steuart's Virginia infantry bivouacked in the town, searching out and taking even well-hidden goods, en route to the impending watershed battle in Gettysburg. Steuart's men would enjoy the fruits of the well-stocked larders of outraged Mercersburg citizens. But many of these uninvited guests would soon come to a deadly end at the hands of the Federal Twelfth Corps on the slopes of Culp's Hill.

In June of 1864, twenty-two troopers of the Sixth U. S. Cavalry under Lieutenant McLean surprised Confederate General McCausland's invading cavalry force, twenty-eight hundred strong, as they entered the town using the Blair's Valley route from Maryland that Stuart had used two years before. In a one-hour battle, the little Union scouting force would fire, fall back, charge, then fall back again, bullets flying around the stone Presbyterian Church, the town square, and at the bridge across the run on the north end of town. Once more, George Steiger's home, "Bridgeside" was in the thick of the war. The invaders entered many homes and businesses, some drunk on whisky stolen earlier, and destroyed and stole much property, before moving on to Chambersburg, harassed all the way by McLean's brave troopers. McCausland then proceeded to burn that unfortunate town. The citizens of Mercersburg were fortunate that they had been spared that fate, but felt enough grief at their own losses.

Throughout these wartime turmoils, and for years afterward, life continued its long-established rhythm on the old Meyers farm where the Licking Creek joined the Conococheague. The little springhouse set into the hill continued to see one season after another come and go, its buried gold undisturbed. Soon after the war, J. W. Henkle turned over the mill at Irwinton to Kuhn and Witter. Witherspoon bought the Irwin house and farm. All found a measure of prosperity. Jim Duffield and Robert Brownson, mustered out of the 126th Pennsylvania Volunteers, had returned to their civilian lives, Duffield to run his farm downstream from Irwinton Mills, and Dr. Brownson to return to his medical practice in Mercersburg.

Mercersburg

In the summer of 1883, a red wooden covered bridge was built over the ford of the Licking Creek. It would assume the name of its color, Red Bridge, and from the name of the major local landowner, Witherspoon's Bridge. The farmer who had bought the Meyers farm let the bridge's sweaty work crews store their water jugs and lunch pails in his cool springhouse, only ten yards up the slope from their work site. Men who were happy to make a dollar a day set their lunch pails over a cache of gold coins worth more than a lifetime of bridge building.

Chapter Nine
Julia

September 1862

The 137th New York Volunteer Infantry Regiment was gradually coming together in its Binghamton encampment, set up at Rockbottom Flats on the south shore of the Susquehanna River. The new recruits followed an established routine—rigorous drilling by day, then getting acquainted in the evenings. Though nominally a regiment from Binghamton, the men of the 137th were drawn from a wide area of New York's Southern Tier, as far east as Windsor in the foothills of the Catskill Mountains and as far north and west as Ithaca and its surrounding villages just below the Finger Lakes.

Luke Kellogg and Billy Weed felt somewhat the outsiders in Company F, where most of the men were from the area around Binghamton and in many cases had known each other from childhood. A few of the men in his company had been as far as Utica on the Chenango Canal, and some had "taken the cars" as far as Cortland or Ithaca. None had ventured north into Finger Lakes country so far as to pass by the mill at New Hope. Luke struck up acquaintance with some of the recruits from Ithaca in Company H. A few of them had made an occasional journey northeast to Luke's home countryside on the west shores of Skaneateles Lake. Yet to most of his mess mates, "water" meant the Susquehanna, Chenango, or Tioughnioga Rivers, or perhaps one of the small lakes that dotted the hill country just to the south, in Pennsylvania.

But Luke was a likeable sort, and his stature—a bit over six feet, a good four inches taller than most of his fellow soldiers—lent him a naturally commanding presence. Billy Weed, while much shorter than Luke, had a quick wit and a ready laugh. Very quickly, they were accepted by their mess mates, most of whom, like Newt Hunt and George Kilburn, had known each other for years. Albert Hughes, a life-long Binghamtonian, was especially friendly to the newcomers. These three had hit it off almost immediately with Luke and Billy, found they had much in common, and enjoyed each other's company.

The young women of Binghamton were as caught up in the excitement as were the young male recruits. In the evening, after supper, the girls often strolled across the bridge to the Southside—in groups, of course—walking to Rockbottom Flats to meet and talk with the younger new recruits. Later they would return to their homes to sit on their porches and gossip about the attributes of their favorite soldier.

Julia Stow was a particularly beautiful young woman. At eighteen, she was tall and shapely, with fine posture, a long slender neck, a face that a sculptor would love, with full mouth, high cheekbones, firm chin, and large expressive brown eyes. Her lustrous blonde hair, swept up and braided, accentuated her height. Julia's father adored her, and her mother doted on her only child. Julia was strong-willed and unabashed about expecting to get what she wanted.

Julia was not a happy girl. None of the young men who had paid her court suited her. They were too short, or too stuffy, or too boring, or too easily intimidated by her stature, her beauty, her strong will. Yet she wanted a beau. Her friends teased her about it, except for her best friend and confidant, Polly Bird. Polly had been sweet on Albert Hughes for years. At any gathering, Polly and Albert were together. It was commonly assumed that in due course they would become man and wife. Julia envied their closeness and longed to find her own love and soul mate. Polly understood, and never teased her about it. Instead, she reinforced Julia's discrimination. "Don't settle for just any old boy,

Julia. Wait 'til you meet the man that makes your heart flutter. Then don't let him get away!"

One evening, Polly and two of her friends came over to the Stow house on Front Street. Julia sat on the porch, feeling alone and melancholy. Polly walked up and spoke firmly to Julia.

"Jule, this just won't do. You can't sit here and pine away for the rest of your life. If none of our boys suits you, come with us to Rockbottom Flats. Bert has met two boys from up in the Lake Country that he says are really nice. He thinks you'd enjoy meeting them. It's certainly more interesting than sitting here alone in the evening, isn't it?"

The other girls talked excitedly about the boys at camp, telling her about this tall, broad-shouldered recruit from up in the Lake Country. "Julia, he's so strong, so handsome, and so much fun, but we can't seem to get him interested in any of us. But you might be able to. Do come and try. Please?"

"Oh, all right, Pol. I've got to do something, I guess. Let me go tell Father I'm going to cheer up the new recruits."

Bert Hughes was expecting Polly as usual that evening. He persuaded Luke to come with him to the camp gate. "Who knows, Luke. Tonight there may be some new girls." Bert was in on Polly's ploy to get Julia to the camp, figuring she'd finally find an appealing possibility in the tall man from New Hope. Bert figured Luke had more than enough strength of character to deal with Julia's willfulness and certainly wouldn't be intimidated by her. Luke would have to be impressed by her beauty.

At the gate, the crowd of young men and women mingled. Bert and Polly quickly embraced, then he grabbed Luke's arm, leading him over to where Polly was pulling a reticent Julia away from her friends. Julia and Luke looked at each other, tall soldier to tall maiden. Their eyes met in a deep, searching look as Polly introduced them.

"Luke Kellogg, I'd like you to meet my best friend, Julia Stow."

Luke stood transfixed, stunned by the beauty of the girl.

"It's a pleasure to meet you, Mr. Kellogg. You are so brave to go off to war. I admire your courage. Are you enjoying Binghamton?"

Julia smiled at him. She knew even before he answered her that this was the man she had long envisioned in her fantasies—tall, strong, solid, unafraid.

"At this instant, Miss Stow, I am enjoying Binghamton very much!" He reached out and took her slender hand in his, holding it in a gentle but firm grasp. "I'd be pleased if you would call me Luke, Miss Stow." He continued to look at her intently, the trace of a smile on his face as she responded with a squeeze of her own on the large hand holding hers.

"Then you must call me Julia, Luke."

Polly and Bert grinned at their handiwork as Julia put her arm in Luke's and led him off on a private stroll, talking animatedly to her tall escort.

"Albert Hughes, I think you have found her the man she's been waiting for. You are such a dear!" Polly led Bert off on their own little walk, grinning in satisfaction.

Julia quickly drew out Luke's story of his abortive earlier attempts at enlistment, and how he and Billy Weed had arrived in Colonel Ireland's Regiment here in Binghamton. She in turn shared her thoughts about the war, her admiration for his bravery. In short order, the pair knew with certainty that God had intended them to meet and to spend their lives together in spite of the separation of war that would come. It was because of the war that they had discovered each other. The pain of separation would be a small price to pay for a lifetime of happiness. Neither cared to think of the separation by death that would be a constant shadow over them while Luke was at war.

Julia walked home from Rockbottom Flats feeling above and beyond her surroundings, transformed by an unfamiliar yet magnificent feeling of love and desire. Polly, of course, was dying to talk to her after the other girls had left them. Once safely home on her porch, Julia poured out her feelings to Polly, the only person she dared trust with her explosive desires.

"Oh, Polly. I want him. I must have him. And I want him to have me. In every way. Body and soul! And the regiment is leaving in only a week! I won't be able to bear our parting unless I've known him, and he's known me. Fully and completely." Julia looked earnestly into her friend's eyes.

"I know how sinful this must sound to you. I don't care. God can't let me finally meet the one man I can love with all my heart and soul and body, and not let me be fulfilled. So it can't be sinful. It must be right! It must! Polly, you're my truest friend—closer to me than a sister. You've got to help me figure out how I can get Luke to myself!"

"Oh, Julia. This is so wonderfully romantic! Of course I'll help. After all, didn't Bert and I bring you two together? I think I have just the way for you and Luke to slip off together. Saturday night, the Roses are letting Millie have some of the boys to a farewell party at their new house by the river. Millie told me to ask you to come, and Millie's brother Tom would invite Albert, I'm sure. And Tom won't object if Bert brings his best friend from the regiment. Bert and I will cover for you while you and Luke slip down to the riverbank. It's still warm, the bank is mossy, it's wooded and private—a perfect place for your tryst. But you have to promise to tell me all the details later. Agreed?"

"Oh, yes, Pol. Thank you! But are you sure the spot on the river is safe? I would die if anyone other than you knew what I had done!"

Polly grinned broadly. "Do you remember the party Millie had on Independence Day? How you wondered where I'd disappeared to? Now I'm swearing you to secrecy, Jule. Bert and I were down on the riverbank, in that very spot. I guess you could say we tried it out for you that night. And oh, Julia, it was wonderful!"

Julia joyfully agreed to keep her friend's secret. The next two days she spent planning what she'd wear, what perfume to use for her seduction, how she should wear her hair. Each evening she practically ran to the Rockbottom Flats camp gate, rushing into Luke's enfolding arms, spending the next hour in rapturous communion with her newfound love.

Friday night, Luke lay in his blanket, deep in thought. Deeply concerned. This lovely vision, this magnificent young woman, had confided in him her desire, her need to join with him in physical union. Luke was completely inexperienced in these matters. He hadn't spent much time with girls his age, growing up as he did in a sparsely settled area of the Finger Lakes. He'd sure never known a woman so forward. But Luke Kellogg, at eighteen, was a vigorous young man, in the prime of his youth. His body wouldn't let him ignore her invitation. He knew he couldn't refuse this beautiful girl. He'd already decided that as soon as the war was done he'd take Julia as his wife, if she'd have him. With war's dangers ahead of him, he realized it would be folly to ignore what might turn out to be their one chance to give each other such happiness. Luke allowed his thoughts to turn to anticipation of the delights of her loving that awaited him. He soon drifted off to a deep, contented sleep.

Saturday evening the Rose house was brightly lit with candles, the fiddler was playing, and young women were flirting coquettishly with young men about to go off to war. Involved with their own romantic preoccupations, they took no notice when Julia led Luke out into the garden and down to the riverbank.

Julia had chosen for this most special of nights to let her hair spill gracefully in a golden cascade to her shoulders. She wore a prim high-collar shirtwaist under the flatteringly low-cut bodice of a burgundy velvet gown. Not wanting to be encumbered by the bulkiness of a hoop skirt, she had chosen to wear but a single petticoat. It filled out the long skirt as a small concession to the dictates of fashion, while still accentuating her willowy yet curvaceous figure. Luke gazed at her and thought that this must be what a Greek goddess would have looked like.

Reaching the tree-lined riverbank, he saw she had led him to a secluded mossy spot, away from any prying eyes. The night was warm. The quarter-moon's light shimmered across the flowing water. Luke embraced Julia and she responded passionately to her lover. He stroked her long hair, reveling in its silky texture. Her perfume had the subtle scent of lavender, enticing him to kiss her cheeks, her earlobe, her full moist lips. She pressed her lips to his, her mouth slightly open, and ran the tip of her tongue over his lips, searching, until he responded with his own tongue. While holding her close with his left arm enfolding her slender waist, he allowed her to place his eager hand on her breast. "Let me," she whispered.

Julia swiftly undid the buttons on her gown and slipped out of it, laying it over the low branch of a nearby tree by his dark blue uniform jacket. Seconds later, she had undone each of the whalebone buttons on her shirtwaist. She slipped quickly out of the petticoat and spread it on the ground. Standing in the moonlight, her skin milky white, her hair framed her lovely face like golden silk on fine porcelain. Luke stood transfixed by this vision that surpassed any image of female beauty that he'd ever imagined, let alone seen. "My God, but you're a vision!" She pressed herself tightly to him, then leaned back, took his hand and placed it again on her breast. "I'm yours, Luke. Come to me, quickly! Now!"

She knelt down in front of him and began to unbutton his light blue trousers while he tried to focus on pulling his shirt over his head. His mind was dazed with desire as he felt her hands on him.

Julia was amazed at the effect on her senses of his reaction to the gentle touch of her slender fingers. She'd only imagined what it must be like, this instrument which would soon transform her from maidenhood to womanhood. Luke somehow got his shirt off, and followed Julia down onto the petticoat "bed," fighting to keep under control the urges her stimulation had created already in him. Inexperienced though he was, his love for her told him to delay his release until she could achieve her own, simultaneously with him. Julia was ecstatic at the long-awaited sensations her lover was creating in her. Luke marveled at the love of this amazing young woman. His low moans, almost guttural, mingled with her sharp little cries as she urged him on, fearing his restraint might deprive her of the last little measure of delight. All too soon, they reached the peak in an explosion of release. He started to rise, but she pulled him back, with kisses and murmured words of love and encouragement. The desire of a young man is readily rekindled, and Luke rose to the occasion. This time their lovemaking was slow, as they relished the motions of each other's young bodies, until once more they achieved the deep fulfillment of full release.

"Oh, Luke! That was the most wonderful moment I've ever experienced! I wish we could stay here and make love in the moonlight all night! Tell me you loved it too, my darling Luke! And tell me you won't hate me for this tomorrow, or think I'm cheap. For this is only for you, my darling. No other man shall ever know me as you have tonight!"

"Dear, dear Julia! I've never known such a feeling of happiness and fulfillment. I could never think of you as anything but the highest value, a love beyond price. I will love you forever. I could never join with another woman as I have with you tonight. I wish we could stay here 'til dawn, but I fear we will be missed and your reputation endangered. We must get back to the others, before Bert and Polly run out of excuses for our absence."

And so they ran down to the water, cleaned up hurriedly, dressed, each helping the other to remove any traces of dishevelment that might betray their activity. They managed to slip unnoticed back into the garden, where Bert and Polly found them. Polly took one look and saw the changed demeanor of the lovers, and with a grin and a smile, said, "Well, you two seem to have enjoyed your walk in the moonlight."

Chapter Ten
Bolivar Heights

October 1862

It had been an eventful four weeks for the men of the 137th New York Infantry. After the weeks of recruiting and training, the regiment was officially mustered in on September 25. Two days later, Sergeant Major Joseph B. Abbott marched the boys in blue through the streets of Binghamton to the Erie & Western station. Cheering citizens waved flags and handkerchiefs. Fathers proudly watched their sons doing their family name proud, while mothers dabbed their tear-filled eyes with hankies. Wives stood holding their children by the hand as their husbands marched off to an uncertain fate. The rest of the crowd was stirred by the patriotic martial music of the regimental musicians. Luke scanned the crowd until he saw Julia standing with Polly.

Seeing him, Julia cried out. "Luke, take this!" She ran up, and while walking alongside the marching soldier, tucked her scented kerchief into his inner breast pocket, kissed his cheek, and ran back to Polly, not letting him see the tears welling up in her eyes.

Luke had felt torn by the conflicting excitement and anticipation of what lay ahead and the realization that he may have seen his newfound lover for the last time!

He'd felt lucky on the train trip south. Many of the men had ridden in freight cars, some even on open platform cars, but his company had been assigned to the few passenger cars. The boy from the Finger Lakes had never been farther south than Binghamton. Now he was crossing the whole of Pennsylvania and traveling south of the Mason-Dixon line.

It was late afternoon when the train rattled down the tracks by the Susquehanna where it cut through Tuscarora Mountain north of Harrisburg. The mixture of sun and shadow on the broad river expanse reminded him of the warm August evening only a month ago, when he lay on the shore of Skaneateles Lake at Glen Haven and watched the shadow of the ridge behind him drive the sunlight off the water and up the ridge on the far shore. Then, of course, he had only brother Andrew for company. Now he had the whole regiment!

They had reached Washington, expecting to go into camp across the Potomac, when orders arrived sending them back north halfway through Maryland to Frederick. On the train ride, much of the talk had revolved around the reports of the terrible battle of September 17 on the Antietam Creek at Sharpsburg. Now here they were, only twenty or so miles to the east of that battlefield. They were seeing firsthand the deadly impact of war—the churches and public buildings were filled with the maimed and wounded.

They had barely settled into their tents, hastily set up in a cow pasture east of Frederick, when orders came to move out. The men boarded the Baltimore and Ohio cars and rode the twenty-two miles west to Harper's Ferry. They marched back across the Potomac River bridge to encamp at Pleasant Valley, in the shadow of Maryland Heights, where the Potomac River split South Mountain from Virginia's Blue Ridge. There Colonel Ireland continued to drill the regiment, imparting yet more of the skills, knowledge, and attitudes his men would need to win battles and survive.

The men of the 137th didn't lack for motivation, and didn't need to be taught responsibility. While some, like Luke Kellogg, were barely old enough to make the eighteen-year-old age requirement, others were old enough to be their fathers. Luke's company commander, Captain Henry Shipman, was fifty years old. Colonel Ireland was still a relatively young man of twenty-nine. Privates Brad and John Harris were in their early forties, and they were not atypical, though the average age was twenty-seven. By comparison, the average enlistment age for the Union Army from 1861–65 was only nineteen and a half. The 137th was quite senior by comparison. Sometimes they were from one family, like the five Mabee boys from Ithaca, the eldest thirty-four and the youngest eighteen.

These were serious men, citizens who believed strongly in the Union and were determined to absorb every bit of training they could get. They wanted to do the job right, get it done, and get home. And so they worked hard at learning drill, formations, and the other myriad details of the military arts. They learned how to fire their Enfields, and how to use the bayonet in close combat drills. Most of these men were hunters and marksmen. Proper care and respect for knives and firearms was second nature. In camp, they learned the idiosyncrasies of the government-issue weapons, until their care and use had become routine. Now they were itching to teach Johnny Reb a lesson.

In October, Colonel Ireland's regiment joined four other New York regiments to make up General George Greene's Brigade, Second Division, Twelfth Army Corps. They marched across the Potomac through Harper's Ferry and up the hill to set up camp at Bolivar Heights. On October 29, not yet settled into camp, the men of the 137th got their first chance to engage the enemy.

For the past few weeks in camp at Pleasant Valley, Privates Luke Kellogg and Billy Weed had listened enviously to stories about skirmishes fought with Virginia cavalrymen up and down the Potomac and Shenandoah Rivers. Now they were getting their chance for action. Orders had come to send out pickets to ward off surprise attacks on the camp by roaming bands of rebel horsemen. Leaving all their gear at camp, Luke and Weed joined a handful of Company F men heading off in the twilight, led by Lieutenant Marshall Corbett.

As the sky grew dark over the Charles Town Road, the pickets were surprised by a patrol from the Black Horse Troop, Fourth Virginia Cavalry. Sergeant Jack Lewis and the newly enlisted Private Lathrop Emmons were among them. The Black Horse troopers exchanged shots with the New Yorkers, who quickly retreated into the darkness of the woods by the side of the road. Seeing one Bluecoat run off down the road alone, apparently disoriented by darkness and unfamiliar surroundings, Jack and Emmons ran him down. The lone soldier stumbled and fell into the roadside ditch.

Jack barked out a demand: "Surrender or be killed, Yank!"

Emmons laughed. "Well ain't he somethin', Jack—layin' in th' ditch on his back like a damn dead groundhawg."

With his unloaded musket lying useless in the ditch, Private Newt Hunt knew he had no choice. "I surrender. Don't shoot!"

"Well you ain't no damn groundhawg, Yank. Git up out o' th' ditch an' start walkin'. You're a prisoner of the Black Horse Troop, Fourth Virginia Cavalry." Jack was a bit irritated by Emmons's groundhog comparison. His new private would learn soon enough to have more respect for the enemy's ability to deal death. Hunt stood up and began to walk slowly down the road in front of the two horsemen.

"Do we really have t'walk this prisoner all way back t'Charles Town, Jack? I could take care o' this right quick." Emmons raised his naked saber high, intending to deliver a quick and fatal blow to their captive. Then a single shot rang out. A bullet hit Emmons's upraised arm. Emmons gave out a howl of pain and his saber fell harmlessly to the road. Another volley followed from behind a low stone wall on the embankment just above and behind the men in the road.

A full moon had risen, illuminating the startled faces of the rebel troopers and the grim visages of Yankee riflemen at the wall. As Newt Hunt dove back into the cover of the ditch, Luke Kellogg stared at Jack and Emmons. They returned the look, images forever burned into each man's memory. Jack fired his carbine at the men on the embankment, then the rebel troopers wheeled about, spurred their horses, and were galloping away when the second Yankee volley erupted from behind the wall.

"Jack, I'm hit!" Emmons cried out, while spurring his horse to flee faster.

"Hang on and ride, man! We're soon out of range." Jack guided his mount alongside Emmons's, ready to hold him if he started to slide out of the saddle.

Meanwhile Private Hunt, his captors well away, scrambled up the bank and jumped over the stone wall into the midst of his liberators.

"Thank God you boys came back—that one Reb was set to kill me for sure, surrender or not!"

Lieutenant Corbett patted him on the back. "We just circled back through these woods when we saw you weren't with us, figurin' the Rebs might've caught you. But you really need to thank Kellogg here. He got off some shot, to hit that Reb right in the arm before he finished swingin' that saber. Like Captain Shipman says, us men of Company F have to look out for one another! Now, is everyone all right? Anybody get hit by them Rebs?"

"Luke—you're bleedin'!" Bert Hughes was pointing to Luke's shirtsleeve, which was growing red with blood soaking through. His mind flooded by the excitement of this first enemy encounter, Luke hadn't even felt the blow. Now he looked down at the bloody sleeve. He took out his sheath knife and cut away the sleeve.

"Aw, it's nothin' much. Just grazed me."

"Well, Kellogg. Looks like you got and gave first blood in the regiment. Bind it up and let's head back to camp." Lieutenant Corbett led the now-blooded patrol back to camp, where he reported to Captain Shipman and Colonel Ireland. The two officers made it a point to commend Corbett for his coolness in rescuing Hunt, and then went looking for Private Kellogg to praise him for his marksmanship. They found him being treated by assistant surgeon Steven Hand while John Farrington, Chief Surgeon of the 137th, examined this first regimental battle wound.

A little knot of men gathered around Luke, Weed and Hunt when they got back to their tents, anxious to hear all about this first combat engagement. Sergeant Will Dodge spoke up.

"You got them Rebs good, Luke. They likely ran them horses full out back to Charles Town!"

Luke couldn't help but enjoy all this adulation, but he was thoughtful. The pain throbbing in his arm reminded him that war wasn't going to be fun and games. The next few years would be hard, and the casualties far more severe than this first flesh wound. When Lieutenant Corbett was promoted in May of 1863, Luke had a notion it was a result of their successful rescue of Newt Hunt on the Charles Town road.

In the early morning hours, Luke awoke, seeing again in his mind's eye the moonlit faces of the two Virginia cavalrymen, especially the face of Emmons. There was a mean and violent streak shining in the man's dark eyes. And the red hair, prominent nose, and jug ears outlined in the moonlight made for an easily remembered impression. The other man's visage was more solid, the expression one of fearlessness, yet somehow reflecting the prudence and respect of an experienced professional soldier. *In another lifetime,* Luke thought, *I think I could like to know this man. But "jug ears" I'd just as soon not run across again.*

Down the road in Charles Town, Jack Lewis watched Lathrop Emmons being treated for the wound to his forearm. The bullet had passed through, damaging neither bones nor tendons. "You're damn lucky, Lathe. And that Yank ball that hit you on the way down the road was nearly spent. The surgeon dug it out of your shoulder easily. Hardly even bled. Next time you may not be that lucky. You're just startin' out at soldierin', Lathe. Be more respectful of the enemy, more watchful. We need you to survive." Privately, Jack was concerned. Lathe appeared to be more than a little hot-headed. Was he just over-enthusiastic, or did he have a real mean streak? Jack remembered his father. Surely Lathrop Emmons couldn't match that man's downright ugly mean nature—could he? Jack figured he'd best keep an eye on Lathe.

"Tell ye what, Jack. Some day we'll meet up with those boys agin. I can see the face o' that Yankee sonuvabitch that shot me, clear as day. One day I'll repay him, in spades! Mark my words." Emmons gratefully swallowed another big slug of whisky as the last bandage was wrapped around his right forearm.

"Well just keep your eyes open for any Yank. Any of 'em can kill you. I can see that fella's face too, Lathe. He must be a helluva good shot, t'hit your arm instead of killin' you. Maybe you oughta thank him if you ever do see him again."

"I'll thank 'im, a'right. A thanks he'll not likely fergit!"

"Anyway, Lathe, you're lucky. I just got told the regiment's ordered back over the mountains. We're to be patrollin' home in Fauquier County for a time. You can have a couple days at the farm at Upperville. Mrs. Pettis'll surely feed you up and get you fit as a fiddle real quick."

Fauquier County had so far largely escaped the devastation of the war. The Pettis farm at Upperville was a storehouse of harvested grain, hay, vegetables, fruit, and freshly butchered pork. Sergeant Jack Lewis accompanied Private Lathrop Emmons to the farm, enjoying a hero's welcome. The two troopers enjoyed the delicious dinner prepared for them in Mrs. Pettis's kitchen. The considerate Minerva Pettis had sent a buggy to bring Rachel Lewis to the farm for dinner with the son she seldom saw in these war times.

After dinner, they sat around the fireplace and listened to Jack's recounting the raid around the Union Army. Harry Pettis laughed when Jack told of "repatriating" his horses sold to Pennsylvania farmers. "I'm glad someone else is finally supplying you with horses, before I'm totally cleaned out!" Jack was mum on the encounter at the Licking Creek.

"I found Sally. Left Brunebaugh's farm. She's in Chambersburg, workin' for a lawyer named Baird and his wife. I was able to spend a few hours with her, an' I guess you could say we're engaged. Soon's this war's done I'm bringin' her back here as my wife. I know you all will like her. She's hard working, and good as gold. Pretty to boot. A real peach, Mrs. Pettis. Would you like to see her?"

Jack pulled Sally's locket from under his shirt, slipped the chain from his neck, and pressed the locket's hidden catch to pop open the case. He handed the locket to his mother, who gasped in surprise, then passed it on for the others to see. Rachel, a small happy tear in her eye, spoke first.

"Jack, she's so purty. I'm s'happy fer ye, son. I cain't hardly wait t'meet her. Oh, how I wish this here war'd be done with."

The others chimed in, agreeing with her sentiments, awed by the tintype, but more by the girl's beauty. Emmons was impressed by the size and quality of the gold locket, but said nothing, even though he was curious about the strange markings on the back of the case. Someday he'd have to ask Lewis about that. When the locket made its way back to Jack, he put the chain back around his neck and slipped the locket back under his shirt, next to his heart. He looked at his mother, then to the Pettises, and finally to his cousin Will Gresham.

"I'm glad you can see her picture, but she's even prettier in person, an' as sweet a gal as a fella'd ever want. An' she loves me. Now if anything should happen to me, I'll count on you to somehow get word to her. I'd want you to treat her as my wife. An' Will, I'll depend on you t'see she's taken care of."

Harry Pettis was quick to respond. "Ye can count on us, Jack. Your Sally will be looked after as best we can." That done, Pettis turned his attention to Emmons.

"Now, Lathe, tell us how you managed t'get wounded after only two weeks in the cavalry!"

"Mr. Pettis, we routed a bunch o' green Yankee infantry near Charles Town, an' they got me with a couple o' lucky shots. But give me a day's rest an' I'll be fine."

Harry Pettis thought he'd ask how come one of the shots was in Emmons's back, if they were routing the Federals. But he wisely decided not to dispute the issue with Emmons.

That night, asleep in his bed in the bunkhouse, Jack thought of Sally. "Wish this damn war would be over soon, so I could ride back north, get the gold, get Sally, and buy a farm and settle down. Lord, how I love that girl!" He fell asleep with a smile, warmed by the fresh memory of their lovemaking those few weeks ago.

Awakening in the night, Jack saw the image of the soldier from New York. He saw a strong and determined face, with steely eyes that showed conviction. He thought to himself, *In another time, another place, I think I might like this man. But maybe Lathe's right—I have a feeling we may just cross paths with this man again. If he's any guide to Federal strength, we may not win this war anytime soon.*

Ten days later, while the Black Horse Troop was patrolling on the opposite side of the Blue Ridge, General Greene led his brigade of New Yorkers on an armed reconnaissance to Charles Town, finding it recently vacated by the rebels. Entering the town, they got a hostile reception from the citizenry. The same women who had cheered their Virginia cavalrymen, baked willingly for them, and offered such comfort as they could, now looked with open contempt and hatred at the column of blue-coated Federals in their midst.

Standing in shadowed doorways, half hidden in the windows of upstairs rooms, these ladies made no attempt to hide their feelings. "Damn Yankees. You'll soon enough feel Gen'ral Jackson's steel and skedaddle back up north where you came from. An' good riddance! Ya'll ain't wanted here."

Colonel David Ireland responded with restraint when an elderly woman spat at his horse as he passed. He graciously tipped his cap and, making a slight bow in her direction, said, "And a good day to you too, ma'am."

Luke Kellogg thought Surgeon Farrington had a fitting response to the Charles Town community's insults. Luke held open the doors to the vacant Jefferson County Courthouse and watched his regimental surgeon ride a horse right up the steps into the courtroom and up to the judge's bench, where he turned and faced front. As he did so, his thoroughly patriotic steed deposited a large, dark, fragrant memento! Luke laughed as the doctor rode back out on to the street while the ladies of Charles Town gasped at the disrespect shown to their seat of justice.

On the way back to camp at Bolivar Heights, the boys liberated cattle from pastures by the road, encouraged by several of the officers. Luke and Billy Weed were helping Hunt and Kilburn herd the beasts up the road when General Greene, riding back along his brigade's column, came upon the happy cowherds. The stern commander spoke loudly. "All right men, none of that. We are not here to plunder civilians. Turn these animals loose immediately!"

Back in camp, wishing he'd been able to enjoy the beefsteak they so nearly obtained, Luke wrote a letter to his Julia, pining for him back in Binghamton.

Camp of the 137th N.Y.S.V.
Bolivar Heights, Va., December 10, 1862
Dearest Julia,
Your men of Binghamton have acquitted themselves well in their first encounter with the Secessionists. We bested some of their cavalry last month. I wounded one rebel who tried to slash Newt Hunt who they had cornered, but we drove the rebels off. I was slightly wounded, but don't be worried, for it's soon healed.

Last week outside Charles Town we helped some of our officers rustle up some Secesh beef. First time I ever helped a Methodist class leader, a Presbyterian deacon, and a Baptist minister steal a cow! But General Greene made us give them back.

There is much sickness in the camp. This is not a healthy place. Our friend Richard Hall, and Lt. George Spencer got the typhoid and are in hospital at Harper's Ferry. They don't think Hall will make it back to action, even if he recovers. Poor Jeremiah Dimon they say is near death, suffering dysentery after the fever.

I hear we will be moving out of here in the next week. It won't be too soon!

In the night, when I don't sleep, I think of you and our short time together. I hope this war will be over soon, so we can be together always. But these rebels look to be a tough lot, and it may take some time before we make them stop this rebellion.

Last Sunday, at services, our Chaplain Washburn preached from John's Gospel. The message was, God demands much from those who serve his cause. I fear he means there will be more hardship, more sickness, more fighting, more death before God will grace us with victory!

I must end now, dear Julia. Pray for me always, as I do for you.

> *Affectionately*
> *Luke*

Chapter Eleven
137th New York

June 13, 1863, Aquia Creek Landing, Virginia

Billy Weed looked around one last time at the winter camp of Greene's brigade. The neat streets and rows of canvas-roofed log shanties that had made a comfortable winter home for the men of the 137th New York were finally to be left behind.

They had gotten over the low morale of the winter, brought on by long, often boring hours in camp, missing loved ones, reading papers filled with Copperhead propaganda such as, *"The states have a right to set their own destiny. The tyrant Lincoln is killing our men to set himself up as emperor. Our armies can't defeat Lee and Jackson. Negro servitude is no concern of ours. The Union is well-rid of the secessionists."*

Angry as it made them, feeling that their risking life and limb for their country was unappreciated by these naysayers, they grew even more determined to show up these unpatriotic ignoramuses. At one point Billy Weed made his feelings abundantly clear.

"Them people's nothin' but free-loaders. They expect to have their freedom to say whatever they want, no matter how dumb, long as they don't have to fight to keep it! Then they got the gall to yell at us who do!"

When President Lincoln came down from Washington in mid-April to review the Army of the Potomac, the men of Twelfth Corps cheered their commander in chief. Gaunt and haggard, Lincoln appeared more care-worn and exhausted than any of his troops. The New Yorkers of Greene's brigade were heartened by the presence of this man. Again, Billy Weed said it for them all.

"Look at him, Luke. President Lincoln looks more worn down than us. He's carryin' our troubles an' a whole lot more besides, yet he comes down here to be with us. Tells me he gives a damn about us boys. Don't need words to see he's showin' us respect and thanks. Them so-called 'Peace Democrats' can heap all the scorn on him they want, but we can see how false that is. Ol' Abe's showin' us he's sure we're gonna win. Now it's up to us to prove he ain't wrong!"

From then on, the troops were renewed in their eagerness to get moving, to take on Lee's army, to show the country and the world that Southern invincibility was a myth, that the rebel idols Stonewall Jackson and Jeb Stuart had feet of clay, that, given the right leadership, the boys in blue would win the day and the war.

In May, Greene's New Yorkers got their chance. Moving out of camp, the Union Army under General "Fightin' Joe" Hooker took on Lee's Army of Northern Virginia once again, at Chancellorsville. The New Yorkers of General Greene's Third Brigade showed their mettle in this, their first major battle. Crouching in hastily dug trenches, they listened to shells whistling overhead and exploding around them. If the primary objective of artillery bombardment is to terrorize the enemy, it failed with Luke and his fellow soldiers. They waited coolly until the order was given to move out by the left flank. Luke was duly amazed at seeing a nearby soldier grab a cannonball, its fuse still lit, and throw it back out over the breastworks.

Back in camp the men of the 137th, while regretting their losses, were impressed by the protection the trenches and breastworks had given them. They were justifiably proud of the praise given them by their commanders. Second Division Commander Geary had written, *"The conduct of Greene's Brigade...was admirable. Although exposed for quite a length of time to the fire of the enemy, where they could neither shelter nor defend themselves, nor return the assault, they bore themselves with the calmness and discipline of veterans.*" And Brigade Commander Greene had singled out the boys from Binghamton: "*The One hundred and thirty-seventh New York, commanded by Colonel Ireland displayed great coolness and good discipline in all its movements.*" After going through this ordeal by fire, Luke Kellogg and Billy Weed knew they were ready, just waiting for the chance to really deal the rebels the knockout blow.

This June morning the order had come that would move the Army of the Potomac into collision course with the Army of Northern Virginia. The New Yorkers of Greene's brigade threw off their camp mindset and prepared to live and fight on the move. They'd been issued eight days' rations and turned in all but their essential gear, lightened up for a hard march to who knew where. Billy Weed's knapsack was heavy, but his friend Luke Kellogg had helped him make shrewd choices about what to take and what to throw away.

"First, Billy, get rid of that fry pan an' plate. I'll give you my extra pan. One of the Syracuse boys in the 149th showed me how to make this. I took an extra canteen, put a little black powder in it, put it in the coals, and blew the two halves apart. Then the coals melted all the solder off the edges. See this wood stick I made? It slips right in the end and holds it secure, and you don't burn your hands. This'll serve for pan and plate, and it's lighter'n either."

"Pretty slick, Luke. Thank you."

"We'll share and split up some of the load, Bill. You take the coffee. I'll take the salt pork. I already cooked up a batch and wrapped it in this cloth sack, so it's ready if we're marchin' and don't get time to cook. I wrapped up a piece of it for you to go with your own hard biscuits in your haversack, so you got somethin' to eat quick if you need it."

In each case, Luke had taken on the heavier items. *But then,* thought Weed, *he's much bigger and stronger, so maybe it's only fair.* Luke, on the other hand, knew that if Weed's load got too much for him, he, Luke, would wind up carrying both knapsacks before he'd see his friend drop out and be labeled a straggler. Weed packed his knapsack carefully, folded the gum blanket he'd sleep on, and the tent half he'd sleep under, and went to strap them on the outside of the knapsack to go next to his back. Luke did the same, but took Billy's gum blanket and strapped it with his own. Each took their wool blanket, folded it, rolled it up, and strapped it on the top.

Knapsack set comfortably high on his back, Luke slipped his cartridge box strap over his left shoulder, tightened his belt around his waist, and sheathed the bayonet in its scabbard. He slipped the haversack strap over his right shoulder and the canteen strap after that, so that both were set comfortably on his right hip, canteen above haversack where it wouldn't bounce and bang. He was carrying a lot of material, but everything was in the right place for easy access and comfortable carrying. Then he checked out Billy Weed to be sure he was as comfortably rigged for a long march as one could be. Their brogans were well worn, but not worn out. Their feet would, they hoped, stay in good shape. Still, with all the weight strapped on them, and each carrying a ten-pound Enfield musket, Luke figured they'd need all their strength and endurance for the marching that lay ahead.

The word had been given at muster that morning. They were off on a long march, and stragglers would not be tolerated. Commanders would be held accountable. The men of the 137th had too much pride in Colonel Ireland to see him bear the consequences of their weakness. Besides, these were mature men, firm in their belief in themselves, their regiment, their commander, and their country. They'd borne hardship countless times before enlisting in this war, and the winter's trials only toughened them further. They'd stick together, help each other, march as far as was necessary, then fight and beat the secessionist army.

But first, a lot of hard marching lay ahead. The Army of the Potomac would march more than one hundred miles from Fredericksburg, Virginia to Frederick, Maryland, searching and probing, spoiling for a fight. And they wouldn't stop there. They'd continue on, fanning out from Frederick, the seven different corps heading north over various roads, eventually converging again forty miles north in Pennsylvania. There they would finally find the invading Army of Northern Virginia. Seventy thousand Confederate soldiers moved west from York, southwest from Harrisburg, south from Carlisle, and east from Chambersburg, those four roads converging at a peaceful Pennsylvania Dutch village just north of the Mason-Dixon line—Gettysburg.

A new commanding general, named by President Lincoln while the army was crossing the Potomac, now knew that the huge rebel army was thrusting into the heart of the Union—a dagger aimed at Philadelphia or New York. And if this son of Pennsylvania didn't deal it a mortal blow, the invading army could capture Baltimore and Washington at its leisure. All the world would then have to recognize as legitimate the Confederate States of America. Secession would have succeeded. General George G. Meade had been surprised that this gravest of responsibilities had been taken from "Fightin' Joe" Hooker and settled on him.

Some of the men in Fifth Corps had earlier looked at their commander's stern visage, with balding head and prominent nose, and dubbed him "the old snapping turtle." Not complimentary to his looks, perhaps, but not far off the mark as to his character. Private Luke Kellogg had heard that nickname given to his new high commander, and made some insightful comments to Billy Weed. "You know how snappers work, Bill. Trailin' along, layin' low, unseen by their quarry 'til they get 'em where they want 'em. Then zap, snap—the snapper's got his prey by the leg and draggin' him down to make his meal. I have a feelin' those rebels are gonna be dragged down by our old snappin' turtle, and right quick!"

Indeed, Lee's army lay spread across a hundred miles of southern Pennsylvania, sitting above the Mason-Dixon Line like so many ducks on the surface of a pond. And Meade had his army gathered together in Maryland, following Lee just below the Line, like a gigantic snapper just beneath the surface, looking for the right chance to strike its prey.

Chronically short of food, shoes, and clothing, the basics any army needs to sustain itself, Lee knew his men needed plenty of territory to forage. He would spare Maryland, many of whose inhabitants were sympathetic to the Southern cause. His armies quickly crossed the state, moving in less than a day from the Shenandoah Valley of Virginia into the Cumberland Valley of Pennsylvania.

There Lee's restrictions were off. Thrifty farmers by the Mason-Dixon Line and shops in Mercersburg, Greencastle, and Waynesboro were the first to feel the ravages of seventy thousand hungry, ill-clothed rebels. Then so did their cousins, all the way up that wide fertile valley to the banks of the Susquehanna overlooking Harrisburg. Lee's lieutenant, General Ewell, marched his corps east from the main army at Chambersburg, across South Mountain through Gettysburg and York, gathering food, shoes, and clothing as he went, demanding gold where he could get it. His men were only too happy to exact tribute from prosperous Yankees who had so far escaped the kind of devastation felt in their Southern homelands. Ewell's men made it all the way to the Susquehanna, and might have continued to Lancaster and even Philadelphia, had not the green troops of the Pennsylvania militia burnt the bridge at Wrightsville.

Meade might be a newcomer to the top spot, but he was an experienced, battle-hardened combat commander. Before the war, he had been a railroad engineer and knew this terrain well, on both sides of the Mason-Dixon Line. He held another advantage—he knew generally where Lee was, while Lee, out of contact with Jeb Stuart's long-range cavalry, had no accurate knowledge of where the Federals were. In the past two years, Lee's invincibility was based on one simple principle—to force the Army of the Potomac to attack from an unfavorable position, while he kept the advantage of the terrain for himself.

Meade wasn't going to repeat his predecessors' mistakes. The new army commander quickly came up with a brilliant plan. Meade laid out a defensive line along a stream called Pipe Creek, in the foothills of the Catoctin Mountains north of Frederick. He'd probe north, find Lee, and draw him back down to the Pipe Creek line. His troops would be defending high ground, while Lee's men attacked across exposed fields of fire. He'd inflict such casualties as would make Antietam's carnage of the previous September seem ordinary. A severely weakened Lee would have to pull back west and south, the long way, across the Potomac. Meade could swiftly move his forces the short way down through Washington and into Richmond before Lee's surviving forces could reinforce their capital's defenses. The war would be quickly ended.

While chain-of-command generals Slocum, Geary, and Greene may have had some insight into Meade's strategy, and had perhaps passed some of their knowledge down to Colonel David Ireland, ordinary soldiers like Luke Kellogg and Billy Weed had no clue. They just knew

Lee's army was in Pennsylvania, and that they were marching hard and fast to catch the rebels before really serious mischief occurred.

Sergeant Major Van Emburge told his men, "If rebels get to Harrisburg, what's to stop 'em from foraging up the Susquehanna all the way to Owego and Binghamton, and up to Ithaca, for that matter! We're fighting for our homes, now boys! Let's go get them rebel sonsabitches!"

Meade had kept his cavalry on a tighter leash than Lee had his. While Lee had Jenkins' West Virginia mounted infantry close at hand, he was depending on General Stuart's cavalry division to probe in force at a distance. Lee expected Stuart to track Hooker's (now Meade's) army, informing Lee of the enemy strength and disposition at all times. Such information was crucial to an army on the move deep into hostile country, well away from home support. But when Lee began his invasion, he gave Stuart a disastrous amount of discretion as to how to maneuver. Instead of the buffer between the opposing armies, Stuart's brigades of horsemen became a strategically useless distraction beyond them both.

In contrast, Meade's cavalry commander, General Pleasonton, employed his three divisions very effectively. He sent the tough, experienced General Buford north from Frederick toward Harrisburg to probe for Lee's forces and Generals Kilpatrick and Gregg north and east to look for Stuart. So Meade had probes out to find either of the forces that could surprise his army. On June 30, they all made contact.

Meade didn't just dig in at Pipe Creek and wait. He continued to pursue Lee while always keeping his seven corps between Lee and Washington. Slocum's Twelfth Corps had marched into Pennsylvania on the morning of June 30. Luke and his comrades were finally able to take a breather, resting that pleasant afternoon at Littlestown, unaware that twelve miles to their west, Buford's cavalrymen had run up against the leading edge of the rebel army spilling east out of South Mountain. A brigade of barefoot North Carolinians were bent on commandeering boots from a Gettysburg store when they saw the dust of the Yankee cavalry fast advancing from the south. No shots were fired, but the mystery was over. Both sides finally knew just where the other was—converging on Gettysburg. Buford dismounted his men and established a defensive line west of the town to await the expected rebel attack. His couriers were swift in returning to Meade at Taneytown, who was equally swift in ordering his corps to converge on Gettysburg.

Wednesday morning, July 1, General Reynolds was first of Meade's corps commanders to arrive on the scene, meeting Buford in the cupola of the Lutheran Seminary on the west edge of town. Rapidly seeing the disposition of forces, Reynolds ordered the men of First Corps into position to relieve Buford's dismounted cavalry, which had thus far held back the Confederate advance. Not long thereafter, a rebel sharpshooter's bullet took Reynolds' life. That day the battle raged on the west and north sides of the town. Union troops continued to arrive, but too late to hold back Lee's Second Corps arriving from the north and east.

Union Fifth Corps commander General Hancock had arrived later in the day in advance of General Meade. He quickly saw the superb defensive position the terrain south of town provided him, where his brigades were now arriving. There he positioned the new arrivals and the survivors of the battles north and west of town. By Wednesday night, a strong Union defensive line was in place on the heights south of Gettysburg. The Union left flank was anchored at Little Round Top in the southwest. From there the line ran northeast on Cemetery Ridge to the edge of town, then curled back south around the crest of Culp's Hill, the Union right flank anchored on its lower summit, just west of Rock Creek. Day One had ended with Lee pleased that his men had been victorious in forcing the Federals back into a passive, defensive posture. The great Southern general was confident that, on the following day, his men would crush the Blue Army like a walnut in a nutcracker—Hill's corps pushing down from the north, Ewell's corps pressing from the east, and Longstreet's corps squeezing in from the west, forcing the Federals to run out to the south, Meade's army crushed into a torrent of crumbled and broken blue-clad fragments.

On Thursday and Friday, Lee would discover that this walnut shell might crack—but it would not break.

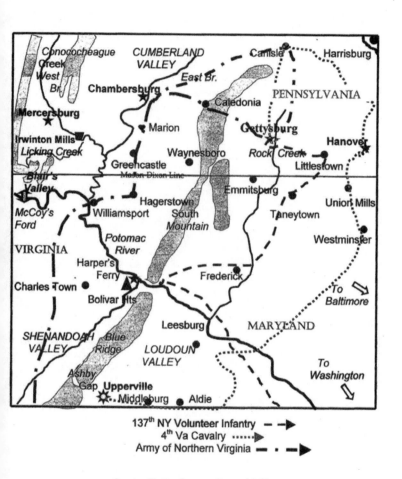

137th NY Volunteer Infantry — →
4th Va Cavalry ·····▶
Army of Northern Virginia — · — ▶

On to Gettysburg, June 1863

Chapter Twelve
Emmons

June 1863

It had been an eventful spring for the men of the Black Horse Troop. The Fourth Virginia Cavalry had numerous encounters with the enemy as the Army of the Potomac and the Army of Northern Virginia continued grappling across the Virginia countryside between Richmond and Washington. Sergeant Jack Lewis was developing more confidence in Private Emmons with each skirmish, as the new recruit learned to be more disciplined in his attack. Several times there were lulls in the fighting that gave Jack and Emmons a chance to return to the farm at Upperville, where they were able to rejuvenate themselves and their horses. While Jack and Lathe ate and rested, Harry Pettis had his black servants see to it that their horses were re-shod and their saddles and gear cleaned and burnished.

Jack had no interest in the pretty girls in the Loudoun Valley. His love was focused solely on Sally, his secret wife in Pennsylvania. In contrast, Emmons was only too happy to respond to the attention of the young women of the area eager to show their affection for their fighting men. When several showed willingness to entertain the men in the seclusion of the barn loft, Jack smiled and demurred, remembering his own tryst with Sally in the Pennsylvania barn before the war. Lathrop had no such restraint, and was pleased to demonstrate his manhood with any girl willing to yield herself to his lustful desires. He was rough and demanding, only caring for his own pleasure. In short order, the word got around among the girls—avoid that man!

Carrie Payne was a sweet young girl whose father owned a small farm nearby. Her mother had forbidden her to accompany the little group of girls who had been fawning over the cavalrymen furloughing at the Pettis farm. Yet when Mrs. Pettis invited the Paynes to dinner, Mrs. Payne accepted, so as not to offend her wealthier neighbors.

Around the table that evening, Jack was gracious, and young Carrie was smitten with him. A plain-faced but sturdy and hard-working girl, she assumed that his lack of attention to her was because she wasn't sufficiently attractive for the tall, handsome cavalryman. Lathrop Emmons, on the other hand, was most attentive, and she soon focused herself on gaining his favor. Emmons was stocky, a good two inches shorter than the slim and wiry Jack. Lathe's red hair was unruly, sticking out beyond his prominent ears. His nose was quite large, in contrast with his small, thin-lipped mouth, nearly hidden by his moustache and the narrow beard on his chin. Lathe Emmons was not a handsome man. But he was fighting for Virginia, and was a hero in the eyes of Carrie Payne. She could think of nothing but this red-headed cavalryman.

Poor Carrie didn't realize that Lathe had earlier had his way with one of the other girls out in the barn and had no interest in her as a romantic match. He was interested in her father's farm. Knowing she was an only child, he was already planning to entice her into marriage so he could gain control of the Payne property. After the war, Emmons figured, a shrewd man could parlay that property into bigger holdings and gain real prosperity. He could build a place even Harry Pettis might envy.

On each later visit back to the Pettis farm, Emmons made it a point to stop at the Payne's to call on Carrie. He achieved his goal. Young Carrie fell in love with Lathe and dreamed of the day when the war would end, he'd marry her, and they would have a life together.

In March of 1863, Jack and Emmons returned to Fitz Lee's brigade, fit and ready for action. It wasn't long in coming. Pickets on the Rappahannock discovered Federal cavalry crossing at Kelly's Ford.

From dawn to dusk, the battle seesawed back and forth. For once, Jeb Stuart's vaunted cavaliers had met their match.

Near dusk, the Fourth Virginia troopers tore down a fence and charged the Yankees. Private Lathe Emmons spurred his horse forward, riding far out in front of his comrades. He found himself surrounded by the enemy with no choice but surrender or die. As the blue-coated horsemen were escorting their gray-jacketed prisoner toward the rear of the Federal line, Jack and a squad of Black Horse troopers charged into the group, sabers slashing. In the melee, Private Emmons spurred his horse and galloped away to freedom, followed by Jack and the rest of his rescuers. "I owe you, Jack," said Emmons with heartfelt relief at escaping a Northern prison.

"Now look here, Lathe, I know you hate Yankees, but you've got t'be less hot-headed. Stay with the squad. Otherwise you'll get taken again, and next time we may not be so lucky in getting you out of the kind of scrape you got into! There's a big difference between courage and foolhardiness, Trooper."

The next day, around their fire, Emmons and Jack talked about the courageous Black Horse commander. Lieutenant Colonel W. H. F. Payne had been twice cut by a Federal saber, shot once, and then captured. In spite of his wounds, Payne had managed to escape and then walk twelve miles to rejoin the regiment. "Now that's courage," Jack maintained.

"Yes, but it also shows how dumb them Yankees are!" And Lathe went quiet, gnawing on a hard biscuit.

A week later, Jack was talking to Lathe. "I guess the good Lord didn't like us attacking Federals on Sunday! I'm told the regiment lost twenty-seven men, captured up on Telegraph Road. The Yankees always seem t'be able t'call up more Bluebellies from somewhere, while we keep losin' men. I'm tellin' you, Lathe, fightin' Yankee cavalry ain't the turkey shoot it used t'be." They were sitting around in a disagreeable rain, short of rations, already missing the good and plentiful food of Mrs. Pettis's table.

"I hear the regiment's got less'n half the roster able t'ride an' fight," Lathe grumbled.

"I know our Black Horse only got a little over a hundred left on the roster, an' only a little better'n half of that fit t'go," Jack commented.

"It's a good thing any one of us can lick ten Yankees!"

Jack didn't respond, but thought to himself, *Lately I'm not so surprised we're not getting' the best of 'em. We're short of horses, short of men, and short of rations, and the Federals always seem to pile on more of everything. Maybe what we need is another good raid north, an' take what we need away from 'em.*

On the ninth of June, Federal cavalry crossed the Rappahannock at Kelly's Ford to attack Stuart's unsuspecting cavalry. Hurriedly reacting to the sudden threat, Stuart sent his regiments to meet the blue-coated horsemen. At Stevensburg, the advancing Fourth Virginia was thrown into utter confusion when the retreating Second Carolina rushed back up the same narrow road, colliding with the Virginians. Despite Colonel Wickham's best effort to rally them, his men wheeled their mounts and galloped away from the attacking Federals. Eventually Wickham was able to gather enough of his men, including Jack and Emmons, to mount a countercharge and drive the Bluecoats back to Kelly's Ford. But Colonel Wickham, who up to this point had utmost confidence in his men, now felt disgraced by their actions that day. Jack particularly felt stung. The regiment had let their commander down, and Jack vowed to regain the colonel's trust.

Five days later came the chance for redemption. The Black Horse Troop had moved through Upperville to Middleburg. Jack and Lathe had just enough time at the Pettis farm to sit down to a good meal while their horses were reshod. Cousin Will was eager to hear of the recent battles.

"We sorta let you all down for a while at Stevensburg last week." Jack began his narrative between mouthfuls of food. "But Lieutenant A. D. Payne got us together an' we chased the Yankees back across the river. Still, we're smartin' from that first lickin' from any Yankees. We aim to show'em they can't do that to us without payin' for it!"

Will listened to his cousin with rapt attention, then announced he intended to enlist come September when he turned eighteen. Jack later took him aside and reminded him that he was counting on Will to look after Sally Keefer if anything should befall him. Will again promised he'd somehow get to Chambersburg, if the need arose, and see that Sally was taken care of.

Jack and Lathe had then mounted up and ridden off to rejoin the Black Horse outside Middleburg, just as a brigade of Union cavalry entered the town. In the sharp clash that followed, the Virginians escaped without the loss of a man. Jack felt that the action had partially avenged their humiliation at Stevensburg.

On June 17, Fitz Lee's brigade was ordered to the little village of Aldie to deny the Federals passage into the Loudoun Valley through a gap in the Bull Run Mountains. Around noon their forward pickets encountered an unexpectedly strong force of Union cavalry—two brigades.

Colonel Wickham positioned the Fourth Virginia athwart the Middleburg Road, and led the First Virginia into the village. Lieutenant Payne took a squadron of thirty men of the Black Horse, including Jack and Emmons, off to the left up the hill to the Snickers Gap road. When the order to charge came, Lt. Payne's men rode forward, letting out their fearsome rebel yells, sabers raised. Though greatly outnumbered, they rode downward into the massed Union column. Jack's strong, broad-shouldered mount easily brushed aside any Federal horse it slammed into, while its rider delivered a rain of deadly saber slashes on the blue-coated enemy. Horses went down, throwing their riders under the deadly pounding hooves of terrified animals. As the Union column broke up in confusion, the rest of Fitz Lee's brigade came riding in, pursuing the fleeing Bluecoats back east through the village.

Fitz Lee's brigade had not only completely routed a superior enemy force, they had captured a number of horses. Now a number of the Virginians who had lost horses in earlier clashes and had been fighting dismounted could resume their full function.

Jack and Lathe were nearly exhausted, but had escaped with only minor scratches. They were elated at their success, Colonel Wickham would later write of his regiment, "*Suffice it to say, that its conduct gave me entire satisfaction.*" Later that night, in bivouac at Rector's Crossroads, Sergeant Jack Lewis would state with his own great satisfaction, "Now, Private Emmons, we can hold our heads high again. Stevensburg has been avenged!"

On Tuesday, June 23, 1863, General Robert E. Lee ordered General Jeb Stuart to cross the Potomac into Maryland. The long-awaited raid north would finally come. Stuart was to shield the move north of Lee's army by riding to the east while feeling out the location of the Army of the Potomac. In his controversial order, Lee gave Stuart perhaps too much leeway. Instead of placing his riders between the armies, Stuart had swung far to the east, with the north-marching Union forces between himself and Lee. Stuart lost all contact with Lee's army and never found the main body of the Union Army.

Arriving in Chambersburg deprived of Stuart's reconnaissance, Lee was late in finding that the Union Army was close at hand in Maryland, just below the Pennsylvania line. By the time Lee had regrouped his strung-out infantry corps, Union forces were occupying the heights south of the little village of Gettysburg. Instead of forcing the Federals to attack him in a place of his choosing, Lee was now forced to attack them where they held the terrain advantage.

Jack knew none of this, of course. He was just elated that they would be off on his long-anticipated raid north. Would that it could be as successful as Stuart's lightning strike of last October! He thought of Sally Keefer in Chambersburg and wished that Stuart would take his brigades there once again. He longed to see his pretty wife, and hoped that there might be time to re-consummate their union. So many times he'd opened the locket and gazed at her image, longing to see her again. So many nights he'd lain in his blanket reliving the memory of her body pressed to his, of her eager movements as they reached the climactic release of their wedding night. Now perhaps, a forgiving God willing, he and Sally could once more join in passionate embrace. And who knew, maybe the same forgiving God would provide him the opportunity to retrieve the hidden gold and give it to Sally for safekeeping. Then, if anything should happen to him, at least he'd gain comfort knowing he'd provided for her.

As the brigade passed through Upperville on June 24, Jack and Lathe received permission from Lieutenant Payne to make a brief stop at the Pettis farm. Harry Pettis and Will Gresham related the story of the June 21 Battle of Upperville, when Wade Hampton's brigade fought the Federal cavalry of General Gregg's division at Goose Creek, in the fields just one farm over from Pettis's. "An' you boys from the Black Horse weren't here t'defend us! Lucky fer us Gen'ral Robertson's cavalry drove them Yankees off 'fore they could mess up our place!"

Harry insisted that Will get them fresh horses and tack, while Mrs. Pettis fed them one last substantial meal. While Lathe was still eating, Jack rode off quickly to make one last visit to his ailing mother, still living with Will's parents at their small farm nearby. He kissed her goodbye as she asked God's blessing on her dutiful son. Somehow he knew this was the last time they would be together.

At midnight on Saturday, June 27, after driving the Federals out of Fairfax Court House and helping themselves to the abandoned government supplies, Stuart's cavalry crossed the Potomac into Maryland. His latest "ride around the Union Army" had begun. For the next ten days, his men would never unsaddle their horses.

Sunday, the raiders captured a large government wagon train, chasing the Union escort back to the gates of Washington itself. Taking the captured wagons with them, the raiders rode north, destroying telegraph lines as they went. Riding northeast, they reached Frederick at midnight. At daylight Monday, reaching the Baltimore and Ohio railroad at Hood's Mill, they spent the morning tearing up tracks and cutting telegraph lines. Showers made the day muggy, the roads muddy. Lathe grumbled to Jack, "Prisin' up these here rails is even harder'n plantin' fence posts. I'm sweatin' like a damn hog!"

"Beats bein' shot at, don't it?"

In the afternoon they got that, too. Riding on to Westminster, Stuart's men encountered a small body of Federal cavalry guarding the supplies sent forward to support the advancing Union Army. In a pitched battle with the badly outnumbered men of the First Delaware Cavalry, the Fourth Virginia drove them from the field, but at the cost of two lieutenants killed.

Lathe Emmons was riding just behind when he saw his lieutenant cut down by a saber slash. Emmons spurred his mount forward and gave out his best rebel yell. As his horse rammed its broad shoulder into the mount of the lieutenant's assailant, Lathe thrust his saber forward, running it clean through the blue-coated trooper. Yanking the sharp steel back out, Lathe wiped the blood off on the man's back as he fell out of the saddle. "Gotcha, ye murderin' Yankee bastard!"

When the Black Horse Troop regrouped, both Jack and Emmons and their horses had once again escaped injury. The regiment rode on to Union Mills, a few miles below the border from Hanover,

Pennsylvania, where they bivouacked in the rain and tried to catch a few hours' sleep.

Chapter Thirteen
Hanover

June 30, 1863

Jack Lewis crawled out from under the gum blanket he'd rigged as protection from rain the night before. The sky had cleared and the morning star was visible above the eastern horizon. Someone had made coffee, real coffee, and the aroma drew him to the small fire and the blackened pot from which it came.

"Have a cup, Sarge, you'll need it if'n you're as tired as me." Josh Martin handed Jack a well-dented tin cup of the black liquid.

"Thanks, Martin. It's right welcome this mornin'. But you better get that fire out an' get packed up. We're back in the saddle at first light."

A friendly Marylander had gotten word to Stuart that Federal cavalry was camped in Littlestown, Pennsylvania, just seven miles northwest of where Jack Lewis was drinking his coffee at Union Mills. General Stuart was intent on joining Lee's army and figured he'd find them at York, near the Susquehanna River, heading for Philadelphia. He didn't want to be further delayed by skirmishes with Federal cavalry, so he'd ordered his three brigades to avoid Littlestown and head for York by way of Hanover. His men were tired after three weeks of hard riding, but keen on raiding into Yankee country once more.

General Judson Kilpatrick had heard that a large Confederate force was in York. He ordered his Union Third Cavalry Division into their saddles at dawn. The two brigades of Federal horsemen left Littlestown on the road to Hanover, heading for York, one brigade led by General George Custer, the other by General Elon Farnsworth. Their men had been on the march for three weeks and were nearly worn out with riding.

A pale pink glow in the eastern sky greeted the columns of cavalry—tired men in gray coats making their way north to the Mason-Dixon Line; drowsy men in blue coats marching east just above the Line toward unexpected collision.

By the time the Virginians reached the Pennsylvania line, the early morning sun was shining brightly in a clear blue sky. The road rose and dipped over the low rolling hills. Cattle grazed in pastures lush with new grass. Split-rail fences lined fields of ripening wheat and rows of corn growing tall. Jack leaned in his saddle toward Lathrop Emmons, riding alongside. "Gonna be a nice day, Lathe. That rain's left us for a spell, maybe. This here's pretty country, ain't it? Great for horses. I was up here 'fore the war with some of Pettis's horses so I know some of these farmers got some good stock. Our mounts are gettin' a mite worn. I'm thinkin' we can swap 'em fer fresh horses from one of these farmers—with a little persuasion."

Kilpatrick's Federals reached Hanover at eight o'clock, ahead of Stuart's rebel columns.

General George Custer led his Michigan Brigade into the little town, stopping briefly before continuing on toward York. General Elon Farnsworth next led his brigade into town. He allowed them to stop and eat, fed generously by the grateful citizens of Hanover. Two of his regiments had ridden on toward York, while the Fifth New York was dismounted, standing on the streets, devouring slabs of smoked ham on thick slices of fresh bread slathered with rich butter, and washing it down with cider or cold water from the town pump. The Eighteenth Pennsylvania was still entering the town, serving as the rear guard for the division's wagon train. Scouts from the Eighteenth had skirmished with Stuart's advance party a few miles back, killing a Confederate near Gitt's Mill. The battle of Hanover was about to start.

Confederate Colonel Chambliss, leading Fitz Lee's brigade, drew up his men in the fields south of the town on either side of the road they'd ridden up from Westminster. Two companies of the Eighteenth Pennsylvania were spread out in front of them. Chambliss ordered his men to attack.

Jack and Emmons were approaching Hanover on the road from Union Mills, their Fourth Virginia Regiment part of General Fitz Lee's brigade, when they encountered the Eighteenth Pennsylvania's rear guard. They had reached the Littlestown Road junction next to the Karl Forney farm. Forney's two young boys, Sam and John, were hoeing corn early that morning in a field that lay between the two roads. Something on the Littlestown road caught Sam's eye.

"Johnny—look there! On the road! Cavalry! Our soldiers—see our flag? Something will perhaps happen. Let's go over to the fence rail and watch them go by," an excited Sam told his brother.

"Hooray for the Union! Hooray for the cavalry!" The boys waved their flat-crowned, broad-brimmed straw hats enthusiastically until the last of the mounted troopers passed.

"Johnny, I see nothing more but wagons up the road. We'd best get back to hoeing."

At a little past ten, the boys heard whooping and hollering across the fields to the east, toward the Westminster road. The Thirteenth Virginia was galloping toward the Eighteenth Pennsylvania, firing their carbines as they came.

Quickly the fields were filled with mounted horsemen in deadly combat. The Fifth New York had returned to join the battle. Bullets were flying everywhere.

"Johnny, quick, help me get the team unhitched! Hear that whistling? Bullets! It must be rebels, come up from Maryland! Our barn will not be safe; let's quick get over to Geiselman's. Let the plow be. Just get the team and run!"

Sam led his brother and the horses across the field to safety, never realizing just how closely death had passed them by.

When the skirmish started, the Black Horse Troop had ridden up the road and joined the fighting, firing as they came. Private Lathrop Emmons's horse Salem sensed his rider was in a truly ill temper—tired, hungry, and angry. The Bluecoats weren't yet in range. Spying the

Forney boys running through the young corn leading their team, Emmons raised his carbine and aimed it at Sam. "Git them an' we git their horses!"

Sergeant Jack Lewis, riding his mare Ivy just off Emmons's left side, saw and instantly drove Ivy's shoulder into Salem's flank. Emmons's arm flew up and the carbine discharged, the bullet flying harmlessly over the Forney boys' heads.

"What th' hell?" yelled Emmons, angry at having his aim spoiled.

"What in Sam Hill you tryin' to do, Lathe? They're just boys! Save it for the Federals, man." In a blinding flash, Jack Lewis saw the innocent face of the Mercersburg boy he'd shot back in October. "Well, boys, at least I saved you from that cruel fate," he said quietly. Maybe God would count this as a partial atonement, a step toward redemption.

The fight moved on up the road in front of Karl Forney's farmstead on Frederick Street. The Forney family lived in a large two-story brick house with chimneys at either end and three dormers across the front of the attic, five windows on the second floor, and four below, centered by a transomed entry framed by a hip-roofed porch. The always-observant Jack took in the sight at a glance, admired the handsome structure, and immediately refocused on the deadly task at hand.

Among the combatants in front of him, Jack recognized his old commander, Fitz Payne. W. H. F. Payne had co-founded Jack's Black Horse Troop, had fought hard and was promoted to Lieutenant Colonel, and had just been given command of the Second North Carolina. Now Jack saw Lt. Col. Payne at the front of his new regiment, in the thick of the action. The men of the Fifth New York were giving no ground as they fought in close quarters in front of the Winebrenner Tannery, just up the road from the Forney farmhouse. Jack saw Payne's horse rear up and stumble. Payne was thrown off the horse, unluckily falling right into a tanning vat. Frustratingly far from the action, Jack could only watch as a New Yorker hauled Payne from the vat. He saw the Union trooper hustling his prisoner back toward town, Payne spitting vile fluid from his mouth, his gray uniform now brown with tannin.

"Emmons, Taliaferro, you four, follow me." Jack jumped Ivy over the stone wall, around the back of the Forney house, behind the tannery, into an alley leading into town. Turning the corner, he saw the bedraggled officer stumbling up Frederick Street, surrounded by his blue-coated escorts.

"There he is, boys. Get those guards!"

Emmons got off a shot with his carbine, felling one. The New Yorkers returned fire. Payne started to break away toward his would-be rescuers, but the escorts dragged him back and hustled him farther into the center of town. By now, Custer's Michiganders were entering the battle, charging down Frederick Street from the center of town.

"I'm hit, Sarge!" Black Horse Trooper John Taliaferro took a bullet in the arm, and only a quick grab by Jack kept him from being unhorsed.

"Damn! There's just too many of 'em, boys. Get back up that alley an' out of town. I'll cover your backs." Jack fired his carbine at the oncoming Federals until his men were safely up the alley, then beat a hasty retreat himself.

The battle at Hanover continued back and forth, but in the end Stuart's Division was forced off the main roads, away from the town. Cut off from Lee's army, not knowing where the main Federal forces were, Stuart decided to ride north to Carlisle where he hoped to find elements of Lee's invading army. Meanwhile his men went foraging through York County.

"Lathe, we was just lucky to get away with our skins back there. I just regret we lost Col. Payne t' the Yankees. But my poor horse is showin' the wear of it all. They hardly had a break these last three weeks. Don't think ol' Ivy can go much further without some rest."

"Salem's the same, Jack. Only so much ye kin ask of a horse. Why don't we go lookin' fer fresh mounts on one o' these here farms?"

"Pettis had me take three fine horses to a farmer named Dubs just a little ways southeast of here, on the Codorus Creek. A black stallion called Midnight, a bay, and a sorrel mare. I trained Midnight, an' he was one of the strongest, fastest, most fearless animals Pettis ever had. Let's go see if they're still there, Lathe."

Mrs. Dubs had hidden Midnight in the vaulted basement of the farmhouse. To no avail. Jack knew what to look for. When the barn revealed only the gray and the mare, he strode across the yard, saw the hoof marks leading to the cellar door. Jack called, "Midnight!" and heard the horse's answering whinny.

Mrs. Dubs protested vigorously. "Jack Lewis, I thought you were an honest Christian boy when you brought us that horse in '58. But you rebels are no better'n horse thieves!"

"Now, Miz Dubs, I'm no thief. This is a requisition. Someone'll be along to give you a receipt for the horses. You'll be properly paid once we win this war. An' we're leavin' you our mounts. With a little rest and feed, Ivy and Salem will be good as new." Jack felt only a small twinge of guilt at taking the woman's horses—why should only Virginia farmers bear the cost of this war the tyrant Lincoln had brought on them all! With strong and rested new mounts under them, the two troopers rode off to rejoin the Black Horse, finding the Fourth Virginia bivouacked at New Salem. Once more up before dawn, Jack found himself riding over narrow winding lanes through a succession of tiny villages on the way to Dover.

The long columns of gray cavalry continued their relentless northwest march on through Wellsville and Dillsburg. They rounded the stub end of South Mountain to enter the Cumberland Valley, passing through Boiling Springs and reaching Carlisle after dark. In the midst of a pitched battle with the militia there, Stuart was found by Lee's courier and ordered to move immediately south to Gettysburg.

"Emmons, wake up! You damn near fell out of your saddle, man!"

"I'm s'damn tired, Jack, but I'm jes' restin'."

The weary columns were headed back south, moving slowly in the moonlight over South Mountain through the gap at Mt. Holly. When daylight came, they picked up the pace and moved on toward the rendezvous with Lee at Gettysburg. Reaching New Oxford, they met Kilpatrick's Hanover-encamped Federal troopers once again. Delayed by having to fend off Federal attacks there and again at Hunterstown, Stuart drove his men once more to ride at night, moving back southwest to arrive at Gettysburg the morning of July 2. There the thoroughly exhausted Virginians dismounted and, after seeing to their horses, slept the sleep of the dead.

General Kilpatrick's Union cavalry had shifted west from Hanover to protect the Union right flank from attack by Stuart's brigades. General David Gregg had positioned his Federal cavalrymen and horse artillery three miles east of town on the Hanover Road. Included was the Michigan Brigade led by the brash young General George Custer.

In the late morning of July 3, General Jeb Stuart's brigades had moved into position on Cress Ridge, near the Rummel farm just north of the Hanover Road. Stuart intended to lead his brigades into the rear of the Union Lines behind Culp's Hill. He would use dismounted skirmishers to occupy the Federal cavalry while he led the main body of his troops south, hidden in the woods and using Cress Ridge to hide his southward movement. Then he could attack in force right into the heart of the undefended Union rear.

Past Rummel's wooded lane to the east were broad open fields—ideal for mounted cavalry operations. Gregg's Federals were in the woods to the east of these fields. Federal skirmishers approached Rummel's lane and were driven back by rebel sharpshooters in Rummel's barn. To drive the Federals back and shield his movement south, Stuart ordered his cannon into action. That only served to reveal his presence to Gregg, whose artillery responded vigorously. The opening shots had been fired—the prelude to the largest cavalry battle of the war.

Sergeant Jack Lewis shook Private Lathrop Emmons awake. The sun was high in the sky, the day hot.

"Get up, Lathe. Listen to that! That's horse artillery firin' just south of here. Gen'ral Fitz Lee's got rest of the brigade down there somewheres. Cap'n Payne tells me our Fourth Virginia's just s'posed t'wait in reserve. This's gonna be like Antietam again, when we missed all the action. Well I ain't gonna sit here waitin'. I'm gonna get the Cap'n's permission t'ride down there. I've had some sleep, an' I got a pretty fresh horse. Are you with me, Emmons?"

Jack rode swiftly to the Black Horse commander and asked permission to ride south and join the battle in progress. "I've got a fresh horse, I'm rested—let me go!" Permission was given.

"I'm comin', Lewis!" Emmons leapt into his saddle and followed his sergeant.

The two men drove their horses hard down narrow dirt lanes, crossing the York Road and reaching Cress Ridge to join General Fitz Lee's other Virginia regiments, waiting at the tree line at the edge of the open fields.

"You boys itchin' t'fight? Ain't had enough yet? Well, looks like this's gonna be some battle. See all them Yankees down there? Spoilin' fer a fight? Well, we're about t'whup 'em!

To Stuart's dismay, instead of moving south behind Cress Ridge, General Wade Hampton led his brigade of North Carolinians in a charge east out across the open fields. Seeing this maneuver, Fitz Lee's brigade surged forward, covering Hampton's left flank. The initial charge blew right through Custer's Seventh Michigan Cavalry. Jack and Emmons, first firing carbines and then slashing with their sabers, had cut through the Bluecoat defenders. They found themselves behind the enemy line just as Custer, calling "On, you Michiganders!" led the First Michigan in a gallant countercharge that broke the Confederate charge and forced them to retreat back to the northwest.

"Emmons, we're cut off. No way back through all them Yankees now. Follow me!"

Jack spurred his horse over a low stone wall into the woods. They had no idea if there were Union reserves waiting there, but they knew hundreds of Federal troopers were now to their north. Dodging branches, they quickly emerged from the wood at the Hanover road, crossed it in an instant, galloped through a field for a hundred yards and turned southwest down a narrow path into some woods. Once they saw that no Union horsemen were pursuing them, they slowed their sweating horses to a walk, moving quietly down the woodland trail, listening intently for any sound of enemy soldiers.

Jack had a finely developed sense of direction that even the stress of hard riding and intense combat hadn't dulled. He knew that, given the lay of the land, with the low ridges running southwest, they should soon encounter the broad stream called Rock Creek that Fitz Lee's brigade had crossed just hours before, up near the York Pike. A few brief minutes after rejoining the brigade on Cress Ridge, Jack was able to scan the terrain, see the hill to his southwest (Wolfe's Hill), and could figure that Rock Creek lay in the valley between it and the hill west (Culp's Hill).

Jack now figured they were headed in the right direction to skirt the western base of Wolfe's Hill and should come up to Rock Creek on the left flank of Johnson's Confederate infantry. With any luck they would evade any outlying units of Federal cavalry and be able to swing back north under their own infantry's protection, to rejoin Fitz Lee's brigade before nightfall. Ironically, Jack was taking the same route Stuart intended his two brigades to follow into the rear of the Union lines.

They were lucky. Between them and the Hanover road lay the Sixteenth Pennsylvania Cavalry, General Gregg's reserve. But the Sixteenth's attention was focused on the noise of the battle that was still going on, on the fields to their north and east. They made final checks of their carbines, expecting the call to ride forward at any minute. If any of them heard the occasional snapped twig or muffled hoof-fall of the two rebels passing down the wooded trail a few hundred yards to the south, they put down it down to deer fleeing the noise of the cannonades on the other side of the Hanover Pike.

Jack and Emmons were soon out of hearing and into a wood free of soldiers. Unfortunately, unbeknownst to them, Johnson's badly banged-up infantry had by now pulled back well to the north of Wolfe's Hill, beaten back by the Union counterattack at Culp's Hill that morning. So when the two riders finally reached Rock Creek, the only signs they saw were of abandoned positions and the battle-devastated woodland on the slopes to the west. Realizing that only Union troops were across the creek, and quite likely in the immediate vicinity of the opposite bank, they turned their horses southward. They stayed in the woods, out of sight of the opposite bank, for about a quarter of a mile, until the quietness of the evening gave them confidence it was safe to return to the creek.

It was now late Friday afternoon, the sun getting lower in the western sky. On the east bank of Rock Creek, Stuart's two brave outriders were now facing the infantrymen of Slocum's Twelfth Corps. Of the two brigades Jeb Stuart had intended to be crossing Rock Creek at that very spot, only Sergeant Jack Lewis and Private Lathrop Emmons had made it there. History would never record their achievement. On this last day of the Battle of Gettysburg, they had survived combat with Custer's Michigan Cavalry. They wouldn't be as lucky with Greene's New York Infantry.

Chapter Fourteen
Culp's Hill

July 1, 1863

General Henry Slocum had the Twelfth Corps on the move early Wednesday morning. The 137th broke camp at Littlestown and marched five miles west on the Baltimore Pike to Two Taverns. They spread out along the road, made fires, and cooked dinner.

Luke and Billy Weed were out ahead scouting when they came up on a large brick farmhouse set just off the road. The smell of fresh-baked bread arrested their attention. "My gawd, Billy, that smells like my mother's kitchen Saturday mornings. Let's go see if we might get some bread."

They followed the delicious aroma right up to the kitchen door. Ella Hartman, helping her mother, had just taken the last loaf out of the oven when she heard the tread of boots on the porch. Looking up, she saw two very hungry-looking young men in bright blue uniforms. Luke smiled at the shiny-eyed girl wiping her hands on her apron.

"Might we purchase a loaf of bread, miss?" He held out a fifty-cent piece.

Ella smiled back at the handsome soldier in his fresh uniform, issued just last night to replace the one dirty and torn from days of hard marching.

"Indeed you may not! We won't take your money. But you can have two loaves and this crock of apple butter, with our thanks. Just chase those rebels out of Pennsylvania!"

Luke thanked her and gratefully took the sample of country cooking back with him. "Oh, Billy, smell that bread. I don't know what we're headin' into up the road, but home cookin' sure makes it worth the march to here!"

Luke and Weed were enjoying the last of the fresh bread and apple butter they'd been given when the order was given to resume the march. As the column moved toward Gettysburg, the men began to realize that a major battle was taking place up ahead. Puffs of smoke in the distance marked the explosions of artillery shells. Whole families passed them, hurrying away from the town, seeking safety, fear in their eyes. Wagons and artillery caissons, wounded men and prisoners, shell-shocked stragglers gave way as the Twelfth Corps marched by. Disillusioned soldiers mocked the new troops. "You just wait. You boys're gonna get all the fightin' you want, an' then some!"

By three o'clock, their column was a little east of the stone bridge at Rock Creek. The men could hear the rumbling thunder of cannon fire up ahead. Slocum gave the order to move rapidly in the direction of the firing, sending his two divisions in divergent directions.

The First Division, General A. S. Williams commanding, turned off to the right, heading up a wooded lane on the east side of Rock Creek, north toward Wolf's Hill. Bert Hughes, now a corporal, watched them go off and whispered irreverently, "There goes Shakey Williams, leavin' us to do the fightin'!"

General John Geary's Second Division continued up the Pike before turning west to join the troops already forming the left flank of the Union army in the rocky flats west of Little Round Top. The men of the 137th spread out and rested on their knapsacks, rifles close at hand. They could hear the noise of the battle to their north, but had no idea of the chaos occurring as the outnumbered First and Eleventh Corps survivors were driven back through the streets of the town to Cemetery Hill.

Day One of the Battle of Gettysburg having ended, Luke Kellogg slept fitfully in front of Little Round Top that night, turning occasionally to relieve the ache from the hard rocky ground beneath and the chill of the night air above.

At daybreak on Thursday, General Dan Sickles's Third Corps came up the Emmitsburg Road and went into line on the Union left. With the left flank thus covered, Geary's men shifted across the Baltimore Pike to take up position on the southeast end of the Union line. Facing them across the little valley of Rock Creek was Johnson's Division of Stonewall Jackson's Corps, led by General Richard Ewell since Jackson's death at Chancellorsville in May.

General Meade had formed a strong defensive perimeter shaped like a fishhook, anchored at the town's Evergreen Cemetery on Cemetery Hill. To the north, in the town, lay A. P. Hill's Confederate Corps. To the east, Meade controlled the heights of Culp's Hill, blocking Ewell's Confederates. To the southwest, Meade had men covering the heights of Cemetery Ridge down to Big Round Top, facing the Confederates of Longstreet's Corps. This gave Meade many advantages over Lee. Meade held the high ground. Lee would have to march his attacking formations uphill, directly into the Union guns. Meade was inside the fishhook, which gave him the advantage in speed of command and control. He had but a short ride to see for himself the disposition of forces. He could then readily shift his forces to repulse an attack on any front. Lee, on the other hand, had to spread his men the long way around outside the fishhook. He or his couriers had a long way to ride to reach Ewell's troops well to the east of town, Hill's on the north, and Longstreet's to the southwest. As a result, the Confederate attacks Lee wanted to be coordinated were not. Meade was able to shift his men to repulse each attack in turn.

When he arrived at Culp's Hill on the morning of July 2, General John Geary called his brigade commanders together. "Gentlemen, I put the question to you—shall we have the men entrench the line? Now, you know I do not favor such, since once used, our men may hesitate in future to fight without them."

The commander of the Third Brigade, General George Greene, was the oldest Union general at Gettysburg. "Pop" Greene had no hesitation about making his opinion known, and in no uncertain terms.

"John, I'm more interested in saving my men's lives than in theory. My men will dig. This hill has everything needed to quickly erect strong breastworks—logs, rock—and my New Yorkers know how to build strong walls. Now I'm off to walk my line and lay out the works."

Luke Kellogg and Billy Weed were able to lay their hands on some axes, and set rapidly to work felling trees.

"This ain't much different than what we were doin' last year this time up by Bear Swamp, Luke."

"But we didn't have a few thousand men comin' at us with guns at Bear Swamp, Billy. Just keep choppin'!"

Meanwhile Pop Greene and David Ireland were walking the terrain of Culp's Hill. Greene was summing up the advantages and disadvantages of their defensive position.

"David, I'm going to place the Seventy-eighth on our left, tight to the Eleventh Corps position. Then the Sixtieth, 102nd, the 149th, then your 137th anchoring our right flank, tied to Kane's brigade. I understand that First Division is covering the line beyond Kane. You've got the harder ground to defend, David. My other regiments are at the top of a steep wooded slope. The rebels will have a trying time, keeping line of battle coming up through all those trees and boulders. Now, with our breastworks in place, those regiments are in a nearly impregnable position. But your men are down into the saddle between the upper hill and the lower hill where Kane's line is. Rebels will have an easier time coming at you. Of course, with Kane's line angling off to your right and ahead of you as it goes up around the crest of the lower hill, his brigade ought to provide you with fire into any attacker's flank. But just in case the Rebs break through Kane's line, I want you to have a fallback position. Have your men build a traverse, a line of breastworks angling back west on the side of the hill, separating your men and Kane's. Then if Rebs do break through, you can swing your men into those works and defend our right flank."

Colonel David Ireland, born and bred in Scotland, still had a bit of his native Scottish burr. "Aye, General. My lads'll get the traverse in place 'fore noon."

"One more thing, David. I'm sending Col. Redington out with men from the Sixtieth as skirmishers across Rock Creek. Apparently, it's Johnson's division of Ewell's corps facing us, and I want to know when they're coming at us. Pick a handful of your best men, good woodsmen, to go with Redington, but tell them to fall back to your position when the rebels come at us. Now, David, you understand. We must defend this hill at all costs. If the rebels take it, they can fire cannon right into the heart of our lines. We will not allow that to happen."

"Aye, General. You can depend on the 137th to hold the flank." Ireland finished walking his line, satisfied that his breastworks were solid. He had placed Company A on his extreme right, the end of the brigade's line.

"Captain Shipman, I need four good men, good woodsmen, to go as skirmishers. Kellogg for one; you pick the others."

Luke and Billy Weed had eaten a few hard biscuits with the last of the Hartman apple butter and taken a quick nap when they were tapped to go skirmishing. Luke was bone-tired from past days of hard marching and the sweaty exertion of the morning's breastworks construction, but he felt his blood coursing through his veins at the prospect of impending combat.

Reaching Rock Creek, Luke slid down the steep west bank, waded through the waist-deep water, and clambered up the east bank. He could hear occasional cracks of musketry up ahead. Lieutenant Colonel Redington's New York skirmishers were trading fire with rebels probing out in front of their lines. Redington soon realized an entire Confederate division was coming up behind the rebel skirmishers he was facing, and sent couriers back to alert General Greene to the enormity of the threat to the Culp's Hill defenders.

Meanwhile, the salient of Sickles's Third Corps, way out in front of the Union defensive position on Cemetery Ridge, was coming under intense fire from the front and both flanks. General Meade rode out to look over the situation, saw Sickles in a desperate position, and realized it was too late to order Sickles to break off and pull back to the Cemetery Ridge line. His only choice was to decide which of his other corps to pull in to reinforce the salient long enough for an orderly pullback. Meade directed General Slocum to divert men from his Twelfth Corps positions on the right flank to cover Sickles withdrawal. Henry Slocum, seeing no immediate threat from Ewell's troops on the east, did as he was ordered. He pulled his First Division away from Rock Creek, and the Second Division away from Culp's Hill.

Pop Greene went looking for General Geary. "John, my skirmishers are in the thick of it with Johnson's division. You can't pull us out and leave this hill undefended!"

"All right, George, you can stay in place. But Kane's brigade and Candy's are on the move to back up Third Corps, and First Division is being moved there as well."

Greene quickly got his regimental commanders together.

"Men, Slocum's pulled damn near the whole corps out and moved them west. We're all that's left on this line. Johnson's rebels are already driving Redington's skirmishers back, but he's buying us a little time. Godard, you spread your men of the Sixtieth across the works of the Seventy-eighth and your own. Von Hammerstein, you take your Seventy-eighth and head down hill to support Redington's withdrawal. Everyone else, move to the right so that we cover the works as far as we can man them."

Up and down the line, the command was heard: "By the right flank, take intervals."

On the right, Colonel Ireland marched his men out of their works on the high knoll, while the men of the 149th New York spread out to fill in after them. The men of the 137th, even spread thin, could cover only the north half of the works vacated by Kane, across the saddle then up and over the crest of the lower knoll. As it was, one regiment was covering works vacated by three of Kane's. Beyond that, the First Division works were completely vacant. Greene's men were spread thin, with no one behind in reserve. The risk of a rebel breakthrough was very high, and the results would be catastrophic. The Confederates could roll through unimpeded right into the heart of the Federal army!

Colonel Ireland strode along his new line, talking to each of his company commanders.

"We're spread thin, and there's no reserve behind us. Spread the word. I want each man to understand that he holds the responsibility for the success or failure of this battle—we hold this ground, or lose the Union!"

The former farm boys, mill hands, and grocery clerks from New York's Southern Tier, now battle-tested soldiers, understood their commander's order. They knew what they had to do, and were fully prepared to pay the price. Victory tonight would not come cheap.

Colonel Ireland knew the situation was grim. His regiment, while still sheltered from direct fire by Kane's breastworks, defended a much shallower slope than before. Moreover, Ireland was well aware of the danger on his right flank. If the rebels crossed Rock Creek to the south, they could move unhindered into the vacant works on his right. There was an old stone wall to his south, running east west, that also concerned him. It could provide cover for an enemy move to his rear, forcing him to defend against attack on three sides—an untenable position.

The commander of the 137th was a smart tactician. As night's darkness deepened, he knew exactly where his fallback positions were. He was prepared. He passed the word to his company officers and non-coms, who in turn briefed their men. Ireland had confidence in his men. Well trained, well briefed, well informed, the men of the 137th would be ready to meet whatever challenge they faced. Even under fire in the dark.

At 7:00 P.M., Redington's skirmishers were up to their ears in combat. Luke, Weed, and the others settled into a steady rhythm. Load, fire, draw back. Load, fire, draw back. While one loaded, another was firing. They had plenty of gray-clad targets, and fortunately plenty of trees and boulders to duck behind. They crossed back over Rock Creek and worked their way up the slope, stopping to pick off as many as they could of the rebels wading or clawing their way up the steep creek bank. Von Hammerstein's men, halfway down the hill, had to hold their fire, for fear of hitting their own skirmishers. But once the skirmishing men had passed behind them, the Seventy-eighth New York fired deadly volleys into the rebel formations, if you could call them such any longer. With the woods and boulders to negotiate, formations quickly broke into disconnected groups, moving and firing upward into the Federal lines.

By now it was getting dark, and more so in the woods. Luke and Weed were in a skirmish line well to the south of the Seventy-eighth New York, giving way grudgingly to the overwhelming Confederate advance. Ireland's men held their fire, awaiting the return of their skirmishing comrades. They watched their men trading fire with the advancing rebels, nervous fingers on their triggers. When Luke and Billy Weed finally tumbled over the wall to safety, the 137th unleashed a deadly storm of lead into the oncoming rebel formations.

Ireland's Regiment was facing not one but three Confederate regiments of General George Steuart's brigade of Virginia infantrymen. Though vastly outnumbered, the 137th New York managed initially to stalemate the rebel attack. Advancing in the dark against an enemy protected by breastworks, Steuart's men didn't realize their numerical advantage over the defenders. But those on their left soon realized the works in front of them were undefended, and they moved in unhindered. Moving north in the vacant trenches, they soon encountered Ireland's men and began to pour fire into the regiment's flank.

"Company A, refuse the line!" Ireland was ordering his right-most company to pivot their line around at a right angle to the works, the better to counter the enemy's flanking fire into the brigade's men firing at the frontal attackers. This worked until Steuart's men discovered the stone wall that would cover a rebel advance well beyond the "refused" company's line.

Colonel Ireland moved swiftly down his line, passing orders to his company commanders.

"We're taking fire from the front, the right flank, and now the rear. In good order, have your men pull out of the works and fall back to the traverse."

In the dark, under enemy fire, Luke Kellogg, Billy Weed, and the rest of the 137th continued to load and fire while they backed out of Kane's now untenable works and worked their way up the slope and tumbled over behind the wall of the traverse.

Steuart's men were right behind, smelling victory. Corporal Aaron Benn stumbled and went down.

"Kellogg! Weed! I'm down. Cover me!"

"Surrender, Yank, or be killed!" The Virginians had overrun the hill around the corporal.

"Luke, they've got Benn. We got to get him back!"

Luke turned and fired.

"Bill, it's too dark, too much smoke. I can't see. Don't want to hit Benn. Move back up to the traverse!"

He and Weed vented their anger and frustration at the loss of their friend by speeding up their rate of fire until their muskets were so hot they could barely touch them. They were nearly out of cartridges. Their muskets were fouled by the residue of the black powder, built up over so many firings with no time to clean the barrel.

"Where's Bert Hughes, Bill?" Luke looked around for their friend who had been near them as they rotated the line back up to the traverse.

"Over here, Luke. I'm hit, but I'll be all right, I think. But Sergeant Dodge here, he's hit bad!"

"Fix bayonets, Bill, we're gonna have to stick 'em when they come over the wall!"

"Luke—look over there! Cap'n Gregg's leadin' a squad of Ithaca boys. They're chargin' the Rebs with bayonets! Let's go help him!"

"Hold position, Bill! There's nobody behind us yet, and we got to hold this line until some reinforcements get here!"

"Oh, no, Luke, Cap'n Gregg's been hit, an' his men are havin' to fall back, carryin' him!"

In the nick of time, reinforcements moved into the works. Men of the Fourteenth Brooklyn slid into the traverse beside Luke and his comrades and began to fire.

It was now ten o'clock. The full moon's light could not penetrate the smoke and the shadows of the woods enough to allow Steuart's rebels to continue the attack. His regiments fell back, to spend the next few hours of darkness in the works Kane's brigade had constructed. Confident that the Fourteenth Brooklyn could hold the line, Colonel Ireland ordered his men to move back into the small hollow behind the crest of the hill.

"All right men, clean your muskets, refill your cartridge boxes, and get a bit of rest. We've stopped the rebels, for now. You've done everything we've asked. We've held the hill!"

Thanks to their commander's smart tactics and their own bravery, self-sacrifice, and discipline, one New York regiment had stymied the aggressive attack by an entire Virginia brigade. Meade's right flank was secure, at least for the night.

At 3:00 A.M., Colonel Ireland strode down the line of his troops as they lay on their blankets in an exhausted sleep, passing the word to his company officers and non-coms. "Corps artillery will commence bombardment of the enemy positions at three-thirty. Have the men prepare to meet the enemy assault."

By this time, General Geary had Kane and Candy's brigades back from Cemetery Ridge. The Union breastworks were now well fortified with riflemen, more than compensating for the losses Greene's brigade had suffered that night. Come daybreak, they would damn well drive the rebels from their works!

Luke Kellogg leaned against his knapsack. The night was hot and muggy, and the moonlight filtered through the trees. The smell of powder mixed with the putrid smells of burned wood and burned flesh, of coagulated blood, of his own dried sweat. The moans of the wounded and dying on the slope of the hill below him were accompanied by the occasional crack of a musket, fired at a shadow in the trees, at an enemy moving from behind a boulder below. He'd slept for two hours, exhausted after the night's fierce battle.

He itched. He hadn't had a bath in a week, what with the hard march up through Virginia and Maryland. No railroad cars this trip! He and his comrades had "ridden Shank's mare"—walking on their own two feet—for three weeks, the last at nearly quick march to join the battle.

Someone had made a little fire, and coffee was boiling. Luke rolled up his blanket, walked over to the fire, and filled his tin cup with the hot, black man-fuel. Then he strode back to his regiment's new position, now in the middle of Greene's line, looking down on the steepest slope of Culp's Hill. He set the cup on a rock and checked his weapon and bayonet one more time. He crouched behind the breastworks, gazing intently down the slope. Scattered shots rang out as pickets probed in the shadowy moonlight. A scant few dozen yards below, Luke could see gray-clad men partially hidden by trees, rocks, and the breastworks.

Luke took a quick gulp of the hot coffee, leaned to his right, and whispered. "Bill—watch me wake up a Johnny." He picked up his musket, loaded it, aimed, and fired. Gratified by a yell and curse down-slope, he ducked behind the works, Weed already there. The answering shots passed harmlessly over his head, thudding into tree trunks behind. "That's my hill you're on, Reb. Best get out now, 'fore you're blasted out!" Another answering minie ball whistled harmlessly overhead.

And then the cannonade began. The ground shook. Men screamed in agony as hot metal tore through Confederate uniforms and burned rebel flesh. The 137th fired a withering volley into the charging gray ranks. Leaves and small branches showered down in front of Luke. The roar, smoke, and debris of the bombardment to the south continued for nearly an hour. The Virginians who'd spent the night in the First Division's trenches were really catching it! As the sun began to rise, through the haze and smoke Luke could see the dead and wounded Confederates littering the slope. Still the rebels kept coming. The Binghamton men continued their deadly fire into the attackers. Unlike the night before, when they were on their own, this morning they had support. As their ammunition ran low, and the muskets began to overheat and foul, they fired one last massive barrage as the men of the Nineteenth Ohio ran up out of the hollow in the rear and jumped into the trenches. Then the Ohioans fired, covering the vacating men of the 137th. When their muskets were cleaned and cartridge boxes refilled, the New Yorkers ran back into the works and covered the Ohioans as they dropped back into the hollow to refit. They continued this alternation until the rebels finally realized the Federal line was impregnable, broke off, and retreated down the hill and across Rock Creek, leaving their dead and wounded behind. At eleven o'clock, when the embattled New Yorkers realized that the attackers had retreated off the hill, they raised a loud cheer, one that could be heard on Cemetery Hill. The last desperate attack on the Union right flank had failed. Culp's Hill was secure.

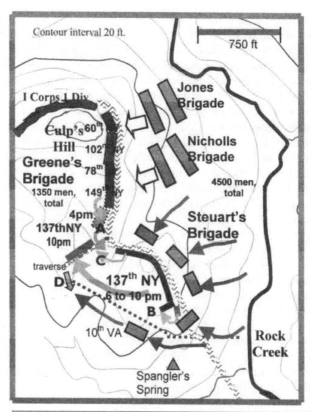

stone wall ■■■■■■■■▪

breastworks vacated by XII Corps 〰〰〰〰

A - 137th NY undoubles its line, shifts to single line in vacated
trenches over lower slope of Culp's Hill
B - 137th Co. A "refuses the line" – turns to face flank attack
C - 137th rotates the line to the traverse, in the dark, under fire
D – Capt. Gregg leads squad in bayonet charge on 10th VA

**Defense of Culp's Hill by Greene's Brigade
6-11pm July 2: Movements of 137th NY
Regiment**

Chapter Fifteen
Spangler's Spring

Noon, July 3

The men of Second Corps watching Longstreet's rebels from Cemetery Ridge heard the cheer behind them on Culp's Hill and realized that it must mean they were now safe from a surprise attack from the rear. They had no inkling that Lee had ordered Jeb Stuart's Cavalry to mount an attack from the east that afternoon. So they waited and rested until the fierce cannonade began at two o'clock from Seminary Ridge, answered immediately by their own artillery. Once more, they would endure a Confederate charge. Lee, unsuccessful with the attacks on the Federal right and left, ordered Pickett's division to charge the center of the Union line on Cemetery Ridge. Once more, the Union defense held. Rebel soldiers still alive fled back to their lines. By four o'clock, the fields in front of Cemetery Ridge were littered with their dead and wounded.

Back on Culp's Hill, the men of Twelfth Corps listened to sounds of the fierce combat to the west, fully expecting to be diverted there once again. The New Yorkers of Greene's brigade were easy to spot. Their faces were black with the remains of gunpowder from near-continuous firing of their muskets the night before and this morning. Lips were cracked and near bleeding from the saltpeter off the cartridges they had to bite open for each shot. As one sergeant had told them early on, "To join the army you only need two teeth—long as they be opposites!" Their uniforms and bodies were grimy from the construction of breastworks and the fighting afterward. Most men had come to accept the condition. Others, like Luke Kellogg, longed for a chance to scrub away the thick layer of dirt, sweat, and gunpowder residue.

Meanwhile, some rested, while others carefully probed down the east slope, retrieving their wounded comrades, awed by the destruction of the lush woods and by the number of dead rebels littering the hillside. Some heard the artillery fire off to the east and wondered at what action was taking place there. Later they would hear about the fierce and bloody cavalry battle in which Jeb Stuart's cavalry was driven off by the Union horsemen of General David Gregg.

Colonel Ireland tapped Lieutenant Marshall Corbett of Company B on the shoulder. "Mart, form up squads of any of our men still in one piece and go gather in our wounded. We've lost too many good men. Let's save those we can."

"Yes sir, Colonel. Right away." Corbett saw Private Kellogg, remembered his action months ago on the road to Charles Town, and immediately wanted him for his detail. Luke, for his part, was happy to once again serve under this officer who had earned his respect during that first incident in 1862.

Luke helped carry the regiment's wounded soldiers back to the little swale west of the hill's crest to await transport to a field hospital. Charles Covert, a private in Company B, leaned on Luke as he limped back. Luke helped Covert sit down, his back up against a hickory tree. "Here, Charlie, take a good slug out of my canteen." Covert gratefully drank deeply, emptying it. "Wish it was whisky for you."

"No matter, Luke. Right now this water tastes better'n any whisky. I was so damn thirsty in that fight I was ready to kill a Reb just to get his canteen!"

"Think you'll be all right, Charlie?"

"Yeah, I think so. Reb's ball passed clean through my leg. No bones broken. Surgeon's got no excuse to cut my leg off. So I'll be ready to go again shortly—count on it!" As he considered Charlie's bravery, and that of those who had paid the ultimate price, he recalled Chaplain

Washburn's sermon back in Harper's Ferry—"God demands much, and victory has a price!"

In the next couple of hours, Luke found a small patch of bare ground in the swale west of the brow of the hill, lay down, and slept, oblivious to the distant din of battle that would come to be known as Pickett's Charge. At around four o'clock, he was awakened by a nudge from Sergeant Aldrich. "Get up, Kellogg. I got a job for you."

Aldrich directed Luke and Weed to take as many canteens as they could carry and go get much-needed water. Luke and Billy were at least somewhat refreshed after the brief nap, despite the incredible drain on their energy from the violent battles the night before and this morning. Besides, they were young and had the reserve stamina for the task they'd been given. Luke and Weed worked their way south, behind the east brow of Culp's Hill, shielded from any Confederate rear guard sharpshooters.

When they got to Spangler's Spring, there was a long line of Union soldiers with the same mission, waiting their turn to get the cool, clear spring water. The wounded had been carried off by now, but dead Confederates still lay about the area.

"Billy, I'm feelin' so itchy an' dirty I can't hardly stand it. I'm goin' down to Rock Creek and wade in. You want to come too? Then we can come back, fill up these canteens, and get back to our company."

"If it's all right with you, I'll just wait for you here. You know me, Luke, bein' dirty never bothered me none. It ain't like I been muckin' out the stables. This is just good clean smoke an' black powder! Naw, you go. I'll stay here, get these canteens filled soon as it's my turn, an' wait for you to come back an' help carry 'em back up the hill.

"Of course, Luke, Sergeant Aldrich told us to stay together, 'cause there may still be Johnny Rebs around. You could get into a fix if there's any of them Rebs still down to the crick there."

"Well, I figure I can handle myself if any Rebs want to get any more of what we've given 'em already! Lookin' at the line of fellows ahead of you, it'll be at least an hour before you get your turn. I'm gonna go down into the First Division before I cut over to the crick. Oughtn't be any Rebs down that far, I figure. Anyway, I got my musket, my bayonet, and a Reb officer's pistol I picked up earlier when we were gettin' our wounded on the hill. I'll be all right."

After a brisk ten-minute hike down along the First Division's lines, Luke cut east toward Rock Creek. He worked his way over downed trees, past shell craters from errant artillery rounds, through briar bushes that tried to tear at his blue pants—not that he noticed. He'd been through much worse thickets as a boy in the woods around Bear Swamp. After the ordeal of the fighting the night before and this morning, a few thorn scratches were nothing.

Soon enough, he saw the gray-olive green water of Rock Creek ahead and eased forward carefully, using the numerous old oak and hickory trees and the large, lichen-covered boulders as concealment. If there were any rebel sharpshooters on the slope beyond the creek, he'd not be an easy target.

After the heat of the day, his body felt encrusted with dried sweat, mixed with the grime and blood of battle, just adding to the itching layers accumulated over the previous day's marching and fighting. His face was black from gunpowder, his lips cracked from hours of biting off the ends of the saltpeter-laden cartridges. Now he was eager to clean up.

Not seeing any sign of rebels on the far bank, he set down his gear, took off his boots, rolled up his pants, stripped off his shirt and jacket, and waded into the stream. He bent down and dunked his head and upper body in the cool water. It felt like his life had been restored to him. After what he'd been through, this was even more refreshing than a hot summer dive into the cold, clear water of Skaneateles Lake.

Luke eagerly scrubbed the grime out of his hair, then off his face and arms. He bent down to rinse off, then sat on a boulder at the water's edge and just enjoyed the feeling of cool water soothing his sore and aching feet. Those feet had served him well and had lots more hard marching ahead. He wanted to do everything he could to keep them healthy.

"I promised Weed I'd be back in an hour. I'd better get dressed an' get crackin', or he'll have the whole regiment come lookin' for me!"

He dried off with his shirt, wrung it out, and put in on loosely. The temperature of the air was still in the low eighties. He knew he'd be dry soon enough.

Picking up his musket and the pistol he'd found earlier, Luke walked back along the bank, picking his way carefully so as not to step in some hidden muskrat hole. "The fellas would josh me forever if I did something stupid like steppin' in a hole and breakin' a leg after comin' through the battle without a scratch! But I'd better be lookin' around, too. Don't want to get caught unawares by some Reb."

Just downstream, the creek began to widen out, backed up by the dam at McAlister's Mill. He looked back, then across the stream ahead of him. On the opposite bank, he saw two gray-clad horsemen emerging from the wooded slope. Rebel cavalry! Luke ducked behind the thick trunk of a fallen tree and quickly loaded his musket while he figured out what to do—lay low, or fire on the enemy.

Chapter Sixteen
Rock Creek

6:00 P.M., July 3, 1863

Sergeant Jack Lewis and Private Lathrop Emmons of the Black Horse Troop, Fourth Virginia Cavalry, carefully guided their horses through the underbrush on the east bank of Rock Creek. Tired, hungry, and exhausted after the excitement of battle had worn off, they wanted to find a moment's rest in the shade from the July heat, still oppressive in the early evening. Above all, they urgently needed cool water for their horses and themselves. They had found it here in a grassy glen under the sycamores on the bank of the creek. They intended to let the horses immediately drink from the stream, then dismount, fill their canteens and quench their own overwhelming thirst. Here was the chance to wash the dirt and blood off their faces, to wipe down the horses and let them rest a bit, before moving on.

As his black stallion lowered its head to the creek's water, Jack turned to Emmons.

"By God, Lathe, I thought we were dead back there for sure."

"We woulda been, Jack, if you hadn't cut down those last two blue-bellies with your saber. When we jumped that there rock wall and made it into them woods, I knowed we was safe."

"Ain't safe, yet, Lathe. This whole area's crawlin' with Federals that'd shoot us in an instant. We got to get over into Maryland and down back 'cross the Potomac. I reckon we can follow this here crick south into Maryland an' stay behind Meade 'til we hit the river. We done it last fall after we raided Chambersburg, an' I reckon we can do it again."

"I don' know, Jack. Seems like we're a long ways from our boys, an' too damn close to the Fed'rals. I don' want t'wind up in some Yankee hellhole of a prison! "

"Well, it's time you begun to worry some, Lathe! We just been damn lucky. But better to take a bullet here then to rot in Fort Delaware. So let's let the horses finish drinkin', fill up the canteens, an' get on out of here, 'fore some bluebelly off that hill 'cross there comes lookin' for water and takes a notion to bag us." Jack turned to his comrade.

"Now, Lathe, listen careful to me. If I should catch a bullet, you gotta take this here locket off my neck an' get it back to Cousin Will at Upperville." Jack reached into his shirt and pulled out the locket, letting it rest outside his shirt where Emmons could see it. Then he pulled the gold double eagle coin from his pocket—the only one left from the handful he had kept from the sacks he had hidden in the springhouse. He held it up for Emmons to see.

"Remember I told you 'bout a trooper took sacks of gold coins off a man when we raided Mercersburg last October? When he took the man's horse and found the sacks of double eagles? Well, that was me, Lathe. This here double eagle is one of 'em I kept. I hid them sacks in a springhouse close by a stone bridge over a crick east of the town, and ain't got to 'em yet. When I got this locket from my Sally there in Chambersburg, I scratched a map on its back of where I hid the sacks, case I had to get someone else to get them coins back for me."

Jack didn't quite trust Emmons enough to tell him he was talking about the bridge at Irwinton Mills. But Cousin Will could figure it out, using the map on the locket. He held up the locket for Emmons to see, then let it fall back onto his chest, held by the thin gold chain around his neck.

Lathrop Emmons stared intently at the gleaming gold coin in Jack's hand, his mind visualizing the fortune that a pile of these double eagles represented. "I remember you tellin' us 'bout the locket last month back at Pettis's, Jack. Don't worry. If'n anythin' bad happens, I'll git the locket an' git it back t'Will fer your Sally. An' if I should git captured an' you git away, you tell Carrie t'wait fer me, hear?"

Across Rock Creek, Private Luke Kellogg of the 137th New York was hidden from their sight behind a fallen tree, watching them, listening to their voices as the sound carried across the water. Luke listened intently, catching bits and pieces of the Virginian's conversation—"Mercersburg...sacks of gold...springhouse...stone bridge...map...Sally's locket...." His brain, tired as it was, tried to process all this. It certainly seemed that Sally's locket was the key to finding something truly valuable.

But this was no time to dwell on such thoughts. Luke's battle-tested reflexes took over. Outnumbered by their two to his one, he felt certain the rebels wouldn't hesitate to shoot him first, if they saw him. He intended to take them before they got him! Musket loaded and ready to fire, he cocked his pistol and set it carefully on the fallen trunk. Raising his head, cap off, he had a clear view of the two Confederate horsemen ten yards upstream. Deeply tired, they had let their guard down. They hadn't looked carefully across the creek. Nor were they looking his way now.

"Halt and surrender!" Luke's shout rang across the water. The startled Virginians looked up, raised their carbines, and fired in the direction of the voice. The low sun's rays reflected off the water, nearly blinding them.

"You had your chance!" Luke had already rested his loaded Enfield on the fallen log and had aimed carefully. He fired.

A trooper jerked up, then pitched forward. Lathrop Emmons had been hit. The minie ball cut a deep furrow on the side of his head with enough impact to rattle his skull. Emmons passed out, slumped down in the saddle. His horse reared up in terror, plunged into the creek and splashed downstream for a few yards until the deepening water diverted the animal up onto the bank and into the woods in a headlong rush toward the Baltimore Pike.

Jack Lewis drew his saber and spurred his horse. Midnight splashed across the creek, turning to avoid a midstream cluster of four large boulders in the shape of a cross. On he came toward the downed tree and the figure in blue half-hidden behind it. Luke was hastily reloading his musket. Jack raised his saber, meaning to deliver a mortal blow to the Yankee.

Luke raised his musket and fired a minie ball into the horse's head as it neared the creek bank in front of him. The magnificent black stallion's left shoulder dipped down as it stumbled and fell near the bank. Water flew. The Virginian dropped his saber and grabbed for the saddle's pommel with his right hand. Too late. Jack felt himself thrown through the air, overhanging sycamore branches tearing at him, ripping Sally's locket from his neck before he hit the water. The locket fell with a splash and was carried a little way downstream by the current as it sunk and was wedged under a rock near the bank.

Jack, half-stunned and sputtering water from his mouth and nose, wiped the water from his eyes, raised himself up out of the water, yanked his pistol from his belt holster, and fired.

Luke, seeing the trooper's action, fired his own pistol, the ball hitting Jack in the chest below his left shoulder. Jack cried out as he staggered, blacked out, and fell face-down into the water.

"I've got to admire your courage, Reb, but you should have surrendered 'fore I had to shoot you. Yet I'll not leave you to drown in the crick."

Luke waded out and dragged the trooper up onto the bank. Luke was startled when he looked at Jack Lewis's face.

"You're one of those Reb cavalry we fought last fall above Harper's Ferry!"

Jack spit out water as he regained his senses and looked at the man who had first shot him then hauled him out of the water. He too was startled when he looked closely at Luke's face.

"Remember me, Reb? Last October on the Charles Town road? My name's Luke Kellogg, with the 137th New York, Greene's Brigade. We were in camp at Bolivar Heights."

Jack was on the brink of unconsciousness, but he was alert enough to realize this was the Yank that had shot Lathe Emmons!

"I remember you, all right! I'm Jack Lewis. Lathe Emmons an' I are with the Fourth Virginia Cavalry. You're the Yank that shot Emmons on the Charles Town road 'fore he could cut down that Yankee that fell in the ditch. An' now you just shot 'im again!"

"Well, Lewis, I wish you would have surrendered 'fore I had to shoot you. I'm afraid you're hit bad. But now you're my prisoner, and I'll see you get to a surgeon. But first, what was all that about your locket and the gold sacks? Who'd you take 'em from? Where are they now?"

Jack felt for the locket and realized it was gone. "Damnation! I lost my Sally's locket! Must've come off and fell into the crick. Yank, you got to help me find it!"

"First let's get somethin' on that wound, Lewis."

Luke tore off a piece of shirttail and placed it over the wound under Jack's shirt.

"Let's hope that your shirt'll hold that cloth in place until the surgeons can get to you."

"Please, Kellogg, see if you can find my locket in th' crick."

"Not likely I can find it. Water gets deeper here near that mill dam. But rest easy there while I look some."

Luke looked into the water downstream from the fallen horse, and even waded in and felt around the rocks in places a locket might have caught, but with no success. Now the light was fading, the sun lower in the sky, deep shadows falling across the stream. No point in searching any further. Back on the bank, he cut a cross and his initials into the bark of the same sycamore that had ripped the locket from the falling man's neck. He noted the unusual pattern of the four boulders that lay midstream in the form of a cross. If he ever had a chance to come back to Gettysburg and look for the locket, at least he had landmarks to remind him of where it had fallen into the water.

Luke turned to Jack and started to tell him he'd had no luck, but his new prisoner had passed back into unconsciousness.

"What do I do with you now, Lewis? And how many more rebels are ridin' up through those woods that'll be lookin' to pay me back for shootin' you two? Well, you're not gonna answer me now, I guess. But it sounds like I got company." He turned toward the sound of boots tromping through the thicket behind him, presumably men from the First Division drawn by the gunshots at the creek.

Not wanting to risk being shot by someone from his own Twelfth Corps, Luke called out.

167

"Halloo, I'm Ireland's Regiment. Greene's Brigade. Got a Reb prisoner here."

"All right, Private, we're from the 123rd New York. First Division. We'll take over for you with this Reb."

"Thanks, Sergeant. I'm long overdue back to Culp's Hill and my Regiment."

Luke hurried back toward Spangler's Spring and an anxious Billy Weed.

"I thought rebels had got you for sure, Luke. I was jus' gettin' ready to give up on you an' go back for help. What took you so long?"

"Rebels, Bill. Cavalry. Two of 'em. Same two we shot back above Harper's Ferry last fall. Can you believe it? Now how strange is that!" On the way back up the hill, Luke filled Weed in with the details, leaving out the overheard conversation of gold and the locket.

About the same time Luke was dealing with Jack Lewis, a column of ambulances escorted by an infantry detachment was headed east on the Baltimore Pike. They had just crossed the bridge over Rock Creek when Emmons's horse dashed out of the woods with its semi-conscious rider. One soldier grabbed its bridle and brought the frightened animal to a halt. Another caught the rider as he fell from the saddle. The wounded Confederate was loaded into an ambulance that continued on down the Baltimore Pike, later depositing him in an improvised field hospital hastily set up in the church at Two Taverns. He was lucky. Not many rebel wounded were getting any kind of treatment by the overworked Union surgeons.

Jack Lewis was in worse shape. The minie ball had missed his lung but was lodged below his collarbone. He'd lost a lot of blood, and moved in and out of consciousness. He was fortunate the First Division was close to the Baltimore Pike. The sergeant who'd taken him over from Luke wanted to do the right thing, and had taken him directly to the Pike and flagged down one of the many ambulances heading for the field hospitals east of town. Jack was loaded aboard.

The column moved slowly east in the twilight, stopping at the field hospitals set up well to the rear of the Gettysburg battlefield. By nine o'clock Jack was deposited at a field hospital set up in a large barn on the Jacob Hartman farm, between Two Taverns and Littlestown. A weary Union surgeon bandaged Jack quickly, then continued with his assembly-line amputation of limbs. Lanterns, hung from the beams overhead, cast a hellish glow over the bloody scene.

Jack Lewis regained consciousness only to be staggered by the screams and moans of the amputees and the sight of a pile of their bloody limbs. Overcome by pain and overwhelming exhaustion, the valiant Virginian silently slipped into a feverish sleep.

Chapter Seventeen
Littlestown

July 4, 1863

This was a cheerless Independence Day at Gettysburg. It rained all day long on the bloody battlefields. The wounded and dying moaned and cried for water. The survivors trudged through the muddying fields, gathering the wounded and carrying them back to improvised field hospitals. Details of men dug shallow graves to bury the dead as best they could in the face of an overwhelming task, given the carnage of the past three days.

General Meade realized Lee's Army of Northern Virginia had been badly bloodied and was withdrawing back across South Mountain. He also knew his own casualties made a pursuit through the mountain gaps dangerous. If he attacked, Lee would be defending the high ground, and the Union forces exposed—just the reverse of what had given Meade his victory at Gettysburg. He refused to risk more losses and the exposure of Washington to the Confederates. His troops instead were gathering up the wounded from the battlefield, recovering from their exhaustion, and preparing to withdraw back through Frederick toward Washington, continuing to shield the capital from Lee's army. If, when rested, his troops could catch some of the Virginia Army before they crossed the Potomac to the west, so much the better.

Private Luke Kellogg and the other survivors in General Geary's Second Division spent most of the day burying the dead that littered the slopes of Culp's Hill. At one point in the hubbub of activity, Luke was able to venture once more to Rock Creek. The rebel trooper's dead horse was still on the mid-stream boulders, but with the hard rain, the creek had already risen. The rocks were covered. Luke sensed the futility of the search. He noted the landmarks, forming a picture in his mind. He knew it might be months before the Secessionists gave up and he could return to search in the creek for the Virginia cavalryman's locket. If the locket had been carried deeper into the mill pond.... Well, perhaps some time in the future another opportunity might arise. Meantime, he still had a war to fight, and there was the grim duty of burying the dead.

Sunday, the men rose to another gloomy, rainy day. Their rubber blankets had provided minimal protection during the night. The sputtering fires sent out acrid smoke that hung low to the ground. Hot coffee helped the men wake up, but the physical and mental exhaustion of a week of virtually unbroken marching, digging, fighting, and now burying had taken its toll. They stumbled around, not eager to resume their grim task. Before they had done much more, orders came to move out. The Second Division packed up and marched down to the Baltimore Pike, leaving scores of rebel dead on the slopes of Culp's Hill.

On the way to Littlestown, Luke and Billy Weed dropped out of the line of march as they passed the large brick farmhouse of Jacob Hartman. Slipping around to the back porch, they knocked on the kitchen door. Mrs. Hartman opened the door. "Oh, thank the Lord you boys are still with us!" Wiping her hands on her apron, she invited the boys into the kitchen.

"Thank you, ma'am, but we're dirty and wet to boot. We'll stay here on the porch. We were hopeful we might be able to buy a loaf of your wonderful bread to take with us." Luke stood there in his muddy boots, water dripping from the rubber blanket he'd thrown over himself like a poncho.

"You'll do no such thing. Pay me, indeed! Why you boys are heroes, chasing that rebel army back out of here. You just set down on those rockers while I fix you a plate. The bread will be out of the oven in a short while."

Luke and Billy almost fell into the comfortable rush seats of the ladder-back rockers on the broad porch. For a few short minutes they dozed, until their hostess's voice roused them.

"I had some scrapple and fried potatoes and biscuits left over from breakfast, and I fried up a few eggs to go with it. You poor boys look half-starved! You eat up good, now, and the bread will be done shortly." With a motherly smile, the stout farm wife set the heaping plates in their laps. They'd never had scrapple.

"Tastes like griddle cakes an' sausage all in one," said Weed with his mouth half-full. Luke was too busy wolfing down the hearty fare to answer at the moment. He refilled their tin mugs with hot coffee from the pot she'd set on the porch rail for them.

Wiping the remaining syrup and egg yolk from his empty plate with the last of the biscuits, Luke leaned back and belched happily. He popped the biscuit into his mouth, savoring the last tasty bite. "Miz Hartman sure does know how to cook, Billy. I feel like a new man!"

The screen door banged and Mrs. Hartman emerged with two sacks filled with loaves of fresh bread. The delicious aroma almost made the two soldiers hungry all over again. But their stomachs were full, and they knew that they'd be grateful to have such a treat as fresh soft bread instead of hard tack when they camped that night. So the sacks went into their knapsacks.

"There's some cold smoked ham in there, too." Mrs. Hartman told them. Luke leaned over and, careful not to drip on her, kissed her cheek. Billy Weed did the same.

"Miz Hartman, we'll not forget your kindness to us. God bless you and Mr. Hartman!"

"And may God bless you, boys, and our country. You take care, now." She waved to them as they rounded the corner of the house, marching double-quick to rejoin their regiment. She went back into her kitchen and took down the sack of flour, beginning again to make the dough, to replace the bread she'd given away, humming happily with satisfaction for having made some small gesture of thanks to her nation's defenders.

That evening, Colonel Ireland's regiment camped once again at Littlestown. Luke and Weed shared their tasty bread and the delicious Hartman ham with Newt Hunt and George Kilburn.

Swallowing a mouthful, Billy Weed shook his head, his face showing sadness.

"The regiment lost so many good men here, Luke. Brave Cap'n Gregg, Lieutenant Van Emburge an' others dead, Aaron Benn captured; Bert Hughes, Will Dodge, an' so many others wounded an' in hospital now. Almost seems disrespectful to be enjoyin' Miz Hartman's good bread like this."

"Billy, they're all heroes, every one. They did their duty and did it well. I honor them for it. We did ours too, and we owe it to the others to keep doin' it. And we got to stay strong to do it right. I believe the good Lord wants us to take what strength we can from good people like the Hartmans, an' accept it gratefully. Tonight at meeting, just thank the good Lord for his protection, and say a prayer for those that are no longer with us."

Later, they walked to a nearby barn where Chaplain Eli Roberts had set up for a Sunday service for the men of the 137th New York. The men were dog-tired, but these were God-fearing men, grateful to their Maker for having been spared the fate of so many of their comrades during these past climactic days.

The local Lutheran minister had been asked to give the sermon. Presaging the words that President Lincoln would use a few months later on the hallowed field of Gettysburg, Pastor Knecht began to speak with a booming voice. Luke fought the temptation to doze off and managed to absorb most of the pastor's words as they echoed off the barn walls, and seemed to rise to heaven, or at least well into the hayloft!

" 'Greater love hath no man than to lay down his life for his brother,' said the Lord. You men have offered your lives for your comrades, and for your nation—for all your brothers, and sisters, mothers, wives, children. Many of your comrades have made that last great sacrifice, here, a short distance away, for you, and for us. They have not died in vain. They, and you, are the true soldiers of the Lord."

Pastor Knecht's voice rose to a crescendo, and all eyes were on him as he concluded in his stentorian voice.

"You have fought valiantly, in the words of our nation's Constitution, 'to preserve a more perfect union.' You have fought to insure that we remain one nation, under God, with liberty and justice for all!"

A heartfelt "amen" resounded through the barn and out into the muggy night as the men of the 137th New York rose and left the barn.

Billy Weed had something on his mind, troubling him.

"Luke, we got to get word 'bout Albert to Polly Bird back in Binghamton. Let her know he's captured, but alive."

"I know, Bill. I got a scrap of paper from Chaplain Roberts so I can write to my Julia, let her know we're all right. I'll ask her to tell Polly. Colonel Ireland says he's gettin' married next month to Sara Phelps, Julia's friend. Anyway, he's ordered me to go with him back to Binghamton to help with recruiting. I'll spend time with Julia, of course, but I'll make sure to tell Polly how brave Bert was at Gettysburg."

Some years later, Luke Kellogg would read the official reports of his commanders recounting the performance of the 137th New York Volunteers at the crucial battle of Culp's Hill.

The commander of the Third Brigade, Second Division of Twelfth Corps, General Greene, said of the battle on the night of July 2:

The First Division and the First and Second Brigades of the Second Division were ordered from my right, leaving the intrenchments of Kane's Brigade and Williams's Division unoccupied on the withdrawal of those troops. I received orders to occupy the whole of the intrenchments previously occupied by the Twelfth Army Corps with my brigade. The movement was commenced, and the One hundred and thirty-seventh Regiment on my right was moved into the position vacated by Kane's Brigade. Before any further movement could be made we were attacked on the whole of our front by a large force, a few minutes before 7, and the enemy made four distinct charges, which were effectually resisted.

About 8 p.m. the enemy appeared on our right flank in the intrenchments from which Williams' Division had been withdrawn, and attacked the right flank of the One hundred and thirty-seventh New York. Colonel Ireland withdrew his right, throwing back his line perpendicular to the intrenchments in which he had been in position and presenting his front to the enemy in their new position. The officers and men behaved admirably during the whole of the contest. Colonel Ireland was attacked on his flank and rear. He changed his position and maintained his ground with skill and gallantry, his regiment suffering very severely.

Colonel Ireland, in his report of the battle, said of the regiment's officers who were killed:

Captain Gregg with a small squad of men charged with the bayonet the enemy that were harassing us most, and fell mortally wounded, while leading and cheering on his men. Captain Williams I had thanked for his coolness and courage but a short time before he fell. Lieutenant Van Emberg, acting adjutant, was everywhere conspicuous for his bravery, and fell while cheering his men. Lieutenant Hallett fell doing his duty. Our regiment's loss was 40 killed, 87 wounded, and 10 missing. The Confederate force against which our regiment and brigade fought was Johnson's Division of "Stonewall" Jackson's old corps, then commanded by General Ewell.

In the next few weeks, the 137th finished its Gettysburg campaign, marching south to Frederick, west over South Mountain, then south to the Potomac to camp briefly at Pleasant Valley, across from Harper's Ferry, where they had camped eight months ago as a new regiment. Luke thought to himself that night in camp, "It seems a lifetime ago we were here, ignorant of war. Now half of us are gone. And we still have a war to win!"

A few days later, the regiment moved across the Potomac, through Harper's Ferry and into the Loudoun Valley of Virginia, setting up camp at Hillsboro. Here the men finally had a chance to wash themselves and their clothing of the dirt and grime of a month of marching and fighting. Luke luxuriated in the water of the cold stream, thinking of the last time he'd washed, in Rock Creek at Gettysburg. It brought back vivid images of what had happened next—the faces of the two Virginia cavalrymen, the sharp brief conflict, one wounded and carried off by his runaway horse, another wounded and now prisoner.

He thought again of their conversation of hidden gold, of the search for the fallen locket, of how strange a coincidence it was that these were the same two horsemen he and Weed had fought at close quarters last fall at Bolivar Heights. He had no idea of just how intertwined his life and theirs had been, and would continue to be. He had no idea he was now in their Fourth Virginia Cavalry home area, and was bathing in a creek not more than twenty miles from their home at Upperville.

It would be nearly two more years until his soldiering was done. The men of the 137th New York would ride railroad cars west across southern Ohio, then south to Nashville, marching east to join the Union forces at Chattanooga. There, in the Cumberland Mountains on the Georgia border in November of 1863, they helped turn the tide at the Battle of Lookout Mountain. In the late summer of 1864, after the Atlanta campaign, they would lose their beloved Colonel David Ireland to disease, mourning his loss as the train bore his body back to Binghamton. In December of 1864, the regiment was assigned to General William Tecumseh Sherman, joining in Sherman's March to the Sea.

When the regiment was mustered out in the spring of 1865, Luke would return to Binghamton, marry his beloved Julia, join her father's business, and live a peaceful existence for eighteen years, until fate brought him back once more to the bank of Rock Creek, in the shadow of Culp's Hill.

Chapter Eighteen
Camp Letterman

July 17, 1863

For two weeks, Sergeant Jack Lewis moved in and out of feverish delirium. While the bullet had missed his lung, it was still lodged in the muscle under his collarbone, and infection had set in. In his delirium, he talked not about battles or home, as others around him did, but about Sally, her locket, two creeks, a springhouse, and gold.

Ella, Jacob Hartman's daughter, had been spending long hours tending the wounded in her father's barn. Today she was relieved to hear the wounded would be moved to the new general field hospital that had been erected east of Gettysburg on the York Pike called Camp Letterman. She hoped that more of the men would survive there. She was becoming emotionally numbed after seeing so many fine young men die of their wounds there in the barn, despite her best efforts to sustain their lives with loving care, and with little else but laudanum to dull the pain.

Ella was puzzled by the rebel cavalryman's delirious words. Who was Sally? What locket? What creeks? Why a springhouse? Gold what? When Jack was lucid, she would ask him, as she placed a cool wet cloth on his feverish forehead—about the only treatment she could offer him. While Jack was lavish in his thanks for her attention and care, and smiled when she mentioned Sally, he disavowed any knowledge of lockets or gold.

But the next morning, after another delirious night, he called Ella to him. He was lucid, and asked her why men around him were being taken away. She explained that they were all being moved to a real field hospital on the York Pike, where they could have better medical care. Jack felt the dull throbbing pain of his infected wound, and the ache in his head from the fever. He realized he was dying.

He had no choice, now. He'd seen Lathe shot, and presumed he was dead. Sally must be taken care of—must be told of the gold hidden not far from her. He must confide in this young woman who, in spite of being a Unionist, had been so kind to him. He must trust her to send word to his cousin Will, after the war if necessary.

"Miss Ella, ye been so good to me, and I should ask ye no more favors. But I surely must. Ye been askin' 'bout my locket an' th' gold, and I ain't been tellin'. But I got t'trust ye now, 'fore I meet my Maker. Pray I don't go t'hell!" In his illness, Jack's carefully learned "King's English" veneer had given way to the language of his boyhood years ago on Lost Mountain.

Ella looked down at the gaunt, hollow-eyed, grizzled cavalryman with deep concern, and with the affection that comes with being a constant caregiver. "You'll not go to hell, Sergeant Lewis. Not if my prayers are heard. And I trust God to hear them for you. You killed, but only because you thought your cause was right, not because you're evil. God understands, I'm sure. He will not deny you redemption. And you can trust me. What can I do for you?"

Jack turned his head away from the earnest young Pennsylvania German woman. He couldn't bear to let her see the shame he now felt.

"Oh, Miss Ella. It ain't fer battle I'm concerned. I only done what needed bein' done fer Virginia t'be free of the Washington tyrant Lincoln. No, it's what I done out o' carelessness that'll send me into hell, I'm afeared. But what's done's done. Cain't undo it now. But I need ye to know some things, important things, an' t'tell my cousin Will Gresham of Fauquier County Virginia after the war's settled.

"I kilt a civilian—just a boy—an' hid his gold in a springhouse by two cricks near Mercersburg durin' the raid north last October tenth. I drawed a map, scratched onto the back of a locket give t'me by my sweetheart in Chambersburg the next day. Kep' it 'round my neck up 'til that Yank shot me at the crick. It come off an' fell into th' water when my horse went down and a tree limb snagged it offn me. But Will won't need no map if ye tell 'im whar t'look. Tell 'im to go t'th' mill on the crick east o' Mercersburg, go over th' stone bridge, across the ford, and into the springhouse on the far bank. The sacks o' gold're buried inside, front o' th' back wall. Will ye promise t'tell Will fer me, Miss Ella?"

"Oh, Sergeant. How can I? If it's stolen property, and I tell your cousin, I'm a party to your deed. But I can tell him about the locket, and where you lost it. And I will. I promise. If I can find him, after the war. But if you are truly repentant, you must ask God's forgiveness for what you did that day."

"Many times I've asked God t'forgive me. But pray fer me, Miss Ella. Pray fer my redemption."

Jack realized he'd get no better commitment from her. In his heart, he hoped that somehow he'd survive, against all the odds, to recover the gold himself or at least to get word to Will by some other way. He had seen the murky water of Rock Creek, the jumble of boulders just downstream of where he had fallen, and figured the odds of the locket being recovered were slim to none.

On July 21, a few weeks after Jack's plea to Ella Hartman, a young Gettysburg woman walked down the York Pike to the field hospital called Camp Letterman. The tents laid out in neat rows made a small city on the George Wolf farm near the railroad. Wounded men were carried there and shipped off to other, more permanent hospitals as soon as they were able. Entering her assigned tent, sixteen-year-old Liberty Augusta Hollinger walked down the aisle between the rows of bandaged, maimed, moaning men—survivors of the horrific three-day battle. Libby was tired and nearly exhausted, both physically and emotionally. Yet she kept a smile on her face and radiated the kind, gentle spirit that she was. She had been helping to tend the wounded and dying since the first day of the battle—a little bit of brightness and comfort for these men in their agony of mind and body. As she wrung out a cloth to place on the feverish forehead of a man in a butternut cavalryman's breeches, she could see the blood caked on the bandage that wrapped his head. It didn't concern her that this man was among those who had stolen her father's horse and ravaged his warehouse downtown. Now he was just one of God's creatures who needed her attention.

"What's your name, sir?" she asked as she laid the cool cloth on his forehead.

"Lathrop Emmons, miss. But the boys call me Lathe."

"I hope your pain has eased, Mr. Emmons."

"Private Emmons, miss. But I'd sure be pleased if ye was to call me Lathe. Ye remind me so of my sister Lucy back home in Virginia. Yes, miss, my pain is eased, I'm feelin' some better t'day. Miss, my sergeant, Jack Lewis, was with me when we was shot. Have ye any idea whar he might be?"

Now, Lathe had no sister Lucy, but thought his young nurse would be less wary of him if he used that little ploy. He figured this might be his last chance to find the exact whereabouts of Jack's plundered gold.

Libby felt overwhelmed by the thought of finding one man among the large number of wounded, but promised to inquire of the presumed wounded Confederate prisoner named Lewis. To her amazement, she found him within the hour, on a cot in a tent nearby. She hurried back to Emmons's tent to report her success.

"I know it's a big favor t'ask, miss. But could ye he'p me up so's I could walk over t'see Sergeant Lewis?

With considerable reservations about the effect on Emmons's health, Libby helped him sit up, pull himself upright by his cot, then got his arm over her shoulder and walked him slowly to Jack's cot. Emmons was shocked when he saw the bloody bandages around his friend's chest and listened to the wheezing, gasping, breaths that came from his mouth. Emmons bent close to his ear.

"Jack, it's Lathe. I'm here. We made it!"

Wheezing, his words a mere choked breath, Jack gasped out his last words.

"Lathe, I'm dyin'. Find my locket. Git it to cousin Will. It come off there in th' crick where we was shot. Somewhere near that there pancake-shaped rock by th' bent sycamore tree. Caught under them rocks, prob'ly." He choked, coughed weakly, and continued.

"Th' money sacks is buried in a springhouse right by the ford, close by th' stone bridge over the Conococheague Creek east o' Mercersburg. Tell Will I drawed th' map on th' back o' th' locket. Tell Will t'tell Sally I loved her!"

By sheer cussedness, Jack had willed himself to stay alive until he'd been able to pass that message to Emmons. Now it was done, and after one last gasp, he allowed himself to slip into the void.

Libby felt the tears welling up once again. So much death she had seen in these last few weeks. So many good and brave men dead, blue and gray, in this terrible war. So many loved ones who would mourn them. Jack Lewis's last words would remain with her—"tell Sally I loved her!"

As Libby walked him back to his tent, Emmons knew what he had to do—find that locket. He knew as soon as he was fit, probably within the day, he'd be put on the train with other prisoners of war and would spend the rest of the war in some Yank prison. But when the South won, he'd be released, and then he'd get back to that creek at Gettysburg and find the locket. Recovering Lewis's gold stash would follow, and he'd have his own horse farm in the Loudoun Valley below Ashby's Gap. The thought of wealth and power would sustain him even in his imprisonment.

For the past few days, two well-dressed ladies from Baltimore had been walking through Camp Letterman, distributing gifts to the patients. Ostensibly there to boost the morale of the wounded of both sides, their real mission was to aid the escape of as many of the Secessionists as possible.

Lodging in Gettysburg was difficult to find in the aftermath of the battle. Hundreds, if not thousands, of families of the wounded and dead, do-gooders like the Baltimore ladies, and just plain curious onlookers had descended on the small town. The locals had enough problems trying to deal with their own straitened circumstances, let alone provide for this invasion of well-meaning people. Scarcity drove prices to unreasonable levels, severely stretching the patience of both locals and visitors. The Baltimore ladies had been fortunate indeed to find lodging with Jacob Hollinger's family. The house was neatly kept, the food delicious, if not sumptuous, the family polite and considerate of their Maryland lodgers. Still, after a day of observing their activities,

Jacob developed a suspicion they might not be what they claimed to be. He shared his misgivings with his daughter.

"Now, Libby, just keep an eye on them out at the hospital."

"All right, Father, though they seem to be such nice ladies."

That afternoon, the Baltimore ladies entered the tent where Libby had just brought Lathrop Emmons back from the visit to the dying Jack Lewis. Libby was at the far end of the tent, away from them as they talked at length with Emmons.

The next morning, the ladies left the Hollinger house early and were soon at Emmons's tent, carrying their usual bundles. This time, however, the bundles included civilian clothes sized to suit him. The suit coat contained train tickets and false papers identifying him as one Charles Randell, purveyor of fine cutlery, with letters of credit on a Philadelphia bank. In a minute Emmons was out of his hospital garb, into the clothes, and away with a Baltimore lady flanking him on either side. An hour later, he was on the train headed for Baltimore.

Just before noon, Libby Hollinger returned to Camp Letterman. In the course of her rounds, she entered the tent Emmons had earlier vacated. Lathe's bed was empty. Surprised, Libby turned to the soldier in the adjoining cot.

"I'm surprised to see Mr. Emmons gone. Has the provost taken him?"

"Why, no, miss. Two fine-lookin' ladies brung him a new suit an' shoes. He changed quick an' left with 'em."

"Oh my stars!" Libby exclaimed, and went looking for the provost.

"Mr. Emmons has apparently walked away in civilian clothes, sergeant."

"Damnation! Another one! We've lost some others this week like that. The guards down at the station caught a few of 'em, but most just mingle in the crowds of visitors and get away clean. Well, thanks for keeping track and telling me, Miss Hollinger."

That evening, Libby told her father of the apparent role of their Baltimore lodgers in aiding Emmons escape. An angry but unsurprised Jacob Hollinger then informed the ladies they were no longer welcome in his house. They offered to pay double to stay, but Hollinger refused to yield. He could have used the hard cash they offered after the financially ruinous devastation of his warehouse and its contents of molasses and flour by the rebels. But he was a man of stern principles, on which he would not yield. In the morning, the Baltimore ladies were gone.

Three days later, Emmons had made his way back to the Pettis farm in Upperville. He spent several weeks recuperating, enjoying the attention of young Carrie Payne, who treated him as her conquering hero. He related the events of the fighting at Hanover and Gettysburg, and of the final skirmish at Rock Creek where he and Jack had been wounded. Rachel Lewis and Minerva Pettis cried on each other's shoulders when Emmons told them of Jack's dying in Camp Letterman.

"Our brave Jack! To die so young. But a hero, never to be forgotten! And his poor Sally. We must get word to her. Oh, it is so sad. How I wish we could have brought her to us before this. I fear she has no one to console her. We must pray that she's strong, Rachel."

A tearful Minerva sat down and wrote her sad letter to Sally Keefer. Pettis knew a farmer who had a cousin just over the Potomac in Maryland, a secessionist sympathizer. The farmer carried the letter to the cousin, who in turn was able to post it to Chambersburg.

Will Gresham was deeply affected by the death of his cousin, best friend, and hero.

"Mr. Pettis, now it's my turn t'fight. Jack's dead, an' the Yankees got t'pay fer it. You got to let me go jine the cavalry! When Emmons goes back t'the Black Horse, I mean t'go with him."

In the course of time, Emmons felt himself fit enough to return to the fighting, full of hate for the damn Yankees and eager to find ways to avenge the death of Jack Lewis. With fresh new horses supplied once again by the patriotic Virginian Harry Pettis, Lathe and Will rode off to rejoin the Black Horse Troop.

In the subsequent campaigns, Will acquitted himself well. The men made approving comments on their new recruit.

"Gresham's well on th' way t'bein' a fine trooper, Emmons."

"That boy sure does have a way with horses."

"Give 'im time, he's like t'be near as good as Sergeant Lewis, rest his soul."

In October of 1864, the Fourth Virginia was fighting General Phil Sheridan's Union cavalry in the Shenandoah Valley. It was almost precisely two years after Jeb Stuart's October 1862 raid into Pennsylvania, when Jack Lewis had found and hidden the gold, and married Sally Keefer.

On October 8, a bitter fight ensued outside Strasburg between Sheridan's dismounted troopers, firing in large numbers across Tom's Creek at the charging Black Horse Troop.

"Charge on, you Black Horse! For Virginia!"

"This saber's for you, Yank! This's from Jack Lewis!" Saber raised high, Will spurred his horse into the waters of Tom's Creek; Lathe Emmons rode beside him, firing his carbine at the blue coats among the trees.

Will gave out a loud cry and fell dead, a minie ball in his chest. Emmons reached out to steady his friend in the saddle.

"Will, I got ye!"

Emmons jerked back, struck in the head by a ball that cut a deep furrow in his scalp. He fell off his horse into the cold water of the creek, and was knocked unconscious. Private Rob Martin saw him fall and jumped out of the saddle into the creek. He hauled Emmons out of the water, hoisted him sideways across his saddle, then quickly leaped back into his stirrups to carry the wounded man back out of danger.

When Emmons came to, Martin was standing over him.

"Lathe, Gresham's dead. You're just lucky you're not."

"What? Will Gresham's back at Upperville, ain't he?" Emmons's vision was blurry as he tried to register what Martin was telling him.

"Lathe, you was ridin' right beside 'im when he took the ball in the chest. You must o' really taken a lick in the head, man!"

"Oh no! First Lewis an' now Will! Them damn Yankees're gonna pay fer this. I swear t'God, Martin, I'm gonna see t'that. Sooner or later!"

The realization slowly dawned that the bullet, or the fall, had caused a problem with his memory. Whole episodes, and parts of others, seemed to be missing. He could no longer remember how Jack Lewis had died at Gettysburg. Try as he might, Emmons could not dredge up the facts now pushed back into the deepest recesses of his mind. As the war ground on and the chance of victory grew dim, his concern for lost memories was pushed aside by an abiding hatred of the Northerners who had brought this defeat upon him. He felt an overpowering resolve to survive, rebuild, and somehow, some time, make the detested Yankees pay the price.

Redemption

Chapter Nineteen
Reunion

October 1882

A handful of men were gathered in the American Hotel on Court Street in Binghamton, New York. These veterans of the great War of Rebellion were proud members of the GAR, the Grand Army of the Republic. At about the same time, another group of veterans of the War of Secession, the United Confederate Veterans, UCV, was meeting in Warrenton, Virginia. Each group, unaware of the other, was considering how best to commemorate the upcoming twentieth anniversary of the greatest battle of the war, the Battle of Gettysburg.

For some time, various efforts had been proposed to erect monuments to the heroic men from both North and South who had fought so valiantly on that hallowed ground. The Gettysburg Battlefield Memorial Association had purchased key tracts of land on which the battles were fought, and a few Northern states had erected marble and granite monuments there, honoring the men of their regiments. The Southern states, their economies made poor by the war's devastation, had only just begun to recover sufficiently to consider raising money for monuments to their fallen heroes. In 1882, the war had been over for just seventeen years. Hard feelings and bitterness were still strong in many quarters, even as a minority of veterans worked to put the past behind them and work toward a full reconciliation, based on the brotherhood of shared heroism in the face of death. In New York and Virginia, as well as other states, this movement had begun. These men understood that for the nation to achieve redemption for the horrors inflicted in the terrible conflict, forgiveness was the first step.

The men in Binghamton had served in several infantry, artillery, and engineer regiments that were in the thick of the three-day battle at Gettysburg. Henry Shipman, now sixty-nine years old, had been a fifty-year-old captain in Company F of the 137th New York Volunteers, fighting valiantly in the victory at Culp's Hill. He felt strongly that there should be a proper monument erected there, commemorating the regiment's heroism for future generations to see and be reminded of Binghamton's crucial role in winning the battle. Shipman had gathered the little group to propose the raising of funds for the memorial, to which all enthusiastically agreed.

Then several voices spoke up. "We should go down there in July, as a group, and pick the exact spot for the memorial." Colonel Milo Eldridge chimed in. "Great idea! I've never wanted to go back, but now maybe it's time."

Starting with this nucleus of support, Shipman convinced the membership of the local GAR post to hold their Eighth Encampment at Gettysburg on July 2–3, 1883, inviting all the other New Yorkers of Greene's Brigade to join them. Others were invited to join, to make it a reunion of all GAR members for the twentieth anniversary of the battle, but interest was lukewarm. It seemed that the prospect of a full national celebration in 1888, the twenty-fifth anniversary, had broader appeal. Nonetheless, Shipman decided to go ahead with just the local group. Instead of "roughing it" at a tent encampment, the smaller group chose to stay at the Hotel Gettysburg, meet there, and hire horse-drawn omnibuses to tour the battlefield.

The Virginia veterans gathered in Warrenton had a different slant on things. While they also wanted to see a monument raised to the Confederate Cavalry and would enjoy the opportunity to meet old comrades on a field of battle, the time and place was very much open to question. Given all the many locations of cavalry battles where they distinguished themselves, they had many choices. It seemed as if every man in the room had a different idea. Several wanted the monument and reunion to be at one of the numerous Virginia locations, all of which were relatively close to Warrenton—Dumfries, Brandy Station, Middleburg. Others wanted it to be in locations where Stuart's cavalry had brazenly carried the war into Yankee territory—Mercersburg, Chambersburg, Hanover, Carlisle, all in Pennsylvania. But when it came down to making a practical choice, each location was found to have too many drawbacks, at least in the opinion of the majority.

Finally, someone mentioned Gettysburg. It was in Yankee territory, there was an established battlefield preservation organization, monuments had already been located there to other combatants, and they knew the United Confederate Veterans was considering a major reunion there in 1888, on the occasion of Gettysburg's twenty-fifth anniversary. That would be a perfect time to unveil a major monument honoring the cavalrymen. Besides, military historians at West Point and the Virginia Military Institute were now declaring the Gettysburg cavalry battle of July 3, 1863 as the greatest such engagement ever fought in North America, the like of which would never be seen again.

"Besides. With all the monuments t'Yankees goin' up at Gettysburg, folks'll come t'think Lee got whipped bad. We got t'make sure Virginia has monuments there t'our boys, so they'll know we licked our share o' Yankees."

After some little discussion, the men agreed that Gettysburg was the right place for a monument.

"Why don't we all join together an' set up a UCV encampment at Gettysburg next July? It's the twentieth anniversary of the battle, an' we'd get lots o' publicity. It'd be a perfect time to scout for the best place for a monument, an' if need be, purchase the land if it's still in private hands."

They agreed that this made sense, and established a committee to plan and organize the event and to set up a United Confederate Veterans encampment on land held by the Battlefield Association.

Chapter Twenty
Binghamton

June 1, 1883

Luke Kellogg sat on a bench behind his new house at the end of Chapin Street, gazing down at the swiftly moving water of the Susquehanna River. He had a lovely view. South Mountain rose beyond the opposite bank, its forested slopes lush and green. The water sparkled in the warm sunshine. The rhododendron bushes around the house were a blaze of brilliant red blossoms. The fragrance of white peach blossoms filled the air, drifting over from the little orchard he'd planted. He knew any other man would be counting his blessings, having such a lovely prospect.

But Luke was deeply depressed. The beauty of his surroundings just served to deepen his melancholy. Julia should be here, by his side. How she had loved the view, the murmur of the rippling water, the scent of new blossoms—the fruits of her careful planning for their new home. She had immersed herself in the planning and planting of the gardens, trying to pull herself out of the deep sadness of the loss of their children. Michael, five, and Hannah, three, had died of scarlet fever in the winter of 1881. Luke had fended off his own depression by focusing on ways to help Julia deal with their tragic loss. He had encouraged her to turn her thoughts and energy into putting new life in their gardens.

Then last summer Julia had discovered a lump in her breast. Dr. Ayers had tried not to show her the alarm he felt, but told Luke there was little he could do except give her laudanum to ease the pain that would come. Luke hired nurses to care for Julia at home and spent every available moment he could spare with her. She read to him, or he to her. He taught her to play chess, a game he'd learned in the long days in camp in the war.

In this terrible time, they had regained the deep and abiding love for each other that had receded under the daily routine of his business responsibilities and her preoccupation with children and household. Julia ignored her illness and responded gratefully to Luke's physical love. They would talk of the time of their first meeting, and their passion on the riverbank. The memory awakened a near re-creation of the physical and emotional passion of their youth. Spent, they would lie in each other's arms, hearts full of deep love, not allowing each other to give in to the fear of parting.

Often, in the darkest hour of the night, Luke would awaken and lie there sightlessly, dreading the loss of his wife, his lover, his best friend, his partner in life. On one particularly troubled night, he could see the Grim Reaper with his scythe, just waiting in the distance. The hazy, macabre image took his thoughts back to the time nearly twenty years ago in Gettysburg, on the banks of Rock Creek, when a Confederate cavalryman's saber was poised to strike him dead. Then, he'd prevailed over the Reaper, his pistol shot defeating the impending saber blow. But now it was Julia who was in Death's line of vision, and neither Luke nor any man had means to deflect it.

On his riverside bench in the June sunlight, with rippling blue water in front and lush green all around, Luke let his mind slide back in time, to last November when the maple trees were nearly bare, and their fallen red and orange leaves carpeted Spring Forest Cemetery. Dull brown oak leaves still fluttered through the air and skittered across the ground like so many pairs of buckskin gloves. On the side of the hill, a small group stood by the open grave of Julia Stow Kellogg, buried next to her children and her parents in the Stow family plot. The damp chill of the glum, gray, overcast day just accentuated the grief the mourners felt. Luke listened to the Reverend Stocking deliver his brief eulogy and prayers, asking God's mercy on her soul and His comfort for those who mourned her.

Luke stood among caring family and compassionate friends, but in his grief, he barely heard the pastor's words. He was deeply grateful that Andrew had come down from the farm at New Hope with Billy Weed to stand by him. Albert Hughes, Luke's old friend from the 137th New York, was handing his wife Polly a second clean handkerchief as she continued to weep for her dearest friend. And Luke was conscious of the concern and affection shown him by Julia's brother John, Luke's partner in the Stow & Kellogg family business, and by John's wife Emma. But no one and nothing could begin to make a dent in the grief he felt in the very deepest recess of his soul.

"Ashes to ashes, and dust to dust," Reverend Stocking intoned. In hushed tones, the mourners expressed their sympathy to Luke and returned to their carriages or buggies, their horses waiting stoically behind the black-trimmed hearse and its shiny black-coated team. Luke dreaded having to maintain his composure when the mourners gathered back at the parlor of his new home. He wished he could dismiss them all and just be left alone with only his own deep sadness as company. But he knew that convention demanded they, and he, follow through with the post-interment gathering.

He leaned over to his brother-in-law.

"John, would you and Emma please see the crowd back to the house, an' serve as host and hostess until I get there? I would like to linger a little while alone with Julia, one last time."

Emma dabbed a handkerchief once again at her moist eyes. "Of course, Luke. We understand. Come when you are ready."

She turned away quickly, so as to spare him the sight of a fresh cascade of her tears. "So sad, so sad," she murmured to John as he led her down the hill to their waiting brougham.

Luke stood, head bowed, hat in hand, by the fresh grave of his wife and the graves of little Michael and Hannah. There were no tears, just a numbness in his soul. The pain had become a constant in his life, starting with the loss of the children, a pain shared with Julia, a pain that grew as he watched her life slowly slip away in these past heart-breaking weeks.

Luke had often wondered if God was testing him as he had tested the biblical Job, visiting on him the death of those closest to him. Or was this retribution visited on Julia, and hence on him, for their tryst on the riverbank so many years before? Was this the price demanded for redemption? He quickly dismissed the notion. He didn't subscribe to the fire-and-brimstone preachers whose Old Testament God was a vengeful deity to cower before. No, God was a loving God, a forgiving and patient God. Julia and he had long ago made peace with Him over that one indiscretion of youth. Her many and constant acts of love and charity had surely long since achieved her redemption. He had no doubt whatsoever that his beloved Julia was now with Him in Paradise, reunited with her innocent children. He could only pray that he would be dealt with as mercifully. He prayed that Julia would somehow intercede with Him, that God would in time lift his burden of deepening melancholy.

In the early years after the war, Luke had often walked through Spring Forest. He found it a peaceful respite from his business cares. At the end of the war, Julia's father had taken his son-in-law into the Stow wagon and plow manufacturing business. Luke had found it a rewarding challenge and enjoyed it. He invented a new plow blade that was well received by farmers, and the business grew rapidly. Julia's younger brother John joined Luke in running the company, and the elder Stow retired. Eventually the press of business and family matters had caused these visits to the cemetery to become infrequent. As he turned from his wife's gravesite, he realized how long it had been since he'd paid his respects to his friend and regimental commander. Julia would certainly approve his taking the opportunity now. He made the short walk past the imposing Phelps mausoleum to the low granite crypt with the Union officer's saber perfectly carved on its top, and the engraved name on its east face—*COL. DAVID IRELAND U.S.A.*

Setting aside his grief for the moment, he stood at attention and rendered a salute to his wartime commander. The memories came flooding back. How much he, and indeed Julia, owed this man. He thought back to his arrival in Binghamton twenty years ago as a young lad of eighteen, fresh off the farm. He recalled how swiftly his life had changed in those following months. How then-Captain Ireland had officially recruited him, then trained him in the basics of camp life, military drill, and basic military discipline. How Colonel Ireland had kept the 137th New York Volunteer Regiment in fighting trim, had kept their morale high through the dreariness of winter camps, the bone-wearying long forced marches, and the potentially devastating impact of seeing the horrors of war for the first time. How Colonel Ireland had led them to victory on Culp's Hill those fateful days of July 2 and 3, 1863. How his quick tactical moves and his inspiration to his men had beaten back the almost overwhelming rebel onslaught that, if successful, would have rolled up the Union right flank. The rebel hordes would have poured into the very heart of the Union lines. That would have made Gettysburg an unmitigated disaster for the Army of the Potomac, and very probably would have resulted in a permanent Confederate States of America. But Ireland's men of the 137th had held. Luke recalled how they had endured another two years of bitter warfare before General R. E. Lee finally acknowledged the defeat that had begun on Culp's Hill, and surrendered at Appomattox Court House.

Luke recalled the grand wedding in late August of 1863. Colonel Ireland was granted furlough. He came back to Binghamton, accompanied by the newly promoted Sergeant Luke Kellogg. Luke escorted Julia Stow as she attended her friend Sara Phelps's marriage to Colonel David Ireland at her uncle Sherman Phelps's ornate mansion at the corner of Front and Main. The Colonel had only a few short weeks with his new wife, and Luke with his beloved Julia, before they had to board the cars, the train that would return them to the regiment in Virginia.

Luke thought back to that October of 1863. The 137th New York had yet another battle to win, at Lookout Mountain, on the Tennessee-Georgia border near Chattanooga. Following their brave commander's lead, Luke and the rest of Ireland's stalwarts used their great speed and strength to repel a surprise night attack by the rebels, and so turned the tide of battle. Luke vividly remembered how near a disaster it had been. He was running out of ammunition, all of them were. The colonel rode up and down the line, braving the rebel fire, exhorting his men: "Fight on! Get ammunition from the dead, boys! We will not retreat!" When the battle ended, When the battle ended the men inventoried their ammunition, there were fewer than two hundred cartridges in the entire unit. Afterward, Colonel Ireland took command of the New York brigade replacing the wounded General George Greene.

Luke remembered the sadness they had all felt one year later, as their beloved commander died a prolonged and painful death from dysentery. David Ireland's final march was a slow train ride bearing his casket to Binghamton. There the hero's body was reverently entombed on the Spring Forest hillside where Luke now stood. Julia had sent Luke the clipping from the Binghamton Republican which began, "*It is our painful duty to announce the death of Colonel David Ireland...*" and concluded with "*...his memory will be cherished as one of that 'noble army of martyrs' who have nobly fallen in the defense of their country.*"

Some years after the war, Sara Phelps Ireland had Luke and Julia to tea at Sherman Phelps's new mansion on Court Street, where she now served as her widower uncle's hostess. She showed them the treasured letter written to her by the regimental doctor who had tried in vain to save her husband's life: "*his death produced a great shock to his Brigade, who placed the greatest confidence in his fidelity and courage.*" To which sentiment Luke fervently added his heartfelt affirmation.

Now on this November day, Luke stood, head bowed, by the granite tomb with the saber carved on top and said a prayer of thanks to God for this great and good man. David Ireland had trained Luke well, had led him well in battle, and had done him the great kindness of letting him return home to Julia on the occasion of his colonel's wedding. Luke felt that he owed his very existence, and much credit for the time God had allotted him with Julia, to the man whom he here honored. But that part of his life had now ended. A new chapter of his life awaited him. It was time to return to the unhappy present, and do his duty.

These recollections served to steel him for the public appearance his guests were waiting for him to make. He walked back over to his trim little buggy, climbed up, and, with a quiet "gee-up" to his horse, drove on down Front Street toward home and the waiting assemblage in his parlor.

Now it was eight months later, and though the June day was bright and sunny here on the riverbank, the gray November gloominess of the cemetery was still embedded in his soul. Yet he felt more than a little ashamed for feeling sorry for himself. Julia had always been so optimistic and cheerful in the face of adversity. When little Michael had died, she gave even more love and attention to Hannah, instead of moping. When Hannah died, she grieved for a week, then turned all her love and attention to her husband and her gardening. Even in her final fight with cancer, she maintained a positive outlook, not fearing death, looking forward to Paradise, loving her husband with even more intensity, packing every possible bit of living into each day left to her. If she were here now, she'd be jollying him out of this morose mood, not letting him wallow in it.

"Hello, Luke." The familiar voice jarred Luke out of his self-absorption. He turned his head and saw the gray-haired gentleman standing beside him, looking at the swirling water of the river. "Water's up today," said his visitor.

Twenty years ago, Henry Shipman had been his company commander in the 137th New York Volunteers. After the war he'd resumed his life in Binghamton, and over the years the two men had maintained the friendship welded so firmly by the shared danger of battle.

"Hello, Henry. Yes, the river's as high as I've ever seen it."

Henry saw the trace of a smile on Luke's lips, and chuckled. "You've said that every time the river's been up, even in the worst drought, for as long as I've known you!" It was a running joke with them. Henry was glad, in any event, to see it had perhaps stirred Luke out of his depression.

"Luke, come with me to Gettysburg next month. It's been twenty years since the Regiment licked Johnny Reb at Culp's Hill. A number of fellows have told me they're seriously considering going down there on the train. Fellows from Tioga, Tompkins, and Cayuga County that we haven't seen since we were mustered out. And don't you think it'd be instructive to meet some of those Southern boys we damn near hand-wrestled by the rock wall, Luke? I wonder if any of 'em will show up.

"At any rate, a change of scenery might do you some good. I tell you from experience, sitting around dwelling on your loss is no good. I know what you're going through. I suffered it too when my dear wife

Mary died in '66, and then two years ago when my daughter died. Believe me, it's no good to get bottled up in loneliness. Get out, be with friends, build on the positive. Don't let yourself turn into a lonely and bitter recluse." Henry sat down beside Luke and gazed at a broken leafy branch floating by on the water.

Luke lifted his head and gazed off into the distance.

"Thank you, Henry, for wanting me to go with you. Maybe you're right. Maybe it would be good to get away for a bit. And it would be good to see some of the fellows from the regiment again. I don't much care about seein' those fellows that were so hell-bent on killing us, though. Tell you what—I'll sleep on it and stop by your place tomorrow to let you know. All right?"

"Fine, Luke. It should be really interesting to see the battlefield, see if any of those trees our minie balls and cannon shot cut down on Culp's Hill have grown back at all. And I hear some states have put up monuments to their regiments. Be interesting to see them, don't you think? I'd like to drive out to Littlestown, too. There was a Hartman woman at a farmhouse on the Baltimore Pike, toward Two Taverns, who must have stayed in her hot kitchen all morning baking bread that she shared with us. How good that apple butter was on them! And she wouldn't take a penny from us. And then gave us cold buttermilk from the springhouse to boot. She was a saint! If she's still alive, I've got a special present for her."

"You mean you were at her kitchen, too, Henry? We must've been ahead of you, but Billy Weed and I were fed by the Hartmans, too. Now you make me feel guilty if I don't go, Henry. You're right. Her kindness after those forced marches across Maryland was just the tonic we needed. Who knows—maybe it was her bread, apple butter, and buttermilk that gave the extra energy we needed to win that fight! But I remember best her pretty, young daughter Ella, that served Billy and me. If it weren't for my own lovely Julia here, I think I'd have been back there after the war sparking that sweet girl! Wonder what's happened in her life after the war? All right, Henry. You've sold me. Count on me. By George, we'll just make it a high old time!"

"That's the ticket, Luke! You'll not regret it. Stop by my place tomorrow and we'll make arrangements together. I'm just tickled that you're coming with us!"

When he'd walked his friend back to the front gate, he went inside the house and sat down in a maroon plush chair in the new parlor. He'd been given a box of fine cigars, made right over on Pennsylvania Avenue, their wrapper leaf grown on a farm at the base of Ingraham Hill, just across the river and downstream a mile. He had been meaning to try one. Luke took a cigar from the humidor, inspected it, and clipped off the tip. Striking a wooden match, he singed the end, then closed his lips over the tip, held the match to the end, sucked in, and puffed contentedly as the fragrant smoke rose through the room. Julia hadn't liked the odor of cigars, especially the stale odor of the smoke that lingered long after the tobacco had been extinguished. In the months since her death, Luke had allowed himself the indulgence of a good cigar in the late afternoon. But he left the windows open, not wanting to invoke the silent rebuke of his housekeeper.

Savoring the aroma, he thought again about this so-called reunion. Would it be a problem for him to be away for four or five days, or even a week? Not really. Julia's younger brother had been running the business more and more lately. Truth be told, Luke realized, it might be better for all concerned if he turned the business entirely over to John, who had earned Luke's complete confidence over the years.

The realization hit him that he'd really become bored with the business, now that Julia was gone. *Truth is,* Luke thought, *there's really nothing for me here now. I remember Great-uncle Charles Kellogg moving west to Michigan way back in '38. The far west is opening up. Maybe I should sell out here, make a fresh start in a new part of the country. Perhaps that's the key to redemption, in this life at any rate.* The idea suddenly seemed very appealing.

"But first," he said aloud, "I will go back to Gettysburg."

He sat in his comfortable chair, a wispy wreath of cigar smoke lingering above, little moved by the slight breeze from the windows. He closed his eyes, leaned back, and allowed his mind to go back in time, to the hot summer days in the small Pennsylvania town by the Mason-Dixon Line. He saw again the gun smoke, heard the explosions of cannon fire and the whistling of minie balls, the crash of breaking trees, the rebel yells of the attackers charging over the rocks and through the trees up the hill toward his crude but effective revetment. Heard the screams of the wounded, the cries for help, for water, for God. Felt the ground shuddering under the weight of the cannonades. He saw again the blood and gore and broken bodies, felt again the anguish over a fallen comrade, the rush of fear, overcome only by the instinct to fight and survive, to never give in to fear or to any attacker.

After a time, those vivid images receded. They were replaced by the image of Rock Creek, placidly flowing through the wooded glen below Culp's Hill before rushing through the rocky flume as it swept under the bridge on the Baltimore Pike. He saw again the gray-coated cavalrymen, felt again the quiet calm anger, relived his unerring shots, the rearing and charging horses, the upraised saber, the horse, dying in the stream. Clear as if it were in the room, he heard again the Virginian's drawl, telling about the locket, the map drawn on its back, the plundered gold hidden in the springhouse by the creeks shown on the map. He remembered his brief, unsuccessful search for the locket in the murky water of Rock Creek. He remembered wondering if the Virginian would survive his wound, not giving him much chance of it. And what of the other, the one with the red hair and jug ears, whose horse had bolted after Luke's shot?

Luke led his mind back to the present, sat up in his chair, and stubbed out the cigar in the oversized ashtray beside him. *I wonder if the horse soldier did survive. If he did, he's long since retrieved the gold he talked about. But if he didn't, and didn't tell anyone else any more than what his partner and I heard there at Rock Creek, that locket's the key to anyone recovering it. Of course, just finding a locket in that murky water and boulder-strewn creek is a tough problem in itself.*

His excitement began to rise. *This is just the challenge I need! By heaven, I will go back down there with the boys. I suppose there'll be some Southern veterans meeting there. I'll inquire amongst them to see if any of them know if that fellow survived. I think I remember him saying something about Black Horse Troop, Fourth Virginia Cavalry before they took him away. Yep, I'm almost certain that was it. And then I'll search around some in the creek for the locket. Even if I don't find it, just the bits I heard him say might provide enough clues. I'll go off to that other town, Mercersville—town—burg—something like that, I think I remember him saying. I'll ask around, see if anyone recognizes the two creeks and springhouse. Then I'll just go exploring, and maybe I'll find it. In any event, this will be an exciting venture!*

Chapter Twenty-One
Carrie

June 1883

Carrie Emmons watched her husband coming across the side yard. In a moment he'd be in the house. She saw an all-too-familiar scowl on his face. Whatever his problem was, he wouldn't confide in her. But she knew he'd be only too ready to take out his frustration and anger on her. Why was God demanding so much pain from her? How had she managed to so anger Him? Was it her growing disrespect for her husband? Or that she no longer loved Lathrop Emmons? She thought she hid it well enough from her sons and her husband, holding it deep inside herself. But she knew she couldn't hide it from an all-knowing God. Would she ever find peace in this life? Or would her redemption come only in the hereafter? But she'd better pay attention to the here and now, for Lathe was nearly in the door.

Lathrop Emmons walked slowly from the barn to the house. The weight of his debt felt like the proverbial millstone around his neck. Another foal stillborn. Another lost chance to sell a colt for enough to make the bank payment due the end of July. And those damned Pennsylvania farmers refuse to buy any more animals from him.

It was Emmons's own fault. Before the war, Harry Pettis had sent Jack Lewis north with excellent horses, fairly priced. Pennsylvania's thrifty farmers were only too happy to continue their business relationship with Pettis. After the war, Emmons had begun to travel the same routes, with some initial success. While his stock wasn't the best and his prices were too high, horses were scarce and the economy was booming. The farmers paid what they had to, grumbling. Emmons tried passing off some substandard animals as top quality. Serve these Yankees right if they weren't horsemen enough to spot the difference. Eventually word got around that the man couldn't be trusted, and his sales dropped off.

Five years ago, life had seemed to be going so well. The carpetbaggers were gone and Virginia's economy was growing, the war's devastation in the Loudoun Valley largely repaired and rebuilt. Emmons had married Carrie Payne after the war, and in 1873 they had inherited her father's small farm. With a bit of luck, a prodigious amount of hard work by Carrie, and some shady, if not totally dishonest, horse-trading by Lathe, they had expanded the farm and developed a profitable horse breeding operation. They'd rebuilt much of the house, hired several servants, and generally led a comfortable life. Carrie soon realized there was no love for her in Lathrop. She contented herself with building up the farm, while enduring if not enjoying the infrequent times when her husband took his pleasure with her in bed. Carrie often thought that she and her sons could run the farm better, more profitably, if somehow freed of the reputation of shady dealings that Lathrop had brought upon them.

Their twin boys, born in 1867, had developed into fine horsemen and often won races at local fairs, riding the thoroughbreds from the farm. They had a much better way with horses than their father, who could be brutal to the animals in training them. Carrie had come to think the family would be better off if he turned horse training over to the boys. The twins had recently returned from the private school in Staunton, set up after the war by Jedediah Hotchkiss. Emmons had opposed sending the boys to study with Hotchkiss, since he'd heard the man was a damned Yankee from Windsor, New York. He relented only when Carrie gently countered that prejudice, citing the man's loyal service to Virginia during the war as Stonewall Jackson's own chief engineer and mapmaker.

The twins were full of plans to attend the College of William and Mary in Williamsburg.

How am I going to tell them we can't afford to pay the tuition? That we are in serious danger of losing the farm? Emmons felt hemmed in by responsibilities, overwhelmed by his debt, frustrated at his inability to pay the bank, let alone educate his sons. His anger began to build. While Emmons struggled to keep it under control, the horses often bore the brunt of his anger.

At the dinner table, the boys talked eagerly about their plans for the summer and their anticipated fall at college. Carrie listened and smiled, proud of her boys' achievements and promise, until she saw the scowl on the face of her strangely quiet husband. She wisely said nothing to show her concern until that night when they lay abed. With some trepidation, for Lathrop could erupt unexpectedly, and on more than one occasion had threatened her with physical violence, she now spoke softly to him.

"Lathrop, what is so troubling ye tonight?"

He put her off, protesting that it was nothing, trying to keep himself under control. But later as he lay awake listening to her light snores, he thought about their situation. Something drastic must be done. Tossing and turning, his mind struggling to come up with a solution to this dire problem, he sat bolt upright in bed. It had come to him. The answer! An image, long-submerged in his memory, appeared to him as clear as if it had been painted on the wall in front of him—a gleaming gold double eagle coin!

Carrie turned her head to him, wakened by his sudden movement. "What is it, Lathrop? What's th' matter?

"Nothing you need t'be concerned with! Go back t'sleep."

Lathrop Emmons now knew what to do. The solution had been there all along. Hidden away somewhere north, just over the Line in Pennsylvania, was his salvation. The long-forgotten gold of his wartime comrade-in-arms, Jack Lewis. The Mercersburg plunder. Four sacks of twenty-dollar gold pieces! All he had to do was figure out exactly where Lewis had hidden them.

The key was Sally's locket, lost in Rock Creek there at Gettysburg. His mind churning, memories of the confrontation at Rock Creek flooded back. All those memories, lost to him for so long after the head wound had buried them so deeply into the farthest recesses of his brain, were coming back. Apparently the heightened stress of his current predicament had finally broken these old memories free and sent them bubbling up into his consciousness.

Damn, he thought. *I could've got that gold found anytime in the last eighteen years if I just could've remembered these details. Just damn lucky I remembered it now!* He started to form a plan to search out the gold's exact location but soon fell into a deep sleep, palpably relieved by having seen the end to his dilemma.

The next morning, the Emmons men went vigorously about the business of running the horse farm. The boys were happy to be home, out of the classroom and back on horseback. Their father was relieved, knowing he'd uncovered a way out of his financial box. While the boys mucked out stables, he sat in the small office where he maintained his records and did his accounts. Looking through his mail, he found a letter from Williams Carter Wickham. He had held Wickham in the highest regard as the commander of the Fourth Virginia, fully intending to vote for him for state senator that fall. "Now, I wonder what th' colonel wants with me after all these years? I expect he's calling on his old regiment fer support in th' election. Well he needn't have bothered—we're all fer him, I'm certain."

Emmons was half right—Wickham did ask for his support. But not for the election. For attending a reunion of sorts, a gathering of cavalry veterans of the Battle of Gettysburg. The letter invited all men of the Fourth Virginia to join their former comrades at a United Confederate Veterans encampment on the battlefield, July 1–4 of 1883—the twentieth anniversary of the battle. As he read the letter, he felt a definite mix of emotions. The events of June and July 1863 flooded back and he felt again some of the excitement of the battle. He'd long since resumed commerce with men of the North, but now they were shunning him. He presumed there would be Union veterans gathering on that anniversary also, and he wondered if he was ready to see them once more on the battlefield. The memories of seeing comrades killed, captured, and suffering cruel imprisonment at the hands of Union forces were still strong—the hatred still lying just beneath the surface of his soul. He thought in particular about the one who'd shot him and killed his friend Jack Lewis there at Rock Creek. The same Yankee sonuvabitch who'd wounded him in '62!

Then he remembered the locket, with Jack's map scratched on it, the key to finding the gold. It was still lodged somewhere there on the banks or in the crevice of a boulder in Rock Creek. Surely it was too big, too heavy to float all the way to the Chesapeake Bay, deep on the bottom, guarded by blue crabs! Here was an opportunity to find it. To use it to home in on the hiding place, to finally uncover and retrieve Jack's gold. He couldn't allow himself to consider that the locket was impossibly hidden itself, or that even if found, would lead him to an empty hole, the gold long since removed by some lucky accidental finder. He needed the hope, the emotional lifeline that a quest for the gold provided him.

He'd go to that reunion. There was a possible buyer for a horse in Frederick County, Maryland. He'd firm up that sale, deliver the horse himself, and then go on to join his fellow veterans at Gettysburg. Emmons had felt a bit guilty anyway, about never having visited Jack Lewis's grave. Lathe knew that Lewis's body hadn't been returned to Virginia, but lay buried somewhere at Gettysburg. Lathe had a lot of character flaws, but disloyalty to his comrades from the Fourth Virginia cavalry regiment wasn't one of them! Jack Lewis had saved his bacon more than once. Perhaps he owed it to his dead comrade to go back to that battlefield and pay his last respects.

He wondered how many others would be returning to Gettysburg. Was it possible that that Yankee who'd shot him would be there? Made no difference, really. Lathe figured he'd spend most of his time at Rock Creek, up from the stone bridge on the Baltimore Pike, below Culp's Hill, searching. Searching for a glimmer of sunlight reflected from a gold locket. Then he'd be off toward Mercersburg. Guided by the locket's map, he'd retrieve the gold and ride triumphantly back to the farm. With luck, he'd pay off the loan. Freed of the crushing burden of payments, he'd easily be able to cover the boys' tuition. Life would be good again!

Chapter Twenty-Two
Hotel Gettysburg

July 3, 1883

Henry Shipman sat back in an overstuffed armchair, blue clouds of fragrant cigar smoke spiraling toward the ceiling. He looked around the room at the men seated there, puffing away contentedly after the good dinner the veterans had enjoyed in the hotel's banquet hall. "Well, men, I judge this a very successful reunion."

"Yes, yes indeed," came back the nodding agreement.

"We've gotten commitments for major donations from a number of the men. The Binghamton Republican has agreed to do a series of stories on our reunion, on the battle at Culp's Hill, the history of the 137th New York Volunteer Regiment. They've said they'll do an editorial urging community support for funding a monument here. We've all had a fine time together, to boot!"

Marshall (Mart) Corbett exhaled out a large aromatic puff of smoke before speaking. "I for one thank you, Henry, for setting this up. The tour of the battlefield today was quite an amazing experience. I hadn't fully appreciated just how hot the battle had gotten to the west of us. We had enough glory to gather in our own fight there on Culp's Hill. Can you just imagine that Pickett's charge? So brave, so foolish. But by

God, the 'old snapping turtle' did the job! General Meade finally showed Robert E. Lee the Union Army wasn't something he could push around any more. Twentieth Maine stopped the Rebs on the left at Round Top, we New Yorkers stopped them on Culp's Hill, and the whole damned Army of the Potomac stopped them in the center on Cemetery Ridge."

"What about our cavalry, Mart? Seems they showed Jeb Stuart who was boss, too, over there off the Hanover Road. Gregg and Custer's men drove 'em off when they might've run right up into the back of our lines."

"Kellogg, didn't you have a little run-in with a couple of Stuart's stragglers down on Rock Creek that evening?"

"Interesting you should bring that up, Mart. Yes, I was down washing some of that black powder off me when these two Reb cavalrymen showed up on the other bank, watering their horses after that battle, I guess. They must have made it through Gregg's line, then couldn't get back to their own lines. Anyway, they wouldn't surrender. When they fired at me, I shot 'em both. One took off, and one came at me with his saber. But I got him before he got me. Horse went down, threw him in the water. He would've drowned if I hadn't waded in and hauled him out. Funny thing about the two of those fellows. They'd been the ones tried to slash Newt Hunt on the road above Harper's Ferry back in November of '62—remember? I'd shot one of them before he could strike Hunt—the fellow had jug ears and red hair, and damned if he wasn't there at Rock Creek, and I shot him again! I suppose both of 'em got taken prisoner. I know the one fell in the creek did. Don't know if either of them survived."

Luke Kellogg mused to himself as he remembered these details, now vividly refreshed by being back where it had happened. "There was a gold locket lost in that scuffle, and I aim to go down to Rock Creek at sunup and see if I can find it. I noticed the water level's down quite low, with this dry spring weather they've had down here. Should make it easier to search, if anything can be found after twenty years. Remember how damn hard it rained on the Fourth back in '63? Couldn't find anything in the high water then, that's for sure."

"Always thought they were right when they said the cannonades of July 3 caused that rain. Never heard so many guns firing for so long in all my years in the army." Corbett nodded his head to emphasize his point.

"Maybe so, but that shelling we took at Chancellorsville in May of '63 was pretty bad," Shipman countered.

"Only because we were under it! No, this was worse. I doubt that many guns had ever been fired at one another before or since."

The old battle veterans' discussion continued well into the night, stimulated by the large jug of Maryland rye whiskey one of the men had brought to the room. Luke Kellogg had excused himself early and gone to his room. He wanted a good night's sleep. He had a premonition that the day after would be a very demanding day.

He rose at 4:00 A.M., dressed in an old shirt and pants, and pulled on the sturdy leather boots he'd brought along. Luke walked downstairs, through the deserted lobby, and out the door to the sidewalk. There, waiting for him on the Gettysburg Square, was the buggy and driver he'd engaged.

"Chilly mornin' for July, ain't it sir.?" The black man greeted Luke with a smile.

"Just feels pleasant to me, Isaac. You'd sure not much like our upstate New York July mornings, if you think this is chilly!"

Isaac Watson laughed. "Yessir, that's fer sure. I don' want t'git no further north than right here! An' you can call me Ike. Ever' body does."

Watson drove his buggy around the center of the square and out Baltimore Street toward Evergreen Cemetery, Culp's Hill, and Rock Creek. The two men fell into easy conversation.

"You here in the war, Mister Kellogg?"

"Yes, up on Culp's Hill. Got pretty hot for a while. Were you in town at that time, Ike?"

"Yessir. Bad times, those were. Them Virginia boys tried to take a lot o' our folk back with 'em, callin' 'em 'contraband.' Dragged me with 'em back almost to the Potomac River, but some o' our cavalry attacked the Rebs an' we ran off in the ruckus. Walked back up t'Waynesboro, then over the mountain back here t'home. Lucky! My cousin James, his whole fam'ly been here free fer two generations. They took 'im back an' sold 'im down Miss'sippi. Never heard no more of 'im. You know there's Confed'rates meetin' here this week too, camped over on the Battlefield Association land, jus' past the cemetery. One o' them wanted t'hire me t'drive 'im t'Rock Creek this morning. Mean lookin' fella. Red hair, jug ears. I done tol' 'im I was booked up. Not me. Not any o' us. We don' want nuthin' t'do with those fellas." Isaac shook his head emphatically. The memories of the Confederate Army's treatment of Pennsylvania's free blacks as mere chattel was still strong, even after twenty years.

Luke had been half-dozing, listening to Watson's soft voice, lulled by the gentle swaying of the buggy. The mention of the redheaded man with large ears brought him to full alert. "You say a man tried to hire you, to take him to Rock Creek this mornin'? Red hair an' jug ears?"

"Yessir. Big nose, too. Mean-lookin', like I said."

"Would you believe I met that fellow in the war? Twice? Shot him in Virginia, shot him here, at Rock Creek! Now he's back here lookin' for the same thing I am, I'll just bet. It's worth an extra dollar if you'd get this horse of yours into a trot, Ike. I want to be at Rock Creek at sunup, and before that Reb vet gets there!"

"Yessir, Mr. Kellogg!" Watson cracked his whip above the horse, which broke into a brisk trot. At Luke's instruction, he turned the buggy left up a narrow lane off the Baltimore Pike, shortly after they'd passed the imposing brick archway of the Evergreen Cemetery Gatehouse on their right.

"This'll be fine, Ike. I'll walk from here down to the creek. Here's the money we agreed on, plus an extra five dollars. Thank you for the ride, and for the information. I'll walk back to town when I'm done here. Good day, and God bless!"

Watson turned the buggy around and disappeared up the Baltimore Pike toward town. Luke walked carefully in the light of false dawn, through the brush, stepping over fallen trees, carefully avoiding putting a foot in the varmint holes, walking around the big boulders, until he got to the bank of Rock Creek. He followed the bank until he spied the distinctive cross shape formed by four boulders in midstream. In his mind's eye he saw the cavalryman's black stallion lying dead on the bank, those boulders midstream behind it. Looking about, he saw the sycamore and found the faint mark he'd blazed on its trunk twenty years before.

Well, here we are again, Private Kellogg, Luke thought to himself. He knew from his boyhood days at Skaneateles Lake that the best time to see clearly below the surface of the water is early morning. This was the time to be here. He was gratified to see that the water level in the creek was far lower than it had been on that day twenty years ago. Then he realized the mill dam had virtually disappeared, and that Rock Creek was down into its original bed. The mill pond downstream didn't exist anymore! Conditions couldn't be more favorable for finding a gold locket in a wide creek. Now he just needed to wait for sunlight. It was brightening noticeably, and very soon the sun rose brightly above Wolf's Hill, sparkling off the rippling water of Rock Creek.

Luke peered down into the water carefully as he walked slowly along the bank. Conditions were indeed good. He could see small minnows swimming over crystalline pebbles scattered on the bottom around the base of the large boulders in the stream. But where was that locket? He continued his search. Looking, looking, but not yet seeing what he wanted to see—the yellowish sheen of gold metal burnished by years of water flowing over it. *I must be patient,* he thought, *and not get discouraged. I'll take all day if need be. The fellows can march in the Fourth Parade without me.* But deep down, he knew his chances would dwindle as the sun rose higher and surface glare obscured the view.

The chances of anyone finding a lost gold locket in the water of Rock Creek, especially twenty years after it entered the water, are slim to none. Luke understood that. Under normal circumstances, he'd never have embarked on what was clearly a wild goose chase. But his circumstances weren't normal. His family was lost to him. His business had lost whatever appeal it once held. If ever he was going to take a flyer in his life, this was the time. So here he was, gambling that he'd find this locket, and that it would lead him to the stash of gold. His carefully-timed persistent search was about to pay off. For the rising sun's reflected rays flickered and shone off something yellow barely under the surface of the water between two large rocks, just as Luke looked that way.

"Eureka!" yelped Luke. He waded into the shallow water, bent down, and with a gentle tug freed the oval object from its rocky trap. The locket! It had been wedged securely in a rock crevice against the current for twenty years, burnished by the flowing water, shining in the sunlight.

Luke rubbed it off on his shirttail, held it up to the light, and saw the markings scratched on its smooth back cover. It was clearly a map of some kind. Just as the cavalryman had said! Now he'd hurry back to the hotel with it, get his things together, and set out for Mercersburg to continue the final stage of his search. Undoing his wide leather belt from the first two pant loops, Luke slipped the locket carefully into the pocket cleverly hidden on the inside of the belt, reinserted the belt into the loops, buckled it, and began to walk along the bank, heading back toward the Baltimore Pike.

Hearing a noise behind him, Luke turned his head to look. A sudden blow to the head sent him face-first into the water. Trying to fight his body's need to pass into unconsciousness, trying to get his head up out of the water, trying to fight off the hands that were rifling his pockets, vaguely realizing that his last glimpse was of the red-headed, jug-eared rebel soldier, Luke gave out one last loud shout, then passed out.

Chapter Twenty-Three
Rock Creek

July 4, 1883

Well before dawn, Lathrop Emmons awoke in his tent at the Confederate Veterans' encampment on the grounds of the Gettysburg Battlefield Association. The three other veterans in his tent were snoring loudly. They'd had a big night last night. The warm July night around the campfires, the jugs of whiskey passed around, the stories shared, the lies told, the fallen mourned—all had taken their toll on these men reliving the awesome experiences of their youth. They were content to renew memories and enjoy the company of old comrades, and slept peacefully. Lathe was driven by different demons—revenge, greed, survival, all aggravated by his mean nature, which was rarely apparent but always submerged just beneath the surface, waiting to manifest itself.

Lathe had been angered the previous day when he found that none of the black drivers would take his custom and used one flimsy pretext or another to turn him down. "Shoulda taken 'em all an' shipped 'em t'Mississippi or Alabama back in '62 or '63! That woulda knocked the sass out of 'em!" Every other conveyance had long since been booked by other veterans. "T'hell with it! I'll walk over there. Shoulda just ridden one o' my own horses up here, then I wouldn't have t'deal with these damn nigras anyway."

And so this July Fourth morning, Lathe had dressed in the dark, pulled on his boots, and set out across the fields, crossing the Taneytown Road and more fields, past the Evergreen Cemetery, across the Baltimore Pike, through the trees, and past the boulders to Rock Creek, where he waited for the sun to come up. His memory was still mighty hazy. The wound he'd suffered there at the hands of that damn Yankee, then the twenty-year amnesia following his later injury, had fuzzed up the details of where the locket had fallen. He just hoped that the sight of Rock Creek would revive his memory of Rock Creek, 1863.

In the dark, Lathe had wandered too far north, almost to the base of Culp's Hill. As the false dawn improved visibility, he realized his error and began to carefully work his way downstream, skirting swampy areas, cursing at the thorn bushes that seemed to be everywhere, tearing at his clothes and, worse, his face and hands. As the sun rose, he realized that downstream he could see boulders in the stream in the shape of a cross, an image that he seemed to recognize. Then he saw the man, wading in the shallows, bending down, then standing up, holding something.

"Damn! That damnable Yankee found it! Well, good. He saved me the trouble. All I need do now is go take it offn him."

Emmons bent down, picked up a cannonball-sized rock, and crept forward through the undergrowth. As he closed in on his quarry, his foot crushed a dry branch with a loud crack. The man turned his head toward the noise. Lathe leaped forward, the rock raised high, and brought it down with a sickening thud on the man's skull.

Lathe looked at Luke Kellogg's inert body on the ground and recognized the face as that of the man who'd shot him on the road to Charlestown back in 1862!. "Why, that's the Yankee sunuvabitch shot me twice!" Greed overcame revenge as Emmons rifled Luke's pockets without success. "Where'd the bastard put that damn locket?" Lathe turned Luke over, practically ripping his pockets off trying to find it. Luke stirred, then tried to get up.

"Where's the locket, you damned Yankee? I saw ye with it! *Where in hell is it?*" Overcome with anger, Emmons was shouting the words.

Half-dazed from the blow, Luke still managed to shout in an equally loud voice, hoping to attract someone's attention before this half-crazed man could deliver a last, fatal blow.

"You're insane, man! Ike! Get help!" Luke knew Ike Watson was long gone, but knew his only chance was to make his attacker think he was about to be discovered.

As Lathe hit him one more time, Luke let out a fearful yell and fell into the water.

Lathe was torn. What to do? His initial impulse was to just hold the man under until he was drowned, then strip him and rip his garments apart until the locket was found. A swiftly following thought said, *No, bring him around, then beat him until he tells you where he has the locket.* And the next thought said, *Don't risk being discovered here. Wait for a better chance to get it from him.* Trying to sort it out, he began muttering to himself.

"What if someone heard that yell? They'll be over here in a minute. And a Southerner up here won't get much but trouble. Seen that already! Let the bastard drown. I'll get well away 'til I'm sure nobody's comin'. I kin come back here in a bit an' search his body. If anybody catches me then, I kin say I was comin' t'see what the shouts were about an' found him drowned in the crick. An' if worst comes to worst, I think now I kin figger another way t'locate that gold o' Lewis's."

With that, Emmons ran back through the trees and underbrush, around the boulders, until he reached the path back to the Baltimore Pike. As he ran across the road, he saw the black buggy and heard the driver call out. Lathe ran harder, into the cornfield where he stopped and crouched behind the stalks, hidden from the road.

Chapter Twenty-Four
Baltimore Pike

July 4, 1883

Doctor Harry Hartman rode slowly up the Baltimore Pike, dozing as the first rays of the July sun turned the eastern sky to pale rose. The horse walked slowly as the buggy gently swayed, adding to the doctor's drowsiness. After a long night of waiting in the brick farmhouse, he had finally delivered a whimpering whelp of a ruddy son to an exhausted Minnie Shultz. Now, worn out from a long day of dealing with patients' problems and a night of obstetrics, Doc Hartman was only too happy to nod off and let his faithful horse Jim navigate back to the stable behind the house and office on Gettysburg's Baltimore Street. But at the edge of sleep, the doctor was rudely brought back to full alert by the sound of a man's tortured shout coming from somewhere toward Rock Creek. Jim reared up and snorted, Doc pitching forward and catching himself on the buggy's dash. "What the Sam Hill?" As his mind flushed its cobwebs, he saw the running figure that had startled Jim dash into the cornfield to his left. Pulling on the reins, he brought Jim and the buggy to a halt at the side of the roadway.

"Stop! What are you doing?"

The gray-clad figure ignored his challenge and vanished into the woods beyond the rows of knee-high corn. A quick look around told Doc Hartman they had come well past the stone bridge over Rock Creek. He turned the horse a few hundred yards up the little lane to the right. He hopped down from of the buggy and walked quickly down the path to the creek's edge, following the tracks the running figure had made. Reaching the muddy bank, he followed the footprints upstream until he saw a man lying facedown in the water. He grabbed hold of the man's legs, pulling him back up onto the bank. Quickly bending down and pressing his fingers on the carotid artery, the doctor felt the weakest of pulses. He reached in the mouth, cleared the tongue, pressed on the abdomen and pushed the water out of the lungs. He was rewarded by a face-full of spit-water from his coughing, hacking, newfound patient. Wiping his face with his shirtsleeve, Doc saw the blood oozing from the hair on the side of the head. A quick look told him the blood flow wasn't arterial, not an immediate life-threat.

He gave the figure a quick looking-over with his professional eyes. The man was in his late thirties, in good shape to all appearances. That probably helped him to stay alive until the lucky accident of Doc Hartman's finding him. He sat up groggily and looked at his rescuer. "Who're you?"

"I'm a doctor. Can you stand up?"

"I think so." But as the man attempted it, his knees buckled. Doc caught him under the arms, put the man's arm around his shoulder, and half-carried, half-dragged him back through the underbrush to the buggy. With a combined lifting and pushing, the doctor got the man up onto the floor of the buggy between seat and dash, then clambered up and shook the reins. "Yo, Jim, home—hyaah!" Breaking into an unaccustomed trot, Jim swiftly covered the miles past the battlefield, through the Steinwehr Avenue intersection, and up the two blocks to the doctor's solid brick house on Baltimore Street. Doc tugged on the reins to slow Jim and turn him into the alley that led to the stable behind the house. His elderly stableman Frank emerged from a little shack in the backyard, rubbing the sleep out of his eyes. "Late night, Doc!" he muttered, but quickly grabbed Jim's bridle and led him to the little granite step used by folks to alight from a carriage. But the doctor had already leapt down and was tying the reins to the hitching post.

"Give me a hand here, Frank." Frank was momentarily startled at seeing the man on the floor of the buggy. He pulled himself up the left side, bent his knees, hooked his elbows under the man's shoulders, and eased the man forward. Doc grabbed the ankles and together they got the man down onto the ground.

"Go get my stretcher." Frank propped open the back door to the office, went in, found the stretcher in the closet, and hustled back with it. Together, Frank and Doc set the prone man on the stretcher, carried him into the office, and slid him off onto the examining table.

By the time Doc had finished cleaning and bandaging the wound, the man had returned to consciousness, moaning softly. "Where am I?"

"I'm Doctor Hartman—you're in my office in Gettysburg. You've had a nasty blow, but with a little luck you're going to be all right. You'll have quite a headache. These pills will help. Can you tell me who you are?"

"My name's Luke Kellogg. I fought on Culp's Hill with the 137th New York in '63. Here for a reunion."

"Well, Mr. Kellogg, someone nearly killed you this morning. I found you facedown in Rock Creek, unconscious. You would have drowned."

"I owe you my life, Doctor. I won't forget this. But let me pay you for what you've done. I'm all right now, no need to bother you further."

"Not so fast, Mr. Kellogg. This is attempted murder! I'll have someone go down to the courthouse and ask the sheriff to send a deputy over here—now!"

"I'm sorry Doctor, but I can't wait around for that. I'll take care of this myself." Swinging his legs down off the table, Luke pushed past the doctor and went out the back door, into the stable yard, and disappeared down the alley into the town.

Luke felt a little woozy, but walked as quickly as his wobbly legs could take him. Even in his shaky condition, it took only a few minutes to walk the length of the block, go around the corner of the square, cross York Street, and get into the Hotel Gettysburg. In the lobby, he plopped down into a leather chair and signaled to the bell captain. "Please have a boy go tell Ike Watson I'd like to hire him an' his buggy for a few days."

Henry Shipman and several other veterans came down the stairs and saw their friend Luke sprawled in the chair, head bandaged. "What in Hades happened to you? You find a way to fight the war over again? That's not a gunshot wound, is it? We saw more'n enough of that here twenty years ago! Don't tell us you got into it with one of our Virginia friends."

Luke grinned at them, feeling a bit sheepish. "Well, I'd ask you all to keep it to yourselves, but yes I did, as a matter of fact. Early this morning I went back over to the place on Rock Creek where I shot those two Virginia troopers. Damn if one of 'em didn't show up an' crack my head, with a rock, I guess it was. He must have come for the United Confederate Reunion, went back to the creek just as I did and saw me there. Must have decided it was a good time to pay me back for what I did to him back in '63. I fell into the water and probably would have drowned. Lucky for me, a Doctor Hartman was traveling up the Pike, heard my shout and came to check. Must have scared the rebel off. Anyway, he took me back to his office up the street here and patched me up. Saved my life! He wanted to call the sheriff on the man, but I asked him not to, then left to come back here. No point in rehashing it all again."

"Well, I think you should get the sheriff on him! He tried to kill you, Luke! How do you know he won't try it again?"

"Look. I shot him once in Virginia—remember that time on the road when we were in camp at Bolivar Heights, above Harper's Ferry? And I shot him again, here, in '63. He surprised me this time. He won't surprise me again. And if he tries anything, I'll shoot him again! I've got my pistol up in the room, and this time I'll make sure I carry it on me."

"Well, dammit, man, just watch your back and be careful. I gather you're not planning on marching in the parade. You know we're supposed to form up in just a few minutes." Shipman was concerned for Luke, but he also wanted to make sure his Binghamton contingent was in place, on time, and looking sharp.

"No, I'm feelin' better by the minute, but I don't much feel up to marching. You fellows will have to carry the honor of our 137th without me. I won't be going back to Binghamton with you, either. As it turns out, I've had some unfinished business come up that will likely keep me down this way a few more days. But thank you. Henry, for convincing me to come to this reunion. I've enjoyed being with everyone. I'll send a telegram home to my brother-in-law that my return's been delayed. Just don't tell him about my little fracas this morning. No need for him to be concerned." Luke gave his comrades a last salute, then stood up and walked gingerly up the stairs to his room.

A bellboy carried his bags down to the lobby while Luke held onto the stair rail and carefully walked down, step by step. Ike Watson was waiting for him in the lobby. "What you have in mind, Mister Kellogg? I came right over when the boy tol' me you wanted t'hire my rig again. Oh my goodness, what happened to yo' head?"

"Happened down at Rock Creek, Ike. It's a long story—I'll tell you while we ride. If you're agreeable, that is. I need to get over the mountain to Chambersburg, then on to the town of Mercersburg on the far side of the valley. And I'd like to get there this afternoon. Can you take me?"

"That's quite a trip. More'n forty mile, I'd guess, each way. But yessir, I'll do it for you, Mister Kellogg. We'd best get out quick, though. The parade starts soon an' we'll not get through town once it starts." Watson picked up Luke's valises and took them to the buggy, Luke following behind fast as he could manage. He knew he'd get to his destination faster if he hired a horse and rode, but he knew that was more than his banged-up head would allow.

"I'm deeply indebted to you, Ike, for doin' this for me. I know you're passing up good business here in town, and I'll make sure you're properly paid." With Watson's assisting arm, Luke hoisted himself up onto the buggy's seat. Watson climbed up next to him, and, as the bands began to play, shook the reins and started up the horse with a cry of "hyaah, Blossom!" Taking a series of back alleys and side streets, Watson took the buggy to his house off West Middle Street, threw a few clothes in a bag, and hopped back up beside the waiting Luke. The sound of a band playing "Marching Through Georgia" made Luke think of the years after Gettysburg, when the 137th New York fought at the battle of Lookout Mountain, at Resaca, and then marched to the sea with Sherman. He reckoned the men at the Confederate encampment would be less than thrilled by the sound of that particular tune.

Chapter Twenty-Five
Caledonia

July 4, 1883

Ike Watson's buggy went up the hill of West Middle Street and at the crest turned right on Seminary Avenue, past the buildings of the Lutheran Theological Seminary, and then headed west on the Chambersburg Pike.

The sun was high in the sky, and the day's heat was getting uncomfortable. Luke loosened his collar, tried to ignore the throbbing of the wound on his head, and shifted in his seat to try to find a more comfortable position. Watson held the reins loosely, letting the horse set its own pace. He glanced at his passenger, who was dozing, apparently done in by the events of the morning. As they passed through Cashtown, a welcome breeze came down off the mountain. Luke stirred, adjusted his position, and dozed off again. He slept the whole way up the eastern slope, across the summit, and woke only as they descended into Caledonia. The hemlock and pine forests made the ride cool, shady, and pleasantly scented. "This sho' is pretty country through here," remarked Watson to his awakening passenger.

"Yes, it is," answered Luke. "Reminds me of the pine woods on the ridge by Bear Swamp up in Cayuga County when I was a boy."

Looking around, he savored the loveliness of his surroundings, and contrasted his pleasure at the sight with the terrible agony the retreating Confederate wounded must have undergone passing on that same road, in the dark, in a drenching downpour, that night twenty years ago. He said a silent prayer for his fallen comrades of the 137th New York, and for the souls of all the brave men and women who'd suffered through the terrible agonies of civil war.

Luke mused as he gazed at the changing views. *In one sense, the war seems like it was only yesterday, while in other ways it seems like a lifetime ago. So much has changed. Twenty years ago, I wasn't much more than a boy, and had only the basic concerns of getting a hot meal and a little sleep, staying alive, and of course, saving my country! Since then I've had a beautiful wife and lovely children—all gone. Now I'm back to those same basic concerns—food, sleep, an' staying alive. Well, I'm jolly well gonna find that gold, too. Not that I need the money, Lord knows. But it's a challenge. And I'm hanged if I'll let that jug-eared, redhead Reb have it without a fight!*

He loosened his belt until he was able to extract the locket from its hidden compartment. Holding it to the light, he scanned the marking on the back. He tried to decipher the meaning of the lines etched onto the back of the gold case. A circle, not much bigger than a dot, on the left. A straight line leaving the circle to the right. An irregular line crossing it headed down, then bent up and went down again on the right. Another irregular line coming up from the bottom left, joined the first in the middle. Stubby vees, facing each other, set across the upper bending line, near the joining of the two irregular lines. Another line starting at the near right edge of the straight line, going downward slanting slightly to the left, crossing the higher bending line at the twin vees, then crossing the lower irregular line, with an x inscribed on the right just after it crossed.

Watson had been paying close attention to the road during the descent from the South Mountain summit. Now as the road leveled off, he looked over at Luke and saw the locket in his hand. "Nice locket. Somethin' special?"

Luke grinned at him. "I suppose it is, Ike. It almost cost me my life this morning." He proceeded to give Watson a brief summary of his encounter with the Virginian, without divulging the real significance of the locket. "The cavalryman I shot back in '63 lost it in the water at Rock Creek, an' I happened to spot it this morning. I guess the redheaded Reb thought since it was his partner's, he ought to have it 'stead of me."

"What's the marks on the back, Mister Kellogg?"

"I think it's some kind of map, but I can't place anything on it."

Seeing that Watson was very curious but much too polite to ask his passenger to show it to him, Luke decided there was no harm in having Watson take a look.

"Recognize anything, Ike?"

"Cain't say as I do. Don't think it's nowhere 'round Gettysburg. But sho' appears like maybe the circle's 'sposed to be a town...the straighter lines roads, an' the crooked ones are mebbe cricks, d'ye think?" Watson turned the locket around in his hand, looking at it from other angles, as if some magic script might appear in the proper light.

"I was thinking about the same, Ike. I think once we get to Mercersburg, someone might recognize and be able to identify the cricks and roads. Hope it's not too dark when we get there."

"What 'zactly are you lookin' for, Mister Kellogg?"

Luke figured he'd better tell a little white lie here, so as to not expose Watson to any problems if the Reb redhead should reappear. *What he doesn't know won't hurt him,* he thought to himself.

"I'm not exactly sure myself, Ike. But I'm sure interested in finding out. Especially if it's these markings that made Johnny Reb so hot to get his hands on this locket."

Still examining the locket, Watson spotted the tiny catch, and pressed it. The front popped open, and Sally Keefer's long-concealed note almost fell out and was lost, but Watson caught it in time. He handed the locket and folded slip of paper to Luke. Luke was momentarily taken aback—something about the image of the girl in the tintype reminded him of his own Julia as a young woman. "Why, it's a picture of a girl, Ike. Pretty girl, too. Must be his girl back in Virginia. But wait, I heard him say he got it from a girl in Chambersburg. A Virginia rebel with a girl in Pennsylvania? Seems strange. Let's see what this paper says." He carefully unfolded the little scrap, and read from the fading ink: " 'To Jack with all my love, Sally'."

Thinking for a second, Luke continued. "He'd told me back after I'd shot him he was Sergeant Jack Lewis of the Fourth Virginia. He must've met her when Stuart made that lightning raid into Pennsylvania in '62. Jack Lewis was some quick worker!"

"D'ye s'pose she's still in Chambersburg, Mister Kellogg? Wouldn't it be somethin' if we was to see her there this afternoon?"

"Yes, it would be quite a coincidence, Ike. With this tintype, we know what she looked like twenty-one years ago, but odds are she looks more than a little bit different today. And who knows if she's still alive, or living there still? No, not too likely, Ike."

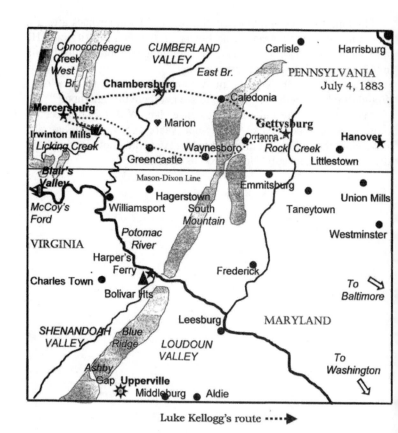

Luke Kellogg's route ⋯⋯▶

Lathrop Emmons route ⋯⋯⋯▷

From Gettysburg to Irwinton Mills, 1883

Chapter Twenty-Six
Gettysburg

July 4, 1883

Lathrop Emmons crawled behind the rows of young corn until he figured he was well out of sight of the buggy on the road. He turned, listened, but no one was following him. He was able to slip back to the roadside unseen. He watched one man help another into the buggy, then climb up and drive the horse and buggy up the pike toward Gettysburg.

"Damnation! He's pulled that Yankee out o' th' crick an's takin' 'im off in that buggy. An' that locket with 'im!"

Emmons trotted along the road, well behind the buggy, keeping out of sight of the driver. His fury drove him forward.

He'd been so close! Yesterday he'd gone off on his own, telling the others that he wanted to revisit the spot on Rock Creek where he'd been shot twenty years ago. He left their tour omnibus at a point on the Baltimore Pike that he thought was close to his destination, then walked east through the woods until he reached the west bank of Rock Creek. For several hours, he wandered up and down the bank, peering into the water, reaching down under rocks that might have a chance of hiding a locket. Eventually he became frustrated and gave it up.

"Damn it all! Maybe th' light's not right. I bet I'd see better with th' first rays of the sun shinin' across. That'd be more likely to shine up a gold locket so's I could see it."

Standing on the bank of the creek across from the place where he and Jack Lewis had been shot, Lathrop stood, head bowed, and offered a silent tribute to his friend. "Jack, ye were th' best friend a fella coulda had. I wish I coulda found yer locket, and I wish ye could somehow lead me t'that gold ye hid. But I'll keep tryin'. I wish somehow I'd get another crack at that damnable Yankee that shot us, t'pay 'im back fer what he done."

Now, as Emmons watched the buggy moving briskly up the hill past Evergreen Cemetery's arched gatehouse, he only regretted that the payback hadn't been final. But now he knew for sure the Yankee shooter had indeed overheard Jack Lewis telling Emmons about the locket and the hidden gold. The locket had been found, and had to be somewhere in the Yankee's possession. Emmons had no intention of giving up. One way or another, he was going to get Lewis's treasure. But maybe he didn't need the locket. Surely the Yankee wouldn't leave Pennsylvania without continuing to search out the locket's prize. If Emmons could just follow him, he might be led to the hiding place.

Making sure he couldn't be seen by the buggy's driver, the Virginia veteran strode quickly along toward town. He watched the buggy crest Cemetery Hill and disappear down the hill into town. He reached the top of the hill and looked down Baltimore Street toward the square. The buggy was several blocks away, nearly obscured by people milling about making final preparations for the big Fourth of July parade. He caught just a glimpse of the buggy as it turned right and disappeared between the buildings. As he passed each side alley and street, he looked for any sign of the vehicle. At High Street, he found what he was looking for—fresh horse droppings.

He walked slowly down the sidewalk for about fifty feet—there in the yard across High Street, behind the big house on the corner, was the black buggy that had interrupted his work at Rock Creek!

Emmons crossed the narrow street to the yard and the buggy, when an older man emerged from the back of the house and headed to the little barn at the end of the yard.

"How-do, sir," Emmons offered. The older man caught the Southern accent, turned, and replied, "Doin' right well, thank you. You a Southern veteran here for a reunion, I expect."

"Yessuh, Virginia Cavalry, United Confederate Veterans, camped on the battlefield lands down off Taneytown Road."

"You boys'll be marchin' in the big parade in a short while, won't you?"

"Not me. Got me some important bus'ness to tend to 'cross the mountain past Chambersburg. Any idea where a fella might hire a horse?"

"Why, just over there, cross the street, at Buehler's Livery Stable."

"Well now. Couldn't get much handier'n that. Nice lookin' buggy. Local fella own it?"

"Why this's Doc Hartman's buggy. This here's his office and home. He just come back from deliverin' a baby. I helped him with a poor veteran he picked up off the Baltimore Pike down by Rock Creek. Said he'd been hit in the head by some fella with a rock, tried to rob him. Went through his pockets 'fore he got scared off. Didn't get nothin', though. Nasty bump on his head size of a goose egg. Doc's in there fixin' him up right now, I expect. Hasn't asked me to fetch the sheriff yet, but I expect he will shortly. Sheriff's only just down the street. Fella's a GAR man, down from New York. Said he fought on Culp's hill, had been lookin' at where he shot a couple of Reb cavalrymen back durin' the battle. Fella named Kellogg. Reckon he'll be tellin' all his boys 'bout how he took a rock at Rock Creek!"

Emmons took it all in. Inwardly, he laid out his plan: *So the Yankee's a New Yorker named Kellogg. Good to know. Make it easier to follow his trail, if I have to. I'd still like to git that locket off o' him if I git the chance. But I reckon I'll hire a horse an' ride on t'Mercersburg, see if someone don't recognize the description o' the place as I remember Lewis tellin' it.* Still feeling a smoldering anger at not having gotten the locket, but beginning to develop more positive feeling about finding the gold, Lathrop went back across High Street to the livery stable.

He found there were only a few horses left, most having been hired by veterans to ride in the Fourth of July parade that was now forming up. With the practiced eye of a long-time horse breeder, he examined each animal carefully. "None o' these nags'd git me to South Mountain, let alone git up over it t'the Cumberland Valley an' back," he complained to the liveryman.

"All we got. Take 'em or leave 'em. 'Course, if you was to ask me politely, and was willing to pay me a bit extra, say five dollars, I'd let you take one of these and ride it out to Bream's horse farm, by Orrtanna, just this side of the mountain. You can leave my horse there and hire one of his. They're too high-spirited for most folks in town, but they're young and strong, and like a good hard ride."

"Now that sounds some better. I heard o' Bream. S'posed t'have good stock. All right, I'll do it. Here's money fer yer horse, and five fer you. Now tell me how t'git t'Bream's place."

After listening carefully to the man's instructions, Emmons mounted up and rode back to the Confederate Veterans encampment. He made his excuses for not staying, then packed up his gear and loaded his saddlebags behind his saddle. He'd brought along the saber he'd kept after the war, thinking that if he rode in a parade, it would mark him as the Black Horse Trooper that he had been. Now he thought it might serve a more useful purpose, and hung the scabbard from the saddle as he had done for those three years of the war.

Looking more and more like the Black Horse Trooper he'd once been, he rode back into town, skirting the parade route until he reached Middle Street and followed it west to the Fairfield road. Just before reaching Fairfield, he turned right on the road that followed the base of the mountain toward Orrtanna. When he reached the Bream farm, he turned down the lane, crossed the little creek, and rode into the yard by the stables. Half an hour later, after a careful examination of the proffered animals and some intense negotiations with Jacob Bream, money changed hands and the veteran cavalryman rode out the lane.

With a spirited animal, a sorrel named Pickett, under him, Lathrop felt the old familiar blood-rush of the excitement of battle, and with it the complete recall of Jack Lewis's last words to him: "I hid them sacks in a springhouse close by a stone bridge over a crick east of the town...."

Now he felt certain he'd find the place where Lewis hid that gold, even without the map on the locket. He'd damn well recover it, as reparations for all his losses in the war and since that had been inflicted on him by these smugly prosperous Northerners. And if that New Yorker Kellogg got in his way, well, his saber had cut his way free from Yankees many times before!

Emmons had looked at several maps before he'd left home and had determined that the shortest route to Mercersburg was through Monterey, up over the Blue Ridge Summit, down into Waynesboro, then west on the pike to Greencastle and on to the outskirts of Mercersburg.

He paused for a minute at the summit of South Mountain before descending. The view out across the broad Cumberland Valley was so beautiful this Fourth of July that it demanded Emmons's attention. Rolling hills green with growing corn and timothy, fields gold with ripe wheat, and the blue Tuscarora Mountains in the distance. The beauty must have triggered some small voice of conscience in the deep recesses of his soul. He began to consider what he was about to do. For lack of a better listener, he began to talk to his mount.

"Here I am, hot on th' trail of a fortune in gold, hidden by my truest friend in th' war or since. I honor Jack Lewis's memory. Twenty years ago at Rock Creek he tol' me t'tell his cousin Will t'git th' gold an' give it t'his wife Sally. So, by rights, I guess it's her gold, an' if I find it I should give it t'her...but why din't Jack ask me outright t'git th' gold an' git it t'Sally? Din't he trust me? That don't sit too well, horse. Now Will's long dead, an' if anybody's gonna git that gold, it's gonna be me! By rights, I s'pose it really ain't Jack's gold. It's some poor fella in Pennsylvania that's out his coins. By now prob'ly no one remembers whose it was. So why should Sally git it, anyway? I'm th' one doin' the work here, riskin' jail, prob'ly, fer bustin' that Yankee Kellogg this mornin'. Sorry Jack, don't mean you no disrespect, ol' friend, but that gold's gonna be mine."

The horse just snorted and pawed the ground as if to say, "Whatever you say, boss. Let's just not stand here all day thinking about it, let's get on down the mountain!"

At Waynesboro, Emmons headed west on the Greencastle Pike, passing up a chance to eat at the Anthony Wayne hotel, not wanting to risk the New Yorker beating him to the gold. In Greencastle he watered the horse, but again passed up food, this time at the Antrim House. His only hunger now was for gold! West of that town, he crossed over the east branch of the Conococheague on a stone arch bridge, but saw nothing other than the creek and bridge that matched Jack Lewis's description of the gold's burial place.

At the tiny crossroads community of Upton, in Peters Township, he stopped at the little store, tied up the sorrel horse to the railing in the side yard, and walked up onto the porch. Two old men leaning back in their chairs, smoking cigars, looked him up and down. "We ain't seen the likes of a fella like you for near twenty years. You been to some battlefield havin' a reunion? Antietam? Gettysburg? You weren't one of them West Virginia ruffians come with McCausland an' burnt Chambersburg, were you? Must say, though, that's a fine lookin' sorrel you're ridin'."

"No, I warn't with McCausland. I was at Gettysburg with Stuart, though, back in '63. Come up from Virginia to a reunion. Twenty years now. Come over here lookin' fer somethin' a friend lost when he was with Stuart in Mercersburg in '62, 'fore I jined th' cavalry. Hired that nice sorrel from a fella name o' Bream at Orrtanna, other side o' South Mountain. Raise horses m'self in Upperville, and yer right, th' sorrel's a fine animal." Emmons was on his best behavior. He knew he'd never get any useful information from the locals if he came on too strong. It wasn't that long since men like these had lost horses, livestock, who knows what to the many raids and invasions that touched these border communities. To get himself in a proper frame of mind to gain their confidence, he tried to envision these two Pennsylvania farmers as two of the old men that sat around the general store in Upperville, and talked to these fellows as he would them.

"I'm not as familiar with these parts as I oughta be. Sold some horses south o' here in Maryland, but never quite got up t'here. Name's Emmons—Lathe Emmons. Was with th' Fourth Virginia, Black Horse Troop, back in '63." He hoped neither of these two men knew about the mean-spirited horse he'd foisted off on a farmer named Gipe over in Shady Grove, some ten miles east of where they were seated. When he didn't see them register any recognition of his name, he figured they didn't know about the dealings with Gipe.

"M' friend lost a locket fordin' a crick near a stone bridge somewhere's east o' Mercersburg back in '62. When his wife heard I was comin' up this way, she asked me if I was willin' t'look fer it some. 'Pears it was his wife's mother's, then hers, an' she give it t'him as a good luck charm. He lost it here in '62, an' his luck ran out in '63 when he got shot at Gettysburg. His poor widow'd give most anythin' to have it back, so I tol' her I'd try to find it. 'Fraid it's a little like that ol' needle in th' haystack." Emmons figured these little lies would get their sympathy and enough help without betraying his real objective.

Earl Stickell spit over the railing and nodded his head in agreement. "You got that right. The needle might be easier to find, truth be known. You know how many stone bridges there are over the cricks 'round here? I bet I can count up at least ten 'tween Greencastle and Mercersburg, south of the Pittsburgh Pike an' north of the National Road. You better have some time t'go lookin' in creeks 'round all them bridges. An' you know how many floods we've had since the war? Why, that—locket, you said it was? It could be a mile downstream from where it went in by now. Yessir, you got yourself a chore!"

Surprisingly, Emmons was encouraged in spite of the old fellow's pessimistic warnings. If he could get the location of the likely places down on a piece of paper, he figured he could eliminate some right off, and focus on the most likely ones. And of course he was no longer looking for a tiny locket in a large body of water—he was looking for a springhouse, easily seen from the road once he got to the right spot. He went into the store and bought a sheet of paper and a pencil that he took back out on the porch. "Now, let's see if ye kin draw me a map enough to locate these here bridges yer talkin' 'bout."

Half an hour later, Lathrop rode off with a map showing bridges, mostly crossing the east or west branch of the Conococheague Creek. He ignored for the moment the ones on the East Branch. He figured he'd start first with the ones closest to the town of Mercersburg, then work east. He just hoped the New Yorker was still so hurting from his morning's attack that he would not be able to do any searching yet this afternoon. Otherwise, with the aid of the map on the locket, Kellogg had a real advantage over Emmons.

Emmons picked the stone bridge over the Conococheague that lay just a mile east of Mercersburg on the road to Church Hill. He rode through the fields on the east bank, but there was no lane, no ford, no springhouse—just the steep rocky wooded bluff on the west bank. From there he rode east, turning south at the Church Hill Crossroads.

When he reached the Greencastle Pike, he saw the stone bridge that carried the pike over the Conococheague. There was a large stone house on the bluff west of the creek, by a road that led south, with old log cabins to the right. "Well, damn! These hypocrite Pennsa'vanians had slaves up here, too!" Emmons shook his head, but continued his searching for springhouses and creek fords. The large, prosperous Hiester farm had a springhouse, of course, but there was no ford around. And besides, this just didn't feel right to him. So he turned back and headed east once more.

Chapter Twenty-Seven
Mercersburg

4:00 P.M., July 4, 1883

It was just past four o'clock when Isaac Watson's buggy came down the hill past the tollhouse into the small town of Mercersburg. The wide main street was flanked by handsome houses—some brick, some native white limestone with slate roofs. Their side walls abutted, except for an occasional gated walkway leading to the back yard, and the town's alleys, laid at intervals of six or seven houses. Each house had a large yard in the back with room for smokehouses, washhouses, outhouses, chicken coops, gardens, and stables. Some had shop buildings where the homeowner conducted his trade. Alleys running behind the properties gave access for their horses and buggies or carriages.

If there had been any damage from the war, it didn't show. The town looked prosperous, although in a frugal way—these people were German and Scots-Irish, thrifty folk who took pride in the neat, well-scrubbed appearance of their homes. Near the town square, the Diamond, the first-floor front rooms of the buildings were given over to shops, tea-rooms, and other such commercial enterprises needed by the surrounding farming community. People were walking on the flagstone and brick sidewalks, shaded by the large buckeye trees that grew by the curbs.

Reaching the Diamond, Watson reined Blossom to a halt in front of the Mansion House, the large three-story hotel and tavern that stood on the southwest corner of the square. Luke Kellogg climbed down, passed through the little knot of men standing around and talking on the front steps, and entered the tavern. He sat down at a table and drew a sketch of the map from the locket. Then he stood up and walked over to the bar where the barkeep was bantering with two older men nursing their beers, whiling away the afternoon.

"Afternoon, gentlemen. May I trouble you for some information?"

The bearded barkeep set his rag down on the bar and turned his attention to his questioner. He noted the bandage on the fellow's head but chose not to say anything about it.

"How do, stranger—what can we help you with?"

"I'm looking to find a location nearby. I only have a crude map that was given to me, and I know it's of a location near Mercersburg. Could you look at it and see if you recognize it?" Luke handed his sketched map to the barkeep.

He looked at it, turned it sideways, looked at it again, turned it back and studied it. "Jake, Herb, this mean anythin' to you?"

The two men leaned forward and looked at the paper lying on the bar. A long discussion went back and forth between the three men. Finally, Jake said, "Herb, go get Owen Witter to come in here oncet."

Herb got up, went to the door, and talked to one of the men standing on the tavern's porch. The man turned and joined Herb walking back to where Luke waited at the bar. "This here's Owen Witter, mister. He can prob'ly tell you what you got here."

"Mr. Witter, my name's Luke Kellogg. I'm trying to identify exactly where around here this map represents. I'd be grateful for your help."

"Lemme look at it here." Witter peered at the map then said, "'Pears to be out by my place, past Hiesters on the Greencastle Pike. This here wiggly line's the Conococheague Creek, 'cause that's just the way it bends around down there. See here, this's 'bout the only place where it flows north, goin' past the mill. An' this's where the Licking Creek joins it. Them two arrowheads's gotta be the stone bridge over the

242

Conococheague. Right there by Irwinton Mills. This here straight line at the top's gotta be the Greencastle Pike."

"See, Joe, I told you it was out by Irwinton Mills past Owen's place." Jake looked proudly at the barkeep.

"You was right, Jake," Joe admitted.

"Well, thank you, Mr. Witter, an' all of you gentlemen. Please allow me to buy you all a round." Luke laid a five-dollar bill on the bar. Joe drew beers for Jake and Herb, drew a short one for himself, and poured a double shot of good bourbon for Witter. The men hoisted their glasses to toast their benefactor.

"Don't you want somethin' for yourself, Mr. Kellogg?" Joe poised himself to draw the man a beer.

"Thanks anyway, but I've got to get going while I've still got some light. One more thing—how do I get there?"

"Easy. When you leave the Diamond, go on up Main Street two blocks to the Lutheran church, an' take the left fork on to the Pike. 'Bout two mile out, you cross the Conococheague at Hiester's. Keep goin' a mile or so 'til you see a brick schoolhouse on the right. Turn right there. That'll take you past the mill, over the stone bridge to where they're buildin' the wooden covered bridge over the Licking Creek. Then you're there. Good luck with whatever it is you're lookin' for."

When Luke went back outside, Watson was removing the feedbag, having first let Blossom drink her fill from the public watering trough there in the square. The two men climbed up onto the seat, Ike gave a "gee-up!" call to Blossom, and the buggy moved on up the street. Two blocks later, Luke saw an imposing brick church on the corner. Its slender spire rose from a central bell tower flanked by two large arched wooden doors.

"There's the Lutheran church. Turn left here, Ike."

Blossom easily drew the buggy down the hill to where Fayette Street joined Main, then labored a bit pulling it up the hill to the tree-lined town cemetery. Just past the burial ground, the tollgate marked the transition to the Greencastle Pike. A few miles of ups and downs over the rolling hills, past solid brick farm houses and large Pennsylvania bank barns brought them to the large stone bridge crossing the Conococheague by the Hiester mansion, set well back in the trees on the west bluff overlooking the creek. A mile or so later, Luke saw the brick one-room country schoolhouse coming into view on the right.

"Make a right onto the lane past that schoolhouse, Ike. We're almost there!"

Luke's senses were on full alert. His body seemed to throw off the tiredness of his long day, the long ride, and even the aching of his head wound. After twenty-one years, Jack Lewis's hidden gold would see the light of day!

Watson and Blossom didn't have such an enticing prospect before them to give them a new surge of energy. Both horse and driver were tired, and just wanted to rest. When, after another half a mile's travel, the grist mill appeared on the left, Watson sighed in relief and Blossom whinnied as if she recognized a little rest was finally at hand.

Chapter Twenty-Eight
The Final Battle

6:00 P.M., July 4, 1883

It was almost six o'clock as the buggy neared Irwinton Mills. The sun was getting lower in the sky out toward Cove Mountain. Luke realized that Watson and his horse both needed a good long break.

"Pull in here at the mill, Ike. Let's get some feed for Blossom, some cold water for ourselves, an' see if we could get some supper."

Inside, Luke introduced himself to the miller, a man named Jerry Witter, made arrangements for feed for the horse, and inquired about where he could obtain a meal for himself and something for Watson. Witter called to his mill hand to get a sack of oats and take it out to Watson. Then the miller introduced Luke to the man who'd stood unnoticed back in the maze of slapping belts and whirring shafts and rumbling machinery when Luke walked into the mill.

"Mr. Kellogg, this is Constable Jim Duffield, my neighbor from down the crick a ways. I've asked him to stay to supper, an' you're welcome to join us. My man Ted Price's wife'd be happy to have your man join them, too."

Luke watched the dark-skinned, muscular mill hand carry the sack of oats like it was a feather out to the buggy and the waiting Ike Watson.

"Pleased to meet you, Constable. And thank you, sir, for your dinner invitation, which I gratefully accept. I know Watson will be equally grateful. We've had a long day."

James William Duffield, though his duties as constable were secondary to being a full-time farmer, looked every inch the lawman. His erect posture, firm-set jaw, and piercing blue eyes sent a clear message—no mischief would be tolerated in his jurisdiction. He fixed his stare at the New Yorker.

"Come far, have you? What brings you here?"

Luke returned the constable's appraising look. He had expected he'd need some plausible reason for his presence in this unlikely place, but he wasn't about to entrust the full story to an unknown country lawman.

"I was with the 137th New York, Twelfth Corps, at Gettysburg. Came down for the GAR reunion an' agreed to track down something for a fellow veteran. He was a cavalryman who had come through here in '62 chasing after Stuart's raiders. Said he lost a locket fording a creek. Meant a lot to him. His wounds later crippled him and so he asked me yesterday if I'd come look for it. I want to get to it now while I've still got some light."

"You want some help? Looks like you've already had a tough time today, from the looks of that bandage on your head."

"Thanks, but no. I'm fine. Just an accident early this morning, clambering over the rocks at Culp's Hill." Luke hoped the story sounded plausible, and the constable seemed to buy it. The miller gave the New Yorker a sympathetic shake of the head.

"Well, just be careful. An' don't be too long. The missus'll have supper on the table at seven-thirty. Roast pork, sweet corn, new potatoes an' peas, an' strawberry rhubarb pie for dessert."

"Well, I sure don't want to miss any of that!"

That settled, Luke went outside and down by the millpond where Watson was still fishing.

"Ike, I assume you talked to the mill hand, Price, when he brought out the oats? I've arranged for you to have supper with his family this evening. I'm going to walk on down the road and look for that spot on the map."

"Price already done invited me, Mister Kellogg. I sho' am ready for some fine cookin'! First lemme drive ye t'that new bridge they been tellin' us about."

"Thank you, Ike. I am a bit tired. But then you come right back here and let Blossom rest. I can walk on back, just fine."

So once more Blossom drew the buggy over the camelback limestone bridge across the Conococheague, taking the left fork to the new covered bridge that now carried the lane over the Licking Creek. Luke reached behind the seat, picked up his knapsack, and stepped down. He waved as Watson turned the buggy around, heading back to the mill and an eagerly anticipated supper to stop the growling of his stomach.

Meanwhile, back on the Greencastle Pike, Lathe Emmons turned his mount south on a narrow lane. The men at the store in Upton had told him about a stone bridge past the place still called Irwinton Mills. He figured he'd stop at the mill and inquire.

As he dismounted and was about to enter the mill, he saw a black man fishing down by the millpond dam. Had he looked closer, he would have seen it was the same black man who'd denied him a ride in Gettysburg. But Emmons ignored him and went into the mill.

"Afternoon, fellas. Might there be a ford over a crick near a stone bridge on this road?"

"Well damnation if you ain't the second veteran been askin' 'bout the stone bridge this afternoon. Except you're a Confederate, it 'pears, an' he was Union. Nice fella, from New York, he said. But yeah, there's a ford over the Licking Creek, where the road takes a left fork. 'Course now they're buildin' a nice wood bridge there. Good thing, 'cause that ford gets near impassible in the spring sometimes." The miller looked at the obviously agitated Emmons with a frown. "You all right? What's goin' on here?"

"Never you mind that. How long ago'd he leave here?" Emmons knew he'd been beaten to the gold. Now he just needed to catch up with Kellogg and get it away from him. And this time he'd make sure that damnable New Yorker wouldn't be any further trouble!

"'Bout fifteen minutes, half hour most." The miller responded as Emmons rushed back out the door. "What're you fixin' to do, fella?" But Emmons was already on his horse and galloping down the road toward the stone bridge.

The Virginian had paid no attention to the man lounging in the shadows, listening intently. Constable Duffield came over and spoke to the miller. "Somethin's goin' on here, Jerry. First that Union vet from New York comes in here. Then this Confederate vet takes off out of here like his pants are afire. I think maybe I ought to ride over toward the new bridge and see what's goin' on. Can't have them two refightin' the war over again, can we?"

"Well if they are, Jim, you was in our army—that oughta tilt the odds in the New Yorker's favor!"

"That was almost twenty years ago, and that war's long settled. Except maybe for these two. I'll just go make sure they don't hurt each other refightin' old battles." With that, Duffield went out the door and mounted up, riding down the road across to the new covered bridge.

Luke took in the beauty around him—pale green willow branches dangling over the creek and purple wildflowers carpeting the banks, the water burbling over the rocks under the bridge. But his eyes and attention quickly focused on the springhouse dug into the side of the steep hill above the creek.

His heartbeat quickened as he climbed up the steep grassy slope to the springhouse. This had to be it! The main farmhouse, sited just beyond the crest of the hill, was out of sight of the springhouse. With any luck, he'd not find himself interrupted by an irate farmer looking to chase a thief away from his cream and butter.

Luke pulled the wooden latch peg out of its hasp, swung the little door open, bent low, and went in. He let his eyes acclimate to the dim light. Behind the stone-lined spring pool, he saw covered pails of milk and crocks of butter set on straw. He moved to them, set them aside, took a trenching tool out of his knapsack, and began to dig. It was more like scraping. Only two inches of dirt were removed when he hit metal. A little more scraping, and he saw that this was a lid, probably just like those on the pails he had set aside. Prying with his fingers, he got the lid off and reached in. Leather sacks! He carefully lifted out one, then another, heavy bag. He loosened the drawstring on the neck of a sack, reached in, and drew out a gold coin. Luke looked at the double eagle only briefly before slipping it in his pocket and retightening the sack's drawstring. The leather bags were put into his knapsack, the lids put back on the buried cans, the dirt pushed back, the straw returned on top, and the milk pails and crocks restored to their places. The whole process had taken less than fifteen minutes, he reckoned. Pulling the heavy knapsack behind him, the trenching tool in his hand, he duck-walked out under the low ceiling and out the door into the evening light. He pulled the door shut, replaced the peg in the hasp and half-walked, half-slid down the grassy slope toward the creek and the bridge.

Elated at having recovered a long-lost treasure, Luke walked into the south end of the covered bridge just as a man on horseback entered the north end. Even in the shadows of the covered bridge, Luke could see the man's jug ears and prominent nose, and the saber scabbard hanging from the saddle. Him again!

"Damn you, Kellogg! You got here first!" Lathrop Emmons spurred his horse and jerked his saber from its scabbard in one smooth motion.

Luke had no time to pull his pistol from his knapsack. He shoved the heavy pack to the side where it lodged under a low timber, then held his small shovel ready to deflect the saber's blow.

Emmons raised the saber high, then swung it down at this man who had frustrated him so many times in the war and since. With a loud echoing clang that reverberated inside the wooden structure, the saber bounced harmlessly off the shovel. Luke had managed to parry the saber and frustrate Emmons once again.

In his mind, Emmons remembered the battle at Westminster, in Maryland twenty years ago. He remembered the Federal soldier who had killed Lieutenant Murray, and how he had avenged the lieutenant's death with a savage saber thrust into the officer's blue-coated assailant. It was time to give this New Yorker that same taste of cold steel!

"You Yankee devil, this time yer gonna die!" The thoroughly enraged Emmons swung his saber with slashing blows, again and again, his horse wheeling and stomping on the wooden planks in a deafening clatter of hooves.

"You tried t' kill me twice, now it's Lathe Emmons's turn to kill you, Kellogg!"

Luke ducked and parried. The saber struck the trenching tool, and bounced off the timbers of the bridge as Luke hugged the sides, looking for an opening, a chance to get his pistol, a chance to put a bullet into this crazed horseman.

"Take the money, for God's sake, man! It doesn't mean anything to me. Just stop tryin' to kill me! The damned war's long over, you fool!" Luke was getting desperate, losing energy rapidly. This deadly struggle was more draining than anything he'd experienced in the war, and now he was twenty years older. Still, the will to win, to survive, was strong as ever, and he continued to fight back as best he could.

Emmons turned his mount once more, trying to pin Luke to the wall where he could deliver a fatal blow, but the New Yorker dodged aside. "I'll git the money, a'right. But yer gonna die first!" Emmons began to swing his saber wildly, just hacking away, not worrying about whether he'd hit Kellogg or stabbed him. He knew the man on foot couldn't hold out much longer. Emmons was tired, but knew that the wound from his morning attack would be tiring the New Yorker more.

A hard blow from the flat of the blade smacked Luke on the left shoulder, breaking his collarbone. Luke stumbled, regained his footing, and staggered out the south end of the bridge.

"Got ye now, Yankee!"

Emmons charged, saber raised, to deliver the final, fatal, blow. As he swung the saber, Emmons heard a shot ring out. He felt searing pain, then black nothingness. The heavy blade, with a momentum of its own, cut into Luke's right shoulder and fell clattering onto the stones of the bridge abutment. Luke collapsed in a heap at the side of the road, just avoiding the murderous hooves of the cavalryman's horse as it thundered past.

Emmons swayed in the saddle as his horse charged up the road. Halfway up the hill, he fell from the saddle and was dragged fifty feet before his boot was released from the stirrup. Freed of the weight of its rider, the sorrel horse came to a stop at the top of the hill. It stood there, exhausted from the day's riding and now fighting.

Constable Duffield lowered his carbine. He had been just in time to stop a killing. Duffield rode on through the bridge and reined to a stop by the fallen New Yorker. Quickly dismounting, he bent down and felt his pulse.

"Well, Kellogg, you're alive! But that's a nasty cut on your shoulder. Bet the bone's broken, too. Rest easy, now, while I bandage that cut."

The lawman took a long red bandanna from his back pocket that he kept for use as a dust mask on long dusty trips. Tearing a strip of shirttail from Luke's clothing, he folded it into a compress and held it tightly over the wound to stanch the flow of blood. He was able to get the bandanna under the armpit and tied up over the cloth compress. Taking off the New Yorker's belt, he hooked it around the bandanna at the compress, then passed one end down under the left armpit, bringing it back up and buckling it, thus forming a crude harness to hold the compress securely in place. Then he moved Luke to lie down on the flat capstone of the abutment, head down, as the town doctor, Doc Brownson, had taught him years ago, to keep the flow of blood to the head against the onset of shock.

That done, Duffield walked up the road to where Emmons lay sprawled and unmoving. Once more, Duffield checked for a pulse. There was none. Emmons had fought and lost his final battle. The Virginia cavalry veteran had tried to kill one last Yankee infantryman, and had been foiled by another. And somewhere in the beyond, Sergeant Jack Lewis would be reminding Lathrop Emmons he had told him, long ago, to have more respect for the deadliness of the Yankee soldier.

The constable removed the dead man's belt and carried it back to where Luke lay. Duffield removed his own belt and hooked the two together. Gently he slid the belts under Luke's back, buckling the ends over the chest to secure his arms to his sides and immobilize the broken collarbones.

He looked up the hill to where the dead man's mount stood in the road, and whistled. Surprisingly, that's all it took for the sorrel to turn and walk down the hill to the waiting Duffield. The constable stroked the animal's neck and spoke soothingly until the horse was completely calm. He hoisted the dead man's body up and laid it across the saddle. He mounted his own horse, then taking the sorrel's bridle led him back to the mill, where a startled Jerry Witter helped lift the body off and lay it in the shade.

"Get the man's driver, quick! The New Yorker's hurt bad."

Watson came out onto Price's cabin porch, a half-eaten leg of fried chicken still in hand. "What's happened?"

"Get your rig and head to the covered bridge. Quick now! Your man's been hurt. Bad. We got to get him into town to the doctor."

Watson tossed the chicken leg aside and ran to the buggy. He quickly got Blossom away from her grazing and back into harness. The refreshed horse trotted down the lane toward the bridge with Duffield following, then leading the way to the abutment where Luke lay.

When Watson arrived, Duffield was leaning over the wounded man, who was just regaining consciousness.

"You're badly hurt, Kellogg, but you'll make it. Your attacker's dead. We're going to take you to Doc Brownson in Mercersburg. He's a veteran like us, and a damn good doctor. He'll take good care of your injuries. Later you can tell me what this was all about. For now, just rest easy."

Ike Watson and Constable Duffield carefully lifted Luke into the buggy. Ike saw the knapsack on the planks against the side wall of the covered bridge, picked it up, and set it carefully behind the seat of the vehicle. *Sho' seems heavy!* he thought to himself. *Wonder what he got in there?*

The sun had descended behind Cove Mountain by the time the buggy passed Fairview Cemetery and descended the hill into Mercersburg. Constable Duffield had ridden on ahead and alerted Doctor Brownson that he had another war casualty coming in. That done, he took the dead man's body to the undertaker.

Ike Watson had been told where to go, and he tied up Blossom at a hitching post outside the doctor's office on Main Street. His office was in the house the doctor had grown up in, a large imposing stone house with broad porches on the corner of Oregon Street. The doctor met the buggy outside, with two men who helped him when called upon. These men had a stretcher onto which they carefully transferred Luke and then transported him into the doctor's treatment room, where they laid the patient on the examining table.

252

Brownson carefully removed Duffield's crude harnesses from Luke's torso. Luke winced in pain when the doctor gently pulled the bloody improvised compress from the wound. Brownson looked at the ugly gash and the white exposed collarbone the saber blow had laid bare.

"A nasty blow, Mr. Kellogg. During the war, this one might well have been fatal. In those days, we thought putrefaction of the wound was necessary to healing. But thanks to the English doctor Lister, we know better now. I use carbolic acid solution to clean my instruments and your wound, to prevent the infection we now know is the real killer from most wounds. It saddens me to think of the men who died in the war from our ignorance of infection." The doctor began to swab out the wound with cotton cloth liberally doused in the carbolic acid disinfectant solution.

"So we'll clean out your wound, sew it up with a drain in it, and it will heal nicely. Can't do much with the collarbones except bind you up and keep you down until the bones heal. You had better plan on spending some time with us here in Pennsylvania, Mr. Kellogg."

The next morning Luke awoke feeling groggy. He looked up and saw Dr. Brownson.

"How do you feel this morning, Mr. Kellogg?"

"Not so well, though I am a little hungry. I'm just lucky to be alive. The constable saved my life out there on that bridge. And I'm lucky he got me to you. But do you suppose I might have something to eat? I've had nothin' since yesterday noon."

"Of course. I'll have Mrs. Crum bring you breakfast shortly. Right now I want to examine the wound." Dr. Brownson removed the bandages, examined the now sewed-up wound, and checked the drain.

"Well, so far you seem to be healing nicely. I am concerned about damage to your ligaments, however. There's an excellent surgeon in Chambersburg that I'd like to examine you. He's had success in repairing such damage. Your man can take you there this afternoon, as long as he drives slowly. I'll give you some laudanum to take along in case the pain returns."

"Where is my driver? I hope he found accommodation for himself an' his horse last night. I'm afraid I've got him into more trouble than he bargained for!"

"Apparently he's staying with the Watson family on Fayette Street. Relatives of his. He said he'd come by this morning to see about you."

While Luke was fed a hearty breakfast, he and Brownson talked about their war experiences and found they had both been at Chancellorsville in the spring of '63. Luke quickly concluded that he'd been extremely fortunate to be under the care of a man who was not only an obviously fine physician, but also one who had been a fine officer. Brownson was equally impressed by this New Yorker who was taking his injuries in stride, who had managed to defend himself successfully until Constable Duffield arrived on the scene and ended the attack.

As Mrs. Crum was taking away the empty breakfast dishes Duffield entered the bedroom and stood by the bed.

"I'll leave you two alone, if you like." Brownson made a move toward the door.

"Please stay, Doc. I'd like to ask Mr. Kellogg what happened and why, and I'd like your opinion as to what we do about it now."

Luke looked up at the man staring intently at him. "It's kind of a long story. Goes way back to the war, in '62."

Luke recounted the history of his encounters with Emmons. He told of the time he shot Emmons when the cavalryman tried to saber-slash Newt Hunt at Bolivar Heights. He told of the encounter at Rock Creek on the third day of the battle of Gettysburg, when he shot the rebel cavalryman near sunset. He left out the part about overhearing the rebels talk about hidden gold. He told about how the two of them had the chance encounter early yesterday morning again at Rock Creek, and how Emmons had become enraged and attacked him with a rock. He told how he'd been saved then by a Doctor Hartman who was passing by. He continued the story of how he'd kept a promise to a fellow veteran to look for a missing locket near the mill at Irwinton. Luke expressed the surprise he'd felt when he saw Emmons on horseback at the end of the covered bridge last evening.

"I couldn't believe he'd follow me all the way from Gettysburg. The man really was intent on killin' me. Can you believe it? The war over for nearly twenty years an' he still harbored that much hate? I tell you, Constable, if you hadn't come along I'd be dead now. I owe you my life."

Duffield and Brownson looked at each other, then at Luke. Duffield spoke first.

"That's some story. Just glad I happened to be at the mill when he showed up. The man did have a wild look to him. Something told me I'd better follow along and see what he was up to. But you did quite a job fending him off before I got there, Kellogg. Now we have to decide what to do with all this. At the mill, the man said his name was Emmons, from near Upperville in Virginia. We'll need to hold an inquest, then we can ship the body back to his family. Could be quite messy. Do we need all that, Doc?"

"Well, I looked at the body early this morning. Your shot didn't kill him. He died when he fell from the horse. Broke his neck. So we could just put him in the coffin and send the body back to Virginia. I can report the death as accidental due to a fall from a horse. No inquest needed." Brownson looked at Duffield to gauge his reaction to the suggestion.

"Thanks, Doc. Sure simplifies things. Unless you want me to make a case of attempted murder, Kellogg?" Duffield turned to Luke.

"No, Constable. Let's let it end here. Call it the final battle, and let it go away quietly. The man's family will have enough to deal with, without thinking his last act was an attempt at murder. He must have been a difficult man to live with, carrying that much hate around with him. No, let's let them have some peace. I'm grateful that you both are willing to let sleeping dogs lie, as it were." Luke lay back, tired after the intensity of the discussion.

"Then it's agreed. I'll say nothing about this in any official reports, and you'll report it as accidental death, Doc. Just glad we saved your life, Kellogg. Now get some rest. You've had one hell of a Fourth of July!"

Luke had just started to doze off when Isaac Watson was shown into the room by Mrs. Crum.

"How you feelin', Mister Kellogg?"

"Tired, but I'm alive, Ike." Luke remembered the sacks of gold he'd stuffed into the knapsack. Where was the knapsack now?

"Ike, did you happen to see my knapsack?"

"Oh, yessir, I did. Layin' on the bridge. Picked it up an' set it in the buggy. Right where 'tis now. Mighty heavy. Thought it might be important, so I took it in and kep' it by my bed las' night. Stayed with my cousin Alexander Watson's family las' night, so I knowed it'd be safe, whatever's in there."

"You didn't look, Ike?"

"Nossir. Didn't figger that was any o' my bus'ness."

"Well, thanks. It's valuable, an' I appreciate your caring for it. I intend to see you're well paid for all this trouble I've put you through, for all the help you've given me." Luke paused to rest, then spoke again.

"The doctor here wants me to see a surgeon in Chambersburg. I was hoping you'd take me there this afternoon. Is Blossom sufficiently rested to make the trip? Then afterward you're free to get back to your Pauline, before she gets too concerned about you running off with some sweet young thing."

Ike grinned at him. "Oh, she knows no sweet young thing'd mess with a ol' fella like me. 'Sides, she knows I like her cookin' too much! No, I'd be pleased t'take you on back t'Chambersburg, if you feel up t'it today. Otherwise, I kin stay here with Cousin Alexander 'til you feel ready t'go."

"Doc says the surgeon needs to see me before the shoulder heals up any more, case he needs to get back into the wound. We must go this afternoon. I'll just have to manage."

That afternoon, after a slow journey up and down the twenty miles of roads across the rolling hills of the Cumberland Valley, Luke Kellogg was lifted from the buggy and carried into Doctor Joseph Hudson's surgery in Chambersburg. Brownson had sent word ahead, and Hudson was ready. The surgeon examined the wounded man and quickly realized the damage was serious, just as Brownson had feared. But Hudson knew his business, and an hour later Luke lay in a recovery bed, still under the knockout effect of the anesthesia, his damaged shoulder ligaments carefully sewn together by the skilled surgeon. When Luke awoke, groggy but lucid, Dr. Hudson was leaning over him.

"Good. You're back with us. All went well. In a month or so you'll be good as new. You'll need to stay here in town for a while to recover, and so I can monitor the healing. There's a woman named Barnes who has a boarding house on King Street. She's very capable. Could have been a nurse. She has a room for you, for as long as you need. Your man is still waiting here. He wanted to make sure you were all right before he went on back to Gettysburg. He can take you to the Barnes house now, if you feel up to it. I've got you properly strapped up, so moving won't tear the stitches or separate the broken bones." The doctor had confidence in the compassionate, confident woman who had served him as a recovery nurse on numerous occasions in the past. He knew Sally Barnes could restore this New York veteran to full health as quickly as was humanly possible.

Chapter Twenty-Nine
Chambersburg

July 5, 1883

The late evening shadows were deep when Ike Watson helped a groggy Luke Kellogg into the Barnes House.

Mrs. Barnes and Watson steadied Luke on either side as they slowly made their way into a back room off the main entry hall, where a comfortable bed awaited. With great care, they managed to get him onto the bed between crisp white sheets. Despite the lingering warmth from the July afternoon, the high-ceilinged room felt cool, with a refreshing breeze from the tall opened windows at the back of the house.

Seeing the feverish beads of sweat on her patient's forehead, Mrs. Barnes left Watson alone with Luke for a moment, and returned with a basin of cool water and a cloth. Wringing the cloth out after dipping it in the basin, she laid it on Luke's feverish forehead.

"Oh my, that feels good. Thank you."

"Mr. Kellogg, I'm Sally Barnes. This is my boarding house. Dr. Hudson has engaged me on your behalf, to nurse you back to full health."

Hearing the name Sally, looking at her face, he recognized something familiar about this woman, but with the lingering effects of Dr. Hudson's sedatives clouding his mind he couldn't figure out what it was. He was exhausted, but knew he needed to thank his driver and send him on his way home.

"Ike, I'm worn out, dead tired, an' I know you must be too. An' anxious to get back to Gettysburg. I thank you with all my heart for what you've done—you've been the very best friend I could imagine in these few days. But you head on home. I'll be all right. I'm in good hands, as you can see. I owe you far more than I can tell you, Ike. Now go, while you still have a little light. And my best to your understandin' wife, Pauline."

"Mister Kellogg, you one special man. May God be with ye, sir!" Isaac Watson turned and, with a polite half-bow to Mrs. Barnes, left the room to return to Gettysburg, eager to share his stories with Pauline.

Alone now with her patient, Sally pulled up a chair next to his bed, reached out, gently removed the cloth from his forehead, dipped it in the cool water, wrung it out, and laid it back on his forehead.

"Are you hungry, Mr. Kellogg? Can I bring you some nice broth?"

Luke smiled wanly. "Thank you, but right now I'd just like to sleep. Thank you for taking me under your care." And he drifted off into a deep slumber.

Sally couldn't help herself. After more than twenty years of life without a real lover, she'd long since given up the hope of the fiery love she'd known, however briefly, with Jack Lewis. But now she was by the bedside of a man whose handsome appearance and strong body rivaled that of the memory she had of her first, secret husband. The long-forgotten tingle suddenly sprang back into her being. She chided herself for this—she had just met the man, and he was her patient. She had better tend to her proper business and ignore this romantic foolishness. With renewed purpose, Sally freshened the cloth on his forehead, then softly walked out of the room to leave the exhausted man to the healing power of sleep.

Next morning, the sun rose bright and shining on a clear summer day, lighting up the first-floor room of the Barnes House, rousing Luke Kellogg from his deep sleep. His shoulder hurt, his arms ached from their unaccustomed restraints. He twisted in the bed, trying unsuccessfully to find the elusive comfortable spot. Sally Barnes walked into the room carrying a tray of coffee, hot biscuits, eggs, and bacon. The aromas brought up a rumble from his famished stomach. Trussed up as he was, he still managed to wriggle himself into a seated position. Sally sat the tray across his lap. He looked at her smiling face and was struck by the similarity to his mourned Julia.

"Good morning, Mr. Kellogg. How's the patient feeling this morning?"

"Achy, and trussed up like a Thanksgiving turkey. But hungry as can be, and eager to dig into that wonderful breakfast you've brought me."

Severely limited in arm motion by his shoulder bandage and harness, he found it more than a little awkward to feed himself. Hunger overcame pride, and with a slight nod of his head, he accepted Sally's move to assist him. As the mouthfuls of eggs and bacon had their effect, he felt his energy returning, and his mind regaining its sharpness.

Suddenly it came to him. The picture of the girl in the locket. It was this Sally! Matured now, but just as lovely. Jack Lewis's wife!

She reacted quickly to his stunned expression as he stared intently at her. "Are you all right, Mr. Kellogg?"

"I'm sorry. I didn't mean to stare." He thought it too soon to tell her about the locket. He just wasn't prepared to deal with her likely reaction. After all, he had killed this woman's husband! There would be a time, later, to deal with that, if at all.

"You just remind me so of my dear departed wife, Julia, Mrs. Barnes. She was a lovely, caring woman, as you are."

Sally couldn't hide the blush that rose on her cheeks.

"You flatter me, sir. But I am sorry about your wife. I too am a widow. You must miss her."

"Very much." Luke went on to tell her about his attempt to distract his thoughts from the loss of his wife and children, how he had come to Gettysburg for the reunion.

"Surely you didn't get these wounds at the reunion?"

"It's a complicated story. It's enough to say that a Confederate veteran tried to settle an old score. But now that's over, and thanks to Dr. Hudson and you, I will soon put that all behind me."

Sally could see that her patient was again tired. She took the tray and left the room. Luke dozed.

When he awoke she was seated by his bed, smiling.

"Are you feeling better, Mr. Kellogg? Are you ready for some soup?"

"Not just yet, thank you. But please, call me Luke. And may I call you Sally?"

Again she felt that tingle. This time she would not suppress it. She was beginning to feel a much deeper attachment to her patient than she would have liked, but somehow this man was different—someone special. She began to feel an excitement, a sense that perhaps something good was beginning to happen. Something that had been missing from her life for all too long.

Luke saw the radiance in his nurse's eyes. He too began to sense that something promising was beginning here.

"I'd be pleased if you would call me Sally, Luke. I can tell your wounds are bothering you. Dr. Hudson gave me a bottle of laudanum for your pain. Shall I get it for you?"

"No, I don't want to get addicted to that. Saw too many like that in the war and after. I'll be all right with some rest and your good cooking, Sally."

In the next few days, nurse and patient settled into a comfortable routine. Each found themselves wanting to spend their time together, talking about small things, finding more and more common likes and thoughts, gaining joy in each new discovery. As their new-found friendship ripened, each realized it had gone well past a nurse-patient relationship, to their pleasant surprise.

One morning at breakfast Luke felt comfortable enough to tell Sally about his feelings for Julia, the depth of their love, the pain of the loss of their children, the difficult time of Julia's illness, the emptiness he felt after she was gone, his present search for a new life. Sally listened intently, drawn even closer to him by his willingness to share with her these innermost feelings. He had closed his eyes, seemingly drained by the recounting of painful memories. Sally bent down and lightly kissed his forehead as he dozed off once more.

When she brought him his lunch tray, Luke apologized. "I shouldn't have bored you with my past problems, Sally, but thank you for being a sympathetic listener. Now, it's high time I listened to you. Please tell me about yourself." Luke shifted again, trying to find a more comfortable position.

"I'm afraid you'll find my simple life rather boring, Luke. But if I can take your mind off your discomfort for a bit, I'll try to tell my story." Sally began her narrative. Luke leaned back against the bed's headboard, fascinated by her words, and found himself more and more deeply drawn to this lovely woman.

"I was just a young girl when my parents got the fever and died. Our pastor, Reverend Coldsmith, was a fire-and-brimstone preacher, but felt the responsibility to see that I had a roof over my head. He sent me to a farm family to live. They worked me hard, but I had food to eat, a small room of my own, and a few clothes to wear. I was only fourteen when this young man, not much more than a boy himself, came to the farm to deliver a horse bred at his farm in Virginia. He was so handsome, and so strong, and so polite. I fell in love immediately. Two years later, just before the war, he came back to the farm with more horses, and we managed to have a brief moment alone. At that time, I think we both knew we wanted to spend our lives together. When that awful war began, I feared I'd never see him again.

"One night, my master did a terrible thing to me, and I ran away, finding a family here in Chambersburg who took me in as a housemaid and then companion for their children. My mistress was very good to me. She taught me to read, do sums, how to behave in polite society. I loved the children. So in many ways I was very fortunate. But her husband exacted a high price from me. I was forced to serve him in ways no respectable young girl should have to endure. But I was young, and afraid, and had nowhere else to turn. So I submitted, and suffered silently. I went to church every Sunday with the family, and prayed that God would forgive me, and that He'd make my master stop his demands on me. For many months I thought God was ignoring me, punishing me.

"In the fall of 1862, my master and his family packed up hastily and left town, leaving me to watch the house. That evening Jeb Stuart's cavalry entered the town. My dear Jack Lewis was with them. He came to me that night, and we were married without benefit of pastor or witnesses. When he left, I gave him a locket with my likeness in it."

She paused. Memories of that one passionate night with Jack flooded back. For years, she had suppressed her desire for physical love. Now, sitting next to this handsome man, the need to relive that passion began to emerge.

Luke gave fleeting thought to telling her he had the locket, but reckoned it wasn't the right time, and kept his counsel. "I can't have been easy for you, being secretly married to a man on the other side."

"It was indeed a painful time. I constantly prayed for a swift end to the war, with Jack safely returning to me. In '63, when Lee's armies came through on the way to Gettysburg, I questioned the soldiers, especially the cavalry, to see if my Jack was among them. I was told his regiment would be with Stuart, and that no one knew where Stuart was. Later I learned that he had been east, in Hanover and Carlisle, before reaching Gettysburg. When the cavalry came through after the battle, I asked again, but was told Stuart was in Maryland. They told me there had been a fierce cavalry battle east of Gettysburg, but that Jack's regiment wasn't supposed to be involved in it. I could only pray that he had avoided the worst of it, and was safe.

"It wasn't until late August that I got a letter from a Mrs. Pettis in Virginia. Heaven only knows how that letter managed to reach me! I'd had only a few letters get through to Jack, and got only one from him, during the war. The mail didn't easily pass across the lines! Anyway, Mrs. Pettis had heard from Jack's commander that he'd gone missing at the time of that big cavalry battle. A while later she learned that Jack had died in a Federal hospital at Gettysburg. Mrs. Pettis said that Jack had told her of his marriage to me, and that she had promised to contact me if the worst happened. I cried myself to sleep that night. I felt that God was punishing me again. After a time, I came to realize that my marriage to Jack was a gift from God, a gift that I should be grateful for, even though our time together was so brief.

"For the next twelve months I went about my daily routine, deprived of the hope that the war would end, and Jack would come for me. Somehow I managed, though I felt the better part of me had died with Jack. Thank God my employer had long since stopped using me for his gratification. Had he continued, I think I might well have killed him and then taken my own life after I learned Jack had died.

"In July of '64, the rebels invaded again and fired the town. These cavalry were not like Stuart's men. Jack and his troop were gentlemen, in '62. These men of McCausland were brutes. Drunken savages. When they came to us, I begged them not to burn the house, that I was the widow of a member of the Fourth Virginia Cavalry. They just laughed, made rude comments about uppity eastern Virginia cavalrymen, said they were real men from western Virginia. They dragged us all out of the house and put the torch to the curtains and furniture. The house was gutted, along with most of those within two blocks of the Diamond. I feared for my safety with those crude unruly men about. The family fled once more to their mountain cabin. I was left with nowhere to go, and only the clothes on my back." Sally paused and took a sip of tea.

Luke could see she was fighting the emotion stirred up by these bitter memories.

"It must've been terrifyin' for you. I'm sure the town was in an awful uproar. What did you do?"

"There was a woman I knew who worked for an older widower, a very kindly gentleman, whose home was on King Street, on a block that had escaped the rebel's torches. Even the black clouds of smoke that seemed to cover everything somehow had bypassed that neighborhood. Not knowing any other place to go, I went to his house and knocked on the door. She wasn't there. She had fled to her family's farm west of town before the rebels got here. Mr. Barnes took me in, insisted I stay as long as I needed. As it turned out, I never left.

"Unlike all the other older men I had worked for, Henry Barnes was a true gentleman. He never made demands on me, of any kind, and especially none of those indecent demands I'd learned to dread. He showed me friendship, and that grew into love, of a sort. I gave him the respect he had earned and deserved. I suppose he took that for love, and asked me to marry him. Out of gratitude, and I suppose out of fear of what other fate I might otherwise come to, I accepted. We were married in the Lutheran Church in July of '65. I was twenty-one and he was sixty-seven.

"Of course, people gossiped for months about this, an old man in bed with a young girl. He didn't care, and ignored it. I cared, and was deeply hurt by some of the barely whispered comments from unthinking women when I was in the butcher shop, or the dry goods store, or at the bank or post office. The women in church were much more considerate of my feelings, but I'm sure they gossiped about it just as much when I wasn't within hearing. And I don't even dare to think about the comments made about me by the men in the barbershop. But I'd see them looking at me, in that way. I'm no stranger to those looks. I knew they were lusting, and envying Henry.

"I suppose it was a marriage of convenience for us both. I wanted a real home of my own, and he wanted someone to be with him, to care for him. And I did care for him, as a niece would a favorite uncle. I nursed him through the illnesses of his old age. For his last six months, when he was bed-ridden and half-paralyzed from the stroke that ultimately caused his death, I scarcely left his bedside.

"I was still a young woman. I longed for Jack, to fulfill me, to give me babies, to love me fully and completely, heart and body. But it wasn't to be. By day, I showed Henry affection and respect, and tended to his every need. By night, I cried myself to sleep, and dreamed of Jack and the one night we had together.

"In 1870, Henry passed away. He had left me everything. I was able to live reasonably comfortably. I take in a few boarders so that I don't have to draw on the investments left behind by Henry. I suppose many folks would say I have been a fortunate woman. By some measures, I reckon I am. I am proud of my independence, and I try not to take notice of the gossipers."

Sally paused. Luke had been watching her intently as she spoke, and had seen her expression shift from defiance to anger to pride to sadness, in turns.

"I think the men of Chambersburg, except of course for your late husband, have been fools, Sally, that they've allowed you to remain single. You have so much beauty, so much charm, so much strength in your character."

Sally blushed becomingly. "You flatter me, Luke, with such talk. No, it's not that I haven't had men try to court me, or try to get me into their beds. But I refused them all. It always seemed they wanted my money, or my body—to use me for their purposes. They all seemed to want to take, not give. They wanted me, but never genuinely offered themselves. I've been on my own too long now to let a man dominate me. I refuse to be used." The defiant look had crossed her face again, but now Luke thought he saw a deep sadness in her eyes.

Sally thought again of the boy she had given birth to—Jack Lewis's son. Elias. A boy who called Martha Baird "Mother," never knowing that Sally was his natural mother. She had her heart broken once more when the little boy died of fever in early 1867. She hid her grief, never letting anyone know of the secret she shared with the Bairds. Yet perhaps God had now offered her a second chance, however slim, to once more have a child, and this time a child she could truly call her own. Beside her was a man who had suffered the pain of losing his beloved children, who had borne the grief and sorrow as she had. He would fully understand the reason for her sadness. She revealed nothing to him about this, not wanting to reopen painful memories of his own children's deaths. Instead, he saw her expression shift to one of hopeful anticipation.

"I'm not yet forty, Luke. I may still have a slight chance of being able to bear a healthy child. And I long to be with a man I can love and respect, a man I can enjoy sharing my life with, to be a best friend as well as lover. Jack Lewis was the only man who ever met that ideal. I've never met a man in this town who could replace him, no disrespect to my dear Henry Barnes intended. Until now, I despaired of ever finding Jack's like again."

Sally put her head in her hands and tried to fight off the tears that now wanted to pour forth.

"Oh, Jack—I mean *Luke*! Oh my goodness, I am suddenly feeling confused. Luke, please forgive me for talking like this. You must think I am a weak, silly woman indeed!"

"No, Sally, I don't. I am deeply touched that you would mention my name with that of a man you loved so deeply. You are neither weak nor silly. Strong and clear-headed, determined and brave are the right words for you. There's no reason why you shouldn't have a man worthy of your love and respect- to have children with him. You are a beautiful woman, in your prime. Any man who wins your love will be a fortunate man indeed! I can understand your sadness for your past, your desire for a future that holds a new promise of happiness. Before I came to Gettysburg for this reunion, I felt that same sadness, that same feeling that time was running away- that I needed to make a move now, or lose the chance for a truly fulfilling future."

Luke was looking intently at Sally, to see if she was responding in the way he hoped.

She looked back at him, and smiled warmly. Now she realized why she had slipped and called him Jack. This man, here with her this brief time, while physically different, and from a different world in some ways, was so like Jack in the ways that mattered to her. She felt a warmth toward this man, a closeness to him, a building desire to be with him, always- an emotion she hadn't known since Jack was taken from her life. Suddenly she realized that his words, his countenance, his every gesture were genuine signs of his feelings for her.

"Luke Kellogg, you've turned my life upside down. I haven't felt this way in twenty years. I feel like a young girl again—giddy. I can't believe this is happening!"

Luke had rarely been given to impetuous action. Until now. It occurred to him that in a few weeks he'd be sufficiently recovered to leave the Barnes House and return to Binghamton. Back to an empty house and a dull routine with no future. Unless he did an impetuous act. Now.

"Sally, my dear. We're both adults, not youngsters anymore. Time is precious to us. Sally, I won't wait a moment longer. Will you marry me, Sally Lewis Barnes?"

"Oh yes, Luke Kellogg, I will, I will!"

She flew out of her chair to his bedside, bent down, threw her arms around him, and kissed him deeply. Their lips parted, and the kiss grew more ardent. He felt her ripe curves pressed into his chest and began to be aroused. The lingering aches in his shoulder were long forgotten, but when he automatically went to move his arms to draw her even more tightly to him, the restraining harness brought the reality of his condition swiftly home. As she broke the kiss, Luke laughed.

"It's a good thing you hugged me, 'cause I just realized I can't hug you back."

Sally smiled lovingly down at him. She felt full of desire for this man. The urges she had so long repressed, the urges she had not allowed herself to feel, came flooding back. She wanted this man to make passionate love to her, to reawaken the passionate response only

Jack Lewis had ever drawn from her. She looked at him, lying there on the bed, his arms trussed to allow his injured shoulders to heal. Once more, Sally had to repress her desire. She was no longer eighteen. Now she had the patience to wait, to savor the pleasure of anticipating a physical union with this wonderful man. She'd see to his healing, and then share the pleasure with him, the physical expression of love she yearned for.

Still, the urge to physically share her love demanded some form of fulfillment. Good nurse that she was, she knew exactly how to achieve it for them both.

"Luke, darling, how would you like me to give you a sponge bath."

Luke grinned. He knew this was a command, not a question.

"I would love that, Sally!"

She left the room, returning with a basin, a pitcher of warm water, soap, washcloth, and towel.

"Just relax, and let me do the work!"

With great care, her loving hands carefully removed his clothing. Slowly and lovingly, she began to wash his handsome body. Sally felt a sensual pleasure as her gentle hands passed the warm soft cloth over his chest and down to his muscular legs. Luke, injured though he was, found himself aroused. The sight of this lovely woman caressing his body awakened his instincts. She was no longer a nurse but a lover. His arousal was very obvious, and Sally laughed.

"Whoa, mister! You're not in any shape for any of that. Just be patient and heal."

He blushed and chuckled. "Believe me, I'm going to heal even faster, wantin' you as I do."

She put down the washcloth and toweled him dry. "Heal swiftly, my love!" She bent down and kissed him, and again he had to deal with the frustration of arms unable to enfold her as he returned the kiss.

"Now, Luke, I can see that you're tired. I'll close the curtains against the sunlight so that you can sleep, and heal. Sweet dreams, dear."

Sally moved to the windows and drew the curtains. In the dim light she gathered the pitcher, basin, cloth and towel and slipped quietly out of the room, listening to the deep breathing of her now-sleeping patient.

Luke woke up at 3:00 A.M. Restless, he moved his limbs as best he could, restricted by the shoulder harnesses. He lay there, his mind uneasy. *I've asked the widow of a man I killed to marry me. But she doesn't know that. Should I tell her? If I do, when should I do it? What if she learns of it from someone else? Would she ever be able to trust me? Could our marriage survive the shock? Would she marry me if she knew? I don't want to risk losing her.* "O God, help me here." He decided to leave it in God's hands, and soon fell back to sleep.

Luke woke again at seven o'clock, sunlight streaming into the room through the open window. Sally helped him to sit up in bed. "Do you want your tray in bed, or on the table by the chair?"

"I've been too long in bed. It would be so good to sit in a chair and eat normally again." Luke lowered himself gingerly into the chair while Sally set the tray down on a small table and moved it in front of him. She smiled happily at him as he ate ravenously, his appetite returning with a vengeance. While he ate, she straightened up his bedclothes and later took away the tray. When she returned, Luke asked her to sit down. He'd decided he had no choice. He'd have to tell her the truth, and trust her love was strong enough to accept it and move on with her life.

"Sally, dear, I had a sleepless night, trying to decide how to tell you this. When you said 'yes' you made me the happiest man in the world. But now I'm afraid I might lose you, when I tell you the truth about myself and your Jack."

"Luke, darling, I meant it when I said yes. I love you. Nothing you could tell me can change that." She reached out and took his hand in her own.

"Sally, I'm the one who shot Jack at Gettysburg. At Rock Creek."

She gasped, but didn't remove her hand. "How? Why?"

"I was alone. Two Confederate cavalrymen were facin' me across the water. I called for them to surrender. One fired, an' I fired back. His horse bolted off into the woods. The other charged me, saber raised as he came across the creek. I shot his horse. When it went down, he came up with his pistol aimed at me. I shot him in the shoulder. He fell in the water, but I pulled him up onto the bank. Other men were attracted by the shots, an' I turned him over to them. I didn't know what happened after that. Not until you told me did I know he'd died in the hospital there. I'm sorry, Sally. But you need to know that it was my bullet that ultimately caused his death."

Luke wanted to look her in the eye to divine her true reaction, how she felt in the depth of her soul, regardless of what her words might be. But she lowered her head and said nothing for what seemed to him to be an eternity. Finally, she looked up at him, her face showing her sadness. Her hand was gripping his tightly.

"Oh, Luke. I don't know what to say, what to think. I need some time." She gently took her hand away from his, stood up, and walked out of the room. For the rest of the day, she went through the motions, doing what was necessary for his care, no more, no less. Saying little in the process. Avoiding his eyes.

Luke felt his heart aching, only too aware of her coolness. He'd been honest. Done the right thing. Told her the worst. And it had cost them both the chance for happiness they thought they'd finally found. His appetite was gone. He ate little of the food she brought. When he took a nap, his sleep was fitful. That night, too, he slept badly, tortured by a renewed sense of loss. *My children, my wife, now Sally. Lost. Our chance for redemption slipping away.*

Chapter Thirty
Leesburg

July 9, 1883

Lathrop Emmons had died a sudden death, unforgiving and unrepentant in his hatred of Yankees. He died ignoring his duty as a friend to Jack Lewis, unwilling to share Jack's gold with his widow Sally. Choosing to seek gold rather than redemption, Lathrop Emmons had been denied both. Now his earthly remains were in a pine box, headed home for his widow to bury and his sons to mourn.

Carrie Payne Emmons waited apprehensively, watching the black-smoke-belching locomotive and its cars coming up the track. Steam hissing, the locomotive ground to a halt at the Leesburg station. Passengers stepped down and moved quickly into the shade of the station's overhang before dispersing in their various directions. In due course, the doors of the baggage car opened. Two black porters wheeled a large handcart over by the open doors and strained to hold onto the coffin lowered over the sill to them. Gently they laid the coffin on the cart and looked off in Carrie's direction.

"Miz Emmons, you be wantin' us t'load this here on yer wagon, I reckon?"

"Thank ye, porter, yes. Right away, if ye please."

She turned to the two strapping young men at her side. "Boys, git up on t'the wagon and take th' coffin from th' porters, please."

A silence hung in the air, broken only by the sound of the horses' hooves and the creaking of the wagon. On the way over from the farm, not much had been said between the boys and their mother. Carrie knew the boys had taken the news of their father's death hard. Despite the man's moods, they loved their father and mourned his death. The twins had sensed the tension between their parents after coming back from their school in Staunton this summer. Carrie knew they blamed her for it. Her attempts to hide her lack of love for their father were less and less convincing, she knew. *I blame myself for not trying harder to hide my feelings from the boys. Worse, I fear the boys' silence is because they feel I'm in some unknown way responsible for his death. I can't allow that to continue. Somehow, I've got to make the boys understand, without destroyin' the image they cherish of their father.*

She decided that since she was going to have their undivided attention on the twenty-mile ride home, she might as well bring up the topic immediately.

"Jack, Will, it's time ye understood our situation. Ye 're old enough now t'handle it. After all, your namesakes wasn't much older than you when they died in the war. Heroes, both of 'em. That's why yer dad wanted you boys named after 'em. Your father deserved yer respect too. He went through much hardship in the war. Jest he was lucky enough to live through it, else ye wouldn't be here t'comfort me with his passing.

"I don't know why he was in Mercersburg when he died. The men with 'im at the reunion wasn't exactly sure, neither. He jest told 'em he had business there. I reckon he thought he could git payment in advance fer some horses. Whatever took 'im there, you can be sure he had yer best interest at heart. He loved you boys. That's why he was in such bad spirits lately. He was afraid we hadn't enough money fer you boys to go to William and Mary, and he knew ye had yer hearts set on't."

Jack Emmons looked at his brother Will, then back at their mother.

"Why didn't he tell us? We thought we were rich, goin' to Hotchkiss's school an' all."

"Boys, he didn't even want t'tell me. Your father was a good man, in his way, but for quite a spell he hasn't confided in me. I'm afraid we was truly growin' apart. Perhaps I might've loved him more, though sadly I'm afraid he didn't care no more about my affection, and so it withered fer lack o' tendin'. But don't ever doubt that he loved you boys! Now he's gone, an' there's nothin' I can do fer him. But I can forgive him fer the way he treated me. I only hope you boys will forgive me fer not doin' more t'try t'love him these past few years." She dabbed her eyes with a handkerchief.

"You know I kep' the books fer the farm. So I knew there wasn't enough sales t'cover our loan payments comin' due. I guess yer father reckoned he could somehow find enough money somewhere up north t'get us out o' our pinch. But now he's gone. We must give 'im a proper burial, and you boys need t'mourn. But then we got t'get the farm back into soundness."

"Ma, we didn't know. This has to be terrible worrisome for you, now, 'specially with Father gone. But we'll help, won't we Will? We can forget college 'til the farm's back sound again. We'll work hard, and get us back all right, Ma, don't you worry."

"Oh, thank ye, Jack; thank ye, Will. I feel as if a great stone's been lifted offn me. You boys work miracles with horses, an' I got some plans fer how t'raise some cash an' get the bank off our backs for th' time bein'. Thanks be t'God fer openin' up yer hearts. If God was unhappy with me before, thanks t'your goodness I feel his redemption."

She leaned over and gave them each a hug and a kiss. The long ride home was now a journey toward a new and happy future.

Chapter Thirty-One
Redemption

Sally found sleep difficult. Her mind was tormented with guilt. *How can I marry a man who killed my first love? No matter how much I love him, want him, need him. How can I betray Jack?* She dozed off, awoke again. *I love Luke. Even in this short time, I've come to love him deeply. I can't bear to lose this last chance for happiness.*

She thought again of Luke's words. *He's been so honest with me, even at the risk of my reneging on marrying him. And after all, they were at war. They had been on opposite sides, each convinced of the rightness of his cause. Each willing to give up his life for it, if need be. Luke was only defending himself. Even then, he'd tried hard to spare Jack's life, pulling him out of the creek, away from certain drowning. Jack's death was just another cruel blow dealt by fate to warriors. Luke doesn't deserve my blame.*

I've been cruel to Luke these past days, to let him believe he had killed my love by his honesty. She had kept her contact with him to the absolute minimum, and he bore her apparent coldness silently.

Well, I'll not let this go on one moment longer. She rose from her bed, pulled on her robe, and rushed down the stairs and down the hall into Luke's room.

Luke woke up feeling the gentle pressure of warm lips on his. Then he heard Sally's soft voice.

"Luke, dearest. Can you forgive me? I have been terrible to you these past few days. But now I realize how much I love you. I can't bear the thought of losing you. What happened with you and Jack at Gettysburg was terrible, just as the war itself. But you deserve no blame, nor did Jack. Yet I forgive you for it, if you feel you need my forgiveness. You both did what you had to do, for the noblest of reasons. I can only think that somehow Jack has sent you to me, to finish what he started. Jack is lost, but you are here. And I need you. I want to be your wife, to spend the rest of my life with you, my dearest."

Luke smiled, feeling like he could float off the bed now that the night's terrible burden had been lifted. How he loved this woman!

"Sally, I'd marry you this instant if we could manage it. But I can be patient a little while longer, knowing you still love me. Come here and let me kiss you again!"

Sally was feeling intensely happy. All the past sadness of her life was now only a bad memory. For the next week, she hummed happily as she went about her day, spending as much time with him as she could, but encouraging him to rest and sleep as much as possible. With her help, he was able to get up and around. His strength was rapidly returning and he began to urge her to remove his arm restraints. After a discussion with the doctor, Sally agreed to remove them periodically for a short while, as long as he agreed to not use his arms for supporting his weight.

"Doc Hudson didn't say I couldn't hug you, did he?" Luke was standing up in the parlor, facing Sally, who was looking at him as if she could visually determine the extent of his healing progress.

"No, I guess he didn't. But not tight!"

At that, Luke stepped up to her and put his arms around her waist, and bent to kiss her eagerly responsive lips.

"And I'm sure the good doctor didn't say you couldn't now enter my bed, Sally dear."

Smiling, she beamed at him. "No, he'd not have thought to say that, silly. But are you sure you're really healed enough for that?"

"Nurse Sally, your care has me ready for almost anything, and most especially for this. We've waited long enough. Didn't you say you married Jack without benefit of witnesses? I see no reason why we can't do the same. So, here and now, I take you, Sally, to be my wife. Will you take me to be your husband? For better or worse, 'til death do us part?"

"Oh, Luke, I do! I do!"

"Then come with me to our marriage bed, my dear wife. We'll have a formal ceremony as soon as you can set it up. Meanwhile, God has been our witness."

They quickly walked to his bedroom and drew the curtains. She carefully helped him to take off his clothes and lie down on the bed. Sally once more admired Luke's youthfully tight stomach and strong chest with its mat of dark hair, with only the odd white hair giving away his maturity. She swiftly shed her own clothes and slowly turned to face him. Even in the dim light, he could see she had kept the figure of a much younger woman. Luke was in awe at the beauty now fully revealed to him—her slender waist, lovely long legs, and firm breasts, now half-covered by the silky chestnut hair cascading below her smooth shoulders.

"Sally, you are truly beautiful!" This time he felt no concern about his arousal, only impatience at any further delay. "Please, come to me now!"

Sally smiled and went to him eagerly. With mature self-control, she managed to restrain the pent-up passion now raging in her. She tenderly made love to her husband, satisfying their deep and mutual desire, yet mindful of his still-mending shoulders. It had been a long time for both of them, and they soon reached a deeply fulfilling climax.

Afterward, Sally lay beside him, snuggling up to his lean body, her head on his chest. He gently kissed her soft hair.

"Now, Sally Kellogg, we are truly man an' wife."

"Oh, Luke. I am the happiest woman alive!"

"And I the most fortunate of men, dear Sally. I want nothing more than to spend the rest of my life with you."

"And with our babies, Luke?"

"Of course, Sally. If God wills it, our babies too."

On the first day of August, Dr. Hudson came to the Barnes House and carefully examined his patient.

"You've made a remarkable recovery, Mr. Kellogg. Like you were a twenty-year-old! The incisions have healed, muscle tone seems good, bones have knitted properly. Mrs. Barnes, you must have some magic healing potion! Now we'll remove these harnesses, and you should be able to pretty much go about your business, Mr. Kellogg."

Luke paid Dr. Hudson in gold coin, to the good doctor's surprise and delight. His patients too often were slow, if not downright neglectful, in paying him, modest though the country surgeon's fees were. And this New Yorker was paying him in gold. Quick to heal, and quicker to pay what he owed. The pleased physician walked down the hall to the grateful good-byes of Luke and Sally, and went out the door muttering, "remarkable, just remarkable!"

That weekend the Reverend Dr. Jacob Clutz, in town from his church in nearby Newville to cover for the vacationing pastor of Trinity Lutheran Church, conducted a small marriage ceremony before the altar of Trinity. Sally had intended it to be simple and quiet. But Lutheran services traditionally are rich with music, and she gave in to the pleading of the organist to provide appropriate music for the occasion. The musician was proud of his virtuosity, and Sally had always found inspiration in the rich tones of Trinity's massive pipes.

The Lutheran marriage sacrament was brief, its simplicity in stark contrast to the organist's magnificent rendering of Bach's Prelude and Fugue in G Major. The musician's fingers flashed over the keys. His feet danced across the pedals. Bright, sprightly cascades of notes spilling over thundering bass rumbles filled the church, washing over the delighted listeners. Finally, the last note faded and the church grew silent. The small group strolled back to the Barnes House, where Sally had arranged for a small reception.

Luke had related to Reverend Clutz the story of the wartime encounter at Rock Creek that years later had led to his meeting Sally. The minister appeared to be lost in thought as Luke recounted his story. Sally had joined them, her arm in Luke's, smiling happily at her new husband. Reverend Clutz looked at her and began to speak.

"Mrs. Kellogg, this is an amazing coincidence. My dear wife, Liberty Augusta, and I come from Gettysburg. After the battle, she helped nurse the wounded at the army's hospital, Camp Letterman, on the York Pike. Just last week, she was telling our dinner guests about her experiences there. She recalled how she had helped a Virginia cavalryman find his missing comrade in a nearby tent. The two had been wounded at Rock Creek and had been taken prisoner, just after the battles had ended on July third. The man was near death when she found him, but he was able to recount a tale about gold he had hidden near Mercersburg, and about a map of its location inscribed on the back of a locket given him by a girl in Chambersburg. Somehow, my wife felt this brave man was seeking redemption for some past act that he deeply regretted. She remembered clearly the dying man's last words— 'tell Sally I loved her.' It would seem that you are that girl, Mrs. Kellogg. An amazing coincidence! Mrs. Clutz will be so surprised when I tell her that you are the Sally in her story."

That evening Sally asked Luke to explain what Reverend Clutz meant about the locket and the gold. *Now,* thought Luke. *Now is the right time to tell Sally how I came by the locket, and to show her contents of the knapsack, still safely in the closet of the sickroom.* As Luke narrated his story, Sally sat amazed at the tale. Luke took her in his arms, looked in her eyes, and spoke.

"I came to Pennsylvania searching for Jack Lewis's gold. Instead, I found he had left me a far more precious treasure- here, in Chambersburg." He hugged her tightly and kissed her welcoming lips.

Two days later, Luke and Sally Kellogg deposited almost twenty thousand dollars in gold coins in the First National Bank of Chambersburg. Shortly thereafter, the Post Commander of the GAR Post of Chambersburg sat in the parlor of the Barnes House, stunned by the size of the check he held in his hand. Luke spoke first.

"I recently recovered this money from its wartime hiding place. The Confederate soldier who hid it died in the war. My wife and I both agree that the appropriate use of this money is for the benefit of veterans, their widows and orphans. And so we are giving you this check for the GAR's programs that benefit them. There is only one condition—you must treat this as an anonymous donation. We neither deserve nor want credit for it."

Thanking them both profusely, the Post Commander allowed himself to be shown out, and promptly went back to the bank to deposit

Luke Kellogg's check in the post account. He wanted badly to rush to the offices of *The Valley Examiner* and gain the publicity for the GAR Post that such a large donation would provide. But he resisted the temptation, and respected the donors' wishes. Only he would know the source.

From beyond the heavenly divide, the spirit of Jack Lewis gave out a sigh of relief. *At least one of the sins that have weighed so heavily on me have just been expiated. The gold I had taken as plunder would now do a great good—ironically, through the generosity of the man responsible for my premature spirithood. And, of course, the generosity of my own dear Sally. Their generous acts will surely earn absolution for me.*

Spirit-Jack was happy that his Sally had finally found happiness, had perhaps found the redemption so long denied her, even if the man giving her that happiness was the man who'd ended his mortal life. That was one of the good things about the spirit life—no more base human feelings of envy and revenge, just a celestial joy at having led a good man to the woman Jack had loved. The happiness she felt radiated all the way across the heavenly divide to warm his spirit. Jack sensed he'd finally found redemption, through the work of this man and woman, so instrumental in his life twenty years before.

In late August, Luke and Sally Kellogg were standing by Niagara Falls, feeling, like other, younger, couples around them, awed by the power of the great cataracts of the Niagara River roaring over the precipice, carrying Lake Erie's water onward toward Ontario and the distant Atlantic Ocean. Luke held Sally tightly as she snuggled next to him against the dampness of the mist boiling up from the falls.

They had disposed of all their holdings in New York and Pennsylvania, said their goodbyes to friends and family, and boarded the train west. After two enjoyable days at Niagara Falls, they would embark on the grand journey across the vast spaces of the west. A new and wonderful life awaited them in California.

Luke looked down at Sally's upturned face and hugged her even tighter to him.

"Early in the war, our chaplain told us we would have to endure great hardship and pain, some even death. He told us that for us soldiers, and for our families, there would be no easy victories. Jack

Lewis died for his cause; you suffered; I had my trials. We've all paid a steep price, but I believe we have all finally earned our measure of redemption."

Sally looked him lovingly in the eyes, stretched herself up to kiss him, while Luke leaned down to return her kiss.

"Indeed, we have found God's grace, dear." She smiled, her face glowing with happiness.

"Luke, you're going to be a father!"

End Notes

This novel is a work of fiction. Jack Lewis, Lathrop Emmons, and their family and friends at Upperville are fictional characters, as are Sally Keefer and the Brunebaugh, Baird, and Barnes families in Pennsylvania. In Mercersburg, Sam Pine, Nick Mellott, Seth Karper are part of this fiction. In New York, Luke Kellogg, Billy Weed, Julia Stow and her brother John, Polly Bird, and Millie Babcock are fictional characters. Ike and Pauline Watson are fictional. Their story is a tale wrought from the author's imagination.

The surrounding events of the Civil War are real, as are the players in that war. The author has tried diligently to insure the factual accuracy of those events and players. The actions of the men of the 137th Regiment, New York Volunteer Infantry and of the Fourth Virginia Cavalry are drawn from the historical records of those units. The men of the Fourth Virginia and of the 137th New York whose names are mentioned in this book were real people, whose dedication and bravery deserve our admiration. General George Greene and Colonel David Ireland were real heroes of the Battle of Gettysburg at Culp's Hill. Colonel Ireland's wife Sara Phelps was real, a tragic widow of the war, like so many others.

In some cases, the real has been interwoven with the fictional. Liberty Hollinger and her father Jacob were real. She was a teenager who served as a nurse to the wounded after the battle. Her father did expel the Baltimore ladies for aiding the escape of Confederates. Jacob Hartman did own a farm on the Littlestown road. Dr. Harry Hartman, his son, was a doctor living on Baltimore Street in Gettysburg, although his practice was actually begun some years later than the fictional events of this novel. Sam and John Forney were real farm boys in Hanover, fleeing the fields when the battle started there. As a side note, Samuel Forney's daughter Elizabeth would marry Dr. Harry Hartman. The Rev. Dr. Jacob Clutz was pastor of the Lutheran Church of Newville during that era. Liberty Hollinger was his wife.

Similarly, the people of Mercersburg who appear in this story were real, other than the fictional Seth Karper and Nick Mellott. George Steiger's escape from the rebels is a matter of record. Michael Cromer's cradling feat was a source of local pride for many years before the post-Civil War mechanization of farming. Dr. Robert Brownson was a real doctor and soldier. George Wolfe was Mercersburg's constable during the war. James Duffield was a real soldier in the 126th Pennsylvania, though the author has taken the liberty to appoint him constable in 1883. Alexander Watson was a real member of Mercersburg's African-American community. President James Buchanan did own Patchwork Farm. Irwinton Mills was home to Jane Irwin, the wife of William Henry Harrison, Jr. and the mistress of the White House for her father-in-law, while her sister Elizabeth was mother of Benjamin Harrison. The mill, now Anderson's Mill, is in operation today. The covered bridge, now called Witherspoon's Bridge, and the camelback stone bridge, now called Hayes Bridge, still exist. The area around these bridges along the Conococheague and Licking Creeks hasn't changed much since 1883.

In New York, Judge Charles Kellogg was real—Judge and New York Congressman, founder of Kelloggsville, near New Hope, and the founder of New Hope Mills in 1823, a grist mill that exists to this day. Samuel Weed and his American Hotel were real, though their relationships to Luke Kellogg and Billy Weed are in the author's imagination. The Stow family was real, though Julia and her mother and father are fictional members, perhaps cousins twice removed.

Bibliography

Bowers, Dorothy W. *The Irwins and The Harrisons.* Mercersburg, PA: Irwinton Publishers, 1973.

Broome County Historical Society, Binghamton, NY. Muster Rolls of the 137th NY Volunteer Infantry Regiment, 1862. Files of the Broome County Historical Society.

Conrad, W.P. & Ted Alexander. *When War Passed This Way.* Shippensburg, PA: Beidel Printing House, 1982.

Farrington, John F. *137th Regiment Infantry, Historical Sketch (New York at Gettysburg, page 936-950).* Albany: State of New York, 1902.

Fendrick, Virginia S. et al. *Old Mercersburg.* New York: Frank Allaben Co., 1912.

Furness, Judy. *Ledyard News—Ledyard and the 111th NY Volunteers Co. K.* Town of Ledyard, N.Y., 2002.

Hartman, Catherine. *A Personal and Family Memoir.* Mercersburg, PA: Privately printed, 1993.

Heefner, Nancy et al. *The Tuscarora Reader.* Mercersburg, PA: Mercersburg Historical Society, 2000.

Hinman, Marjory. *Diary of a Binghamton Boy.* Binghamton, NY: Hinman, 1982.

Hollinger, Liberty Augusta (Mrs. Jacob Clutz). *Some Personal Recollections of the Battle of Gettysburg.* Gettysburg: Privately Printed, 1925.

Holt, Daniel. *A Surgeon's Civil War.* Kent, OH: Kent State University Press, 1994.

King, Charles et al. *The Photographic History of the Civil War.* Secaucus, NJ: The Blue and Gray Press, 1987.

Massengill, Samuel. *A Sketch of Medicine and Pharmacy from the 15th to 20th Century.* Bristol, TN: S. E. Massengill, 1943.

McDonald, Archie P., ed. *Jedediah Hotchkiss: Make Me a Map of the Valley.* Dallas: Southern Methodist University Press, 1973.

McPherson, James. *Hallowed Ground.* New York: Crown Publishers, 2003.

Murray, R.L. *A Perfect Storm of Lead.* Wolcott, NY: Benedum Books, 2000.

Patch, Eileen. *This From George, the Civil War Letters of George Englis, Annotated.* Binghamton, NY: Broome Co. Historical Society, 2001.

Phisterer, Frederick, comp. *New York in the War of the Rebellion, 1861-1865.* Albany, NY: Weed and Parsons, 1890

Prowell, George R. *Prelude to Gettysburg, Encounter at Hanover.* Shippensburg, PA: Burd Street Press, 1962.

Roy, Paul. *The Seventy-fifth Anniversary of the Battle of Gettysburg*. Harrisburg: Pennsylvania State Commission, 1939.

Schildt, John. *Roads to Gettysburg*. Parsons, WV: McClain Printing Co., 2003.

Stackpole, Edward. *They Met at Gettysburg*. Harrisburg: Stackpole Books, 1956.

Steiger, Henry, ed. *Mercersburg in War Times, by J. Harbaugh, 1902*. Mercersburg, PA: Mercersburg Printing, 2002.

Stiles, Kenneth. *4th Virginia Cavalry*. Lynchburg, VA: H.E. Howard, 1985.

Stoner, Jacob. *Historical Papers, Franklin County and The Cumberland Valley, Pennsylvania*. Chambersburg, PA: Craft Press, 1947.

Thomas, Emory M. *Bold Dragoon, the Life of J.E.B. Stuart*. New York: Harper & Row, 1986.

Trudeau, Noah Andre. *Gettysburg, A Testing of Courage*. New York: HarperCollins, 2002.

Wert, Jeffry D. *Gettysburg, Day Three*. New York: Simon & Schuster, 2001.

Wheeler, Richard. *Witness to Gettysburg*. New York: Harper & Row, 1987.

Wilkinson, J. B. and Tom Cawley. *The Annals of Binghamton of 1840 with an Appraisal, 1840-1967*. Binghamton, NY: Broome Co. Historical Society, 1967.

Acknowledgements

The author is indebted to those diligent historians from whose works were drawn the understanding of actual events and persons described in this novel. In some cases the passage of time has apparently caused some variance in the historical record among the various sources. The author is similarly indebted to the Civil War Reenactors, especially those of the 137th N.Y.V.I., led by Larry Lattin, conveying the life of the Union infantryman. The support and encouragement of the Binghamton Civil War Roundtable is much appreciated.

The author also wishes to acknowledge the assistance in the Mercersburg area given by: Larry and Regina Taylor; Bernice Lowans; Harry and Rollie Anderson and Ruth Anderson Miller; Julia and Cedric Duffield; and in New York by Dale Weed at New Hope Mills.

The author is grateful to Eileen Patch, for her skilled and diligent review and comments on the first edition. Fellow author Bill Giuffre and publisher Thad Floyd of Coastal Publishing, Inc. have made this second edition possible. However the author takes full responsibility for any errors in fact or writing.

Paul and Catherine Hartman Clutz inspired this book, by their life-long love of history and literature. My wife, Terry, has my deepest thanks for her patience and support through the development of this novel, and in encouraging my next project, a history of the 137th New York, in their own words. Thanks are due my webmaster, Annette Brigiotta for a fine website. And to Laura, Dan and Mary, thanks for the constant encouragement.

To the many readers of the first edition who sent me such positive reviews and comments, thanks. I welcome the readers of this edition to share their comments with me as well. Readers will find interesting info on the book's website, including An Auto Tour of the Book.

David Cleutz
dcleutz@stny.rr.com
www.WarAndRedemption.com

About the Author

A long-time resident of Binghamton, New York, David Cleutz is a native Pennsylvanian. Born in Chambersburg, he grew up in Mercersburg , his family deeply rooted in Gettysburg and Hanover. His great-grandparents were direct observers of the battle of Gettysburg – Liberty Hollinger in Gettysburg, Samuel Forney in Hanover, and Jacob Hartman on the Littlestown road.

Cleutz has written several articles on New York regiments at Gettysburg and Antietam. In 2005 he self- published the book, "In Their Own Words – Col. David Ireland and the 137th New York", a volume of letters from men of the 137th New York found in the 1860's newspapers of upstate New York. A comprehensive history of Col.David Ireland and the 137th New York is in the works. This is his first novel.

Cleutz is a graduate of Mercersburg Academy, and holds advanced degrees from Case Western Reserve and Binghamton Universities. A member of the Binghamton Civil War Roundtable, he lectures frequently on the history of the 137th Regiment, New York Volunteers. Cleutz lives with his wife Terry in a circa 1870 home on the banks of the Susquehanna River in Binghamton, New York.